BIRDS IN FLIGHT

ANNI TAYLOR

BIRDS IN FLIGHT

ANNI TAYLOR

The characters in this book are entirely fictional. Any resemblance to actual persons living or dead is entirely coincidental. The town of 'Nautilus Bay' is set in a real area of Australia but the town itself is entirely fictional.

Imprint: Bookish Coast

ISBN: 978-0-6484380-4-5

PROLOGUE

Australia, 1998
Sunshine Coast, Queensland

SERGEANT MULLARD PARKS his police vehicle behind the van. It's just past eleven at night, and it's ink dark. It's not a good place for any kind of drama to play out. He knows that on one side, a cliff edge runs close to the road and on the other side is a thick, dense stretch of everglades. And the sheeting rain is only making visibility worse.

Sitting next to the sergeant, Constable Lea Ramirez gazes straight ahead. "What're you thinking, Sarge?"

"Something doesn't seem right here," he tells her, attempting to peer through the rain. "When the guy called the station, did he sound high on drugs or something?"

"He just sounded, y'know, frantic. And maybe a bit scared about what he'd seen."

"Hmmm. Well, how about I go check it out while you wait here? No point both of us getting drenched like sewer rats."

A nervous smile flits across her face. "Won't say no to that."

Pulling a rain jacket over his head, the sergeant exits the car and tramps through puddles of water to the van. In the driver's seat is a man who looks about twenty, smoking a cigarette and wearing a soaking-wet wifebeater. His shoulder-length hair is plastered in damp skeins to his face. Tattoos run the length of his arm and up to his neck.

"Mr Jared Keller?" asks the sergeant.

The man stubs the cigarette out on the window frame of his van. "Yeah. Yeah, that's me."

"Thanks for waiting for us, Mr Keller. You want to explain what you saw out there, exactly?"

Mr Keller eases his head back. "It was a kid—a little girl—and a woman, running for their lives. Right along the side of the road. They both looked desperate. I thought there had to be someone chasing them. All kinds of things go through your head—like, it could be someone with a knife or an axe. The kid vanished into the bushland, and the woman followed. I admit I was freaked out, but I parked and went looking for them. Couldn't find them. Got driven back by the rain. So I came back to my van and called the police."

"Did you call out to them?"

"Yeah. No answer."

"Right. And there was no one else around?" the sergeant asks.

"Not that I saw."

"Where were you headed at the time you saw the girl and the woman?"

"Just returning home from my girlfriend's house."

"Right. Mind if I take a look inside your van?"

The young man's mouth goes slack, his eyes incredulous. "You serious? You wanna poke around in my van?"

"Just procedure."

Jared throws his hands up. "What kind of procedure is that?"

"It'll only take a minute."

"Go ahead—I can't stop you. It's open."

Sliding back the side door of the van, Sergeant Mullard cranes his head. There are tarps and ropes. He pulls the tarps aside and finds nothing but toolboxes.

"What do you do for work, mate?" the sergeant shouts above the roar of the rain.

"I'm a handyman," Mr Keller tells him, twisting around to look over his shoulder. "I do odd jobs."

A call comes in on the sergeant's radio. "Sarge," says Constable Ramirez over the radio, "a young woman just called the station. A Mrs Deauville. She'd been driving down the same section of road that we're on now, and she saw the same thing the driver of the van did. She saw a woman and child running there. Mrs Deauville had a baby in her car and was afraid to stop, in case someone was chasing the pair. She said as soon as she arrived home, she called the police."

The sergeant slides the door shut and walks back to Mr Keller. "We just had a call from another driver." He relays what Constable Ramirez just told him.

Mr Keller shakes his head. "I didn't see any other cars on the road."

"She's backing up your story, mate. Why argue?"

"What story? And who's arguing? I just don't remember seeing anyone else."

"Well, she saw you. She said she saw your van stop and park by the roadside."

"Look, I think I'm sorry I called the cops. Try to do the right thing and—"

"I'll contact you if I need any more information, okay? You can go." The sergeant stands and watches as the van drives off, the tyres digging into the gravel with a low screech.

He returns to his police vehicle and tries his best to remove his jacket and toss it into the back seat without pouring water on the constable. Wet nights are a pain in the rear end.

"Do you buy his version of events, Sarge?" Ramirez asks, flicking droplets of rain from her sleeve. "I mean, about the woman charging off into bushland with the little girl?"

"On a night like this? Nope. Doesn't add up. Who knows—

maybe Mr Keller called us out as a cover story because he knows another driver saw his van parked."

"That had me worried too."

"We might have to do some follow-up with Mr Keller. Anyway, let's take a drive and see if we can spot the mother and child. That's two separate drivers who saw them, so we know they exist."

"Should we put the lights and siren on? If I was hiding in the forest, I might feel safer coming out if I knew it was the police."

"I like your thinking." Sergeant Mullard begins a slow cruise along the road, lights and sirens on. The rain and the murky darkness affect visibility to the point where this feels like a fool's mission.

Two minutes later, a small shopping centre edges into view around a corner. The centre is closed, with a bare minimum of lights on.

Constable Ramirez points past his shoulder, to the right. "Do you see that? A car in the parking area. It's the only one there."

"Yup. Well spotted, Ramirez." The sergeant turns right and drives in. It's pitch-dark here, save for the soft glow of a streetlight some five metres away.

The car is an old-model station wagon. Sergeant Mullard judges that it maybe came off the factory line in 1985. The front passenger-side door hangs wide open, buffeted by the wind. Rain pelts inside.

Constable Ramirez gasps. "God—that's not looking good. There's a girl in that seat."

"What on earth is going on here tonight?" the sergeant mutters. From what he can make out, the girl is a young teenager. She's slumped over. Is she dead? The victim of a knife attack? Maybe Jared Keller was on the right track, after all.

As soon as the sergeant parks the car, he and Ramirez jump out and race to the station wagon.

The car is empty apart from the girl.

Constable Ramirez lifts the girl's head and touches two fingers to a vein at the side of her neck. "There's a pulse... and she's breathing. I can't—I can't wake her!"

The sergeant casts an eye over the girl as he calls an ambulance.

She's soaked to the skin, her feet sitting in rainwater that's collecting in the floor of the car. Her legs are unusually thin. She is either severely malnourished or has spent years in a wheelchair. He can't tell which.

"Ramirez, listen," he says. "Put her seat right down and then you get into the back seat, ready to do anything for her that the ambulance says. Got it?"

"Got it."

The sergeant scans the interior of the vehicle. A wallet sits in the console. He switches on a light, picks up the wallet, and opens it. There's a licence belonging to a blonde woman named Elsa Jorgenson. After calling for police backup, he asks the station to run a quick background check on her.

"Sarge," Ramirez says urgently, "I found medicine on the back seat. It's insulin. In the name of Grace Lowood."

"Check for a bracelet."

"Excuse me, Sarge?"

"Check the girl for an emergency bracelet."

The constable examines the girl's wrists, pulling back her sleeves "You're right. Her name is Grace, and she has Type 1 diabetes. Going by the birthdate, she's fifteen."

"Good job."

Ramirez answers a callback from a paramedic. The paramedic gives her instructions on what to do for the patient before they arrive. Ramirez bites down on her lip as she listens.

Sergeant Mullard observes the constable. She looks terrified, poor thing. She hasn't been on a callout like this one before. And he has to admit, he hasn't seen many that'd match this one, either.

He answers a call on his radio.

"Detective," says a female voice, "we've run the check you asked for. Elsa Jorgenson is thirty-two years old, from Pennsylvania, United States. She's on a five-year visa. She brought two daughters out to Australia with her—Iris Jorgenson, aged fifteen, and Lily Jorgenson, aged twelve."

As the call ends, he gazes out into the hammering downpour.

Neither of those two girls fits the name or description of the girl in the car or the little girl who was out there on the road.

He updates the constable.

She gazes back at him in the dark light. "That means there are two more missing girls to find tonight—Iris and Lily?"

"Yup. As well as the missing American woman."

"Where do we start, Sarge?"

"We've got to get a search underway. So far, not one thing is making the slightest bit of sense. It's gonna be one hell of a night."

1

LILY JORGENSON, 1998

My mother says I go through life with my fists up. But I don't start fights. It's just that I'm always ready for one.

I got into a scrape at the last place we stopped at overnight. A group of kids were throwing sticks at a mother bird as she tried to defend her nest. I charged at the group, shoving them, yelling at them to quit it.

But the mother bird was no match for the barrage of sticks. They killed her. I climbed up and saved the nest.

I touch each tiny blue egg and then tuck a beach towel around the nest. Gently, I place the nest back into the cupboard where I've been secretly keeping it. A little worry worm burrows into me. The eggs might never hatch without their mother to keep them warm.

I want to ask Mom what to do, but she's not here. She's been out for hours, and she took Grace and Ellie with her. My sister Iris went out too, even though she was told to stay here with me. Iris never does what she's told.

I glance around at a caravan that suddenly feels far too empty—even though there is almost no room to move in it, with the bunk beds and the cupboards and a tiny kitchen all squashed in together.

Mom calls the caravan a travel trailer, but I've gotten used to what they call them here in Australia.

The rain on our caravan's tin roof is still hard enough to sound like drumsticks. It was storming earlier. Pulling aside the curtains at the window, I scan the park, looking for any sign of my mother's old beat-up station wagon. All I see are the blurred lights of other caravans through the night and the rain. Specks of water fly through the narrow opening in the window, wetting my nose.

I shiver in my thin pyjamas. The air isn't cold, not really. But somehow, I feel cold.

A car pulls up, but it's not Mom's. Red and blue lights spin through the tiny window of the caravan. It's the police.

"Open up!" a male voice barks. He rattles and bangs on the flimsy door.

I back away, terrified, pressing my back against the wall of the caravan.

When I don't answer, he shouts, "Police. Open up, or we'll have to force it open."

He gives me no option but to unlock the door and crack it open. A sliver of light from the caravan falls into the night outside. A tower of a man stands there, the downpour splashing on the hood and shoulders of his thick black jacket. Standing beside him is a young woman with dark hair and the same kind of rain jacket as the man.

The man's eyes are impatient. "I'm Sergeant Quincy Mullard, and this is Constable Lea Ramirez. Is your mother here?"

"No... not yet. She went out."

"Out where?"

"To get medicine."

"What's your name?"

"Lily. Lily Jorgenson."

"How old are you?"

"Twelve."

"You're small for twelve." He pokes his large head around me, into the caravan. "Who else is in there?"

"No one."

"I saw quite a few beds. Who sleeps in those?"

I almost stammer as I answer. "My mom, my sister Iris, and two other girls—Grace and Ellie."

"So, five of you?" he asks.

"Yes. Five."

"And... you're all American?"

"No. Just my mom and Iris and me. Grace and Ellie are Australian. They're sisters."

"Why are the Australian girls with you?" Sergeant Mullard asks.

His questions are flying at me like fists. Why are the police here? I'm too nervous to ask him. I don't know where anyone is tonight. Even Iris is missing.

"Grace and Ellie were living with their grandparents," I answer, "but their grandparents got sick. So Mom said she'd take them with us."

"Their full names and ages?"

"Grace and Ellie Lowood. Grace is sixteen, and Ellie is four."

"Okay, got it. You all live here, in this park?"

"No, we just got here a few hours ago."

"From where?" he asks.

"We've been... travelling."

"How long have you been travelling?"

"Almost a year."

"A year?" He frowns, tugs the hood lower over his forehead. "That's a long time. Where have you been travelling?"

"In Australia. Around the coast."

"What do you do for money?"

"We make things to sell. Jewellery and things."

He raises his eyebrows in a sceptical look. The woman police officer shoots me a sympathetic glance, but she doesn't say a word. I want the sergeant to go away. He scares me.

I gasp in relief when my sister comes zigzagging through the rain. She's got a yellow raincoat over her head, wet hair stuck to her face and shoulders.

My relief switches to anger as I run down the steps of the

caravan and into the rain. "Iris, why did you leave me all alone?" I give her a shove that sends her two steps back. "Where did you go? You've been gone for hours."

She combs her hair back from her face with her fingers. "Oh, zip it, Lily. I just went to the block where the bathrooms are."

"No, you didn't, you liar. You've been gone forever."

"Stop spinning out." She looks around. "Where's Mom's car? Isn't she back yet?"

"No," I tell her. "She's not."

Iris turns to the sergeant. "Did my sister get scared and call you?"

"I didn't call the police," I rage at my sister, not giving the policeman a chance to reply. "How would I call anyone? Do you even know what time it is?"

The sergeant's eyes skate from me to Iris. "I'm afraid you girls are going to have to come down to the station with us."

Iris shakes her head wildly. "What? No. We can't do that. Our mom will be back any minute now."

The sergeant holds up a wallet and opens it to show a driver's licence—protecting it from the rain with his coat.

Iris peers at the licence, her eyes large and fearful. "Why do you have Mom's licence? What happened?"

The female officer speaks for the first time. "Iris and Lily, how about the two of you get out of the rain and get changed into dry clothes? Especially you, Lily. My goodness, you're soaked, and you're only wearing your pyjamas."

"Tell me what happened to Mom, first," Iris says to the constable.

She gives us a quick smile. "You need to come with us, then we'll explain."

"Come on, Lily," Iris says, herding me into the caravan. "We don't have a choice."

A few minutes later, Iris and I are travelling in the back of the police car, through the rain and unlit streets.

"It's okay," Iris whispers to me. "This jerk cop isn't saying much, but don't worry. Mom probably lost her wallet, and the police just want to cause trouble."

"But why didn't she come back?"

"I don't know." Iris puts an arm around me, but I shrug it off.

"I thought you ran away, Iris," I hiss.

"Ran away? Don't be stupid. Why would I do that?"

"Because you keep saying you want to. And because you took the pack of cigarettes with you. The whole pack, not just one."

Her voice gets mean. "How'd you find out about the cigarettes?"

"I found them. You hide them underneath our bed."

"Don't tell Mom."

"No promises."

"You dirty little—"

"You left me," I fire at her. "You left me alone for *so, so long*."

"You're acting like a baby. I thought Mom would be back."

"Well, she's not. Where'd you go, anyway? We don't know anyone here."

"I'll say it one more time: I didn't go anywhere. Not for more than five minutes. And don't you say otherwise." She catches hold of my hand and twists two of my fingers until they feel like they're going to break. "Don't you say a single word."

2

Sergeant Mullard takes us to a police station in Nautilus Bay. There's no one inside, apart from a single officer sitting at the front desk. He shoots Iris and me a curious smile before the sergeant leads us down a hallway.

He shows us into a room that's bare apart from a table and chairs. I'm sorry when Constable Ramirez says she has to go. I don't like the sergeant at all, and I don't want to be alone with him.

"You girls want coffee?" the sergeant asks. "I'd offer hot chocolate, but I doubt we've got any."

"We don't want anything," Iris answers sharply.

He gestures toward the chairs. "Then have a seat, and we'll get started."

My sister and I sit reluctantly.

Sergeant Mullard sinks heavily into a chair opposite us. "Let me give you girls the situation. It's taken about two hours to locate you. So, about two hours ago, we had a report come into the station. That report was of a woman and small girl running along the side of a road about fifteen minutes away from here. The two of them vanished into the everglades."

I stare at him in growing shock. "You mean our mother? And Ellie? What about Grace? Where is she?"

The sergeant holds up both of his meaty hands. "Hold on. Let me continue. When the report came in, I was at the station with Constable Ramirez. We went to check things out. We spoke to the driver who saw your mother and Ellie on the road. The constable and I conducted a quick search, but we were unable to find them. But we did find your mother's car, and we did find Grace Lowood."

I suck in an audible breath. "You mean… Grace was alone in the car?"

"Yup," he says. "That's exactly what I mean. Not only that, but the car door was open, and she was getting soaked from the rain. She was unconscious, but she's getting good medical care now."

"Grace has severe disabilities," Iris tells him, her eyes filling with tears. "She wouldn't have been able to leave the car or even shut the door. Where did our mother go with Ellie?"

"That's the million-dollar question," the sergeant replies.

"Maybe Ellie wanted something, and Mom said no, and then Ellie ran off," Iris suggests. "She gets naughty sometimes. She's little."

"Well," he says, "if that's what happened, then she's one hell of a determined little kid, because she ran a long way in the rain and the dark."

I picture my mother before she left the caravan. Everything seemed normal. She had her hair tied up in a bun and her hooded jacket on. She looked pretty—as she always did—but maybe a little worried. Ellie had begged to go, too, and Mom had relented and taken her. What happened to Mom and Ellie?

Fear rattles through me, making me jump to my feet. "You need to take Iris and me there now. Ellie might be scared. She'll come to us. And we need to find Mom."

Iris stands at my side. This time, when she puts an arm around my shoulders, I don't shrug her off.

"My sister is right," Iris says. "We're wasting time."

The sergeant grunts. "I can't let you girls loose in sixty kilometres of everglades—at night, no less. I already have two missing persons on my hands—I don't need two more. And there's a cliff edge quite close to one section of road—it drops straight down to the ocean. You wouldn't want to go stepping off that in the dead of night."

Iris and I turn to each other, our eyes locking in terror. Mom and Ellie are out there, in a place where there is a cliff edge and miles of everglades.

"So," the sergeant says, "there's nowhere for you girls to be right now—other than here. Unless you have a relative who can come get you?"

Iris shakes her head. "No. We have a father in America. Our parents are getting a divorce. There's no one else."

"Right. Well, sit down," he tells us. "I have some questions for you. And you can rest assured that I already have a search party underway. They're out there looking for your mother and little Ellie as we speak."

We return to our chairs, but we're sitting on the edge of them as if we're readying ourselves to flee at any moment.

"Has your mother had any arguments with anyone lately?" he asks.

"Not that I can recall," Iris answers.

He writes that down in a notebook. "Okay, good. So, does your mum have any boyfriends?"

"Boyfriends? No," Iris says.

"Any male friends?" he asks.

"Not for months," she answers.

He lifts his eyebrows. "So, she did have a boyfriend?"

Iris rubs her arm. "Maybe. Kind of. His name was Bennett. We stayed at his farm for a while."

"Where at?" the sergeant asks.

She shrugs. "I don't know—a place called Nimbin, I think."

"Right," he says. "I'll get the details of that farm from you later. So, Nimbin's about four hours south of here. Could your mum have been meeting up with this Bennett guy again?"

"No," Iris answers firmly. "She would have told us."

"Okay," he says. "What about friends? Could she have had an argument with a friend tonight?"

"We don't have any friends," Iris replies from between her teeth. "We're always on the road."

"About that," he says. "Why were you travelling for so long? What about school?"

"Mom homeschools all of us," I tell him.

He blows out a breath and sits back. "That's a big task. Teaching four kids on the road. According to my information, you did have a residential address upon arrival in Australia. On Tiger Street, Nautilus Bay."

"Yes, we rented a house there for the first six months or so," Iris explains. "And we went to school there."

He nods. "I see. And is that where you met the Lowood family—Grace and Ellie and their grandparents?"

"That's right," Iris says. "They lived only a couple of blocks away from us."

He scrawls a few lines in his notebook. "And... you girls didn't answer my earlier question. Why did you go travelling for a whole year? Why did your mother leave Nautilus Bay after only six months?"

My throat constricts. He's asking so many questions. Too many. While Iris seems stumped, I try to find an answer for him. "Mom leaves when things go... when she decides it's time to go." My voice falters at the end.

The sergeant skewers me with his gaze. "Is there something you're not telling me, Lily?"

I turn away, shaking my head and not answering. I shouldn't have spoken. I should have let Iris handle all the questions. *Stupid, stupid, stupid.*

Iris side-eyes me in alarm. Beneath the table, she brings down her foot on mine and grinds her heel into my toes. It hurts—I'm only wearing what Mom calls my strappy sandals. My eyes sting, but I don't cry.

The sergeant hunches his shoulders, twiddling the pen between his fingers. "Hmmm. How were things in your family before you came out to Australia? Paint me a picture."

"How is that relevant?" Iris shoots back. "This didn't happen in America. It happened right here. And you need to—"

"I like to get the full story," he tells her. "I wouldn't be doing my job if I didn't do that. So, your parents are in the process of getting a divorce? There were problems, I assume?"

"People get divorced every day," Iris says, drawing out each word.

"True... true." He nods, still twiddling the pen. "But help me out here. Fill in the blanks. How about you, Lily?"

My hands form fists on my lap. I can't tell the things that boil at the pit of my stomach. I can't tell anyone that there is not one thing normal in my family.

There never *was* anything normal in my family. If anyone were to look at photos of my parents, Iris and me back in Pennsylvania, they'd see an image of a perfect family. And a picture-perfect house.

But inside that house, things were... *dark*. We didn't have people over to visit. My parents' claim was always that our family was too busy for visitors. The truth was that we were too strange.

Mom and Dad would have terrible arguments. After the fights, Dad would start drinking a lot, and Mom would stop opening the curtains in the mornings.

Sometimes, Mom would just pack up and leave us. For days. Or weeks. She never told when she was about to go. Dad would just say she needed to get her head clear. Dad would sit Iris and me down and tell us we needed to treat Mom better, to stop squabbling and stop demanding things of her.

Whenever Mom returned, she'd get back into things in a flurry of activity—baking cakes, digging in the garden, and sewing dance costumes for Iris and me.

Sometimes, our parents would have date nights. But only ever at home. Mom would dress up in a spangly dress and put heavy makeup on. And Dad would wear a suit. He'd get one of his best bottles of wine from the cellar. And they'd have dinner by candlelight. He'd always give her red roses.

But the day after, she'd put the flowers away in a cupboard. And she'd go down to the basement and swim in the pool we had there. Endless laps in the pool, even late at night. We were the only people I knew with a pool in the basement. Our house would smell of chlorine and rotting flowers.

It came completely out of the blue when Mom announced to us that she was divorcing Dad. Iris and I had barely digested that piece of information when she sprang the next thing on us. She stood there in our living room and spun the big, wooden globe—then closed her eyes and stuck a pin in the map of the world. The pin landed on Australia.

She was happy when we moved here—for those first months at least. But then she began leaving the blinds shut all day and acting strange. Iris and I came home one day from our new Australian school to find a caravan parked in our driveway. And then Mom told us that we were leaving.

"Lily? You've gone awfully quiet." Sergeant Mullard rubs the back of his neck, his eyes fixed on me.

I lift my chin, trying to stop my lower jaw from trembling. "What Iris said is probably right. Ellie got naughty and ran off—and Mom had no choice but to run after her. You need to find them."

I can't tell him all our family secrets. Every family has their own secrets to hide, don't they?

3

A LADY WITH A LONG, pinched face arrives at the station. She informs us she's a child protection worker, and she drives Iris and me from the police station to a house in Nautilus Bay. We learn we're being placed with a foster family until the police can track down our father.

I feel like a wild animal being torn away from its home. I'm desperate to return to the caravan and wait for Mom to come back. I want her arms around me. I want her to tell me everything's all right.

A foster couple greet us at the front door of their house. They both look bleary-eyed. It's now four in the morning.

Mr Dawson is a big-boned man with small features swimming in a fair, fleshy face. Mrs Dawson is tiny and wiry, with brown skin. She tells us she's originally from Malaysia. She hugs us and takes us upstairs to a room. There are two mattresses on the floor and a large stack of paintings against a wall.

She gestures at the paintings. "My daughter uses this room as a studio. We'll pull out a couple of beds from the garage tomorrow, but for tonight, I hope you don't mind sleeping on the floor."

"We're fine with that," Iris says in a cold tone. "But we could have slept in our caravan. I'm fifteen. I can look after my sister."

Mrs Dawson smiles tiredly. "Well, the police don't want you doing that. You'll be safe here. If you need anything, just ask."

She leaves us with a stack of sheets and blankets and then exits the room. I'm guessing she just wants to get back to sleep.

I throw myself down on one of the mattresses. "Where's Mom? Where is she? What happened to her?"

Iris tosses me a blanket and pillow. "Try to get some sleep, Lily. She'll come back. She always does."

"This is different."

"Just... go to sleep, okay?"

She switches off the light.

Pain radiates through me. I start sobbing and I don't stop for the next hour, even though Iris keeps begging me to. I keep imagining the worst things. The very worst. In my mind, I hear Mom's voice, saying, "Oh, you worry too much, Lily. Things aren't that bad." She always says things like that. But she's not here to say them now.

The next day, the minute Iris and I wake, we tear downstairs to find Mrs Dawson.

She's in the kitchen, washing dishes in the sink. Turning, she gives us a gentle smile. "Oh girls, I'm so sorry. There hasn't been any news so far. But look, they'll be found. The everglades are so dense—it'll just take a bit of time, that's all."

Her words open up a hole inside my chest. How can they be gone so long? It's been hours and hours.

Mrs Dawson introduces us to her two children, who are sitting at the table having breakfast. The boy, Van, is fifteen—Iris used to be in some of his classes at school. The girl, Anna, is seventeen and has just finished high school.

I hoped the family would have pets to cuddle up with. But they don't. Worse, Iris and I discover that the Dawsons are Sergeant Mullard's family—Mr Dawson is his first cousin. I'm certain this means they'll be spying on Iris and me, reporting anything we say about our mother to the sergeant. We have to be careful.

There is only one thing about the Dawsons that will make staying with them bearable. They live right on the river—their home and family restaurant are located there. I like watching the birds on the water—and the busy restaurant will mean that the Dawsons don't have time to keep a close eye on us.

Iris and I are tasked with helping Mrs Dawson get the tables ready for the customers. She says it'll help get our minds off things. But it doesn't.

The restaurant is called Dawsons Drift. Iris and I have seen it before—when we used to live in Nautilus Bay, but Mom never took us here. She thought it was too expensive.

Iris and I complete our chores and then head down to a quiet spot on the river where we can't be seen from the restaurant. The air is so hot that my scalp is sweating.

We watch the pelicans fighting for the best perches on the fishing boats and the invisible force that snatches up the herons from the water's surface and makes them soar into the blue.

I'm not allowed to return to the caravan. I have no way of retrieving the bird nest of tiny eggs that I have hidden there. Grace is still recovering in the hospital.

Iris stretches her slender body out on the riverbank. Her sundress is pulled up to her thighs, and her skin looks like it's cooking.

"You're getting sunburned," I remark.

"Don't care," Iris says. "Don't care about anything anymore."

I glance back at the house. The Dawson kids are home, and they're both upstairs, watching us. Van Dawson stands on the balcony. He seems embarrassed when he notices us looking back at him—shoving his hands in his pockets and slinking off inside. Anna Dawson is sitting sideways on the wide windowsill of her bedroom, a sketchpad in her hands. She has her thick hair up in a loose knot, locks falling over her face as she sketches.

"Is Anna drawing us?" Iris scowls. "I don't like her. She's a bitch."

"Why's she a bitch?"

"She offered me some of her clothes, as if my clothes aren't any good."

Constable Lea Ramirez had dropped off a bag filled with our clothing from the caravan this morning. I'd bolted out the door, thinking she had our mother and Ellie with her and that the nightmare was over—but all she'd had were the clothes.

"Maybe Anna was being nice?" I suggest.

"I already know my clothes suck. Mom never has any money. But Anna didn't have to make a big thing of it."

Anna's offer doesn't sound mean at all to me, but I know better than to say that to Iris. Iris is always going on about us not having money.

"Mom needs to come back and get us out of here," I say in solidarity. Fresh fear surges through my stomach. "Why haven't the police found her yet?"

Shaking grass from her hair, Iris sits up. "Who knows? Maybe she decided to leave us. It's not like she hasn't left us a hundred times before."

"No. Don't say that."

"What other explanation is there?"

"Someone must have chased her and Ellie down that road. Someone bad."

"Lily, there were two separate people who saw Mom and Ellie. No one was chasing them."

"Something was wrong," I insist, but my voice breaks, and I'm not even sure anymore.

Iris faces me, her nose and cheeks red from the sun. "Maybe she went off to meet up with some guy and then decided to stay with him."

"She wouldn't."

"We don't know that for sure. She hooked up with Bennett pretty damned quick. We were barely at that farm before they were sucking face."

"Iris—no, don't say things like that. You make her sound bad."

"Well, how can she just disappear? Why haven't the police found them? Maybe she did meet someone and then she staged a getaway."

"That doesn't make sense. She'd never do that."

"Our mother doesn't always make a lot of sense."

I shove her shoulder. "I don't have to listen to you."

"Well, like it or not, I'm all you've got."

Anger gathers at the edges of me, pressing in on all sides. "If one person had to be left behind with me, I wish it wasn't you."

She's shocked into silence—but not for long. "Shut your stupid face. And do you have to act like a brat when sour-face Anna is watching?" She flicks her gaze upward to the house.

Her words bounce straight over the top of me. "Why don't you tell me where you went last night? Tell me now. Or I'll punch you in the face—I swear I will. With Anna Dawson watching me do it."

I wait as her expression freezes. But then she just pulls an elastic from her pocket and ties up her hair. "You can't win a fight with me. And I don't have to tell you anything. You're just a dumb kid."

Before I know what I'm doing, I've jumped up, and I'm running. I skirt the edge of the river all the way to the ocean. After tearing off my shoes, I thread through the beachgoers—all the happy families having a day out. I hate all of them. I hate their bright shirts and their stripy umbrellas and their small children enjoying their lazy summer days.

I go where none of them are venturing—over the sharp, uneven boulders to the rock flats. Here, I'm alone. It's just me and the crabs that scuttle into the rock pools.

I get down on my stomach and stare at the reflections of clouds in the rock pools, wishing myself away from here. For the first time since arriving in Australia, I want to go home. Back to Pennsylvania. I miss Dad. He's always been kind of distant—leaving all the parenting up to Mom, but at least he's there. Better still, I want to return to the time before we came out to Australia. I don't even care if the house is all dark, with the curtains drawn. Because the feeling twisting inside me right now is a thousand times worse than it ever was when I was there.

My view of the water's surface passes through to the depths. Tiny plants and creatures decorate the sides and floor of the pool—

spiky purple urchins, orange starfish, bright-red anemones, and constellations of flat, starlike shells.

For a moment, the glittery world reminds me of the dance costumes that Iris and I used to wear. When we lived in Pennsylvania, we performed in child talent pageants. Mom put Iris and me into the pageants when we were very young. The girls were all beautiful, with shiny curls and bow-shaped lips. But Iris and I were not beautiful. One of the star pageant girls once told us that we had plain, spoon-shaped faces that weren't meant for the stage. That had affected Iris way more than me. I didn't care about the pageants like she did. She'd spend ages curling her hair, applying red lipstick and putting on long, stick-on eyelashes that reminded me of spiders. She did look pretty, but it took a lot of effort.

Mom would sit watching as we danced on the stage, but she never seemed to enjoy it, and she barely spoke to the other pageant moms. We'd come home from the loud spectacle of the pageants to our dark house—the house with the curtains almost always drawn.

I tug a strange plant from the rock pool that looks like a string of opaque rubbery beads. Then I drop it when I spot something more interesting. A baby octopus has slithered out from the rocks at the bottom of the pool. I scoop it up and examine it. Its little body is greyish and barely spans the palm of my hand.

"Don't move," comes a voice from behind me.

I turn. It's Van Dawson, sunlight ringing his blond head.

"It's a blue-ringed octopus," he says. "Deadly. Put your hand back in the water. Slowly. Let it swim away by itself."

I fight the sudden urge to throw the creature back in. Van sounds calm but there's an undercurrent of fear in his voice, and it sets my heart banging against my chest wall. I lower my hand into the water. The octopus seems to take forever before it shoots off and vanishes into the depths.

Van's long legs collapse to a kneeling position. "Whew. My heart was in my mouth. Didn't anyone tell you?"

I try to sound brave, attempting a shrug that feels stiff in my shoulders. "Yeah, some Aussies warned us about blue-ringed octopuses once, but that one had no rings. Is it a baby?"

"No, that's as big as it gets. Once you see the rings, it's too late—the octopus is about to inject you with poison. And you'll see the rings, all right—they're neon blue."

Drawing air into my lungs, I consider this. The line between disaster and things being okay is razor thin.

"You won't make that mistake again." He picks up the plant that I abandoned beside my foot. "This is a Neptune's necklace. Seen these before?"

"Don't think so."

"Each of the beads is full of water." Pressing the beads between his hands, he squirts streams of water at me.

"Hey!"

A generous smile reaches all the way into his eyes. "You deserve it for giving me a heart attack when I saw you with the bluie."

I start to reach for the Neptune's Necklace, but then I snatch my hand back. I haven't seen him up this close before. His eyes are dark like olives and his hair curls in caramel waves beneath the straight, blond locks on top. His light brown skin is shiny with sweat. Even the patch of pimples on the left side of his forehead seems like a revelation.

I don't remember being my attention being so captured by a boy before. A strange flush of anger heats my face and throat, as if this is his fault and he's somehow making me stare.

Balling my fists, I put them on my hips. "Did you follow me?"

"My sister saw you run off, and she told me to go after you."

"Oh."

He starts pointing out the names of the creatures in the rock pool. Forgetting myself, I become fascinated with all the things I hadn't seen before and didn't know the names of. Seeming emboldened by my interest, he takes me on a rock pool expedition. Each pool is an entire world, filled with wonderful creatures. Unexpectedly, I'm in a happy bubble.

"I used to love rock pools when I was a kid," he tells me. "Thought you'd like these. Best ones around."

I catch a glimpse of the two of us standing before a large stretch of water. I look half Van's size. I see my small shoulders and skinny legs and straight hips. I suddenly want to be the same age as Iris. The same age as Van.

"I'll walk you back home," Van says.

"It's not my home."

Embarrassed by my outburst, I race from the beach and back to the path that leads to the river. Van catches up to me within a minute. "Hey, things will work out. Things always work out."

I nod rigidly, but I don't believe him.

Iris is both angry and curious when I return with Van. "Did he kiss you?" she demands after he walks away into the house.

Her words make my cheeks burn. "Of course not."

"Did you want him to?"

"Don't be stupid. Anyway, he's your age. You can smooch him if you want."

"He's cute, but he's not my type," she says coolly.

She's lying. Every good-looking boy she's met since we moved to Australia has been her type.

That night, as usual, we have dinner out on the deck of the restaurant after it closes. The salt in the river wafts through the night air. I steal looks at Van and hope he doesn't notice. But Anna and Iris notice. Mr and Mrs Dawson seem distracted, talking about menu plans and orders of kitchen stock.

I fall to sleep quickly once in bed, exhausted from the sun and the beach and the confusing images of Van in my head—and from hearing all the terrible things Iris was saying about our mother.

I wake in the middle of the night with sticky stuff on the sheet under me. When I switch on the lamp, I see that it's blood. My terrified whimpers wake Iris.

She steps from her bed across to mine. "You just got your first period, little sister," she tells me in a sleepy voice, wrapping her arms around my shoulders and kissing my temple. "Are you okay?"

"I want Mom."

"I know. I know you do."

Mrs Dawson comes and changes the sheets and gives me clean clothes and a pad. She doesn't make a fuss, but that doesn't stop me from feeling awful at what I've done to her white sheets.

Anna and Van come out of their rooms to see why everyone's up at three in the morning, but their mother shoos them back to bed.

After Mrs Dawson leaves the room, I curl up in the fresh bedding and cry. Iris says tears will be good for me. But they don't feel good. I've got the sensation that my insides are emptying out. I desperately want to tell Mom what's happening to me. I want her hug. I want her to tell me she's proud of me—just like I heard her tell Iris when Iris got her first period. I feel cheated of that.

"Hey, Lily," Iris whispers. "Is it hurting? I can ask Mrs Dawson for a hot water bottle and a painkiller."

"No. I don't think so. It's just weird... to be bleeding without something being really wrong."

"You'll get used to it. The cramps don't tend to kick in during the first months. Once they do kick in, they can be brutal."

I make a face. "Thanks. Can't wait for *that*."

"Sorry, but someone has to tell you this stuff. When I'm rolling around on the bed at night and I can't stay still, that's what's up."

"I thought you were just a bad sleeper."

"Nope. It's because of periods."

Iris and I had been sleeping head to foot on a single bunk bed for the past year. No room in the caravan for beds to ourselves.

In the morning, I'm too shy to even look at Van or Anna Dawson —especially Van. I grab a drink of juice from the fridge. Van is perched on a stool in the kitchen, shovelling a heaped bowl of cereal into his mouth and watching the TV set that's across in the living room.

My mother's face suddenly appears on the TV screen—her large eyes and sunny smile and yellow sundress. It's a news broadcast:

Police have so far not located the missing Elsa Jorgenson and four-year-old Ellie Lowood, nor has any trace of them been found.

Ellie's sister Grace has just been released from hospital and has returned to her Nautilus Bay home.

The report hits me like yet another punch to the stomach. Why can't the police find them? Why is it taking so long?

I head upstairs and crawl back into bed, curling myself into a tight ball.

4

I WAKE inside a nightmare in which faceless people are chasing Mom and Ellie.

My eyes open to a bright room. Sunlight is draped across my sleeping sister's face. Her mascara and eyeliner are smudged and cakey. I haven't seen Iris without eye makeup since she was twelve.

"Iris," I prompt. "You awake?"

She lifts an eyelid. "Am now. Feeling better?"

"I guess." Pushing my hair back from my face, I roll onto my back. "I saw the news earlier."

She sits up, suddenly alert. "Anything?"

"No."

A flicker of fear crosses her face, and she bites her lip as if she's holding words back.

"Won't be long before they're found," she says finally.

Her words don't comfort me. "Why haven't we heard from Dad yet?"

Stretching, she fakes a yawn. "You know our dad. Every time the police call, he's probably been out in the garage tinkering. I'm sure he has no idea Mom's missing."

"What if he crashed his car coming back from work? The roads are icy this time of year. No one would know. He lives alone now."

"We're both gonna go nuts thinking about this stuff. There's absolutely nothing we can do, little sis'. Hey, wanna get out of this house and go for a walk to the beach?"

"I want to go see Grace." I ache to see her again, but there's a deeper reason. She was there the night Mom and Ellie vanished. I'm desperate to know what she saw and heard.

Iris frowns. "She's in the hospital."

"On the news, they said she went home."

"Really? Well, let's go."

"How? It's too far to walk, and we've got no money to catch a bus or a taxi. Besides, that sergeant told us not to go visiting anyone."

"I've got an idea." Rising from the bed, Iris points to something out the window. "The Dawsons won't even know we've gone anywhere."

Sitting up, I peer through the glass. In the reeds far below, one end of an old kayak pokes out, its red paint peeling.

It's not much, but right now, it looks like freedom.

We get dressed and steal out of the house. The kayak takes a lot of tugging before it gives up its hiding place in the reeds. It's a dirt-caked, cavernous old thing, but when we push it into the water, it seems seaworthy enough.

We paddle it down the river, with Iris doing the bulk of the work. Her careful makeup job swims on top of the sweating skin of her face.

The river is smooth and glass-like, and we share it with the pelicans and ducks. It feels clever to be doing this—almost adventurous. As if Iris and I have snatched back one small piece of ourselves.

It takes just fifteen minutes to reach the part of town where the Lowoods live. After tying the kayak to a tree, we run to Grace's house.

Her grandfather answers the door, leaning on his walking stick. "I didn't expect to see you two."

Iris speaks up first. "Hi, Mr Lowood. We came to see Grace."

He frowns, shuffling as he adjusts his balance. "Oh, I don't think that's a good idea. She's on heavy sedatives, and she's sleeping. Maybe you can see her in a couple of weeks or so."

"We'll be gone in a couple of weeks," Iris tells him flatly.

In all truth, Iris and I don't know where we'll be in two weeks' time. That thought tunnels through my stomach, leaving a horrible, empty space.

A curtain shifts in a front window of the Lowood house. Grace's room.

I whirl around to Mr Lowood. "She's awake."

He winces. "But she's not well. Not well at all."

"Can we say hello—just for a minute?" I plead.

He pushes out a grumbling sigh. "All right, all right. Come in. You both look as if you could use a cold drink before you head off again anyway."

We follow him inside and down the hall. Mrs Lowood is in the sunroom, sitting in a wheelchair and sipping a cup of tea. She stares out the window at the view of their back garden.

We step up softly behind her. "Mrs Lowood?" Iris says.

She awkwardly rotates the wheelchair, and then she stares at each of us with a sad, surprised expression.

I hear Iris take a breath. "How are you, Mrs Lowood?"

Her hands grip the handlebars of her chair. "I'm struggling. I'll recover from the stroke... eventually. But what happened to our Ellie—I can never recover from that."

Mr Lowood pats his wife's shoulder. "I'll get you girls the drinks."

As Mr Lowood leaves the room, a tight smile presses into Mrs Lowood's face. "How are you even managing to deal with all this, you poor girls?"

"I can't bear it," I admit, my voice crushing to a whisper.

Mrs Lowood reaches for my hand. "We'll get through these dreadful days together. Somehow." She glances out to the garden again. "I can't quite believe that Ellie isn't about to skip in through the back door. She used to play out there on the swing every day." Her hold on my hand falls away. "If you girls know anything—even the smallest detail—you must tell the police. Do you promise?"

I switch my gaze to Iris, silently willing her to tell what she knows. But she refuses to acknowledge me. I bump her with my elbow. Iris rubs her arm as if she thinks the bump was accidental. But she knows exactly why I did it.

Mrs Lowood glances at Iris and me curiously.

"Lily and I wish with all our hearts that we knew something," Iris says in a self-assured voice. "Could we see Grace now? We'd like to catch her while she's awake."

"I'm sure Grace would love to see you," Mrs Lowood tells us. "You can go right on in."

When Iris opens the door to Grace's bedroom, I'm immediately struck by how different Grace looks. The last time I saw her, she had colour in her cheeks and her pretty hair was brushed. But now her face is pale and stained with dried tears, and her hair hangs limp. Our mother used to do Grace's hair in different styles each day because Grace loved it. The only thing that's the same about Grace is her wheelchair.

Fresh tears pool in Grace's eyes. "I was so scared I'd never see you both again. I thought you'd be back in America by now."

Iris and I rush to hug her, and the three of us cry together.

As we unlock from each other's arms, Grace draws a deep breath. "I know that you two will want to know about that night."

"That's not why we're here," Iris tells her, brushing her hair back. "We just... miss you."

I say nothing in case I give it away that Grace is right. My stomach tightens and I wait for her to say more.

"I need to tell you something," Grace starts. She takes her time to continue, but I know it's not on purpose. Talking is always an effort for her. I watch her steadying herself, taking air into her lungs.

"I think your mother went to meet with someone," Grace says. "I don't know that for sure. She just... she told Ellie and me to wait in the car. Ellie climbed onto my lap... and I sang her a song. Then her little head popped up and she was looking through the rear window —like she'd just seen someone she knows. She jumped straight out of the car before I could stop her."

Iris sits beside Grace on the bed. "Did you tell the police that?"

With a sigh, Grace nods. "Yes. But Sergeant Mullard spoke to me like... like I'm a child. Like what I say is not important."

My hands are clenched so tight they're sweating. "Did Ellie say anything before she got out of the car? Any clue as to who it was?"

"No clues," Grace replies. "I couldn't see anyone. I wanted... to follow Ellie. But you know I can't. I felt so helpless. I managed to get the door open, but that's all."

I grasp Grace's arm. "Did our mother seem scared at all that night?"

"No," she answers, wrinkling her forehead. "Everything seemed... normal."

Iris moves my hand. "You're squeezing poor Grace too hard, Lily."

"Oh... sorry," I exclaim.

"It's okay," Grace says warmly. "I get it. It's all so awful."

"You know that Mom never would have left you alone like that in the car," I tell her.

"I know," she says.

"How are you, anyway?" Iris asks. "Can we do anything for you?"

Grace's eye grows distant. "There's just one thing... but it seems selfish."

"Anything," Iris tells her.

"I want so much... to see the ocean again. It was like a prison in the hospital." Grace shakes her head. "Never mind. You can't get me there. And my grandparents think I'm too weak to go anywhere."

"We'll come up with something." Iris casts an uneasy glance in my direction.

I know exactly what she's thinking. The kayak. But that would be risky for Grace.

Iris stands. "Lily, go distract Grace's grandpa. And meet me down at the river. Sneak out the sliding doors at the side."

I freeze. "We can't."

Grace stares from me to Iris, looking mystified but hopeful.

"We're doing it," Iris answers, walking to the door and taking a peek up the hallway.

My breath catches tight as I walk out to the kitchen. Mr Lowood has just finished squeezing three glasses of orange juice. I ask him if the drinks can have ice, and I wait while he fetches the ice trays from the fridge. He pops cubes of ice into each drink. Then I take the clinking glasses of juice into Grace's room and place them on top of her tallboy.

After sneaking out through the sliding doors, I run to catch up with the others. Iris has already wheeled Grace to the end of the street and around the corner to the river.

Grace grins widely when she spots the kayak, but I hear just a hint of anxiety when she says, "If this is the last thing I ever do, it'll be a good day."

Iris draws in a long breath. "We'll make sure it's not the last thing you ever do."

We leave Grace's wheelchair behind as Iris carries her to the kayak.

Iris places her on the front bench seat where she can lean against the side of the kayak. We paddle back down the river, praying the Dawsons don't see us as we draw close to their house and restaurant.

"There's Dawsons Drift," Grace says, pointing. "I've never seen it from the water before."

I spot Van on the top balcony of his house. He's with a small group of teenagers. Music pumps from the open French doors of his bedroom.

Iris squints up at the balcony just as Van puts his arms around a girl. "Huh. That's Jaylene Becker. She was in my math class when we went to that school. She's really pretty."

I feel a tiny stab, but I'm not sure why. Jaylene Becker would be about fifteen. Of course Van is interested in someone his own age. Still, my mind jealously catalogues everything about Jaylene that I can see from here—her slender figure, her shiny black hair, the way she's dancing to the music.

We float past the Dawson restaurant, hoping that Van remains distracted and hoping Mr and Mrs Dawson don't see us. Iris guides the kayak into a tiny, sandy cove. There's a short track through scrubby bushland to the beach. Iris and I found this spot when we first moved to town. It's rocky and no good for swimming.

There's only one way to get Grace down to the shore, and that's by carrying her. She's light, but I can see Iris struggling as she carries her along the sandy track.

"This is far enough," Grace says. "I can see the waves. That's all I wanted."

Iris shakes her head, panting. "No, you need your feet in the water."

My sister carries Grace all the way to the shoreline. We sit together with small waves washing over our legs. No one's here, apart from the seagulls.

We talk about the year we spent together on the road, in the caravan with Mom and Ellie. We stick to the good times and avoid talking about what happened on that last night.

"Tide's coming in," Iris points out. "Your skirt will get wet, Grace."

She smiles, closing her eyes. "I don't care. I hereby claim this piece of shore in the names of Iris, Lily, Grace... and Ellie. No matter what comes next, this is forever ours."

"You hear that, ocean?" I yell. "You are ours!"

"You are ours!" the three of us scream together. "You are ours!"

We startle the seagulls, and they fly away from the rocks and over the water.

When we return to the kayak, the water current is running faster —and in the direction of the ocean.

Iris surveys the river with a worried look. "I think we'd better call your grandparents, Grace."

"Do you think you can make it?" Grace asks Iris.

"If it was just Lily and me, yes," Iris answers. "But..."

"Then, no surrender," Grace says firmly. "I don't want to get either of you in trouble."

We set back out in the kayak. The current seems even faster now that we're out on the water. The kayak rocks and pitches about. Iris battles to control it with the paddle.

Tiny bolts of fear pass through my chest as we keep getting spun the wrong way. Iris and I cry out as the kayak half rolls to one side before righting itself again.

Iris jerks her head around to me. "If it should tip, we have to get Grace to shore. We have to."

I nod rigidly, although I have no idea how we'd do that.

"Don't worry," I tell Grace. "We'll get you home. You need to be there for when Ellie is brought back." My words are to soothe myself as much as Grace.

But she seems strangely calm. "It's okay, Lily. Whatever happens, happens."

As I stare at her, I understand something terrible. Grace doesn't think my mother and Ellie are coming back—ever.

We finally get as far as Dawsons Drift. Its decks are now filled with customers, and they all seem to be looking our way.

A small group of people are standing on the jetty, including a woman in a wheelchair. My heart sinks as I see that they are Mr and Mrs Dawson and Grace's grandparents.

A part of me is relieved that this crazy kayak trip is at an end, but I'm also torn up inside at the expressions on the faces of the Dawsons and Lowoods.

Iris attempts to steer the kayak toward the jetty, but the current keeps pushing us out.

Van Dawson appears and hangs himself out on his stomach to catch the side of the kayak. His father holds onto his legs.

Van extends himself so far that he almost falls in. But he's gotten hold of the kayak.

Iris and I step out in disgrace. Mr Dawson lifts Grace out and into her wheelchair.

Mrs Lowood grips the handles of her own wheelchair and turns to Iris and me. "How could you do this to us—stealing our Grace away and then putting her in danger—especially when we already have a granddaughter missing? That's just... monstrous."

"It was all my idea, Gran," Grace insists, but Mrs Lowood doesn't remove her glare from Iris and me.

And she's not finished with us. "There's been a lot of talk around town," Mrs Lowood says. "I haven't wanted to listen to it. But it's all true. Your whole family—no one really knew you. You were barely here in Nautilus Bay before you were gone again on that ill-fated trip. Mr Lowood was in desperate straits when he accepted your mother's offer to take Grace and Ellie. And look where that's all ended up. Don't you two come back to our house. You're not welcome." Her eyes grow wet and her mouth small and tight.

Mrs Dawson is staring at Iris and me in open-mouthed exasperation, her frizzy hair half falling out of its bun. "Girls, what were you thinking? Do you have any idea what could have gone wrong out there on the water? I was completely clueless that you two had even gone anywhere... but then Jaylene told me she'd seen you in the kayak—with Grace."

I look across to Van. Jaylene is standing beside him now. She shrugs at us. "Sorry, but what you were doing was dangerous. Someone had to stop you." She links her hand with Van's, as if for support.

Van nods at us, agreeing with his girlfriend. I want to shove him into the water.

"We're sorry," Iris tells Mrs Dawson. "But you and Grace's grandparents can't keep us all locked away like prisoners."

Mrs Dawson squeezes her eyes shut, shaking her head. "I can't deal with you right now. Just... go to the kitchen and get yourselves some lunch—or breakfast. I don't even know if you've eaten."

Iris and I slink away, under the gaze of every single person who's out on the decks of the restaurant. I turn my head away as we pass Van and Jaylene.

Grace is wheeled away by Mr Dawson, with the Lowoods following.

I see Grace twist herself around and look back over her shoulder at Iris and me, her eyes large and sad.

5

"I THOUGHT Mrs Dawson would punish us," I whisper at Iris as we walk inside.

"Maybe she will later," Iris says. "Trust Jaylene to snitch on us. Anyway, I'm not hungry."

"Me either."

We go to sit on the couch in the living room. Iris switches on the TV and flicks through the stations. As she keeps flicking through the shows, I know what she's looking for. News broadcasts.

She stops on a talk show. We keep watching until the presenter announces the hourly news broadcast. We watch numbly as the presenter reports on international stories–war, bombings, and refugees. All terrible things I barely understand.

The presenter goes local next. Snatching up a cushion from the couch, I hug it tight.

Video of the search efforts to find Mom and Ellie appear on the screen. Police and volunteers are hacking their way through the everglades, their faces red and sweating in the heat.

The next moment, I spot something in the footage that makes my arms freeze on the cushion.

It's a man I know well. He's among the search volunteers. The broad back and thick neck are unmistakable.

I run to the screen and drop to my knees. "Iris! Look! The man in the white shirt at the far right."

"Who? Get your big head out of the way. Oh God... it's Dad."

Iris and I race each other to the phone in the Dawsons' kitchen to call Sergeant Mullard.

He answers us straight away. But he doesn't believe we saw what we thought we did. Half-heartedly, he assures us he'll check into it.

Iris grips my hands and squeezes them. "It was him. Dad. We know it was. We'll be getting out of here any minute now, Lily."

"But... why didn't he tell us he was here?"

From the shadow that enters my sister's eyes, I can tell she has the same question in her mind.

But she throws me a bright smile and then hugs me. "Just... wait for him to get here, and he can tell us himself."

It's late afternoon when the sergeant pulls up in his police car outside the Dawson house. Iris and I have been keeping vigil in the upstairs living room for hours.

We dash outside to meet him.

"Where's Dad?" I cry.

Sergeant Mullard blows out a breath. "I'm afraid it's not that simple."

"What's not that simple?" Iris demands. "We're sure it was Dad."

"That's not under question," the sergeant tells us. "I confirmed that it was, indeed, your father—Frederick Jorgenson."

I nod eagerly. "Everyone calls him Freddie."

The sergeant crosses his beefy arms. "He's been here in Australia for a week. Did you girls know that?"

We shake our heads, casting puzzled side glances at each other.

"You certain about that?" he asks.

Iris straightens. "Yes. But... Dad wouldn't have been here for a whole week without telling us."

The sergeant looks from Iris to me and back again. "Your father told me he flew out here intending to meet up with his wife and daughters. But he couldn't find you. And then when he heard on the news that his wife was missing, he decided to join the search party."

Iris seems stunned into silence. Something feels wrong. Mom was getting us to call Dad almost every week from a payphone. Why didn't he tell us he was coming?

But I push that from my mind. "He can come and get us now, right?"

"Not yet," the sergeant says in a cautious tone that instantly makes me worry. "This is what's happening—we're holding your father for questioning. So just hang tight—might be a while yet before you see him."

Iris's eyes grow huge with horror. "You don't mean he's a suspect in Mom's disappearance... do you?"

In the space that follows, Sergeant Mullard hesitates to speak. Vomit burns the back of my throat. Iris claps both hands over her mouth, shaking her head.

"We're not making any assumptions," he says finally.

But it's already clear. The police think Dad might have hurt Mom and Ellie. But he wouldn't do that. I know he wouldn't.

Iris and I are told we have to remain with the Dawson family. We walk back inside like prisoners walking to the gallows.

As soon as we reach our bedroom upstairs, I pin my sister against the wall. "Did you know Dad was here? Tell me the truth."

She pushes me away. "Are you crazy?"

"You still didn't tell me where you went that night. Did you meet up with Dad? Is that what happened?"

She leans close to my face. "No."

"I don't believe you."

"Believe what you like." She shoves me onto the bed, then spins on her heel and stalks out.

I hear her thud down the stairs. When a crunch sounds from the front yard, I run to the window of the upstairs living room. Iris is wheeling Van's bicycle through the gravel of the driveway. She jumps on the bike and rides away.

Night falls before she returns. We're in even deeper trouble with the Dawsons now. They tell us we're under strict curfew. But when they ask Iris where she went, she just says they can't keep her in and that she doesn't care about their curfews.

In the days that follow, Iris keeps leaving the house and staying away for hours at a time. I hate her for leaving me all alone. When Iris is here, we start having physical fights so fierce that we're pounding each other in the head—and the Dawson couple have to drag us away from each other.

In the early hours of each morning, I wake and cry to myself. The pain twists like a blunt knife inside me, slowly killing me. I miss my mother's laugh, I miss our corny sing-alongs on the road, I miss her lame mom jokes. I never knew I'd miss all of those things about her the way I do now.

A social worker advises that Iris and I return to school. It's the last thing I want. But it's out of my control. Everything is out of control.

Each day in the school corridors, rumours fly thick and fast around my ears. The other kids say all kinds of horrible things. They say Mom and Ellie were running from our dad the night they vanished, and our dad killed them both. They say Ellie ran away from Mom because Mom had been hurting her, and then Ellie fell off the cliff—and Mom fled the scene with our father.

Van Dawson seems embarrassed to be associated with us—he stays completely away from Iris and me at school. He holds hands with Jaylene in the school corridors and quickly turns his head if he sees me. I begin to hate him as much as I hate Iris.

The shame of everything crawls from the pit of my stomach and up into my throat, until I'm roaring at anyone who whispers about me behind my back. I shove anyone who gets in my face, which puts me in front of the school counsellor again and again. Until I'm suspended from school.

Everything, *everything*, has gone wrong. Iris begins refusing to get out of bed in the mornings. And then I do too.

The Dawsons soon give up on us. My sister and I stay in bed

until noon each day, barely eating. We've stopped fighting, and we don't talk to anyone, least of all to each other.

Mrs Dawson calls Iris and me to a family meeting. She's been crying, her eyes all puffy. We sit down at a table in the restaurant, out on the deck. It's Monday, and the restaurant is closed. Mr Dawson and Anna and Van are there too.

"Girls," Mrs Dawson begins, "we can't do this anymore. I did try my hardest. We all tried to help you. But you're going to have to go to another foster family. I'm so sorry."

Anna and Van don't meet our eyes.

I feel nothing but numb inside. It's just another episode inside this nightmare that refuses to end.

The silence is interrupted by a knock at the door. It's Sergeant Mullard, and he wants to talk to Iris and me. I have to fight an urge to run from him. He's always the bearer of bad news.

"Get packed up and dressed," he says in a gruff voice.

"So you can drag us to our new foster family?" I ask in a confrontational voice.

His eyes skate in a slightly baffled glance between us and his cousin, Mr Dawson.

Mr Dawson walks up. "What's going on, Quincy?"

Sergeant Mullard lifts his thick, ragged eyebrows. "I've got their father in my car right now. Time for them to leave."

I stare at the sergeant dubiously. Is he trying to trick us so that we go with him without making a fuss? Is Mr Dawson in on the trick?

My sister and I push past the sergeant and race outside. Dad stands next to a police car, his face bristly with a beard, a little battered and looking as if he's lost a lot of weight. Iris and I hug him on each side, even though it's rare that we've ever done that. Dad has never been the hugging type.

"Where's your luggage?" he asks.

"We don't have much stuff," I tell him. "The police didn't let us take anything from Mom's caravan."

"That's okay," he responds, pausing to squeeze our shoulders.

"You've both sprouted up. I'll get you new stuff. But why in blue blazes are you still in your pyjamas?"

His voice raises a desperation inside me, a reminder of how easy it is to lose things you thought were secure.

"Where are we going to stay?" Iris asks him.

His answer is swift and certain. "We're going home, girls. Got the flights booked for tonight."

Both Iris and I cry out and shrink back. I shake my head. "We can't leave. They haven't found Mom yet."

"The cops have ground me through the mill over the past month," he says. "I'm getting out of here before they find any other reason to try and shackle me. Anyway, they'll keep on looking for your mother whether we're here or not."

Iris draws her dark eyebrows together. "Why didn't you tell us when you first flew into Australia?"

"I was tryin' to find yous," he tells us. "And then when I heard your mother was missing, what could I do? Best thing to do was to try and find her. Maybe I made a big mistake. I'm sorry."

"Why'd you even let us go—I mean, in the first place?" Iris fires back. "None of this would've happened."

He holds the palms of his hands up to Iris in a gesture that looks like defeat. "Your mother had her mind made up. No one was going to stop her. I didn't know what to do. She was unhappy, and I thought—"

"You thought you'd just let her do whatever she likes with us? Take us to a foreign country?" Iris says, railing at him.

I've never heard Iris this angry with him before. For Iris, it's all been about the wrongs our mother committed.

"If I had my time over, I'd have chosen differently," Dad admits.

Iris isn't done. She crosses her arms tightly, shaking her head. "But you didn't."

Dad is definitely done with the conversation. "Quiet down. Go inside and get cleaned up and ready to go. You two look like a pair of ragamuffins."

It's a swift, awkward departure from the Dawsons' house after that. Mrs Dawson and Anna give us hugs, and then Anna gives us a pencil sketch she did of Iris and me on the riverbank. Van hangs back and just gives us a wave. Iris and I don't wave back to him. It's easy to tell they're all glad we're going.

Sergeant Mullard drives us to the airport.

Hours later, Dad, Iris, and I are boarding a plane. As the plane lifts off and heads out over the ocean, I feel nothing but panic. I'm leaving my mother behind in this country. I don't even know what happened to her. But I have no voice in any of this.

Drawing my feet up onto the seat, I lock my arms around my knees and try to hold back the sobs that rattle deep in my chest.

6

LILY JORGENSON

Present Day, Twenty-Four Years Later
NYC

The New York City dark gives way to a misty grey dawn. My twelve-year-old son, Jake, and I stomp through the streets in our boots and puffer jackets, searching for the dead and injured.

"Another one, Mom," Jake calls. He runs on ahead, passing under the Park Avenue Viaduct on Forty-Second Street.

As I catch up to him, he waits patiently by the tiny dead body he's found. A bird.

The birds die every morning during their migration south, flying straight into reflections in the windows. Jake and I have been volunteering with a conservation group to count and collect the dead birds—and find ways of ending the awful carnage. I wasn't surprised when Jake agreed to do this with me. He shares my love of animals.

"Good job, Jake." Crouching to the ground, I scoop the bird into a container.

Jake finds another bird—a common yellowthroat with the trademark bright yellow under its beak and delicate grey feathers on its back. We both think it's dead before we bend down for a closer look. It startles and flaps its wings—and flies away.

A grin spreads across Jake's impish face. This morning, he reminds me so much of his father. Terence has that same kind of unaffected Boy Scout smile that draws people in. Jake also got his father's dark, tight curls and quiet manner of speaking.

It's been years since I last saw Terence. Once, I thought we were inseparable. We were so wildly, crazily in love that we were sure of it, as if our love was an unwritten law. I met Terence on an elephant conservation project in India. Terence was a Californian trust-fund baby looking for a purpose in life. I had a fire in my belly—all my efforts to find my mother had been fruitless, and now I intended throwing myself into saving animals. Terence and I thought we'd travel the world on our big adventure, working for different wildlife foundations. He had been over the moon when Jake was born. But little by little, he started feeling boxed in by life with a young child. And then it was over.

It's strange how things that once seemed so certain can change so completely.

As Jake and I watch the yellowthroat fly high above the city street, one of the volunteers walks up to us, handing over a coffee and a hot chocolate. "Thought you two could use these."

The volunteer has shoulder-length blonde waves falling around pretty features and kind eyes. She looks around sixty years of age. I feel a small stab beneath my ribs. My mother would have been close to that age by now.

I flash a grateful smile at her. "You're an angel."

Jake and I sip our hot drinks as she leaves, steam rising in the air. It's unusually chilly for November, catching me by surprise. It had only been a last-minute decision to throw our winter jackets into the car.

I tuck in a curl that dangles from under Jake's knitted hat. "Are you cold?"

"Nope."

"Hungry?"

"Maybe."

"We'll be heading off in another fifteen."

He shrugs. "I don't mind. Let's find some more birds."

"Have I ever told you what a cool little guy you are?"

"Mom!"

"Sorry."

New York is starting to come alive. The sounds of car horns and roller doors opening punctuate the relative quiet.

My phone rings. I don't recognise the number.

"Hello, is this Lily Jorgenson?" says an unfamiliar male voice.

"Yes, speaking?"

"This is Detective Dawson of Nautilus Bay Police, Australia."

"Nautilus Bay?"

My jaw turns to jelly as I struggle to push out another word. That seaside town is a time and place of my childhood that exists in my brightest dreams and darkest nightmares.

I haven't heard from the police in fifteen years or more. And even then, the last of those calls were just to tell me they had no news. But for them to suddenly call me now, there must be something. I'm not sure if I'm ready to hear what this detective has to say.

"Please go ahead," I finally tell him in a voice that feels rigid on my tongue.

"This concerns your mother, Elsa Jorgenson."

"What have you found?"

"What we've found is a backpack belonging to Mrs Jorgenson."

I inhale a snatch of moist, chilled air. "Oh. Oh my gosh. Where?"

"North of Nautilus Bay and Noosa, in the Toolara State Forest."

A small hope blooms inside me. "How long ago? I mean, how long ago do you think it was left there? Recently?"

A pause comes before he says, "I'm afraid not. We think the backpack had been buried there under a layer of soil for a very long time. We've had some heavy flooding in all areas along the coastline here. Towns have gone underwater. Our best guess is that the floods dislodged the backpack. The bag matches the description given back in 1998."

I stare up at the dim New York sky. "Oh..."

"I'm sorry."

"What's inside the bag?"

"Bits and pieces. A camera. Photographs. Silver jewellery. A pair of sunglasses."

"I remember all those things she had. Did anything provide any kind of clue?" I ask.

"Not so far, to be honest. But we're right at the beginning stages."

I've been waiting so, so long for a call like this. I was almost resigned to it never happening—almost. But this has to mean something. It can't just be that they've found her personal possessions and then nothing more happens for another twenty-four years. I won't accept that.

"My family and I... we need resolution," I state.

"I'll do everything I can to get you that," he assures me. "I'm the detective in charge of this investigation now."

"Thank you. So, what's... what's the next step?"

"A number of avenues. One of the first things will be an intensive search of the area where the bag was located."

"Do you expect... that you'll find anything else? What I'm saying is..." My voice fades. I don't want to say the words *bones, skeletons, remains.*

He pauses before answering. "That I can't say. But I can tell you the search will be thorough."

"Have you spoken with my sister? Her name is Iris. Iris DeCarlo is her married name."

"Lily, I know what your sister's name is," he replies.

"Have we... have we spoken before?"

"This is Van. Van Dawson."

"The boy from my foster family?"

A flush of unexpected anger heats my throat. In an instant, I'm twelve again, feeling the burning shame of him turning his head from me in the school halls and standing there with his girlfriend outside his family restaurant, judging Iris and me for taking Grace away in the kayak.

"Oh, I'm sorry," I say, covering up my thoughts. "I didn't realise it was you."

"Well, Dawson is a common last name."

"You went into the police force?" I ask.

"Yeah. It's kind of in the family—my uncle, Sergeant Mullard, I think you'd remember. Well, he's actually my dad's cousin, but I've always called him uncle."

"Yes, of course I remember him."

"He's retired now."

"I guess he'd have to be in his seventies," I say. I find it distressing being reminded of Sergeant Mullard even more than I do Van Dawson. Mullard's updates about the investigation were sparse and vague. The older I'd gotten, the more I'd felt he hadn't done a thorough job of it.

"Yeah, he is that age," Van says. "About your sister—I spoke with her just before I called you. I... well, I got the impression there's some water under the bridge between you two. She didn't want to pass the news onto you herself."

"I can't say I'm shocked. We haven't spoken in... I don't know how long. Maybe thirteen years." I tried to lighten my tone as I gave him that information, but I failed. The years of silence between Iris and me stretch like a long, dark tunnel.

"Thirteen years?" He sounds surprised.

"I'm afraid so. Iris didn't want to stay in contact."

"That's kind of sad."

"It's just the way it is."

The call ends with Detective Dawson promising to keep in touch during the upcoming search. I'm left holding the hazy but painful memories from the night my mother went missing. And one sharp memory of Iris.

I can see Iris running through the rain, a yellow rain jacket over her head. I tried so many times to get her to explain where she was and what she was doing. But she always stuck to her story that she hadn't gone anywhere.

My sister is a liar.

7

It's a long drive back from New York to our home in Forestview, Pennsylvania. About ninety minutes. We're driving across the Hudson River towards Newport, toward a sky that should be growing lighter by the minute. But the heavy clouds are keeping it gloomy.

Jake looks small in his hoodie and bomber jacket as he sits next to me in the jeep. He keeps peeking at me in the way he did when he was much younger, a lock of hair falling over a large brown eye.

"Mom," he says. "What was the phone call about? Are you gonna tell me?"

"I... I got a call from the police. In Australia."

"Why?"

"It's about your grandma Jorgenson."

His mouth drops open. "Did they find her?"

"The police found something belonging to her. It's a backpack."

"Did she lose it somewhere?"

"They're not sure what happened. But they think it was left behind a very long time ago. Maybe even the night she went missing."

I'm feeling like a lost, lonely child as I explain that to Jake. Ever since that night, I've sensed a place inside me that has been searching for my mother. Constantly, I reached out to her, but no comforting arms responded to me. It's been an ache without an end.

"Oh," Jake says, "but will they be able to find her now?"

"I don't know. I hope they can find out something." My voice cracks, and I cough to cover it up. I want to keep talking, to reassure him, but the right words won't surface. I'm locked up inside myself, trying to process things I can't even name. "Hey... we'll stop for some pancakes at your favourite place?"

"Okay," he answers.

Normally, Jake is way more persistent about things, wanting to know all the tiny details. But he quietens, turning to watch the fields pass by. We stop at Clinton, New Jersey, for Jake's waffles and the second coffee of the morning for me. Normally, I'd grab a cream cheese bagel here, but my stomach is too tight for food.

Jake's eyes are huge as a stack of waffles are brought to our table. This morning, I've allowed him to have ice cream as well as maple syrup. It's the kind of morning to allow a treat.

Iris is on my mind. I have to contact her. Surely, we can't keep up this wall of silence between us. Not now.

Holding my coffee with both hands, I try to eke support from its warmth. I glance up at Jake. "I need to make a call—I'll just be a minute."

"No problem." He digs his fork into his breakfast with gusto.

I walk a few steps to the window of the café. I conduct a search and find a landline number for her and her husband, Gabriel DeCarlo. It's been a very long time since I called a landline.

When I call, I just hear a recorded message. It's a friendly male voice. "Hi, people. This is Gabe and Iris. I guess you've figured out we're not at home. Tell us who you are, and if we like you, we'll call you back!"

I leave a quick, stumbling message: "Hi, Iris. It's me... it's Lily. It's been a minute. I guess we should talk. I mean, we really need to. So, here's my number..."

Ten minutes after that, with Jake's belly full of pancakes and syrup, we head back onto the road. His mood turns from contented to gloomy as we drive through Nazareth and then to Forestview.

I drop him off at the gates of his school. His face seems full of questions as he trudges away. I don't know whether the news about his grandmother has affected him—he never knew her. But I know he never likes to go to school. He's had problems with fitting in.

With a heaviness in my chest, I swing the car around and head home. The house of my childhood peeks through the maple trees. I came back here to live when Jake was four years old, after my relationship with Terence broke down.

Dad has worked hard to keep everything as it was. He's worked too hard at it, actually. Everything is the same as on the day Mom left. The stonework on the chimney is still perfect. The colour of the siding is still the same shade of forest green as it was then. The front lawn furniture is the same furniture. The maple trees are the only things that have changed—they've grown larger, secluding the house even more than they used to.

I park my car and walk along the neat pathway and through the open front door. When I call out to my father, no answer comes back to me. After a search of his usual haunts—the kitchen and the garage—I find him working on the pool pump down in the basement. His face drips with sweat, and his shirt hangs half in and half out of his jeans.

I'm struck anew by how dark it is down here. I rarely ever venture down to the basement. The water in the pool looks murky, its chlorine making my eyes and nose water. The two windows that sit under the ceiling allow some air and light inside, but not nearly enough.

A cold wave of doubt runs over my skin as I watch Dad fixing the pump. He has never given me a sound explanation for that whole episode in Australia all those years ago. He'd been so secretive—flying out to Australia without even telling Mom he was coming. I ended up making a decision to forgive him, and I tried hard to get past it. But Iris didn't. She never made amends with him. Those were awful years after Iris and I came back to Forestview. The rumours about our parents had run deep—through the whole town. Iris had shocked Dad and me when she'd decided to return to Australia, when she was just eighteen. She'd been back in Nautilus Bay ever since. I knew that because I'd kept tabs on her.

Dad grumbles and swears under his breath. "One day soon, I'm gonna drain the pool and concrete over it." He's said that at least a hundred times, though he never does anything about it. Something's always going wrong with the ageing pump system.

"You could get someone else to do this stuff," I point out. "You don't have to do it all yourself."

"Now, why would I do that—go and waste money just to have some turkey come out here and mess things up?"

"Sure thing," I say. His response was the one I'd expected.

"How'd you and Jake do with the birds?"

"It was a low death count, thank goodness. We're at the end of the migration season." I dig my hands deep into the pockets of my jeans. "Dad, did the police call you earlier? From Australia?"

His head jerks up. "Is it about Iris or the kids?"

He still cares about Iris, even if she doesn't care about him. "No. It's about Mom."

His back stiffens, and he drops his head again, twisting the spanner on a rusted bolt. "Oh yeah? I've been out in the garden. Didn't have my phone on me."

He never has his phone on him, but now's not the time to chastise him about it. "They found something belonging to Mom—her backpack."

"Where?" he asks.

"At the side of a road, apparently. Near a forest. The floods brought it up above ground."

"Right... right. So, it'd been buried a long time?"

"The police think so."

"Anything else?"

I know what he means. He's asking if any bones were found. "Nothing else so far."

"Do the police think there's some kind of foul play?"

"The detective didn't say. They're mounting a search... nearby."

His pale-grey eyes fill with scorn. "They didn't do a good job of finding her before. Probably won't find her now, either."

"I know. But there wasn't much for them to go on before. This time, they've actually found something. So, I mean, maybe there'll be some way of tracing her."

He turns back to the pump. "Gotta get this thing going again, or the water'll go even greener."

I know the conversation ends here. Once he's done talking, he's done.

He's the only parent I have left, and he's so... inaccessible. He has a better relationship with Jake than with me. The two of them fall into such an easy rhythm together.

I cast an eye over the opaque water of the pool. I remember my mother swimming endless laps here at night, the overhead lighting so dim I could barely see her. The smell of the pool chemicals would waft up the stairs and through the whole house. Spots of mould would appear on the walls during winter and wet weather, and the odour would get even worse. And then there were the rotting bunches of roses—the ones that Dad would give Mom, only for her to store them away in a cupboard somewhere. And then the stink of rotting flowers and pool chemicals and mould would mix and permeate every inch of the house.

It was Mom who had wanted the pool. Dad had it installed when she was pregnant with me. Perhaps he keeps it in working order because he imagines his wife might come walking back in one day. After Mom left him, he never remarried or had a girlfriend—to my knowledge.

I head out and upstairs for a shower. Afterwards, I tie up my wet hair and change into comfortable clothes and slippers. These days, I work from home except when out on assignment. Today, I'm meant to be writing up an article on an ecotourist resort my company sent me to last week, in Baja, California. The resort offered a world away from the crowds, with rustic accommodation and whale and bird watching.

I'm nervous as I check my phone for a reply from Iris. Nothing yet.

Sitting at my desk, I open my laptop. My focus is all over the place, and it takes me a crazy amount of effort to get started on my article.

Giving up after a few minutes, I stop for a drink and to check the news. My stomach lurches to see an item about the discovery of Mom's backpack in our local media. I'm not ready for that.

Iris still hasn't returned my message.

I force myself to return to writing my article.

But I make no more than an hour's headway before Jake's school calls me.

8

"Ms Jorgenson, it's best you come down to the school as soon as possible," the school counsellor says over the phone.

A breath catches fast in my lungs. "What happened? What's wrong?"

"It's best you hear it direct from Jake."

"Please—is he hurt?"

"He's not hurt. How soon are you able to get here, Ms Jorgenson?"

"Alice, you know me. You don't have to keep calling me Ms Jorgenson."

"Of course. But, well, you know, I think it's best we keep this professional."

I want to yell at her that she's just told me what's *best* for the third time. But she ends the call abruptly.

When I rush into the school twenty minutes later, I've remembered to change out of my slippers, but I'm still wearing the pants with the hole in the left knee. Alice Eloise Dixon is at her desk, with Jake sitting opposite her. As usual, she wears starchy librarian-style clothing and her hair piled on top of her head. She's picking fluff from her cardigan as I enter her office.

Alice regards me through her clear-frame glasses, flattening her lips against her teeth in a beaming smile. “Have a seat. I’ll let Jake explain what went on.”

Jake turns to me with large sullen eyes. “I pushed Waylon."

My chest tightens. "Why?”

“He was sayin’ stuff."

“What kind of stuff?”

Jake draws his shoulders in, shoving his hands into his pockets. “He was sitting behind me in class, sayin' I’m a weirdo. Said my whole family are weirdos. He said... he said that my granddad killed my grandmother and a little girl in Australia and buried them in the dirt.”

I feel a sharp sting in the centre of my chest. Those rumours went around for years after Mom and Ellie vanished. To hear it dragged up again is painful, even if it’s from the mouth of some twelve-year-old kid named Waylon.

The counsellor is shaking her head at Jake. “Children will always say unkind things. What you need to do is to come to us, Jake —come to this office. We can’t help you if you don’t help us.”

I feel as if I'm back at school and I'm Jake's age again. Memories swell and burst in my mind until I have to catch my breath. "It was a few steps farther than just being unkind," I tell Alice. "It was a horrible lie about Jake's grandfather. And we live with him."

Alice's gaze snaps back to me. "You can't assault people for things they say."

"No," I agree reluctantly.

She pulls her mouth to one side. "Well, seeing as this is a first offence, no need for any harsh measures. But I think Jake could benefit from joining our weekly behaviour-management class. It helps children deal with anger issues. It runs after school on Wednesdays, and the classroom is—"

“Mrs Dixon,” I jump in, “are you aware that there has been news —about my mother?”

“Yes, I... I did hear it. Earlier today. This must be a difficult time for your family.”

"Yes, it sure is. And the thing is, that news was only reported this morning, after the kids were already in school. So that news can only have been heard by adults at the school, who have access to their phones and the internet. And this gossip—it has to have come from them. Waylon must have heard them talking. I think you might guess where I'm heading with this."

She tilts her head. "You're insinuating that he overheard some employees of the school gossiping? That's a big stretch."

I hold her gaze. "Let's get Waylon in here, and we'll ask him where he heard it."

"Oh," she answers, her gaze retreating from me. "No, I don't think that's necessary. This is about an altercation between two boys."

Jake shrinks as Alice and I turn to him. He looks about as uncomfortable as he can get with two women studying him.

"Jake," I say, "would you mind stepping out into the hall for a minute? I need to have a private talk with Mrs Dixon."

Alice looks alarmed at the suggestion, but Jake seems only too glad to remove himself from the situation. He jumps to his feet. His expression is both grateful and sorry as he closes the door, and my heart aches for him.

Folding my arms, I return my attention to Alice. "I want to know who said what. You know as well as I do that it had to be members of the school staff. I'll go and find Waylon myself right now, and I'll ask him."

"I wouldn't. That might be seen as a hostile thing to do—for a parent to approach a child in that way."

"Then you call him here to your office."

"I've already stated I don't deem that necessary," she says.

"Perhaps we should bring the principal in on this."

She straightens her stiff lacey collar. "You haven't changed, Lily."

"What do you mean?"

"Well, I... how should I say this? You were kind of... aggressive when you were younger. Perhaps you're not using your fists now, but there are other ways of striking people."

"Excuse me?" My skin heats at her accusation.

"All I'm saying is, children follow the behaviours that their parents model. It's a generational cycle. I know you had a difficult childhood. But you do have a history..."

"What history, Alice?"

"You punched my sister in the jaw."

I gather myself, drawing in a slow breath. "Your sister got a group of boys to surround me and call me the worst possible names. And she told them to say that my mother, Iris, and I paid our way around Australia by sleeping with any man that would have us. I was just twelve, then. *Twelve.* Trixie stood there sniggering, egging them on. Yes, I punched her."

Alice spreads her fingers out on her desk as if to anchor herself. "That never happened. Apart from you assaulting Trixie, that is."

"Oh yes, it did. And you were told about that incident by a few people—not just me."

"I wasn't there, and I believe Trixie's account."

"Of course you do."

She rises to her feet. "I think we should bring this conversation to a close. With all due respect, with this thing about your mother hitting the news again, it's to be expected that some words will be said around town. The best thing you can do is to prepare your son. If he comes and tells me about things being said to him, we'll deal with it. But he can't go retaliating. That just muddies the waters."

My stomach clenches. I desperately want to thump her in the way I thumped her sister all those years ago. But I can't do that.

I turn and stride out of the office. In the hallway, Jake is leaning against the wall, his bony arms crossed. I wrap him in a bear hug, kissing him on the forehead.

"What's gonna happen to me?" he asks.

"Nothing. You were just defending yourself. We'll talk about this later."

It hurts me to have to send him back to class. I've long been fighting the ghosts of a time decades ago, and now my son is caught up in that same fight. It's not fair.

As I head out from Forestview school, my chest feels as if there are ropes tightening around it.

My phone tinkles. I have a message. When I check it, I see if it's from Iris.

In this moment, I wish that the walls between Iris and me would fall away. I could tell her about what just happened with Alice Eloise Dixon. Iris used to hate her too. Iris is the only person in the world who went through the same events I did as a child. Maybe it's time we became sisters again. Maybe I could even find a way to forgive her for holding back the secrets of the past. She was just a fifteen-year-old kid then.

Still, without knowing what she did, how can I decide whether it's forgivable?

I browse to my messages. My heart sinks to see that Iris has barely dashed out a line in reply. It's written exactly the same way she used to text—in her own style of grammar that reads like some kind of word salad:

Lily, terrible time for us for sure, got to run, at orthodontist with one of my twins, talk as soon as I can swing it, ok?

I can tell that she hasn't changed at all.

9

WHEN I RETURN HOME from Jake's school, Dad's in the kitchen, cutting up vegetables to make soup. He rejects my offer to help. In some ways, he still treats me like the little girl who cried buckets every time she tried to chop onions.

"How about I peel the carrots?" I ask him.

He nods. "I want six of 'em."

"Sure." I begin washing the carrots in the sink.

He hacks at a large butternut pumpkin. "What had you rushing out of the house hell-for-leather?"

"Jake got into some trouble. Kids are starting to say stuff."

Dad huffs, shaking his head. "That quick?"

"Yeah. That quick. And then I kind of lost it at the school counsellor—you remember Alice Eloise Dixon?"

"I know the Dixons only too well. Don't have much that's good to say about 'em."

"Me neither," I say.

He makes swift, jerky moves as he skins the butternut.

I touch his arm. "Whoa there."

His eyes focus on me. "She never should have gone."

"Who?"

"Your mother."

"You mean, to Australia?"

Making an affirmative grunt, he keeps working with his knife. "If she needed a break away from here, she shouldn't have left the country. She intended to come back. She had a life here."

He's deluding himself. Mom never planned to come back.

In a careful tone, I say, "I'm sure she missed a lot of things about life here. I did too."

"Damned right. You sure did. You loved fishing in Bushkill Creek with me and hiking in the Poconos. There's nothing like it anywhere else in the whole world. And you and your sister had the pageants."

"I did love all that. Well, I didn't miss the pageants. But I know Iris did."

"Yup. Mystery to me why your mother even put you girls in them. Don't know why women do half the crazy things they do."

I stick my paring knife into a carrot and leave it there. "Oh, not the old *women are mysterious creatures* thing again. That chestnut should have been cracked open a long time ago."

"You're different, Lily."

"No. No, I'm not. I'm just a woman, Dad."

"You're not like your mother. Or like Iris. Could never figure either of them out."

"But you can figure *me* out?"

"You call a spade a spade. You don't dance around the truth."

"People think I'm too blunt," I say.

"People are snowflakes."

After dicing the butternut and the onions, he shuffles over to the pot of water boiling on the stovetop and dumps them in.

"You forgot to fry them first," I say. "More flavour."

He shrugs. "Ah well. It's done now. Get the carrots in the pot, okay?"

As he heads away, I return to peeling the carrots.

I don't think he's ever forgiven my mother for leaving him or forgiven Iris for returning to Australia. Even so, he hasn't forgotten about Iris. He dutifully sends her money each month from a trust fund he's established. He gives me my share in cash.

By rights, Iris should be the daughter he favours. She's exactly what he imagines a good woman should be. She's married with three children, living a stable life, working for her husband's business and looking after her family. And she's happy. A least, her social media tells me she is.

Iris's rejection of Dad stung him hard. I give him updates on her life sometimes, based on what I see in her online photographs. He listens but rarely comments. I'm not even sure why I do that. Maybe I'm trying to string together some semblance of a family, even though the threads of it are just gossamer on the wind.

Six weeks go by. Six of the tensest weeks I've ever experienced.

It doesn't help that the detective leading the case is Van Dawson, because he's all wrapped up with the most raw and painful time of my life. But he does as he promised, and he keeps me in the loop.

Bleak images keep sliding into my mind of what they might find buried there in the forest. I can barely focus on anything else.

Jake hears whispers around him at school and a few jibes shouted at him from kids in the street after school's out. I want to shield him from all of that, but I can't.

I hear the whispers too. I see the glances and the stares. The rumour mill is spinning again. There are articles about Mom in the local media—including old photos of her, Iris, Grace, Ellie, and me. Like it's all still happening.

I drop Jake at school and then go back home to finish an assignment I should have handed in at work weeks ago. I catch sight of myself in the hallway mirror. I'm looking grim and a little haggard. I haven't brushed my hair today or even showered.

When Detective Dawson's name appears on my phone screen, I hold a breath and answer immediately.

"Lily, I wish I could give you better news," he starts.

My mind goes to a dark place. They must have found skeletons. They've found my mother's and Ellie's bones, and this is how it ends. They'll never find their killer because it's been too long, and any possible evidence has now washed away in the floods, and—

"Are you there?" he prompts.

"Yes, sorry. Whatever the news is, I'm ready for it." That's a lie. I'm not ready.

"I've just been out to speak with our forensics team. Today is the last day of operations."

"The last day? Is that because something was found, or—"

"No, I'm sorry. Nothing has been found. It's been an extensive search. The forensic team brought in ground-imaging equipment, and they dug samples from many areas. The decision's been made not to continue searching the site."

A moment ago, I was dreading hearing they'd found bones. Now I'm in limbo again and wondering which scenario is worse—bones or this endless stretch of emptiness.

"So, that's it?" I ask.

"'Fraid so. I wanted to be able to give your family answers, but we didn't get anything. We've come to the conclusion that your mother's bag was most probably thrown from a car. Our best theory is that a vehicle pulled up at the roadside, and someone tossed the bag out. Over the years that followed, soil covered the bag."

"So, what are you thinking—that someone abducted Mom and Ellie and then threw Mom's backpack out of their car?"

I don't voice the in-between stages of that question. Because that throws up terrible mental images of what might have happened to them between being abducted and the backpack being disposed of.

"That scenario is possible," Van admits. "We just don't know."

"Where does that leave us? Nowhere?"

"Don't lose hope. We've got an expert team still looking at traces of DNA inside the bag. And we're very interested in the photographs. Those are still in the process of being restored. And, uh, there is one thing that didn't match with the original file notes of this case."

Every nerve of my body tunes into that last thing he said. "What didn't match?"

"There were a few business cards in your mum's purse. All a bit degraded but fortunately salvageable. One of them is the card of a real estate agency, and it has a name and number written in pen on the back. The name is Silvia White."

I'm disappointed with what Detective Dawson has just told me. It doesn't seem at all important. "She must have been a Realtor."

"Yes, a real estate agent," he agrees. "Silvia apparently moved away in early 1998, to the UK. Now, the original police file states that Elsa Jorgenson was renting the house on Tiger Street—the house you lived in when your family first came to Australia in 1997?"

"That's correct. That's where we lived."

"Okay, well, there was a number on the back of the business card —195000. That had me puzzled. I mean, it's not a phone number. Then I twigged. Maybe it was the price of a house—you know, houses were a lot cheaper back then. So I did some investigating. And I was right. Back in 1997, the Tiger Street house sold for $195,000."

"Okay. So it must have sold sometime before we rented it."

"Actually, the house was sold to Elsa Jorgenson."

"My *mother*? No, that's not right. We didn't own it."

"Yes, you did. I've looked up the title deeds. Your mother did indeed buy it."

I suck in a breath, an image of that house flipping in my mind. That first day that we walked inside it, Mom was so excited. It was a modest house, but it had everything she wanted—a pool and a view of the ocean. But she never once said the house was ours to keep. I distinctly remember her telling us she'd rented it. Did Mom buy the house sight unseen before we even moved to Australia?

"I don't understand this," I tell him. "It doesn't make sense that she kept it a secret."

"Look, the house might not be significant to the case, but I'm guessing it might be very significant to you and your sister."

"But... why didn't the police find this out back in 1998?"

"I don't know the answer to that. But the file does state a full search was carried out on the house. There are notes and photographs here, all documented."

"Yes, I remember they searched the house. I saw that on the news... when I was at your house." I picture myself at age twelve, sitting cross-legged on the couch with Iris in the Dawsons' living room, watching video of police roaming through our old bedrooms and feeling almost violated. Nothing had been private anymore. "Okay, so, I'm just... trying to get my head around this. It's kind of a shock."

"I understand," Detective Dawson says quietly.

"Well... do you know what's been happening with the Tiger Street house all this time? Is it even still standing? It was falling apart when we lived there. It must be an absolute wreck now."

"I actually took a drive past it. It's been kept in fairly good repair by the looks of it."

"Really? But... who on earth has been repairing it?"

"That I don't know," he says.

"So, someone's been keeping it repaired while it's just been sitting there empty for decades?"

"Not exactly. I stopped and spoke to a neighbour. From what I've been able to find out, it's been rented to holidaymakers for a number of years."

"The surprises keep coming. Who's been renting it out?" I ask.

"That's where things continue to get murky. The neighbour has no idea."

"Whoever was renting the house out must have known it didn't belong to them. That's... fraud, right?"

"Trust me, I'm going to be doing some digging. I wanna know what's going on too. It seems it was last rented out about two months ago and has been empty since. That might mean they stopped as soon as word about your mother's recovered backpack made the news."

"Hmmm. It sounds like they were worried someone would find out Mom owned the house. And they were right. Because you did find that out."

"Yeah. I agree. It's a definite concern," he says.

"What did my sister say—about the house? I'm really curious to know."

"I wasn't able to contact her. I left a message. I did catch her earlier, though—she knows that the search at the Toolara Forest site has ended."

"Oh. Okay."

"Do you want me to try again, or are you two speaking now? What's the situation?"

"I tried calling her before, but she just sent me a quick text message back. Look, I'll call her again and tell her about the house. The two of us need to start talking, especially now that there's a house to sort out."

"I have to agree with that. Good luck." He ends the call there.

My heart is going just a little too fast. I remind myself to breathe. It's not so much the news about Mom owning the house that's disturbing me—it's the fact that she hid this from us. Why didn't she tell us?

I pick up the phone again. I need to call Iris. The hell with text messages. For the first time in thirteen years, Iris and I are going to hear each other's voices.

10

I CALL Iris back on the number from which she sent me the text.

I'm coiled up tight like a rusted spring. I've had a million conversations with Iris over the past years—none of them real. I've imagined she's been with me on my vacations, sitting beside me in the car or plane and chatting about the life I see on her Instagram. I've imagined exchanging talk about our children. And in the small hours when I can't sleep, I've confronted her a thousand times about the night Mom vanished.

I'm startled from my thoughts when a woman answers in a breezy tone: "DeCarlo and McKellan Constructions. How can I help you?"

At first, I think it isn't Iris, because the accent sounds Australian and because this seems to be a business number. That can't be my sister. But I remind myself it's been over a decade since we last spoke.

"Hello, hello? Anyone there?" the woman prompts.

It *is* Iris.

"Iris... it's me. Lily."

Silence expands on the other end of the line. "Oh. Goodness. Lily, oh my God, it's been so long."

I'm relieved to be past the first hurdle. And she hasn't slammed the phone down in my ear—unlike the last conversation I ever had with her.

My words rush out. "Yes, it really *has* been so long."

"I meant to call you back. I did. But you know how it is. Things have been hectic. Lily, I so hate to do this, but can we talk a little later? I'm actually in the middle of the school run."

I'm feeling deflated already, anger going on simmer at the back of my mind. She's trying to end the conversation. It's not much different to her slamming the phone down—just a softer version of it.

But I'm not letting her get away with that. "I thought you were at work?"

"Yes, I am. I answer calls from clients and contractors no matter where I'm at. They don't know I'm not in the office. Have to keep the ball rolling. Busy, busy."

"Are you on the road right now?"

"Not exactly. I'm sitting in a slow-moving queue of cars outside the school. But I have to take off as soon as the kids are here. We'll talk soon, I promise. But right now, I—"

"Iris, did you know about the house?"

"What house?"

"On Tiger Street. The one we lived in."

"What about it?" she asks.

"Mom owned it."

"What? No, you're mistaken. She was only renting it."

"I've just spoken with the detective," I tell her. "Van Dawson. He looked into the title deeds. Our mother's name is on those deeds."

"For real?"

"He was certain."

"Wow, I can't believe it. That's crazy."

"Right?"

She releases a long breath. "But... what was Van doing poking around at that end of things? I mean, that's got nothing to do with the search of the forest."

"Iris, does it matter?"

"No. No, I suppose not. It just caught me off guard, that's all. I guess it shouldn't surprise us that Mum bought it. She was so... well, whacky at times."

I catch the way she says "Mum" now instead of "Mom." At least, it's some mix of the two. I picture her kids calling her Mum and Mummy—which they must have done since they were born. It's a small thing but feels large in this moment.

I don't know your children, Iris, and you don't know Jake. We're all strangers to each other. How did we get here?

"Our mother *was* impulsive," I agree, my voice sounding rigid in my ears.

"I didn't think she had any money to buy a house with, though," Iris says.

"I know. I don't get it. So... how have you been these past weeks? I've been on edge, waiting to hear what the police would find."

"Oh, me too. It's been real. After all this time, her backpack gets washed up in the floods. It's just so random and bizarre."

"If only we'd known it was there, like, decades ago."

"Probably wouldn't have helped. The police haven't found out anything new from it. I mean... apart from the house." She groans. "Oh, for the love of—a kid almost rammed his damned scooter straight into my car! So many kids on scooters and bikes. If they ding my car, they'll wish they were never born."

The low rumble of an engine sounds over the phone, and I guess that Iris is edging her car forward.

"The kids are late," she says with a sigh. "They'd better hurry it up. They've got dance, drama, and soccer practice this afternoon. I bet it's Audrey. That girl of mine needs a fire lit under her most days."

"I saw pictures of your kids on Instagram. They're lovely."

"Oh, you found us?"

"Yeah, I did."

"Oh. Well, I've seen your kid online too—Jake. Handsome boy," she says. "He looks like you."

"He's a lot like me in personality, too, poor kid."

Iris's short, snorting laugh fills the phone. It's a sound I haven't heard in a long time. I feel a deep longing, a desire to chat with her like sisters would and have a giggle together. We just admitted that we've looked each other up online. Isn't that some kind of point from which we could start again? Meet up again, even?

"Hey," I start, "maybe I could come there and take a look at Mom's things. I'd really like to do that. And maybe we could—"

"You want to do *what*?" she snaps.

"See our mother's things," I repeat, with less certainty this time. "And now there's the house to deal with too." I don't finish my prior half-said sentence about us meeting up.

"Oh," she says. "Look, I can deal with the house. It wouldn't be a huge bother."

"Deal with it how?"

"Well, sell it."

"Sell it?" I breathe. "Seems a little soon to make any decisions."

"Lily—we have to be realistic. Our mother's not coming back."

"I know." But I feel the spring inside me coiling tighter and tighter. Iris didn't have to say that. And I'm not even sure it's true. I'm not sure of anything when it comes to our mother. I don't think there is anyone in this world who really knew her.

"We're going to have to deal with this like adults," Iris continues. "The media is already dredging up old information about the time Mum went missing. If you come here right now and visit the house, then the news will get out that Mum owned it—and the media will have a field day. They'll go nuts with all the old speculations and theories about what happened to Mum and Ellie. We got dragged through enough of that when we were kids, didn't we? We can just sell the house quietly without it even going to market."

"The media is already digging up old speculations here in PA. I guess that's because Mom lived here."

"Well, there you go. It's already started. Let's not add fuel to the fire."

"Iris... I'd like the chance to see the house before it gets sold."

Her response is as swift and sharp as a guillotine. "You don't have to live in this town. I do."

I catch my breath at her sudden cutting tone. This conversation has all been about her. All about what Iris needs and wants. I have to hold myself back from yelling at her.

"There's something else," I tell her. "Someone's been renting the house out. As a vacation rental. We've got to figure out what's going on."

"Well, I've heard of things like that happening before. People see a vacant house, and they try their luck."

"You don't find it strange?" I ask.

"Not really. This is a holiday town. A prime spot for short-term rentals."

"But I—"

"Lily, for God's sake, let it go. Don't come here right now, okay?"

Pain pools inside me without warning. Dark water spilling in. I don't know what I expected out of this conversation with my sister. But it's a razor-sharp reminder of why we haven't spoken in so long. Everything was always all about her.

"Hey, I've got to go," she says in a slightly softened voice. "My kids are running up to the car. Talk soon."

The phone goes dead, and I'm left with nothing but the sensation of cold water swirling inside me.

11

I DECIDE to look up the old house in Nautilus Bay online.

I've thought about that house a lot but never wanted to see it again—because it haunts me. It's the only touchstone that remains in that whole place—the only tangible thing from back then. But it's a reminder of a place and time I can never go back to. I can never have that sunny, bright sense of home again. Mom, Iris and I were truly happy there. There was always music and laughter and people. A stark change from life in our house in Forestview, Pennsylvania.

I switch on my laptop and navigate to Google Maps. I realise I don't remember the number of the house. The number wasn't important back then. We knew it as the yellow house. That was what the kids on our street called it, and we adopted that name for it too.

My fingers tremble as I type in *Tiger Street, Nautilus Bay*.

I find the street and scroll along it at street level. Everything looks familiar yet totally different. When we lived there, it was a little beach town with faded houses and cracked sidewalks with tree roots growing through them. There'd be beach towels hanging on the street signs. The ocean was everything—the whole reason for the town's existence. It came to life in the spring and summer, full of tourists—families looking for a cheap vacation. I could almost smell the hot fries and hamburgers and hear the music of the 1990s blaring from people's houses and cars.

Tears prick my eyes. I didn't expect the memories of this place to come back to me so vividly.

I keep moving along the street. The houses are larger and far more expensive looking now, most of them no less than mansions. So many of the older homes and blocks of units have been torn down. For a moment, I'm not at all sure if I'm headed in the right direction.

But then, there it is. The house. It's still yellow.

It's still much the same as I remember. The house is tall and narrow with a balcony on the top floor. I didn't know the style of it when I was a child, but looking at it now, I'd describe it as Hamptons style with an Australian-beach-town flavour.

I click on the image to enlarge it. The paintwork on the siding was dull and peeling when I was a child, but it's been sanded and repainted. The yellow is a deeper colour. The garden is tidier, and there is a big hedge hiding the pool from the street. The hedge never used to be there. We used to sit around the pool and talk to everyone who passed by.

The neighbourhood kids were attracted to that pool like ants to sugar. At the time we moved in, the house had been unoccupied for many years, and the pool had been drained. But once we were there, the yellow house was alive again. Mom, Iris, and I scrubbed the pool clean the first week. I remember the day we filled it with water. We were exhausted but happy, jumping in and floating on the surface, watching rainbow-coloured birds fly overhead.

I sit back in my chair, pulling myself to the present, still captured by the sight of the yellow house on my computer screen. But the past is the past. I need to find out more about this house and figure out what to do next.

As soon as I told Iris about the house, she raced straight to the finish line with a suggestion of selling it. I need to be armed and ready next time I speak with her. I decide to start by finding out how much the house is worth.

I browse online to a list of Nautilus Bay's Realtors and call the first one.

A woman with a pert English accent responds. "Hello, Palm Trees Real Estate, Nautilus Bay. Leonie speaking."

"Hi. I wanted to chat to someone about house prices in Nautilus. Who should I speak to?"

"You can talk to me. To whom am I speaking?"

"Katie," I say quickly. Katie is the name of a friend I had as a child. I'm not ready to reveal whom I am.

"Going by the area code showing on my phone, Katie, you're calling from America?"

"Yes, that's right."

"So that I can help you better, can I ask what your interest is in Nautilus Bay?"

"I'm just... looking for a vacation property. I visited the town a long time ago."

"Okay, great. Is there any part of town, in particular, that you liked?" she asks.

"Yes, actually—the street that runs along the main beach."

"Tiger Street? Very nice. Which end—nearest to the river or the national park?"

"Uh, the end up on the hill."

"The hill has great views. What's your price range? I can convert it into American dollars for you."

"Well, I'm not sure. What would a fairly unassuming little weekender cost? I'm talking something that's unrenovated."

"Hmmm. Well, there aren't many of those left. And I don't know if I have any for sale at the moment."

"But if one were to come up?" I ask.

"Okay, in that scenario, on that street and position, for an unrenovated weekender, you'd be looking at somewhere between two and three million. So, in your money, somewhere between one and a half to two million."

"Goodness. That much?"

"I'm afraid so. Real estate went crazy here during the pandemic.

Everyone wanted to get out of the cities and buy a house somewhere with fresh air."

"I can understand that."

"Shoot me your email, and I can put you on our list. As soon as something you like comes up, we can get the ball rolling."

"Thank you." I give her an old email address that I no longer use, which doesn't contain my name.

After the call, I can't help myself from staring at the house on my screen again. The potential price of the house isn't huge by today's standards, but it is still far more than I was expecting. But the money might go to Dad. He and Mom didn't quite get to the point of divorce.

I'm deep in thought, which causes me to flinch when a voice comes from behind me.

"Whatcha lookin' at?" It's Jake. He shouldn't be home from school yet.

As I spin around in the swivel chair, my heart sinks through my chest. Partly concealed by a lock of hair that lies across his face, a purplish bruise runs from his eye to his temple.

12

"WAS IT WAYLON?" I ask, cupping my son's bruised face between my hands.

"Was a few of 'em."

"Who?"

"Waylon and his buddies. Started with them calling me a foot licker."

"A what?" I ask.

"Like... a stray dog that hangs around where no one wants him and licks people's feet to make them like him."

The words tear pieces from my chest. I know instinctively that those holes won't fill themselves in. Not ever.

I notice then that his school clothes are wet. The ground outside is patchy from a light snowfall. I guess that he's been down in that slush.

"Oh, Jake, honey. Where did this happen?"

"In the playground." Jake wipes his nose with the back of his hand.

"This is serious. I'm calling the police."

"They'll all stick to the story that I started it. I can't win."

"They can't get away with this. I'm going down to the school."

"No—don't. I don't want you to. I'll just... I'll just stay away from all of them. They got angry with me today because I was hanging with Jeremy, and they didn't want anyone to hang with me." Jake's shoulder rises in a rigid gesture that is meant to be a shrug. But it fails to look casual.

When I hug him, I don't want to let go, because if I do, I get the sense I'll lose him. He keeps his arms firmly by his sides and doesn't hug me back. I hate what this is doing to him. But I don't know who to turn to. My father will just give Jake advice about how to smack one of the kids so hard that the others will run. And I know that Alice, the school counsellor, will choose to believe the other children over Jake.

"Mom, I just wanna go to my room now. *Space*, okay?"

That had been our code word for the past couple of years. Whenever one of us needed some time out, we used the word *space*.

"No. Sorry, I can't give you that right now. I have to figure out what to do."

"This didn't happen to you, Mom. It happened to me."

"I know," I say.

"I don't want to do anything about it."

"And just let this go on and on? What, year after year?"

His eyes shine wetly, eyelashes clinging together. "You're not in control of what happens to me. You can't make it different."

I don't have a reply to that. The room suddenly feels too warm and devoid of oxygen. It seems as if other people are always controlling the narrative—not just for Jake, but for me, too. Have I retreated too far and given other people too much space? And have I been teaching Jake to do that?

My mind reaches back to the past six weeks. Six weeks of whispers and rumours. Six weeks of Jake having to deal with Waylon and those other kids. Six weeks of the site in Australia being dug up to look for the remains of my mother and Ellie Lowood, with not a trace being found. And what now? Things just go on like this?

I realise that I don't trust Van Dawson with this case. He's related to Sergeant Mullard, after all. All of Van's assurances to me are probably just lip service. What if I go there and try to follow the trail of Mom's disappearance by myself?

The more I think on that, the more it seems like the only way forward. I'll take things into my own hands.

You think I haven't changed, Alice Louise Dixon? Maybe I changed too much.

"Look," I say to Jake. "You know that luggage you have under your bed—that old suitcase of mine that's filled with your books?"

He gazes back at me under a deeply puckered forehead. "Yeah, I guess..."

"I want you to take out all the books and put them away in your closet. Then we're gonna pack that suitcase."

"With what?"

"Your clothes, Jake. We're going away for a little while."

"Going away?" he asks.

"Yeah."

"Where to?"

"Australia."

"No, we're not."

"We are."

"Because of what happened to me?" he asks.

"Yes. And because of Grandma Jorgenson."

"For how long?"

"I don't know. Could be a week or so."

"What about school?"

"Yeah, what *about* school?" I say.

My answer makes a tiny smile appear at the edge of his mouth.

I make a second decision. I'm not going to tell Iris we're coming. I don't know why I stood back when she snapped at me. We're not kids anymore—she can't dominate me the way she used to.

"Come on," I tell Jake. "Let's see about that nasty bruise of yours. I'm sorry, but that means a quick trip to the doctor to see if it's even worse than it looks."

I WAIT until the next day to tell Dad.

As I predicted, he does not take well to the idea of Jake and me travelling to Australia.

"Nothin' you can do there you can't do from here," he mutters. He's digging a path through the thick snow that blanketed our front yard overnight.

I pull the hood of my jacket over my head to protect my ears from the sharp wind. "I just feel like I need to."

"Well, I'm here to tell ya that you don't. And I don't agree with you hauling the boy out of school."

"Jake will be fine. He's only twelve. And I think, considering the circumstances, it'll be good for him to have some time away from school." I shove my hands into my pockets, my right hand curling around a piece of folded paper. It's a list of names I wrote down—a list of every person I intend following up when I get to Australia. Iris is the last name on that list. She's going to tell me what she knows. This time, I'll make sure of that.

Jake is down at the other end of the path, shovelling snow from the front steps of our house. I've never seen him approach this task with so much gusto. I don't know whether he's venting his anger at Waylon on the snow or whether it's some kind of release because we'll soon be leaving town.

"Take it easy, kiddo," Dad calls to Jake, trudging up to him. "You'll dent the shovel. Shovel it in layers rather than attacking your way right to the bottom. Then you don't damage anything or hurt yourself."

"Sure," Jake answers in a noncommittal way.

My father takes the shovel and demonstrates what to do then hands it back to Jake. "Your shiner's really showin' itself."

Jake touches his eye. The bruise has darkened and spread, but the doctor said it should start to clear quickly.

"You shoulda belted the kid that hit you," my father tells him.

"Dad!" I exclaim.

My father doubles down. "Well, he shoulda."

Jake continues shovelling snow. "Couldn't if I wanted to, Granddad. The others were holding me back."

My father grunts. "You were too slow. What you've got to do is get in fast, smack one of 'em into the middle of next week. Be sure to look a little crazed. The others will be too scared to come at you."

It's exactly the advice I thought Dad would give Jake. I can't deny that a part of me wishes that Jake had been able to do just that.

Still not looking up, Jake lifts his shoulders in a shrug. "Dunno how to hit that hard."

"I'll give you boxing lessons," Dad offers. "You won't get through life too well if you figure you can just run away from your problems. You can't go doing that. Some people spend their whole lives running."

I can guess he's talking about Mom now. He thinks that she was fleeing from her problems when she left him. Last night, I asked Dad about her buying the house in Nautilus Bay. He didn't know about it, and he was shocked she'd had the money to do it. He got up from his chair by the fireplace and stormed off, shaking his head.

"Dad, that's enough," I say, walking up to him and Jake. "It was a whole group of kids that had Jake surrounded. There was nothing he could do. Let it go."

My father huffs, but he doesn't say more. He and Jake continue to shovel the pathway. As I turn my head to the street, I catch the sight of the early-morning sun placing thousands of shining diamonds on the snow-covered trees and rooftops. It's a sight I've seen almost every year of my life, and each time, the sheer beauty of it makes me catch my breath.

A tear squeezes from my eye, and I'm not even sure what or who it's for.

13

I'm asleep when the flight touches down in Brisbane, Australia. Jake is sleeping on my shoulder.

Gently, I rouse him. "Jake, we're here."

He yawns, struggling through layers of haze. "Where? Oh. So, is this the last airport we have to go to?"

I laugh. "Yes, the very last one." It's been a long haul, from Pennsylvania to Los Angeles and then across the North and South Pacific Oceans.

An hour later, we've collected our luggage and picked up the hire car. It's a two-hour drive north from here to Nautilus Bay. The sun is warm and welcoming on my back. I'm thankful it's not scorching, as I know the weather here can be. Jake seems shocked by the heat, cupping his hands over his eyes and gazing up at the sapphire sky as if he's wondering where all the snow suddenly went.

For a second, I close my eyes, just drawing in a long breath. When I was a kid, I swore I could detect a hint of eucalyptus candy in the Australian air, and I imagine I can smell it now.

With the luggage packed into the car, Jake and I clip our seat belts on.

"It's funny," Jake remarks. "I'm sitting on the driver's side."

"Yeah, weird," I say, trying not to show that I'm daunted by having to drive on the right-hand side of the car.

But Jake instantly understands. "You're scared to drive this car, aren't you?"

I nod. "I'm exhausted."

"Didn't you sleep on the way?"

"Not much."

"That's the trick. You gotta sleep."

I give a tired grin. "I'll remember that." Sitting there, I try to make the mental adjustments to drive this thing—I have to stay on the left-hand side of the road and make left turns from the left.

Finally, I'm ready to go. I drive off. After a shaky start, I'm surprised by how quickly I get a sense of where I am on the road.

Switching on the radio, I lean back into the seat, relaxing and enjoying the moment. I don't know what lies ahead, but for now, we've got the journey. It's the kind of thing my mother would say.

I pull off the M1 highway and onto the Sunshine Motorway. The road is fairly new looking, lined with green forests. As we pass through the suburbs of the Sunshine Coast, I begin to remember some things. Buildings and bridges. On the GPS, I can see a proliferation of canals and then the ocean to the right.

A memory comes to me of Mom and me singing together as she drove along this road, the caravan bouncing along behind us. Iris, Grace and Ellie were all asleep. A song by the Smashing Pumpkins was playing on the radio—"1979." The song was slow, soft and chill. I remember asking Mom about her life back in the '70s. And she told me about growing up on her family's farm in North Carolina. About her and her brother Davey fishing in the lagoons and climbing the mountains of truck tyres that sat on the property next-door—pretending to be adventurers.

I loved her old stories. And it was always special when it was just me and her. Because when the others were awake, Iris would take up most of the conversation and Ellie was loud and Grace would need a lot of Mom's care.

Jake's eyes light up when we reach the resort I've booked, the

Oasis Dream. The place is a rare one in which the photos match with real life, and it has swimming pools for days. By rights, we should be able to stay at the house on Tiger Street—Mom's house. But I want to slip under the radar for a while. I've been so visible back in Forestview that I don't want to call attention to myself here.

I get us checked in at reception, and then Jake and I head to our room.

“Can we do the slides at the pool now?” Jake asks in a tone that's somewhere between an excited kid and a laid-back teenager. He's fast moving toward his teen years, but he hasn't yet perfected the bored voice of a teenager.

I smile. “Your batteries sure got a recharge somewhere along the line."

"You gonna do the slides with me?"

“Sorry, bud, but I'll sit deck side and look on.”

“That's not a lot of fun for you,” he says.

“I'll be fine. Trust me.”

Jake is used to trips away in which the two of us dive straight into the available activities. But almost all of those were work trips, when I was tasked with reviewing eco-resorts—time was short, and I had to get the experiences and photographs locked down fast. This is different, and I'm unsure if Jake quite understands why we're here.

We change into our swimsuits and summer clothes and head down to the pool area. There are a few families here, but it's not crowded. I'm guessing that's due to it not being peak season yet.

As Jake tears off to the slides, I pick up my phone. I have to steady myself before calling Detective Dawson. Again, I wish he wasn't the one in charge of the case. I wish he wasn't still in town at all.

"Lily," he replies to my call, "how are you?"

"I'm doing okay, I guess."

"There's quite a lot of media interest at the moment. I'm hoping it jogs the memory of someone out there who knows something."

"That would make it all worth it, for sure. I've been keeping up with the stories." I take a breath. "I'd like to come down and take a look at my mother's belongings—in person."

"Of course. I'm afraid the actual backpack and some of the items, such as the bundle of photographs, are still with our forensics teams."

"I understand. So, when would it be convenient?"

"Tell me when you fly in, and we'll sort out a time then."

"We're actually here. My son and I flew in just over two hours ago."

"Seriously? You're here? Okay, uh, well, how's tomorrow—around ten in the morning—work for you?"

"Ten would be fine."

"Just gimme a call beforehand in case I get a call-out."

"Will do. Uh, can I make a request? I haven't told my sister I'm here yet. She wasn't totally impressed about me flying out to Australia—because of all the media attention."

"You got it," he says.

"We went through a rough time when our mother first went missing. Lots of armchair detectives out there. It was kind of relentless."

"I remember. I felt sorry for you."

"Thank you."

Jake and I hang out around the pool for the next hour and order lunch there. Then we go for slow walks around the resort and beach. It feels like forever before it gets dark enough to think about sleeping. I normally wouldn't head off to bed until after ten at night, but I'm craving sleep. Back in Pennsylvania, it was getting dark before five in the afternoon. But here, sunset doesn't come until way after six.

I crawl into bed and sink into a restless sleep.

THE NEXT MORNING is another warm one. I pull on khaki pants, a white T-shirt, and a light denim shirt. It's the outfit in which I feel the most comfortable. And today, I'm in need of comfort.

I do a late breakfast with Jake at the resort. He has a brief moment of protest when I announce I'm heading out for a couple of hours and that I've arranged for him to spend time in the resort's kids' club. But he knows the routine. We've done this many times. It's the deal. Jake gets to come along on my work trips to try out eco-resorts, and he goes into kids' club while I work. It's been a happy agreement so far.

There's no way I'm taking him down to the police station with me. I don't know what depth of emotion seeing Mom's things again is going to dredge up for me, but Jake doesn't need to witness it.

I walk into the police station a short time later. I'm not prepared for the memory of this place to hit me as strong as it does. It's the same station that Iris and I were taken to as children after our mother vanished. I want to run from here.

The officer at the front desk directs me to an internal office. A man in a suit stands in the doorway. He shakes my hand before I realise who he is.

Van Dawson looks very little like the fifteen-year-old boy he was last time I saw him. His once-shaggy hair is now short and neat, and all the blond hair replaced by a much darker colour. The soft jawline of his boyhood has sharpened, and his brown eyes have taken on an intense, searching look.

If he's surprised by how different I look, he doesn't show it. He shows me into his office, and I take a seat.

"How was your trip?" he asks.

I inhale deeply, gathering myself. "I feel smashed, but I'll be fine. I'm a pretty seasoned traveller."

"Can I get you a drink? Water? Coffee?"

"Oh, no—I'm okay. Breakfast and brewed coffee are included at the resort."

"Ah." He scratches his chin, regarding me through his dark eyes. "Been a long time."

"Certainly has. How are your parents? And your sister—Anna?"

Flashes of memory rush at me. Of his family. Of Iris and I staying in that room in his house, feeling so desolate and confused and terrified. And Van watching it all and judging us. Shame and resentment prick my skin.

"Anna moved to England about twenty years ago," he says. "She worked as a graphic designer there. Then she came back when my dad died, two years ago, to help Mum run the restaurant."

"Sorry about your dad."

"Thanks."

A question rises in my mind. Why is Van still here? Does he guess that I wish he wasn't?

"And how about you?" I ask. "Have you stayed in town since... since the last time I saw you?"

"No. I've been all over the place. I came back at the same time that Anna did. To help Mum out with the upkeep of the house and restaurant—on my time off."

"Oh. Well, I guess... I guess I should see my mother's things now."

He nods, then rises to take a shallow plastic box from a shelf. He places it on the desk. "So, this is it."

I scoop a breath into my lungs. "Am I allowed to...?"

"Touch them? Yep, go for it. Forensics is done with these items."

I recognise a lot of the stuff in the box. There's Mom's favourite white cardigan. It's streaked with mud and smells like the earth. I immediately understand why Iris found this so hard. My fingers tremble as I lift the cardigan out. Underneath lies a tangle of silver jewellery and beads, all dulled with time, with dirt caked into the beads and charms. We made so much jewellery that year. We'd bring out the fold-up table and sell our designs at any little market or fair we could find. With care, I lift the pieces of jewellery out. I spot my mother's strawberry lip gloss next—though it's now dried to a paste. Irrationally, I hate it that she didn't get to finish using it.

A lump forms in my throat as I pick up a box of matches.

"Is there anything important you've remembered about the matches?" Van asks.

I shake my head. "No, just... memories. We used to make campfires all the time. Those were among the best times, you know? Just sitting around the fire, talking, toasting marshmallows."

"I bet they were," he says.

I resent Van for being here while I'm looking through Mom's personal items. I want to be alone. The last thing I want is for him to see me cry, but I'm already struggling.

Returning to the box, I find one of Ellie's drawings. The paper is fragile, with dirty stains along the creases of the folds. The drawing is of the ocean with a striped beach umbrella in the foreground. The trees are purple and the ocean bright green. It's wonderful to see one of her pictures, despite the streaks of dried mud.

There is only one thing left to look at now. It's a plastic folder of business cards.

"Can I take them out?" I ask.

"Sure can. We've got photocopies, so it's all good."

The cards show a trail of our lives here—the dealership Mom bought the caravan from, various doctors Mom took Grace to, and trailer parks we stayed at. I wriggle out the card from the Realtor. Just like Van had said, the card has the sale price of the house on the back.

"Were you able to learn any more about who's been renting the house out?" I ask.

"Not so far."

"Well, I plan to find out."

"You should leave that up to me. Whoever's doing this, they might not take kindly to being found out."

I go quiet, not wanting to give it away to Van that I intend to discover as much as I can. Tenderly, I begin packing my mother's belongings away again. I frown as I place Ellie's drawing into the box. There is something written on the back. A name. The letters fade out at the end.

"Did you notice this?" I ask Van. "There's a name here. It says... Rosie More, I think."

"Yes, we saw it. The name ring a bell to you?"

"No. No, not at all."

"I asked your sister the same question when she came into the station, and she didn't know it, either. We tried running it through different databases of names—but we didn't manage to come up with anything useful."

"Let me know the instant you figure out something. I'm very curious to know why Mom wrote that lady's name down. Maybe she's someone we met on the road."

Van nods as his phone rings. He answers the call, raising an index finger to me apologetically.

"I've got to head out," he tells me after he ends the call. "I'll be in contact."

After saying a quick goodbye, I step out into the sunny street. It feels strange to be out here in the sunlight again after seeing the mud-streaked contents of that box in Detective Dawson's office.

The name Rosie More turns over and over in my mind. The more I think on the name, the more familiar it seems. Or am I so desperate for the name to make sense that I'm inventing things?

I remember something as I step into the car. The umbrella in Ellie's drawing was the big free-standing beach umbrella that we kept near our pool. That meant Ellie drew it during the time we lived on Tiger Street. Could Rosie More have lived in our town?

The hot, steamy air inside the car quickly takes my breath. Stupidly, I parked in direct sunlight. I switch on the air conditioning and drive away.

Something else comes to mind. The last letters of Rosie More's name were faded. I'd assumed that was due to the effects of the water that had gotten to the paper, but what if Mom's pen had simply run out of ink? Rosie's last name could be longer than *More.*

Without warning, a name slips into my mind. A memory comes to me of a lady visiting our house on Tiger Street a few times. And the name on her clip folder was Rosanna Moreno. *Dr Rosanna Moreno.*

14

AFTER PULLING the car over into a shady spot, I park and then take out my iPad. I look up Dr Rosanna Moreno online. She's difficult to locate, but I eventually find a listing. She has a practice in the hinterland of Nautilus Bay, and she's a psychologist. She might well be the Rosie whose name Mom wrote on the back of Ellie's drawing.

I waste no time before calling the number of the psychology practice.

The voice that answers sounds weary and rushed. "Yes? Simone Finch speaking."

"Oh, I, um, I was looking for a Dr Rosanna Moreno. Do I have the wrong—"

"No, you've got the right number," she snaps. "But my mother hasn't been in practice for twelve years or more."

"Okay. I'm sorry. I got the number from an online directory. Could I speak with your mother?"

"That's not possible."

"Is she away?"

"No. She's just... not well."

"Oh. I'm sorry to hear that."

"How did you get her number?" she asks.

"I found it online."

"I thought I'd gotten rid of all her listings. Anyway, you'll have to check elsewhere if you're looking for a psychologist."

"It was actually Dr Moreno herself I was looking for."

"Why?"

"My mother used to be a client of hers. I really need to speak to Dr Moreno—when she's able to see me, of course. I want to ask her some questions. My mother is missing. I'm just... wanting some answers."

The woman's tone softens. "My mother has a form of dementia. She won't be able to answer your questions. I'm sorry."

My heart drops through my chest. I should have tempered my expectations before making the call. It's been twenty-four years, after all. But I'd rushed to it like I had no time to lose.

I rub my forehead. "There would be records, though, right? Client files?"

"That's where things get tricky," she replies. "What time period are we talking about?"

"It would have been 1997."

"All the way back then? My mother began typing up her files onto the computer somewhere after 2005. But before then, it was all paper files. And unfortunately, they were water damaged in 2010 and couldn't be saved."

"All of them?" I can't keep the desolation from my voice.

"Yes, all. Apart from some loose papers. But I have no idea what belongs to who with those."

"Is it possible that I could come and look through the loose papers?"

"They're confidential."

"I'm... I'm desperate. My mother's been missing for over twenty years. I really would—"

"Are you one of the daughters of the American woman who's been in the news? The woman who vanished with the little girl, Ellie Lowood?"

"Yes, that's me. My name is Lily Jorgenson."

"I'm sorry about what happened. I'm about the same age as you, and I know what it's like to lose a mother. I mean, it's different for me because mine is still here, but her mind certainly isn't. Look, I'll tell you what—if you come to our house, looking for Dr Moreno, I can look the other way if you should happen to venture into her office area."

"Oh gosh. I can't tell you how much I appreciate this."

"Just... keep it to yourself, okay?" Simone gives me their address. It's at a private home about fifteen minutes from here.

Jake isn't expecting me back until the afternoon, and that's hours away. I've got time to go to Dr Moreno's house now.

I send Jake a quick text: *How's your morning been?*

It only takes a moment before he texts me back: *Any day outta school is a good day. Playing pool and ping-pong in the rec room.*

Great! Have fun. Be back for lunch, I text back.

I steer the car back onto the street and head for the house of Dr Rosanna Moreno. I'm soon driving on the quiet roads of the hinterland. A breeze ruffles the wild grasses on either side. Beyond the grass, gentle hills are coated with a soft green carpet. In the distance, sharp, tall hills rise in isolation. The scenery really is stunning. I don't remember venturing up this way much when we lived here.

The house of Dr Moreno is perched up on a hill on a fairly large lot. A woman who must be her daughter, Simone, waves to me as I make my way up the long driveway. She has olive skin and an abundance of dark hair down to her waist.

"Hello. Simone?" I call as I step from the car.

"Yes. And you must be Lily."

I smile. "Gorgeous property."

"It's beautiful. But the upkeep is a killer. Anyway, come on in. Mum's asleep, but that's her usual. She doesn't sleep much at night."

Simone Finch has dark circles under her eyes, and I guess that she's regularly kept up until all hours, looking after her mother.

The interior of the house is comfortable, styled in a kind of beachy cottage theme. Macramé, rattan, sandy-coloured hardwood floors. The place looks like it might have been built in the 1950s, with its ornate ceilings and mouldings. Large windows frame a view of rolling hills.

"Can I get you something? A cold drink?" Simone offers.

I decline. A restless sensation drums in my chest, along with the headache at my temples. I just want to find out as much as I can and keep moving.

Simone looks a little disappointed, as if she wanted a chat. She's different to how she was on the phone, and I guess now that her abrupt manner was just from fatigue.

She gestures down a short hallway. "I'll show you through to Mum's old office, then."

There's a woman sleeping on an armchair in a sunny bedroom. Her dark hair is peppered with grey and tied back in a long plait. As Simone whispers to me that this is her mother, the woman seems to hear. Her eyes blink open, and she looks at me with interest.

"You're such a light sleeper, Mum," Simone says with a sigh. "This is a friend of mine. Lily."

"Oh, hello!" Dr Moreno exclaims.

Stepping forward, I shake her hand. "Good to meet you, Dr Moreno."

"Call me Rosie," she says, clasping my hand. Her brown eyes are intense in a deeply lined face that holds a quiet beauty.

"Good to meet you, Rosie."

"Do I know you?"

"You knew my mother, Elsa Jorgenson."

"Oh... did I? Is she a nurse?"

"No," I say. "She was a client of yours."

Her forehead creases in a deep frown of concentration. "The birds are noisy today. I can barely hear myself think."

Simone glances at me with a wry smile on her face. "She says that every single day, repeatedly. The ringing in her ears sounds like birds to her. Oh, and she doesn't remember she was a psychologist."

I give Dr Moreno a warm smile before slipping my hands from hers. "It was a pleasure to meet you."

I follow Simone down a set of stairs. The air is immediately stuffy, with a vague mouldy odour. The space here looks like an addition to the main house—far more modern. It's large, with a bank of filing cabinets along the back wall, a desk, and a bookcase filled with psychology titles. The drawers of the cabinets are open, all empty. The walls bear dark stains. A patch in the ceiling has been hastily repaired with timber.

"I've been unable to afford to have this room repaired properly," Simone says apologetically. "I was living in Bali at the time that the water damage happened—I moved there after my divorce. Mum had stopped practicing as a psychologist, saying she was getting too tired. I thought it was a physical thing. But as the months went on, the things she was saying to me, well, they were just getting stranger and stranger. So I flew home to check on her. I discovered that she was barely eating, and she seemed in a confused state of mind. Her office had developed a leak—and rain had been running in all that time." Simone sighs heavily. "Everything was wet and covered in mould. There wasn't much that was salvageable."

"I'm sorry about your mum and everything. A huge thing for both of you to have to deal with."

"Thank you. It was—and is. I never returned to Bali. I've been here ever since." She pauses. "Well, everything that I saved is here in a single cabinet. As I said, it's a hodgepodge of notes and files. I'll leave you to it."

"I appreciate this so much."

"If anyone asks, remember, I didn't know you came down here." Her smile is weary as she points to the lone filing cabinet next to the bookcase. "That's the one."

I get stuck in it as soon as Simone leaves the room. The files are random, as Simone told me they would be—and none of the pages have names to them. All the notes are snatches of people's lives. People with hostile teenagers and cheating spouses and suicidal thoughts. Dr Moreno's careful note taking is impressive—she was good at her job. But none of the notes sound like my mother.

An hour later, I'm sitting on the floor, empty-handed and feeling a hollow exhaustion.

Simone walks down the steps and finds me like that. "Nothing?"

"No. Not even a page."

"Sorry it didn't work out."

"I'm sorry too. But thanks." As I pick myself up off the floor, I run my eye over the bookcase. I gesture to it. "Could I have a quick look through that?"

Simone shrugs. "No point. It didn't get affected by the leak, but Mum didn't keep any client files there."

"Just to be sure—could I?"

Her eyes seem reluctant, but she nods. "I guess. Hey, I'll help you."

We go through the contents of the bookcase together. The shelves mostly hold thick hardcover books on psychology and philosophy. Simone is right—there are no client files here anywhere. But one thing captures my attention—a shelf of yearly planner diaries. It seems that Dr Moreno has kept a diary for every year she was in practice.

I lift out the diary for 1997 and open it up. Within a minute, I find an entry bearing my mother's name. And then another and another. It seems my mother was coming to see Dr Moreno every week.

Simone looks over. "Oh, good find. I'd forgotten all about the appointment diaries."

I squeeze my eyes shut in frustration. "I didn't even know my mother was seeing a psychologist, let alone so often. I wonder why Dr Moreno didn't tell the police Mom was a client—" I jerk my head up at Simone then. "I was thinking out loud. I didn't mean anything bad—"

It's too late because Simone stiffens and takes the diary from me. "Whatever my mother did or didn't do, she would've had her reasons. And she's not in any condition to defend herself."

"Of course. It was a thoughtless comment."

"Well, I've got to get Mum's breakfast ready. I think you've seen everything there is to see here."

"I'll go. And I *am* sorry."

She lifts her shoulders in a sigh. "Look... it's okay. You were in the moment. We've all been there."

As she closes the book, a page slips out. I scoop up the loose page from the floor.

"Looks like a page from a therapy journal." Simone squints as she looks closer. "Isn't that your mother's name at the bottom?"

My eyes mist over, and I can only just read the signature. It says, *Rosie, you said this piece of writing filled your heart. And so I'm gifting it to you. Love, Elsa J.*

Above the signature and dedication is a poem. My mother must have written it. I wished to find much more, but still, after finding nothing at all today, this poem feels like a gift.

"Can I ask you something?" Simone asks. "It's a bit morbid."

"Ask me anything."

"Was your mum's journal found in the backpack that'd been buried?"

"No. I didn't even know she ever had one."

"She would have. My mother insisted on all her clients keeping journals—for their therapy."

"Oh, I see. There was never any journal found anywhere. I'm guessing it might have been here and got destroyed by the roof leak."

"No, the journals weren't kept here. The whole point was for people to carry them at all times and jot down any intrusive thoughts. That means that if you haven't come across your mum's journal yet, it might still be out there to find."

Simone's words catch hold inside me. There could be a journal of my mother's out there somewhere.

15

I DRIVE a few miles down the road, away from the house of Dr Moreno and her daughter.

I haven't read the poem yet. I wanted some space first. I find myself with my foot on the brake now, turning off the engine and parking.

The grass is tall at the side of the road, but I don't care as I blunder into it. I feel like a child again, with all the armour of adulthood fallen away, exposing me.

Mom's poem is tucked in the pocket of my shirt. It's like the page has a pulse as I take it out and unfold it. I practically breathe the words into my soul as I read them:

I have always been running,
especially when I'm at my most still.
I've learned silence is a trapdoor.
You fall into the room made of mirrors
where the stranger watches you
every hour, every minute.
But my mind burns bright.

I'll have a warm body again,
I know I will.
Wind, salt, and sun on my skin,
in my hair, in my lungs.
I've made many wrong turns
—so many,
and one blinding mistake.
But I can't let a mistake
become a life.

16

My HEAD SWIMS with my mother's poetry on the way back to the resort. I feel a little changed by it, but I'm unsure how. And I'm not quite sure of everything she meant to say, but the words cut deep. I can feel the hurt she expressed, raw and visceral.

What was her one big blinding mistake? I don't have a clue. Thoughts whirl in my mind, but nothing becomes clear. I only have more questions.

I ache to share this moment with Iris. But I can't guess at her reaction—and I'd have to get past telling her I'm here in town first. And I'm not ready to do that.

My son is floating in the pool on an inflatable sun lounge when I walk into the resort. A teenage girl floats near him—maybe too close. She looks about fourteen years old. Jake isn't ready for a girlfriend, especially not one her age.

I inhale a quick breath, giving myself a mental slap. The kids are being supervised, and anyway, I have to start giving Jake a little more freedom. I've been on tenterhooks ever since the incidents with Waylon and the other boys at his school. I want to surround him in bubble wrap and keep him safe. But I need to remember that Jake is almost a teenager.

Noticing me, Jake waves.

I go and sit poolside then slip off my sandals and dip my feet in the water. There is a scattering of families under the umbrellas at the chairs and tables. The temperature has heated quite a lot since this morning, the air saturated with the scents of salty French fries and frozen colas.

"Hey, how was your day?" I call to Jake.

"It's okay," he calls back. "Monique smashed me in ping-pong... but I got her back in a pool game."

The girl flashes me a smile I can only call dazzling. She's extremely pretty, her deep-brown skin set off by her red bikini.

I hold up a hand in greeting. "Hi, Monique."

Jake looks a little out of his depth but happy. The concealer I carefully applied to his face this morning to cover the bruise has worn off in the water. By the way Monique is sneaking him glances, I can see that the bruise hasn't put her off at all. I make a guess that Monique is after a little vacation romance, and Jake is it.

The two of them slide from their inflatable lounges into the water and then swim together across the pool.

My phone tinkles with a message. It's from Detective Dawson: *Sorry I had to rush away earlier. My apologies.*

I don't feel ready to share what I've found out with him. My mother's poem is an arrow from the past to the present. And right now, it feels as if it contains clues that I alone need to figure out.

He texts again: *You left something behind.*

I answer him: *I did?*

A list of names, he texts.

I feel stung. The list must have slipped from my pocket when I was in his office. I know all of them off by heart:

Jared Keller—the man who saw Mom and Ellie running down the road that night.

Mrs Deauville—the other witness who saw Mom and Ellie.

Mr and Mrs Lowood—Ellie's grandparents.

Valentina Xiente—the neighbour who lived next-door to us on Tiger Street.

Bennett—the man who owned the farm we stayed at with Mom.

Joyce Simpson—a woman who lived on that farm.

Sergeant Quincy Mullard—who was the first police officer on the scene when Mom went missing.

Constable Lea Ramirez—who was also there.

Iris—my sister, who's been keeping secrets.

I just wish Van Dawson hadn't seen my list. I call him on the phone. "Look, it's nothing. Just some people I remember from back then. I thought it might be helpful."

"Tell me straight," he responds. "Were you intending on looking up the names on that list?"

"This is about my mother, Van. I have a right to talk with those people, don't I?"

"It's not a good idea. And, let me tell you, you can't go talking to the two police officers on your list. Any information they have is confidential. As far as Mrs Deauville goes, she never came forward with her full name—it's frustrating when that happens with witnesses, but it's common. And that first name on your list—he's dead. Jared Keller committed suicide many years ago."

"Oh... I didn't know Jared died. I knew he was a suspect for a long time." I'm disappointed about not being able to contact the others, but I'm crushed by that news about Jared Keller. He was the first one to go looking for Mom and Ellie, and he was possibly the last person to see them that night. I'd wanted to see him face-to-face and decide for myself whether he was lying or telling the truth.

"Yeah, he was a suspect," Van says, "but he was eventually cleared. Lily, it might interfere with the investigation if you go talking with people around town."

"I've already found out something," I tell him hesitantly.

"Oh? What's that?"

I exhale, gathering up some courage. "The name on the back of Ellie's drawing... I worked out who it was."

"Okay. Who?"

"A psychologist. Dr Rosanna Moreno."

"Right," he says. "Well, I'll make plans to pay her a visit."

"I already did."

A short silence follows before he says, "You did?"

Reluctantly, I explain what happened and how I discovered my mother's poem.

"We'd better meet up so I can take a look at that," he replies. "I can come to you. Is six okay?"

"I guess so. We're at the Oasis Dream."

Jake walks up to me as the call ends. "Monique had to go somewhere with her parents."

"Hey, you're flicking water all over me."

"Sorry. Not sorry."

I laugh. "Real funny. How about we go look around town for a bit?"

He shrugs. "Yeah, why not?"

We head out in the car. I'm not even going to try walking around out in that heat. The temperature is too much for this Pennsylvania girl, and it's only getting hotter.

Jake and I spend the next hours looking around all my old haunts—the long esplanade and the caves and inlets. He calls the ocean *the shore,* just like a boy from Pennsylvania would. Just as I used to. It bemuses me that he enjoys the rock pools the most. Is he enchanted by them just like I used to be?

I'm glad to have found something to share with him. It makes me realise, too, that I've spent too many trips away with Jake that were basically just fly-by work trips. We didn't have time to linger and explore and just... exist in the moment.

I avoid the road that leads to Dawsons Drift. I never want to see that place again. I avoid the street where the Lowoods live, and I also avoid going anywhere near the street where Iris lives. I've never been to her house, but I know exactly where it is—I looked it up before I came. I wish things were different. I wish Jake and I could just drop in and spend the afternoon with her and her kids. At one point, Jake asks about them. But I have to tell him the same story I always tell him. That my sister has decided not to have contact with me. It's a difficult thing to say and I know it must be harsh for him to hear.

I have to get braver and confront my past. But I need to bolster my confidence first.

Jake and I end up at an ice cream parlour. It's the same parlour that was here all those years ago. Somehow, it managed to survive.

We stand under a palm tree in the street, trying to finish the ice creams before they melt. I wipe my sticky hands with a handkerchief. "Okay, Jake, one last place before we head back to the resort."

Jake squints at me. "Where?"

"Surprise."

"Hint?"

"Nope." I smile as he folds his arms in protest the way he used to when he was small.

We head across town. Memories swarm me the moment that I turn onto Tiger Street. The thick, old pines that used to line the beach side of the road still stand guard.

Letting the car crawl down the street, I almost catch a vision of fourteen-year-old Iris on her bicycle and tiny Ellie Lowood riding beside her on her tricycle.

And then we're here. The yellow house. I only intended to look at it from the street, without even getting out of the car, but now that I'm here, I want to go in. I feel an urge to see and touch the house that my mother still owns.

My head swims with the sudden memories. It doesn't feel quite real that I'm back here.

Without thinking, I take Jake's hand as we walk up the front steps. He doesn't squirm or protest.

"Whose house is this?" Jake asks.

"You'll find out."

"That pool is yuk."

"Sure is."

The pool in the front yard is in terrible condition. The filter sounds like it's struggling, and the water is murky.

As I reach the house, I notice that the paintwork looks slapdash

—as if it was done quick and cheaply. Everything else seems to be as it was when I lived here, including the front door. Even the door knocker is the same—a metal tiger head and ring that have gone a little rusty.

There's no point in knocking on the front door. The house is empty. Pressing my face up against the clear glass panel beside the door, I get a view of the interior. The living room has new furniture, but the floorboards and stairs look the same.

I gulp down a breath as I notice the painting on the wall. It's a painting of sunflowers that my mother did. My mother loved sunflowers. Whoever's been renting this house out has left the painting there all this time.

"Wait," Jake says, "isn't this the house you were lookin' at on the computer the other day? When we were back in PA."

I nod, my eyes brimming with tears.

"This is where you lived when you were a kid, isn't it?"

"Yep."

"You said your mom owned it, didn't you?"

"Right again."

He screws up his face. "Well, can't you just go in?"

"Not yet. I don't have the key."

"If ya break a window, I could crawl in."

"Thanks for the offer, kiddo. But no. Hey, we'd better go."

"You're no fun, Mom." He walks on ahead of me.

I follow him, but then I linger at the pool.

I remember those first hectic weeks after we moved in here. Iris and I were battling with confusion at being pulled from our lives in Pennsylvania and being transplanted here. And we missed Dad. Despite how distant he was, he'd been a constant in our lives. And we did love him—at least, I knew that *I* did.

Mom and Iris and I had set to work cleaning up the whole pool area—getting the water crystal clear and pulling out all the weeds from the surrounds. And we'd soon gotten to know all the neighbours. I can see Mom in my mind's eye—dashing about in her tie-dye skirt, serving watermelon and creaming soda spiders to people. I remember Iris and I being confused by this new and colourful edition of our mother. Had she always been this person underneath, or had moving to Nautilus Bay changed her?

We grew especially fond of two of the neighbourhood children—sisters named Grace and Ellie. Grace was fourteen but looked years younger—she had severe spinal issues and had been in a wheelchair since she was five. She struggled to speak, and she tired easily. Ellie was a confident three-year-old chatterbox. Ellie always seemed to know what her big sister Grace was trying to say, and she'd tell us. All we knew about them was that their father had died, and their mother had abandoned them. They lived with their grandparents a few blocks away.

Mom instantly loved both of them. She'd take Grace into the swimming pool and float her through the water. Grace's whole face would light up like Christmas. Mom taught Ellie how to swim and read.

Iris and I had Spice Girls mania back then, and we blasted their songs constantly. Each day, after all our neighbours and friends had gone home for dinner, Grace and Ellie would often still be there with us. We'd sit outside in the night, listening to the ocean and the crickets and eating homemade pizza. Ellie would giggle in hysterics when Iris and I would protest that pineapple didn't belong on a pizza, and she'd keep sneaking it back onto our slices.

Those were fun days. The best. In those months, it was as if we'd hit a slipstream of warm air and we were all just floating in a capsule of time removed from everything else.

Our idyllic summer went on and on, the warm weather lingering months past the summer season. It seemed like it would last forever. It didn't. We spent less than six months here before things somehow turned bad and Mom dragged us away from yet another home.

I'm drawn away from my memories as I notice a woman peering over the fence at me. I half expect her to run away when she catches me looking her direction, but she doesn't. With her dark hair and olive skin, she looks familiar.

"Lily?" she calls in a husky Latino accent. "Lily Jorgenson, is that you? No, it can't be... is it?"

"Valentina?" I say in surprise. Valentina Xiente is one of the people on my list of names. I wasn't sure at all if she'd still be living next door.

She nods. "It's me, sweetheart."

She rushes around the fence to me. Her hair is as long as it used to be, only streaked with grey. She'd be in her mid-sixties now.

We hug, both of us immediately crying.

"Oh, look at you," she exclaims. "I can't believe it. You're back, sweetheart. After all this time."

"I'm so happy you're still here. I came to show my son my old house."

"Oh, honey, I have to tell you that the police have been poking around. A detective came to ask me some questions the other day. I don't know what's going on."

"I've spoken to him—Detective Dawson. He said he'd spoken to a neighbour. I didn't realise that was you."

"Yes, it was me, sweetheart. I'm not sure if I said something wrong now. I don't want to cause trouble for anyone."

I give her a warm smile. "You didn't cause trouble, Valentina."

"Good. Come and sit with me a while. I want to catch up on your news."

I brush the leaves off the pool furniture and sit down with Valentina. After I introduce Jake to her, he wanders across the road to look at the ocean.

"Beautiful boy," she says.

Valentina and I chat for the next half-hour.

She was the first person we got to know when we moved here. I remember her as an energetic woman with a thousand stories about growing up in Columbia. She had a tribe of kids who became the first friends Iris and I made. She and Mom would sit by the pool, laughing together and drinking coffee liqueur and milk on ice.

Questions begin to gnaw at me—questions that I hope she can answer.

"Valentina," I say, "did you ever notice my mother writing in a journal? Like, some kind of diary?"

She looks back at me curiously. "A diary? No, I don't think so."

"Can I ask you something else? When my mother left this house, do you know why? Did she say anything to you?"

She nods, sighing. "Yes. And I told Sergeant Mullard this. Elsa was worried about someone hanging about the house. I never saw them myself. But it was real to Elsa. I'm not saying this person wasn't real—I don't know. But she grew frantic about it. And then she decided she had to go. I was so, so sorry to see your family leave town. A big sorrow to me. Especially after... well, you know, especially after Elsa and the little girl went missing."

I'm startled by her words. I remember Mom getting increasingly anxious. Her old patterns had returned. She started leaving the blinds shut all day and drinking wine early in the afternoons. Had she been imagining a stalker?

Valentina and I hug with tears in our eyes, holding tight to each other.

17

Jake and I head back to the resort after my conversation with Valentina. He can tell I've been crying, and I hate that. I decide that later, I'll dine with him at one of the nice restaurants in town as a special treat.

Detective Dawson turns up at our door at twenty minutes past six. "Sorry I'm late," he says. "I was on a call. A guy turned up at the company he was just fired from—and he was threatening a co-worker."

I wince. "Oh no. Did he have a weapon?"

"A knife. Luckily for him, I was able to talk him into dropping it."

"Must have been a big relief."

"All in a day's work."

Despite Van's smile, he has distinct questions in his eyes as he glances at me. I show him inside, intending to get this conversation over quickly. I shouldn't have to account for what I've been doing since I've been here.

He spots Jake focusing hard on a game on the PlayStation.

"Hey there. Whatcha playing?" he asks Jake, walking up to him.

Jake looks up with a shy grin. "Uncharted."

"Uncharted, eh?" Van replies. "So, you like adventure games? I've played every one of the series."

"Like 'em?" Jake asks.

"Love 'em," Van answers.

Jake looks happy with that answer.

"Jake," I say, "this is Detective Van Dawson. Detective, this is my son, Jake."

The three of us have a cold drink together and a little chat, and then the detective and I head out to the balcony, which overlooks the hinterland. There's a small table and some wicker chairs. It's serene, quiet. Unlike the conversation I'm about to have.

I slide my mother's poem across the table to Van. I hate letting it out of my hands, feeling as if I need to guard it and keep it safe.

He reads it quickly, murmuring the words to himself. "Sounds like she had her mind made up—to change her life."

"She certainly did. It was the year of huge changes."

"Do you know what the specific lines mean? Like, what's the room of mirrors? And what was her one big mistake?"

"I wish I knew. I don't."

"And the psychologist herself—you told me she has dementia? And all her records sustained water damage?"

I nod.

He exhales. "And this page is from a journal, you said?"

"Apparently."

"Well, it'd certainly be interesting to know where that journal is."

"The journal should have been in one of a few places—Mom's backpack, her car, the caravan, or her house. It was in none of those places. So someone must have it. Maybe someone stole it from her?"

He raises his dark eyes to me. "There's a good possibility that no one has it. Your mother might have lost it. Or she might have decided to destroy it."

A bitter feeling twists inside me. He seems cut from the same cloth as his uncle–Quincy Mullard. Not willing to look into things deeply enough for my liking.

"But it might still exist," I argue.

"It might." He hands the poem back to me. "Oh, and this." He takes my folded list of names from his pocket and gives that to me too.

I don't meet his eyes as I take the two items back.

"I passed you on the street earlier," he says.

"Oh?"

"You were with your son, turning down Tiger Street."

"Oh. I, uh, I did take Jake to see the old house."

"Just a drive-by?" he asks.

"We might have stopped."

"Did you get out of the car?"

"Briefly."

"Long enough to go having conversations with the neighbours?"

I stifle a gasp. "You were following me?"

"Not exactly. I reviewed my surveillance footage before I came here. I had a camera set up as soon as I found out your mother owns the house."

"Oh. Okay. Good idea about the camera. I just really wanted to show the place to my son. And yes, I spoke with Valentina."

He chews on his lower lip. "What about?"

"I haven't seen her since I was a kid. It was just a catch-up."

"She's on your list."

I inhale the night air deep into my lungs. "I might have asked her a couple of questions."

He runs a hand through his hair in a way that I'd seen him do as a teenager. "We could work together, you know."

I debate whether to tell him what Valentina said or not. But I make a guess he's going to go there and ask her if I don't.

"Valentina told me that Mom thought she had a stalker," I tell him. "And that's why she bought a caravan and left the bay."

He straightens, his expression switching to what I was coming to know as his professional detective face. "Can you give me the details?"

I relate what Valentina told me. "Do you think it could be relevant?" I ask.

"I don't know," he says. "That happened a long time before your mother vanished. And we don't know whether—"

"Don't know whether my mother was in her right mind or not? Is that what you were going to say?"

"Not in those words. But she was seeing a psychologist at that time, right?"

"Yes. But we don't know why she was seeing a psych. And we can't ask Dr Moreno, either. If your uncle had been doing his job all those years ago, he would have found out about her. Back when she was still able to talk to the police."

I sit back in my chair, burning with the words I'd just spoken. I watch him swallow and then shake his head.

"I'm not responsible for whatever my uncle did or didn't do in his investigation," he says in a low, careful voice.

"Can I ask one thing?"

"What's that?"

"That you search my mother's house."

He's silent for a moment. "What do you hope to find there?" he says finally.

"What if the reason the police didn't find the journal is because Mom never took it with her from the Tiger Street house? I never saw her with it. Iris has never mentioned it either. It might still be there."

He draws his teeth along his lip. "I can arrange that."

"You can?"

"Yes. Having learned what I've learned tonight, it seems warranted. I'll have a conversation with Iris first though and see if she has anything to say about a journal." He pauses. "Can I ask something of you?"

I nod, scarcely believing he'd agreed to do the search.

"You're angry," he says, "and I understand that. The police

didn't get anywhere with this case in the past. But I've got a job to do. And I'm trying to do it. And you need to stand back. Okay?"

"Sure. I understand."

I understand what he wants. I just don't know how much ground I'm willing to give.

18

Two days later, I wake in a sweat.

It's the morning of the search.

Van calls me just as I'm clearing my head of the dark dreams I'd been having the moment before. "Lily, I wanted to let you know—you and your sister are welcome to come to the house, but give us a two-hour head start, okay?"

I check my watch. "So, I can come down there at nine?"

"Yeah," he says. "Have you spoken to Iris?"

"No... not yet."

"Well, I've told her about the search today. She, uh, she wasn't happy about it."

"I knew she wouldn't be. Did you tell her I'm here?"

"Nope, that's your business. But Lily, I think you'd better sort that out. It'd be easier on me, too. I'm having to send two lots of messages at the moment."

"Of course. I'll talk to her."

"Good."

He ends the call. In truth, I've been delaying talking with Iris as long as I can. I don't know how to approach her, and I need to muster up some courage. She might completely shut me out.

I head off to have a shower and get dressed. Jake rouses from sleep and asks if he can go to kids' club. At first, I'm surprised, but then I remember—Monique.

I've got some time to kill, and I have a leisurely breakfast with Jake down at the resort's all-you-can-eat breakfast bar. Then Jake smashes me in a few games of ping-pong. I wave him off to kids' club after that.

Cooler air has drifted in on the ocean breeze, along with a spatter of rain. When I return to the hotel room, I decide to dress in jeans and a jacket.

Detective Dawson's search mission is already underway when I arrive at Tiger Street. His car and a white van belonging to a forensics team are parked outside. I can see people moving past the upstairs windows. It feels as if the house is having its old bones stripped. I can't deny that part of me wants it to stay exactly the way it is. But mostly, I'm anxious for the journal to be found. It has to be here. I don't know if I'll be ready for what Mom wrote in it. I have to go one step at a time.

I'm early, and so I wander across to the pool area to wait.

The pool has been emptied—did Detective Dawson organise that? There are patches of slime in the tile grout here and there. I notice a statue half hidden in the tall grass. Crouching, I pull the grass aside, exposing a stone lady in a swimsuit. I remember her from when I was a child. The statue looks like something made in the 1960s, with its polka-dot suit and pointy bra. One of her hands is now gone, and she has lots of chips in her paintwork, yet somehow, she still manages to look serene and elegant.

A voice from behind pulls me from my thoughts. "Lily?"

I twist around. It's Iris. She stands there in a simple white shirt and paisley skirt, her hair dyed a deep red. She's just like the teenage sister I knew... but different. She looks completely like a woman, with her older eyes and flatter cheeks and bright lipstick. Her lips are fuller than they ever were before—from fillers, maybe. She's not as tall as I remember.

I take all this in within an instant.

She presses those full lips together in a harsh expression. "What have you done?"

My back straightens reflexively as I rise to my feet. "What do you mean?"

She waves a hand around at the house. "This. All of this. And how is it that you're here in the bay? You said you weren't coming. You promised."

It's been thirteen years, Iris. Thirteen years. Is this all you have to say to me?

"I didn't promise anything," I tell her.

"I don't understand what's going on. Why is it necessary to search the house?"

"Didn't Detective Dawson tell you about the journal?" I say defensively.

"Yes, he told me."

"Well... don't you think it's odd we never found it?"

"No, I don't," she snaps. "It's not surprising at all, really. Mum obviously didn't want us to know about it."

"But it should still be around—somewhere."

"You talked Van into tearing Mum's house apart... for a journal?" she asks.

"Did he say that?"

"I can guess." She stands back, surveying me intently. "You were kind of sweet on Van Dawson when you were a kid. And look at you now. You've grown to look a lot like our mother. I bet you turned on the charm."

I slip my hands into the pockets of my jacket. My reunion with my sister—if I could call it that—has pushed me off balance, as if I've done something wrong. I close my hand around the list of names I have in my pocket. It feels comforting carrying that list with me, like I have a plan. And Iris's name is on the list.

I'll get to you, Iris. I'll figure out a way to get you to talk to me about that night.

"This news will be over town soon, like a damned rash." She shakes her head, her red bob swinging.

"I can't help that," I tell her. "I'm... I'm going to go ahead and have a look around inside. Van said we could go in after nine o'clock."

"I'm going in too. Last chance to see the place, I suppose, before reporters start showing up."

I don't want her joining me, and I wish she hadn't come. I was feeling a little hopeful about Van finding something—but now, with Iris here, everything feels empty and lost again.

When Iris and I walk in, Van is in the living room talking with two other police officers. He glances at us curiously but says nothing. The noises of things being hammered and sawed echo from the other rooms.

Iris and I walk to the stairs. It seems like a thing from our collective memory—returning home from school and heading straight up the stairs to our bedrooms.

There are two people from the forensics team in our mother's room, so we continue down the hall, ending up in my bedroom. My old wooden bed and the freestanding wardrobe are still here as if no time has passed at all. I lean on my windowsill, looking out. Even though the morning is grey, the wide view of the ocean is beautiful.

"Crazy to be here again," Iris says in a tight voice. Opening the window, she peers straight down at the pool area. "Remember all the parties we had down there? With Mum and Valentina and all the neighbourhood kids?"

"Those were the bright spots," I say.

"Yeah. They were. Hey, remember that day that you, me, and Grace slept in your room, like a slumber party? And when we woke up and looked out the window, we found a dozen or so boys from school in our pool?"

"I'd forgotten that."

Iris screws up her face. "We were in our pyjamas and hadn't done our hair. We were freaking when they saw us."

"Correction. *You* were freaking. I was eleven—too young to care about stuff like that."

"It wasn't your age, Lily. It was just you. I started caring when I was about ten. I wanted to look good every time we left the house. Even if it was just to go to McDonald's. I know I was sneaking eyeliner on from the age of about twelve."

"I remember you wanted to dye your hair back then, but Mom wouldn't let you."

"Yeah. I mean, all the girls on the pageant circuit dyed their hair."

"Yeah, they sure did."

"So," Iris says, "when did you and your son arrive in town?"

"A few days ago."

"Days ago? Why didn't you tell me?"

"It wasn't exactly a great conversation we had over the phone, Iris."

She blinks back tears. "You can't blame me for that. There's a lot going on right now. I've got to think of my family—my kids and husband. You know how bad the rumours about our mother and father can get."

"Of course I know."

"Van told me how you found out about the journal. How did you manage to remember Dr Moreno's name? I mean, I remember her, but I didn't remember her name."

"I'm not sure. I think, back then, I was curious who that woman was that was coming to our house."

"You always did notice the little details. Like, you'd spot a tiny bird's nest up in a tree that no one else could even see."

I take Mom's poem from my pocket. "This is the page from the journal. It's a photocopy."

Iris unfolds the piece of paper and reads it. "Oh God. This is so... sad and strange. The big mistake that Mum talks about in her poem—I mean, what even was that? Did she do something wrong?"

"I don't know. I can't even guess."

Iris folds her arms in close, exhaling. "You know what I think her big mistake was?"

"No..."

"Having children. Having us. We were too much for her."

I shake my head. "That's not true—"

"Think about it. Remember all those times she was in the pool? I don't mean here—I mean back at Forestview. I'd go down there to the basement and try to talk to her—like, about a problem I was having with a boy at school or something—but she'd be in her own zone."

"I know. She was the same with me. But she loved us. I know she did."

"Yes, she loved us in her own way. But it was hard for her. Our mother had severe issues, Lily. She wasn't okay."

"But she got better. The year we went on that road trip, she was okay."

"No. The road trip was just part of her illness. Can't you see that? Her illness probably explains what really happened the night she and Ellie went missing. She left Grace alone in our car, with the rain smashing in, and then she went running along the road with Ellie, who must have been terrified out of her mind."

"We don't know what happened. Something made Mom and Ellie run that night, something so awful they had no choice but to leave Grace behind."

Her mouth twists, and she glances away. "The monsters inside your head can be terrifying."

In that moment, I hate my sister for thinking something that has crossed my mind too. *But even if that is the real story—that Mom was running from demons in her mind—I know something else happened, something involving you, Iris. You're not telling everything you know. What are you hiding?*

Desperately, I want to shake her, make her tell. But I have to take it slow.

"Iris," I venture, "Jake has been asking about his cousins. And... well, I don't know what to tell him. You guys are the only family he has, apart from his grandfather."

She looks back at me, startled. "Oh, of course. The cousins should meet up. My kids have been asking, too. I told them this morning that you were here—I thought they'd hear it on the news, anyway."

I'd been so intent on the search for the journal, I hadn't given much thought to reporters. Iris was right—they probably would be digging around for any morsel they could find on this story. It was a story that was twenty-four years old, but people never seem to tire of a missing person tale. I'd learned that people forget about murders quickly—as long as the murderer is found—but they have long memories for missing persons.

I take a breath. "Well, how about we all, I don't know, meet up in a park or something?"

"Oh, no—look. Come over to our house. For dinner. What are you doing tonight?"

"I don't have anything planned."

"Then it's settled. God, my kids will be so excited when I tell them."

"Jake and I will look forward to it."

I didn't imagine it would be quite so easy to get an invitation to Iris's house. But I don't know if I'm in any way prepared for this. She feels like a stranger to me.

We return to looking out the window at the ocean. Throughout our mother's house, the stomp of boots on the floorboards and the sounds of hammers and saws continues.

19

Jake is over the moon with the plan to have dinner with his cousins, but he seems even more nervous than I thought he'd be.

"Will they like me?" he asks on the drive over to my sister's house.

"Oh, Jake, of course they will."

I hear him inhale and exhale a few times, and it makes my heart hurt.

I park outside Iris's house. Her house has a beach style typical of the area—single storey with a white rendered finish and a tropical garden.

I can hear the yells of excited children when Jake and I walk up the path. I feel as nervous as Jake in this moment.

Iris flings open the door. "Welcome to our humble abode."

The next few minutes are a flurry of introductions. I already know Iris's children's names from Instagram, but I pretend I don't. Kaden, age thirteen, is a handsome kid with a generous smile. The twins, Piper and Audrey, are eleven—and they seem like chalk and cheese in looks and demeanour. Piper has a self-assured manner of speaking and an athletic frame. Audrey is shorter, rounder. She keeps covering her mouth as she giggles. I love her instantly.

The kids herd Jake down the hall to what they call the games room.

I'm sorry that the kids are gone. They filled in all the empty spaces, but now it's just Iris and me.

I glance at the framed photographs on the wall. "It looks like your daughters are into dancing, like you were?" I point to photographs of the twin girls in dance costumes.

Iris nods. "Piper's a natural. Such a talented dancer. But the frustrating thing is that she prefers to run about on a sports field. So she comes home on a Saturday from soccer with bruises and bleeding knees—and then she's got to perform on a stage that night. And then there's Audrey. Bless her little heart, she loves to dance, and she tries hard, but I can't see her getting far with it."

"Oh? Why's that?"

"Well, you know how it is for a dancer. It's all about the line of the body—the grace, the elegance."

I'm reminded of the years Iris and I spent in the pageants. All the dance practice, all the performances on stage while looking out to the audience—most of whom were mothers who were impatiently waiting for their own daughter's performance.

"Aw, Audrey's such a cutie," I say.

"She's cute. But cute doesn't cut it," Iris replies.

"I thought the world had moved past the bad old days of the pageants, when we were all supposed to look like dolls."

"In theory, yes. But the dance comps are still fierce." Iris sighs. "Anyway, let's grab a drink and go sit out in the yard."

My sister leads me out to her enormous chef-style kitchen, with a gleaming benchtop that must be at least ten feet long, where she makes us each a vodka highball with lime and lemon. Cocktails in hand, we walk out onto her back deck.

The yard has everything a family could possibly want. There's a whole outdoor kitchen on the deck and, beyond that, a sparkling inground pool, a half-size basketball court, and a curved seating area with a fire pit in the middle.

"Stunning," I tell Iris.

She beams. "It took a lot to get it to this point. Years of hard work. But it was worth it."

We sit on the edge of the pool and dangle our feet in the water, the same way we used to at the house on Tiger Street. Our dappled reflections in the water look very different these days, though. We're not willowy teen girls in tropical-print bikinis, with our hair hanging all the way to our hips. I wish we could go back to those days and start again. If Iris feels that way too, there's no sign of it.

Iris sips her drink, eyeing me over the top of the glass. "So, tell me about you. What's been happening in your life? And more to the point, is there a special someone?"

I give an awkward laugh. "No, I'm not seeing anyone."

"Well, what do you do with your spare time?"

"I sometimes go hiking up in the mountains or do a bit of kayaking."

She clucks her tongue. "You're not going to find someone out there in the wilds of the Poconos."

It's so like Iris to want people to be in a relationship—the Iris that I used to know, anyway. She was terrified of being alone.

"I'm not looking for anyone," I tell her. "Anyway, how about you? How's the world been treating you?"

"Well, good, mostly. Yeah, can't complain. The business is doing well. We go on a nice holiday each year. My kids have all kinds of opportunities that I didn't have." She looks across the yard as someone walks onto the deck. "Gabe's home."

A man strides across the lawn to us. He looks like the kind of guy TV commercials use when they want to depict a young father—someone with a few wrinkles around his eyes but still unrealistically fit and attractive.

I rise to my feet and give him a hug. "It's so good to meet you, Gabe."

His face cracks into a wide grin. "Finally, I get to meet the fabled sister of Iris's stories. I've heard so much about you."

I smile. "I hope she's only told you the good stuff."

He scratches his chin. "Well, lemme think. What did she tell me? You used to like birds and animals and climbing trees... and, hmmm, Pennsylvania Dutch Chocolate Funny Cake. How'd I do?"

"You did very well. I'm impressed," I say, shooting a puzzled glance at Iris. Why has the sister who refused to speak with me all these years even bothered to tell her husband these things? Iris just shrugs at me.

"So, you run a construction business, Gabe?" I ask.

"Yeah, always lots to do. Keeps me on my feet. Keeps both Iris and me on our feet, actually. We're looking forward to some time off."

Iris nods. "We're off to Thailand in a couple of weeks. The kids loved it last time, so we're heading there again."

"How about you, Lily?" Gabe asks. "What are your Christmas plans?"

Unexpectedly, that hits me square in the chest. Christmas is never anything much. Dad doesn't care for it. So, it's just Jake and me.

"I don't have any plans so far," I answer. "And with everything that's been happening—" I break off. I'm not even sure how to put these past weeks into words.

"Of course." He nods. "It's been an awful time for you and Iris."

He and Iris share a warm glance at each other. I wonder how my sister got so lucky as to find someone like Gabe. She seems to have everything in place. Great husband, great house, great kids. The perfect life.

A stab of guilt works its way between my shoulder blades. How can I force Iris to tell what she did back when she was fifteen? Does it even matter now?

My thoughts are interrupted by my phone buzzing with a message. Iris's phone beeps with a message at the same time.

It's Detective Dawson texting that his team found some things at the house.

My heart sinks when I read the words, *no journal*.

I was so, so sure they'd find the journal. Now that I know of its existence, my hands feel somehow empty without it.

He says they did find a stack of polaroid photographs and a small box of bits and pieces. He wants to see both Iris and me in the morning.

I want to rush straight down to the station. But I can't go and do that. It's late, and Van is probably tired and ready for dinner—and gone home for the day.

The rest of the night at Iris's house, I find myself distracted, thinking about Van's message. Mom never had a polaroid camera. So, do the photos simply belong to one of the many vacationers who've been in the house over the years?

Iris is bright and chirpy during dinner—no hint of the coldness she displayed when she first walked up to me at the Tiger Street house. In fact, she seems almost artificially cheery, giving big smiles and taking her husband's hand when talking about their lives together. It's like she's anxious for me to know how perfect her life has been for the past twenty-four years. I already got the picture loud and clear—she doesn't need to keep showing me.

Jake and Iris's three kids remain excited to be in each other's company. It's obviously a very special night for them—cousins meeting for the very first time.

It's early the next morning when Iris and I meet outside the Nautilus Bay police station. I'm not expecting much, but still, I'm anxious to see whatever it is that the police found.

Iris cranes her head to see if there are any reporters hanging about. "Let's head in. Before anyone spots us here."

I nod. "Let's go."

Van is sitting at his desk when we walk in, waiting for us. "Good morning, Iris, Lily. Have a seat and let's get started."

The first thing he brings out is the set of polaroids. "We found these in your mother's bedroom, inside the headboard of her bed. They were well hidden."

From the serious look on his face, I can tell these are no ordinary photographs. Iris and I exchange tense glances. He places the images one at a time on the desk, side by side.

There are seven pictures, all taken at night from the interior windows of Mom's house. A stranger is hanging about in our yard—a woman. Dangling her feet in the water by our pool or leaning against a tree. She wears layers of loose, cotton clothing, a floppy hat on her head. In one picture, she's directly outside the kitchen window—a pale face staring in, like something from a horror movie. The flash is too bright to see her features clearly.

Iris gasps. "When were these taken?"

"If you look at the date stamp on the photos," Van says, "you'll see that the year is 1997."

I raise my eyes to him. "Our mother took these photos, didn't she?"

He nods. "Seems that way. The pictures were taken with a Polaroid Spectra camera. Do you remember your mother having one of those?"

"She had a Polaroid camera for a little while," Iris answers. "But she sold a lot of stuff before we went away in the caravan."

I turn to Iris. "I don't remember that camera at all."

"I only saw it a couple of times," Iris tells me. "When I asked her if I could use it, she said something about it not working."

"Maybe she bought it just to take photos of this woman," I say to Van. "So, this is proof that Mom had a stalker. This is why she left Nautilus Bay."

Iris nods, picking up the photo of the woman outside the kitchen window. "We need to find out who she is and why the hell she was hanging around our house late at night."

"After all this time, it's gonna be like chasing a ghost," he says. "But it was a good find. And the fortunate thing is that the images were preserved—they were in a dark place away from moisture. Polaroids are even more fragile than ordinary photographs."

A chill invades my spine. "What about the rest of the things you found? Are they connected to this woman?"

"I don't think so," he says. "Everything else we found had fallen through cracks in the floorboards. I was hoping to find credit cards—something with ID on it. But I don't think there's anything useful here."

He pushes across a small box of items that include hair clips, bobby pins, shoelaces, and jewellery. A shock travels down my spine at the sight of a delicate silver pendant in the shape of a bird with a tiny blue gem for an eye. I pick it out and examine it before turning to Iris.

Her blue eyes grow watery with tears. “Oh my, that was Ellie’s.”

Detective Dawson frowns. “Ellie Lowood?”

I nod, a lump rising in my throat.

“Well, I guess it stands to reason,” he says. “She was at your house a lot, wasn’t she?”

“You don’t understand,” I tell him. “This piece of jewellery was made for Ellie the year we were on the road. If this was found at the house, that means she somehow went back there—*after* she went missing.”

Van sits back in his chair, gazing at us with large, thoughtful eyes. “Well, that changes everything.”

20

I END up alone in the afternoon. Iris's husband invited Jake to go out with him and Kaden on his boat, and Jake was more than happy to go. Iris asked if I wanted to join her and her girls on a shopping trip, but I declined. I need some space today.

I feel as if I'm being blown about in a storm. Why was Ellie's pendant at the house? Did Mom bring her back there? I don't understand... anything.

The search of the Tiger Street house has just hit the news, along with the photos of the strange woman who was stalking us. I understand why Van wanted to put that out to the media, but still, it feels intrusive. It's my personal life, out there for people to consume once again.

Leaving the resort, I drive down to the shore. I like the sound of the waves and seagulls and the warm sun on my skin. This place was my home once. This place knows the happiness and heartache of the days I spent here.

After heading along the beach, I end up at the rock pools. I wander around them, stopping to gaze into those tiny, perfect worlds.

I turn as someone approaches. It's Van. In silhouette, he almost looks like the boy he once was. This is the same place where Van had once shown me around the rock pools. A strange sensation passes through me, as if the years have a tunnel between them, passing constantly back and forth.

He looks almost apologetic at having disturbed my peace. "I came looking for you."

"You did? Is there any…?"

"News? No, sorry. But I did want to talk with you and your sister. I did catch up with Iris. and she told me you were at the resort. I tried calling, but your phone was off."

"Oh, damn. I must have left it back in my room. Today's been a bit of a blur. I'd better go grab it. Jake's out boating today, and if there's any problem, then—" I stop. "Wait, what did you want to talk with Iris and me about?"

"About Ellie's pendant. Are you good to talk now?"

"Of course."

"Okay," Van says. "So, you said the pendant was made on a farm you stayed at, by a man named Bennett?"

I nod. "Bennett, yes. He owned the farm."

The mention of Bennett takes me straight back to the months we spent on his farm. He and Mom had grown close so quickly. I'd felt guilt at enjoying seeing Mom happy with him—it'd seemed a betrayal of Dad. But I'd almost gotten used to the farm becoming my new home. And then Mom had abruptly decided to leave again.

"I've tried looking him up," Van tells me. "He seems to have disappeared off the face of the earth."

"I tried to look him up as well, actually," I admit. "No luck."

"He's on your list, right?"

"Okay, yes, he is. But aren't there police files on him at the station?"

"The files are a bit lacking. I don't want to criticise my uncle's note taking, but it's pretty messy."

"Do you have any reason to think Bennett might have done something wrong?" I ask.

"No. I just want to cover all bases. How did the pendant come to be made by Bennett?"

"Bennett did a bit of silversmithing, just as a hobby. He made pendants for all of us. Mom wanted birds." I glance upward at the deeply blue sky. "She liked to think of us as birds in flight—forever free, going wherever we wanted. Silly, huh?"

He smiles. "No. Not at all. It's a nice thought. So, how long were you there, at the farm?"

"From memory, just a little over two months. It seemed long, but it wasn't."

"And there's an entry in the files that says your mother and Bennett had a relationship?"

"Yes, they did."

"And... do you know why your mother left the farm?"

"I'm not sure. It seemed sudden. There was a thing... with Iris. She was fourteen then. She had a crush on Bennett. Mom was horrified when she found out."

"I see. Do you happen to know if anything inappropriate happened between Bennett and Iris?" he asks.

"I hope not. But I don't know for certain."

"Okay. Do you know if your mum ever saw Bennett again after she left the farm?"

"If she did, she never told us. I never saw him again."

"Thanks. That helps me build a better background." He presses his teeth into his bottom lip. "Hey, if you're at a loose end, would you like to come and have lunch with me? I'm about to go on my break."

I'm taken aback by his suggestion. I'm only just getting used to Van Dawson being the one to lead this investigation. And still getting used to the fact that he even became a detective.

"Oh, uh, I'm not sure I'd be the best company," I reply. "I get right inside my head at times. Like now. And I need to go get my phone—in case Jake calls."

He shrugs. "I can divert his calls to my phone."

"You can?"

"Yep. So... lunch? I can make us up something at Dawsons Drift. Not to toot my own horn, but I'm a bit of a whizz in the kitchen."

I stiffen. "No, I won't trouble you." I never thought I'd have a reason to step foot in that restaurant again.

He softens his tone, frowning. "Hey, is it because of...? Ah, how stupid can I get?"

I should have jumped in to say I had plans today. But my mind had blanked. I look away, afraid to let him see what I'm feeling inside. I'm a long way from the child I was when I lived at the Dawsons' home. I can't keep avoiding the things that hurt me the most. After all, I have to reach back to the year that I was twelve and find answers.

I manage a smile. "It's fine. Lunch sounds good."

"You sure? Okay, how about avocado, fried mushrooms and Halloumi on sourdough?"

"Yum. I just have to be at the resort for when Jake gets back."

"You said he's out boating? How big a boat? They could maybe pull up at the jetty outside the restaurant."

"Iris's husband called it a Zodiac... a Zodiac Medline, I think."

"Perfect. Even the largest one of those will get up the river just fine," Van says.

"Okay, sounds like a plan."

"My car? Parking can get a bit tight around town."

"I've noticed how busy it gets these days."

We drive across to Dawsons Drift in Van's car.

His mother and sister aren't here today in the restaurant—other staff members are buzzing about in the large, commercial kitchen. The whole place has been renovated, but the layout is the same. I can't get comfortable here. I second-guess my decision to have lunch with Van.

He grills slices of sourdough, glancing back at me. "So, how long are you planning on staying in Nautilus?"

Despite his casual tone, I sense an undercurrent in his voice. He's seen my list of names. He knows why I'm here and what I've been planning on doing.

"Not sure yet," I say lightly.

"And... you've been living in the US all this time? I mean, since you left Nautilus Bay as a kid?"

I nod. "Mostly. For a few years, I moved from country to country, working on wildlife projects. Either on low pay or as a volunteer. But when Jake was four, I came back to live with my father. How about you—where has life taken you?"

"I went into the police force straight out of school. Did a stint in New Zealand and then in Western Australia. I came back to Nautilus when I was about twenty-five. Got married to a girl named Jaylene Becker. You might remember her?"

I glance out the open window to the river. "I remember her."

A wave of remembered shame crawls down my back. I can see Jaylene and Van standing on the jetty of this restaurant—Jaylene staring daggers at Iris and me.

"Yeah, well, it didn't last with Jaylene," Van continues. "We were two different people. She became a lawyer and started working ten-hour days." He slices Halloumi on a cutting board. "Life just became all work... and little else."

I'm surprised at how open he is about his relationship with Jaylene. But I don't feel ready to share how things went with my relationship with Terence. I haven't talked about that with anyone.

"Too much work is a killer," I reply.

"So, what do you do when you're not writing—for the travel magazine?" he asks.

"You know what I do for work?"

"Yeah. I, uh, kind of looked you up."

I soak that in. "Oh."

"You were not in any kind of conversational mood when you first came back to town. So I filled in the blanks myself. Not that I blame you for how you were. Very difficult time."

"Yes, difficult time," I admit. "Well, I like to get out whenever I can and go kayaking or hiking. I live in a great area for that. It's near the foothills of the Pocono Mountains. There are hiking trails everywhere and white water rafting—and snow skiing in the winter. And the views are to die for."

"Well, next time I'm over that way, maybe you could give me a sightseeing tour. I was planning on a trip to New York soon."

"You were? Any reason you're heading over there?"

He shrugs and grins. "For the heck of it." I can't help but notice the way his eyes crinkle and light up when he smiles.

Skilfully, he plates up the grilled sourdough bread and toppings. I follow him out to a table close to the kitchen. All the tables next to the river are already taken.

I sit down and spread a napkin on my lap. "This looks gorgeous. Thank you."

"Great for a quick meal." Van sits opposite. "Well, I'd offer you a sightseeing tour of my part of the world... but you've already seen it. And there's not much of a line between the seasons here. No snow. But we do have sun. Buckets and buckets of it. The Sunshine Coast has more hours of sun per day than just about any other place in the world."

I spear a tiny tomato with my fork. "Sounds like paradise to me."

He shrugs. "It's just that I'd like to mix things up with a bit more adventure. But I picked the wrong job for that. Well, it depends how you frame adventure. If it's chasing up kids for spray-painting graffiti on the local scout hall, I'm your man."

I smile at his joke. "I'm sure you do more in your job than chase kids."

"Yeah, true enough. There's murders and mayhem in between the graffiti kids."

"So, how'd you decide to go into the police force?" For a moment, I think I've asked the wrong question. His eyes go down, and his jaw is set a little too firmly. "You don't have to tell me," I add. "It's not like it's any of my business."

"It's okay. How do I explain this? The easy way out would be to say I just followed my uncle into the force. And that's what I tell people. But to be dead honest, that's not why. You know how some people will say an event changed them when they were a kid? Well, for me, that was the disappearance of Ellie Lowood... and your mother."

His answer rocks me to my core. "That's why?"

"Yeah. I thought I could make a difference. And having you and your sister stay with my family—even though it was just for a short time—it forced me to see, in real time, the effect on the victims or the ones that get left behind."

I'm stunned by what he's just told me. It doesn't fit with my recollection of him at all. Maybe he just feels bad about how he was back then. Maybe lunch today is his way of saying sorry. But I don't know. And I still don't know if I can trust him with the investigation. The only person I can really trust in all of this is myself.

An older man approaches us. He's tall with a self-assured swagger. Without asking, he pulls up a chair and sits at our table.

"How are you doing, Van, my boy?" he asks.

Van takes a quick sip of his drink and splutters. "Yeah. Doing well. Uncle Quincy, you'd remember Lily—Lily Jorgenson?"

I realise then that the man is the former sergeant, Quincy Mullard. "Hi," I say.

He does a double take as his pale-blue eyes fix on me, but it seems manufactured. "Lily. Well, I'll be. All grown up. And back in town."

"For now, yes." I offer a quick smile.

He lifts his chin, regarding me. "I heard there were some new discoveries at the old house on Tiger Street. I also heard your mother actually owned the house?"

"Strange that we never knew," I say pointedly. He should have found out she owned it back in 1998. And he should have done a much more thorough search of the house.

Mullard rolls his shoulders. "I guess it doesn't make a lot of difference in the scheme of things. Except moneywise, for you and your sister—when you sell the house."

"I'm not sure about that," I tell him. "My parents' divorce was never completed. The money will probably go to our father."

His eyes open fully. "Is that right? Well, hopefully he does the right thing by you both. I'd have a word with him, but he probably still holds it against me that I had him on my suspect list."

Does he think my father is actually guilty of doing something to Mom and Ellie? Is that what he's trying to tell me? I'm feeling twitchy having this discussion over lunch, and when I glance over at Van, I can see he's at odds with it too.

"Uncle Quincy," Van says, "I think Lily needs a break from talk about the case while she's eating. You want me to fix you some lunch?"

"You know me," Mullard replies. "I only eat coffee beans until dinner." He turns back to me. "There was another item in the news. You found a page from a journal your mother was keeping?"

"Yes," I reply in a flat tone.

"That got my interest," Mullard tells me. "What did it say?"

Suddenly, it's like I'm twelve again, alone and terrified in the caravan, with Sergeant Mullard banging on the door and demanding answers from me. But I don't need to answer him now.

"It was just about personal things," I tell him.

He glances back at Van. "You making the page public?"

Van shakes his head. "I don't see any benefit in doing that. It's possibly written about Elsa's life before she ever arrived in Australia."

"Right. And what about the journal? That might be still kicking around somewhere?" he asks, raising a craggy set of eyebrows.

I jump in to answer. "If it still exists, we'll find it."

Mullard shrugs at me. "Sometimes it's best not to poke a sleeping bear. You find out things you didn't want to know. People just go and make a bad situation worse."

Van opens his mouth to respond when a boat putts up the river, capturing the attention of the diners at Dawsons Drift. It's an all-white expensive-looking rigid inflatable. Gabe's boat.

Standing, Gabe throws a looped rope over a pylon at the jetty. Jake and Kaden jump out. I'm relieved to have a reason to say goodbye and walk away from Quincy Mullard. But I won't be walking away from him forever. He's one of the names on my list.

I'll need to be well-armed when it comes time for that conversation.

Van leans close to my ear as we walk. "You want to cross another couple of names off your list?"

I turn to him. "Who?"

"The Lowoods. I've got an appointment with them tomorrow morning. Wanna tag along?"

I exhale. "Sure. Saves me from trying to convince them to see me."

"Nine in the morning? I can pick you up from the resort."

I nod, waving to Jake. "See you then."

There is only one thing I want to talk to the Lowoods about, so it won't be a long conversation. But still, they were livid with me last time I ever saw them. I'm not looking forward to it.

21

It's another overcast, rainy morning when Van and I are standing on the front doorstep of the Lowoods' home. The house looks much the same as I remember. The garden isn't as neat—no one has been clipping the hedges or planting flowers.

"Do they know I'm coming with you today?" I whisper to Van.

"They do. I wouldn't just spring that on them."

The two of them answer Van's knock. I'm shocked to see how much they've changed. It's as if they've shrunk, grown thinner. They look like two people who've had a very hard life. I recall them being around fifty years old last time I saw them, which means they must be in their midseventies now. Mr Lowood is using a walking frame.

They gaze back at me with stern expressions until Mrs Lowood's chest sinks, and she gestures for us to enter. "Good morning, Detective—and Lily. My goodness, Lily, you're all grown up and then some."

"It's good to see you both," I tell her with a quick smile.

The living room is saturated with air freshener to a degree that it's cloying. I notice that Mr Lowood has had half a leg amputated as he sits heavily on a sofa, his trousers riding up.

He follows my gaze. "The doc chopped it about ten years ago.

Gave me nothing but trouble. Joan's not doing well herself. Got problems with her ticker."

Joan Lowood does look greyish as she sits beside her husband. She reminds me of a spindly bird. The Lowoods' appearances seem an unspoken accusation: *See what your family did to us*.

"How are you, Lily?" Mrs Lowood asks in a curt voice. "You look well. I see your sister around town sometimes, of course, but I haven't laid eyes on you since you were a child."

"It's been a long time," I acknowledge. "I have a twelve-year-old of my own now. A son."

Her face creases in a sad expression as her gaze shifts to a large, framed photograph hanging on the wall. It's her own son, the one who died a few years before my family moved to Australia. He is blond and blue eyed, with a dimpled grin and a wave of hair across his forehead. He's very tanned and fit looking.

Beside him are photographs of Ellie and Grace—both blonde like their father. Grace passed away when she was nineteen, of complications from her diabetes. It hurts to see pictures of the two sisters again. This house is filled with painful memories, and I suddenly feel overwhelmed by them.

"I still miss my son terribly," Mrs Lowood says, watching me. "And poor Grace and Ellie too." She dabs at her eyes with a tissue. "Not a day goes by that I don't wonder about our dear little Ellie."

"I loved Grace and Ellie very much," I tell her. "My mother and Iris loved her, too."

Her eyes cloud. "I'm sure."

Detective Dawson leans forward, glancing from Mrs Lowood to her husband. "Well, should we start? As you know, I've reopened the case of the missing Elsa Jorgenson and your granddaughter Ellie."

"I'd almost given up hoping the police would open the case again." Mrs Lowood's voice falters. "It's been so long without the police doing anything. I don't mean that personally, Detective Dawson. You were just a boy when this happened."

He nods. "Well, the discovery of the backpack will hopefully provide some new inroads. Okay, now. Lily and I both have things to ask you about. I'll let Lily go first."

I swallow under the sudden intense attention of the couple. "I just wanted to know if Grace ever remembered any more about that night—anything at all, even the slightest thing?"

Joan Lowood purses her lips. "Grace told her story again and again. I don't know what else she could possibly have said. She suffered greatly for being the one who was left behind that night, not having a clue what was going on."

I look across to Detective Dawson and nod. I'm finished.

Van clears his throat, turning back to the Lowoods. "Okay, next thing. Have you read or heard a news item about a journal Elsa Jorgenson was keeping?"

"Joan can't bear to keep up with the news," Mr Lowood says, "but I heard about the journal."

"Have either of you any knowledge of it?" Van asks. "Ever see Elsa writing in a book?"

They both shake their heads.

"All right," Van says, "I'll move along. Could I ask you to look at these photographs?"

He takes out copies of the seven polaroid pictures that he'd shown to Iris and me.

"Have you seen this woman before?" he asks them. "The year would be 1997. She was hanging around the Jorgensons' house at night."

Mr Lowood looks up with a shocked expression. "Oh dear. I don't remember ever seeing that woman. Used to be lots of her kind around town back in the day, though. Scruffy drug-addict types. Not so much of them here now, thank goodness."

Joan Lowood puts a hand to her throat. "Do you think this woman had something to do with our Ellie going missing, Detective?"

"I don't have any information that points to that right now," Van tells her. "The first step is just to find out who she is."

"I wish we could help you more, Detective." Mrs Lowood closes her eyes as if making a wish. "Please... please find out what happened to our little Ellie."

Mr Lowood holds his wife's hand, his fingers trembling. "Yes... it's been far too many years without answers. Please bring her home. One way or another."

I feel emotionally wrecked as Van and I leave the Lowood couple clutching hands and leaning on each other in their grief. Like me, they've never had any resolution about the disappearance of their missing family member. I understand how that destroys a person.

As we drive away, I send Jake a text to ask how he's doing in kids' club. He sends me back a picture of a sad face. Worried, I dash out a reply with no fewer than five question marks.

Jake messages again to say that Monique and her family are going home today. I should have guessed that was the reason for Jake feeling sad.

"Everything okay?" Van asks me.

"Yeah. I think Jake is just a little besotted with a girl he met at the resort. But she's leaving today."

"Ah. Young love, huh?"

"Yep."

"Well, if you're both feeling at a loose end tonight, how about dinner?"

"Dinner?"

He exhales. "My mother and Anna have been asking to see you. But I... well, I didn't know how you'd feel about that. They've been away on a trip together, but they came back this morning."

My hands clench in my lap. I recall the Dawson family sitting around their dining room table the last time that I'd seen them all. Mrs Dawson had sat Iris and I down to tell us that we had to go to another foster family.

"Mum would really like a chance to make amends," he says.

As an adult, I understand that Iris and I brought Van's mother to a breaking point. I picture Iris and me fighting each other like wild animals in the days before that family meeting at their dining room table, feeling so alone, cornered and panicked. My skin burns hot behind my ears. The sense of humiliation of what Iris and I became is something I've carried ever since.

"She's always felt like she could have done more for you and your sister," Van tells me. "But she was run off her feet with the restaurant back then." He pauses. "Hey... you're not saying anything. Am I throwing too much at you?"

"Sorry. Look, your mother has nothing to make amends for. Really."

"She really wants to see you, though. She called me first thing in the morning to ask."

I feel myself relenting. It might be better for Jake than the two of us just eating alone. "Okay, you've sold me. Jake and I would love to come to dinner."

Van's face breaks into a broad grin. "Mum will be over the moon."

Jake and I spend the rest of the day around the pool, only heading up to our room when night falls. After a shower, I change into a Hawaiian print dress. I wasn't sure if I'd wear it. It was my mother's. I've packed and taken this dress to lots of places before but never actually put it on. Tonight feels like the right time.

The bright colours of the dress have me looking a little ghostlike. My usual routine all year round is a tinted moisturiser and a peach lip gloss, but that's not nearly enough for this dress. I apply a few touches of lipstick, mascara, and bronzer.

For a moment, I catch an image of my mother in my face. It unsettles me. She had looked beautiful in this dress—she'd worn it out to dinner with us just a month before she went missing. I remember her as being happy and contented in her own skin the year we spent on that road trip—despite what Iris says. I'm older than Mom was when she vanished, and I still don't have anything figured out. I want her to have been proud of me, but I have no idea how to measure up. She never saw me grow to become a woman. I had no one to guide me through those years.

A tear tracks down my face, over my carefully applied makeup.

Jake and I meet up with Van at the restaurant. Van's taking orders at a table. It's strange seeing him in that role. He seems a lot more relaxed than he is in his detective role, laughing as he chats with the customer.

He has a big grin plastered on his face as he shows Jake and me to a reserved table right next to the river. It's lovely, with fairy lights strung across the pergola and the rippling water running past. Scents of lemongrass and coconut curry drift in the air.

"Are you working here tonight?" I ask Van.

He shakes his head. "Nah, just helping out until you got here. It's just how it's always been. Whenever I can, I just roll up my sleeves and pitch in."

Mrs Dawson and Anna come rushing up to greet us. Mrs Dawson's dark hair is peppered with grey, and she still wears it up in a bun. Anna, who must be around forty now, looks fresh and pretty in her bohemian-style headscarf, short black dress, and serving apron.

"Oh, Lily," Mrs Dawson says as she hugs me. "You're beautiful. I can't tell you how good it is to see you. I've longed to see you again. I've wanted to know you were okay."

Anna hugs me next. "I've thought about you lots over the years."

"Your family was so good to me and Iris," I tell them. "And we were nothing but trouble."

Mrs Dawson shakes her head. "I won't hear a word of that. I just wish we could have done more for you. I know I felt like I was failing you girls."

"Mrs Dawson—" I start.

She smiles. "Call me Jana."

I return the smile. "Jana. All I remember is how kind you were."

"Thank you," she says warmly. "And this is your son?"

"Yes, this is Jake."

"Wonderful to meet you, Jake," Jana says. "I've got a big bowl of ice cream coming your way after dinner, young man."

Jake grins like a Cheshire cat.

Jana and Anna sit with us for the next fifteen minutes, chatting about the old days of this town. I begin to relax before they head back to the kitchen.

"Told you they'd love to see you," Van tells me.

"You have such a great family."

"Yeah, I do. They've always been there for me. Okay, what are you two hungry for tonight?"

I glance over the menu. "Wow, the dinner selection is amazing."

"A lot of the food is sourced locally," Van tells me with more than a hint of pride. "All organic. The vegetables, honey, macadamias, cheeses, crabs, and prawns... even the coffee." He laughs. "I could keep going and going with that list. The hinterland is a food bowl. And we've got the good stuff to grow it in—ancient volcanic soil."

I smile at his enthusiasm. "It's a wonder you didn't become a chef rather than a detective."

He winks. "Well, it could have gone either way."

Jake tilts his head at me. "This is where you used to live, Mom? Here at this restaurant?"

I nod. "Just for a little while. A few weeks."

Jake looks out at the river. "I'd never wanna leave."

My son will never know what that time in my life was really like because I don't know if I'll ever have the words for it. It seems like another lifetime. Yet at the same time, the past has been rushing back at me since I've been here.

Van and Jake begin chatting about console games.

I turn to watch the river. I remember Grace that day Iris and I took her for the trip in the kayak—how excited she was and how calm she was about the risks. I wish she were still here. I thought I could come back and see her, but she died when I was only fifteen.

It seems that when you're not looking, people can get snatched away, as if on dark river currents deep into the night.

A call comes through on Van's phone. He answers it, his eyebrows drawing together. He ends the call and turns to me. "Lily, I'm sorry. I have to go."

"Is anything wrong?" I say in alarm.

Rising, he gestures me away from the table a few steps. "A man's body has been found on the riverbank—up further," he says quietly. "Technically, I had a night off. But when something like this comes up, then I'm on duty."

Van exits the restaurant quickly. I can tell that Jake is disappointed to lose his dinner companion. We watch Van as he walks out to the jetty and heads off up the river on a small boat.

22

THE AIR FLOATING through the window first thing in the morning is warm and humid. I'd had a sleepless night, tossing and turning until the early hours.

Picking up my phone, I check the news. The man who died on the riverbank last night was apparently beaten to death after an argument over a drug deal.

A twinge of panic competes with the bleary, foggy sensation in my head—this case is bound to take priority over the case involving my mother and Ellie.

When I answer a call on my phone from Iris, I'm sure she's heard about last night's murder incident and wants to commiserate with me about what it'll mean for us. But she has other things on her mind.

"So, you were hanging out at Dawsons Drift all day yesterday," she states abruptly.

Her sharp tone confuses me. "Dawsons Drift? Oh, right, yes. Van asked me there."

"And you were having meetings there with him and Sergeant Mullard?"

"What? No, not meetings. Nothing like that. Anyway, how'd

you—?"

"Gabe told me you were there for lunch—and he saw Quincy with you and Van. And a friend of mine told me you were with Van again at dinner."

"That's true. But it was just—"

"You shouldn't be discussing the case if I'm not there, Lily. This isn't just about you, you know."

I sit upright in bed, waking fully. She's coming at me like a battering ram. "We weren't discussing the case, Iris. Quincy Mullard isn't even a sergeant anymore. He tried bringing things up, but I shut him down."

"You went to the Lowoods' house with Van. You going to tell me that wasn't about the case?"

"Okay, yes. That was."

"Why did you come here, Lily? You said you wanted to see our mother's things and figure out what to do about selling the house. But since you've been here, it's like you've been running your own personal show. With Van at your beck and call."

"That's not fair."

"You even got him to search the house. Now it's all torn apart. It'll be up to us to pay for the repairs."

I inhale and exhale, calming myself. "Don't you think it's important what the police found there? The photos and Ellie's pendant?"

"The photos don't tell us anything except that some weirdo woman was hanging about—a whole year or more before our mother vanished. And as for the pendant, well, I can't explain that. I almost wish it wasn't found, because it's driving me crazy thinking about it."

"The pendant is driving me crazy too."

"Is it? Doesn't seem like it's stopping you from pushing Van to do your bidding. You're just making things worse. Just... go home. You don't belong here. You shouldn't have come."

I recoil as if she'd just hit me. She ends the call before I can even think of a response.

I'm smarting, hurting all over.

A dark thought steps into my mind. Is Iris worried I might be getting closer to the truth—the truth that she's kept hidden from me for so long?

Wrapping my arms around my head, I squeeze my eyes shut. I don't know how to go forward from this point. There are only a few people left on my list of names now. And the most important one of them is Iris. But she's returned to being hostile toward me.

Suddenly, I feel like plunging myself into water—just like Mom used to.

I dress quickly and then leave Jake a note. When I reach the resort's pool area, I'm glad to see no one's here yet. I pull off my beach dress and drop it onto a pool lounge. Then, diving in, I let the cold water close over me and start swimming a lap.

I swim back and forward with long, steady strokes.

My head and body feel so heavy and weighed down, even in the water. Iris is trying to force me to push everything back into the past.

But I can't let go. I won't.

As I glide beneath the surface, the first lines of Mom's poem repeat in my mind:

I have always been running,

especially when I am at my most still.

The words frustrate me, haunt me.

What did you mean by that, Mom? I wish I knew. I wish you told us more. I wish you'd let us in. Is Iris right? Was the road trip just about you taking the four of us girls inside your illness, deeper and deeper, until everything exploded? Where did you go that night when you disappeared into thin air? Where did you take Ellie? Or were the two of you running from someone?

Again, I'm desperate to hold Mom's journal in my hands. I want the rest of the pages—not just this one, tantalising page on which she wrote a mystifying poem. There is so much I need to know.

Maybe the journal isn't here in this town. Mom might have left it with someone else. Maybe even with one of the people from the farm, like Bennett or Joyce.

A startling thought catches hold. I stop swimming, reaching out to grab the edge of the pool, where I gasp and gather my breath.

I could go looking for Bennett and Joyce. I could go looking for the journal. I'll hire a campervan and just take off with Jake. I'll tunnel back through the years, finding everyone and everything I can remember. I'd have to take Jake out of school for an extended period. I know he'd be over the moon at that prospect. Mom did it. Why can't I? Jake's a self-directed learner. We'd be fine. I'd go for as long as it takes.

My thoughts tumble over the top of each other. If I did this, it would have to be done right. Jake and I would stay at every single place Mom stayed at. I'd leave nothing out. I'd recreate the road trip of 1998.

Is this crazy? Probably. But it feels as if the idea is building a life of its own and there's no putting it back in its bottle now.

After lifting myself out of the pool, I wrap my body in a pool towel and dry off. I send off a message to the editor of the travel magazine I do the most work for—letting him know I'll be gone for an extended period. It's just a courtesy message—I've been free-lancing for years and don't need to book in my vacations.

After that, I get busy calling up campervan hire places and getting cost estimates. God, it's going to be expensive. But I have a nest egg built up. Dad hasn't ever charged me rent and he's been giving me money from his trust fund each month. I've been living off that while letting my wages sit in the bank.

Someone has been repeatedly calling while I've been contacting the campervan companies. When I check, I see that it's Iris.

I don't want to hear any more of what she has to say. She's made herself clear.

But when she calls yet again, I decide to answer. I'm guessing she'll be happy I've decided to leave town.

"Lily," she starts, "I didn't mean the things I said. I just get myself into moods and I go straight to the finish line. I'd been stewing all last night about you talking with Van and Quincy, and then I couldn't hold myself back this morning."

"Well, Jake and I will be moving on from Nautilus Bay—probably within the next day or two," I inform her. "So, there's that."

"You are? Please don't do that because of me."

"It's not because of you."

"Well, where are you going?" she asks.

"I'm doing a road trip. The same one Mom took us on."

Her voice falters. "What? Why would you do that?"

"It's just something I need to do. I should have done it years ago. Decades ago."

I hear her draw in a breath. "Lily... are you going to look for the journal?"

She's silent for a moment before she speaks again, in a softened tone. "That's just... nuts. I feel responsible, like I've pushed you towards doing this. Don't do this to yourself. The journal is gone. Long gone."

"Maybe. Maybe not. Anyway, I'm going to look for anyone who remembers our mother. I want to do this."

"Who do you expect to find? They were mostly drifters who we met on the road. Drifters and grifters. Like Bennett. He was just a grifter."

"I don't remember him that way," I say tightly.

"I do. He just used our mother, and used us to sell his jewellery," she says.

"That's not the same memory I have."

"You were eleven when we stayed at the farm," she tells me. "Of course you don't have the same memories as me."

"Iris... I've made my mind up."

"God. I need a stiff drink. How long are you planning on going for? A whole year—like Mum?"

"I don't know."

"And you're dragging Jake out of school for this?"

"I know for a fact he'd love it."

"Lily, it's a flight of fancy. Just like something Mum would have done. No, actually, it's exactly what Mum did do."

"Iris—"

"Maybe that accounts for why we never see eye to eye. You're so like our mother was. You have to realise how lost she was. How she dragged us from pillar to post. I've worked hard to give my own kids all the things I didn't have. Solid roots. Consistency. Opportunities. That's what children need."

I bristle at her words. "And I haven't given my son all that?"

"You gave birth to him on a monkey-rescue project in India."

"It was orangutans, and it was in Sumatra." I look over my shoulder as a family heads into the pool area.

"Whatever," Iris says. "You then took Jake from country to country for the first years of his life. Until you split up with that guy —Jake's father. You two never got married or anything."

"And you know all this how?" I ask.

"I kept track of you. I'm still a big sister."

I digest this information. She tracked me but never bothered keeping in contact? Her years of silence feel even worse now. A bitter kind of anger lodges in my throat.

"I called to congratulate you when Kaden was born," I say. "But I heard nothing from you when Jake was born."

"I suffered from depression for the first couple of years after I had Kaden. Trying to be a mother when I had no role model to follow was damned hard. Try not to judge me."

Conversations with Iris had often followed this route. Attacks followed by defence against any blows.

"I had no role model, either," I say in a dead tone. *You could have been there to help me, Iris—like a big sister would. But you weren't.* "Anyway, Jake and I are fine. We'll be fine." I hang up before she can get another word in.

I head back up to the hotel room. I watch Jake sleeping, the enormity of what I'm planning rushing at me. I know that the odds of me finding any answers out there are low, and this recreation of Mom's trip might be the only resolution I'll ever get. I decide that I need to keep a record of everywhere I go. I'll keep a scrapbook that will form a living record that I at least tried.

I switch on my computer tablet and find the file that I have of the 1998 road trip. Then I send the file through to a store that can print the photos. I'll use the copies of the photos for my scrapbook.

My phone's ringtone sounds, interrupting me. I'm sure it'll be Iris again.

But it isn't—it's Van.

"I have to apologise for running out on you and Jake last night," he says. He sounds exhausted.

"Oh gosh, not at all," I reply. "That must have been a grisly find —that poor guy."

"Yeah, an awful end for him. He's been involved in some low-level crime for years now, but he didn't deserve what happened."

"I hope you find whoever did it."

"I was hoping to make another dinner date with you and Jake, to make up for last night. But I can't do that right now. When there's a murder—"

"I know. I've realised that. You'll be caught up. Van... I've got something to tell you. Jake and I are leaving town."

"Already?" he says in surprise. "Going home to America?"

"No. Something else."

I explain the trip. But Van is even less impressed than Iris.

"There's a possibility of you coming across people who know what happened with your mum and Ellie," he tells me. "You can't—and shouldn't—tackle that on your own. You don't know what you might stir up."

That sounds so much like what his uncle Quincy said to me, I feel like snapping at him. But I hold back. "I wouldn't do anything stupid. I'll have Jake with me."

I bring the call to a quick end. He and Quincy and Iris are all about not poking sleeping bears. But some bears have been sleeping for far too long.

Picking up my computer tablet again, I start sketching out a map of the area where the farm's location could be. That information has been lost over the past years. The farm never had a name. And my own memory is vague.

But I'll find my way there. I'll find my way through my mother's entire trip. And if there are any answers still out there, I'll find them, too.

23

Over breakfast, I tell Jake about the road trip. His eyes light up and he has a dozen questions for me. The thing he likes best is that he won't be returning to school for so long, but he's also intrigued with the idea of searching back through history for clues about his grandmother's disappearance.

I make a difficult call to Dad after that. He tells me, in no uncertain terms, that I'm wasting my time and money. I want to challenge him and ask why he didn't do more to find my mother years ago. I understood that his relationship with her had been over, but he would have plainly seen the effect that losing her was having on Iris and me. It makes me wonder if every family who've had one of their own go missing have these lingering feelings of bitterness toward each other. Who should have done more? Who should have done things differently before that person went missing?

Straight after breakfast, Jake and I head out on a shopping trip. I'd packed light for this journey to Australia, and the clothes we have are not going to last us. In between buying us new clothes, I call in to the photography store and pick up my stack of photographs that I had printed there. Then I head to an art supply store and buy the scrapbooks I want.

We return to the hotel in the late afternoon. My shoulders ache from the armfuls of shopping bags I'm carrying, and I'm exhausted by the thoughts running around in my mind. We eat dinner in the resort's dining room and head off to bed early.

I'm woken by a rap at the door in the early morning. I open up expecting to see cleaning staff, but it's Iris.

She's been crying, her eyes red and her face blotchy. She's wearing an old shapeless tee-shirt and her hair is dishevelled.

"God, what's wrong?" I say, pulling her inside. "Are you hurt?"

She sits on the couch. "I've cancelled the holiday to Thailand."

"Um, what? What are you talking about?" I ask.

She pushes her hair back from her face. "You know how I said that Gabe and I were taking the kids to Thailand for Christmas? Well, we're not going anymore."

"Okay, I remember now. Iris, what's happened?"

"I've just got somewhere else to be—other than Thailand—that's all."

"What does that mean?"

"It means we're coming with you and Jake."

I sink into a chair at the small dining table, staring in shock at my sister. "What? But you—"

Iris jumps in, her words going into rapid fire. "I know. I know what I said yesterday. I've changed my mind. I can't let you go like this. We were just getting to know each other again. I don't want to just let things slide back to how they were between us before. So, let's all go together. It can be one big family holiday. Our kids can have time to connect properly as cousins. It's the start of the school holidays here. My kids have from now until the end of January off school. That's lots of time."

I'm too stunned to properly absorb all she's telling me. "But you had your holiday all booked, right?"

"I always pay extra so I can change the dates of our flights if I want. And I was able to cancel the accommodation. You know, every Christmas we're jetting off somewhere overseas—we just don't spend any time road-tripping around Australia. I've always been against it. Bad memories, I guess."

"Iris... no. This isn't what you want. And anyway, this isn't a vacation for me. It's a serious thing. I intend to find answers."

She crosses her arms tightly, dropping her head. "I thought you'd be happy—not to have to do this on your own."

"You should have talked with me before cancelling Thailand."

"It was spur of the moment."

"What about Gabe—what does he think?"

She sighs heavily. "I haven't told him yet. Gabe's a workaholic. He doesn't even enjoy our holidays. He won't show it, but he'll be happy as a pig in mud to stay here while I go away with the kids."

She's got an answer for everything I throw at her. But none of it makes sense.

"Iris, this won't work. You and me. You know it. Why do you really want to do this?"

Her eyes sharpen. "I just told you why. It's because I care about you. Why is that so hard to understand? I don't want us to part on bad terms again. I don't want that."

"And you don't think that the two of us together on a road trip would be a disaster?"

"We've been together on a road trip before, Lily. We can do it again. Anyway, you're not giving any thought to your son. Won't be much fun for him cooped up in a campervan with his mother."

"Jake's used to just being with me. And he likes exploring."

"He'd have a lot more fun with his cousins. Oh, but I get it. This isn't about fun. You're going to do what no one else has been able to do—get answers."

"You don't get it. You're not going to get it. Iris, you didn't even want me to come here. Like, at all."

"Don't keep holding that against me. Please."

Jake walks out from his bedroom, rubbing his face, his hair askew from sleep. "Oh, hi, Aunt Iris." He looks around the room. "Are Kaden and the girls with you?"

Iris shoots me a *Told you so* glance before she answers Jake.

"Sorry, sweetie. I know you've been having fun together, but they're not with me this morning."

"It's been heaps of fun," Jake mumbles with a smile.

"Your mom and I have been talking about something we can all do together," Iris tells him.

I give Iris a slight shake of my head that says, *This isn't fair*. I can tell she understands me just fine.

"Hey, Aunt Iris, you just said *Mom*, like *we* do," Jake says.

"Did I?" Iris frowns and then laughs. "Being around you two must be bringing out my old accent."

"Go have a shower," I tell Jake. "We're gonna have breakfast down at the resort's restaurant."

"Okay." Drowsily, he wanders off to the bathroom.

Iris waits for him to close the door. "You're doing this anyway—this trip. Why deprive Jake of doing it with his cousins?"

"The cousins that he only just met mere days ago?" I reply.

She doesn't reply to that, instead heading to the balcony and looking out at the view.

If she intended to corner me like a rat in a trap, she succeeded. Because it feels that way. If Jake should later discover there was a chance to have Kaden and the girls along with us and I said no, that could hurt him deeply. And Iris would doubtless find a way to let Jake know.

God, why is she doing this? Is it because she's worried I'll find out something—something she doesn't want me to know?

Another thought comes to me. Could I turn this around on her? A long trip with my sister might give me the chance I need. I might find a way to make her finally tell me what she knows.

I step out to the balcony. "Okay."

She twists around. "Okay?"

"You heard me."

She sniffs and smiles. "We'd better start making plans, then, little sister."

24

I CAN'T SHAKE the feeling of unreality as I walk into the RV lot with Iris. There is a bewildering array of campervans and motorhomes on display. We're greeted by Mr Ackerley, who shows us his vehicles and extols the virtues of each at length. He's delighted when told we're looking for two vans, practically walking with a skip in his step and a twinkle in his eye.

I'm only interested in a small van, just big enough for Jake and me to be comfortable at night. Iris is looking for something much larger. As well as herself and three children, she apparently plans to haul a lot of sports gear and stuff along.

Iris shocks me once again when she points in the direction of a tour bus. "How much is that one per day, Mr Ackerley? It says it's sixty percent off full price."

He scratches his temple, screws up his face. "Ah, you girls don't want that beast. Can't drive it with a normal driver's licence, either. Strike that one off your list."

I recognise the sarcastic look my sister flings at Mr Ackerley. It used to be her signature expression, and it seems she hasn't lost it.

"How much?" Iris repeats.

"Four hundred a day," he says reluctantly. "It needs to get back on the road. It sat there all through the two covid lockdown years and has been there ever since."

Iris folds her arms. "Is it properly converted?"

"Yup," he answers. "Australian regulations are tough for converted buses. This one passes. But—"

"We'd like to see it," she presses.

He doesn't move an inch. "I'd have to get the key."

Iris raises her perfectly groomed eyebrows high in her forehead. "Okay...?"

He seems to have completely lost his skip as he plods away to the office. He returns with a set of keys, and we follow him to the bus. The vehicle is huge. It looks like something a touring band would take on the road. I don't know what my sister is thinking. Is it just a matter of principle because Mr Ackerley called us both girls?

He stands back, his beefy arms crossed tight while Iris and I board the bus. The bus driver's seat is intact, and behind that are two rows of original seats. They're plush luxury models, complete with power points behind each one. All other original seats have been removed. There is a set of new narrow bench seats and tables that I assume are for eating meals. Then there is a bathroom cubicle and, on the opposite side, a small oven and cooktop. Four bunk beds—two on either side—and a bed stretch right across the back of the bus.

Along the length of the bus, the overhead storage has been retained where possible. It has everything you could possibly want for a family, but it's gross overkill for what Iris needs.

Iris and I step from the bus and walk to where Mr Ackerley is waiting. "You say it passes regulations?" Iris asks him.

He nods, casting a dubious eye at her. "Yup. The weight is balanced from front to back. The seats they retained, of course, already passed muster—those don't require seat belts because the chairs are purpose-built for safety."

"Okay," Iris says. "And are those racks inside the only storage?"

"Nah, it's a proper tour bus, so it's got stacks of storage underneath." He walks to the side of the bus and flips up the doors of the luggage compartment.

Iris takes me a short distance away then faces me, squinting into the sun. "What do you think?"

I keep my voice low. "What I think is it would cost you a bomb, and do you really need a whole bus? Who's even gonna drive it?"

She shrugs. "I've got a truck licence. Got that so I could help Gabe in the early days of our business. And if you and I pool together, it's gonna cost less than hiring two separate motorhomes. Plus, we'd get the room to take a lot of gear along."

"You mean, we all go together? In the one vehicle?"

"Is that so radical?"

"Yes," I whisper, but I don't have a good way to explain why.

"Look," she says, "the trip is gonna be expensive no matter which way we cut it. Even when Mom did it on a shoestring, we had to make and sell jewellery at markets just to survive."

"But there were only five beds in there. There are six of us."

"Four bunks and a double," she agrees. "I can have Audrey in with me in the double, and you can snag a bottom bunk."

"We'd be like a... a travelling circus."

"Really, Lily?"

"It's just not what we intended hiring, right? It's not what we came here for."

"Plans can change," she says.

"Would you really be okay with driving a freaking tour bus—every day?"

"I enjoy driving. I did some long-distance runs with the trucks. If you don't believe me, call Gabe."

"I believe you. I just..." I shake my head. "Look, okay. Why not? If you're sure, we'll do it."

Iris goes ahead and signs the papers to hire the bus. Mr Ackerley looks both pleased and confused.

A flurry of organising follows the trip to the RV lot, which is almost all coming from Iris. She wants to pack the bus with sports equipment and games and outdoor seating. I'm just anxious to leave and get started.

In the morning, I check out of the resort and catch a taxi with Jake over to the RV lot. Iris is running late. She and Gabe and their kids finally arrive in their SUV. When we take the four kids over to see the bus, their whoops of delight are ear-splitting. It's been kept as a surprise for them. They're racing about to sit on every seat and lie on every bed. Then they're opening every cupboard and testing out the shower.

"Easy, tigers," Gabe says as he does his own tour.

Gabe then sits the kids down. "Okay, guys, the first rule is to have fun. The second rule is—don't give your mother and Aunty Lily a hard time. Everyone in their seats when the bus is on the road—no playing in the aisle or the bunk beds."

After the family instruction session, Gabe and Iris walk off the bus and hug for at least twenty seconds. The sensation of unreality returns as the bus is packed and everyone's in their seats and Iris is driving us out of the lot. We're really doing this. The kids wave to Gabe as we leave.

Iris proves herself to be a good, steady driver. But it'll still take me a while to get used to seeing her drive a bus. I've seated myself on the seat opposite Iris.

"The kids are still jumping out of their skins," I say to her. "Maybe some music would help settle 'em?"

She points to an MP3 player on the console beside her. "Music for the savage beasts. I brought along a selection. Pick what you want and blast it."

I pick up Iris's player and begin scrolling through her music titles. "These are all old."

"Yeah." She shoots me a wide grin. "The 1990s, baby."

Back in 1998, the music Mom played was almost all from the '90s. It was all new then. Everything for her was always about moving forward, letting the past go. That year we were on the road, music was her answer for everything. Especially on the bad days. She'd tell us to shake out our angry feelings with a song. When Iris and I had been fighting, she'd choose a song from her music collection and make us sing along at the top of our lungs. She had a good collection of '90s music, including Alanis Morissette, Pearl Jam, Radiohead, Nirvana, and INXS.

Back then Iris and I would try to win our fights by screeching the high notes louder than each other. Grace and Ellie would giggle. Often, Iris and I would end up collapsing into giggles too. Sometimes, even the worst times ended up good.

Strangely enough, the kids are on board with the idea of playing music from back when we were their age. It seems that to them, this whole expedition is an unexpected gift and they're prepared to go along with any of the rules that come with it.

Jake, Kaden, Piper, and Audrey sway their heads to the melancholy stringed instruments of the Verve's "Bitter Sweet Symphony" as they settle into playing a card game together.

Without warning, a dark mood descends on my shoulders. I've got nothing to do. I'm used to being the one at the wheel. I drive long distances in my job, always with the hum of tyres in the country areas or the noise of traffic in the city. But there's nothing to distract me from my thoughts now.

25

WE'RE NEARING the first stop on the trip, a zoo. It's the first place that Mom stopped at after we set off with the caravan. If we're going to retrace Mom's steps, we have to stick to the way she did it.

I pull out a scrapbook and mark it as Day 1. Then I paste in the copies of the photographs from when I was last at this zoo. I feel the same aching sadness that I always do when I look at these images of Mom, Iris, Grace, Ellie and me again.

I'm surprised when Iris's kids look on with interest. Iris explains that she's barely kept any of the old photos. I should be shocked by that, but I'm not. She wants to let the past go. We were given the photos by the police sometime in the year 2000, along with other bits and pieces that had been in Mom's caravan.

Iris turns onto Steve Irwin Way, which snakes off the main highway. The entry to Australia Zoo is straight off this road. Palm trees line the entry. An enormous wooden figure of Steve Irwin greets visitors at the gate.

Last time I came here, as a child, Irwin was alive and it wasn't called Australia Zoo yet. It was our first taste of Australia outside of Nautilus Bay. We hadn't planned our trip here. Mom just chanced upon a sign that advertised it, and she followed it. That's how that year went. No itinerary. Just all chance encounters and drifting, as if we were caught up in a slow current.

After leaving the bus, we spend the next two hours walking around the exhibits. The presence of Steve Irwin and the Irwin family is strong here. Long-forgotten memories return to me. Like, which animals were Grace's favourites. And Ellie being so excited about there being tigers here that she ran off to find them. I remember how frantic Mom was when we were all looking for her.

Jake never ran away from me when he was small. He was always too afraid I'd disappear if he let me out of his sight. Back then, that made me feel secure. I didn't have to worry about losing him. But now... now I'm starting to question everything. Did I give him fears he shouldn't have had?

Next, we head to a crocodile show. It's at a stadium they call the Crocoseum. A man-made pond sits in the middle of the stadium. Last time we were here at the zoo, it was Steve Irwin conducting the crocodile show. This time, it's his son, Robert.

Jake is fascinated with all of it. As the show ends and we leave the stadium, he steps alongside me. "Mom, what was it like here when you were a kid?"

"Hmmm. Well, it was smaller. I remember a lot of excitement because Steve and Terri were soon to have their first baby."

Iris overhears the conversation. "That baby was Bindi. She grew up and married an American and now has a little girl of her own."

"I didn't know that," I reply. "Gosh. So the baby now has a baby."

The passage of time seems so swift, running past me. When Mom brought Iris and me here, we were eleven and thirteen. Now we have our own children around that age.

We're all tired when we return to the bus. I sit with my scrapbook, writing down the old memories that have come back to me about the zoo, and the new memories from today. I'll need to paste in today's photographs once I have them developed.

We continue south on our trip, through the Glasshouse Mountains. It's a stinker of a day by the time we reach Brisbane, the capital city of this state. Brisbane is a little distance inland from the coast, built alongside a river.

Drawing out my scrapbook, I add in the few old photos I have of Brisbane. I remember that we didn't stay here long.

Iris instructs us all to wear swimsuits under our clothes before we leave the bus. We take it in turns to change in the tiny bathroom cubicle—the only private place in the bus. Outside, the sidewalk is so hot I think my shoes will end up sticking.

Kaden has a request—that we visit the art gallery. Everyone is in immediate agreement. Anywhere to get out of the sun.

The temperature in the gallery is beautifully cool—so cool we end up deciding to have lunch in the café. Kaden seems in his element among the artwork, studying each painting and sculpture. I'd thought of him as a sporty kid, and it surprises me to see him show this level of interest in art. I don't know Iris's children at all. They're like strangers to me, even though they're my nephew and nieces. Every little reminder of that feels like a jolt in my chest.

We head out of the gallery and back into the South Bank area. I find it interesting how different the city looks to the picture I had in my head. The place now has a fresh, youthful, almost arty vibe. Back when I was a kid, I remember people cynically calling this city Brisvegas, due to the big casinos that had been built here. It wasn't known for its cultural refinement then.

Iris leads us to a beach in the middle of the city. I have only a vague memory of it. It's a huge man-made swimming area, complete with sand and palm trees. Currently, it's crowded with kids and families—small children shrieking. The sound is like a field of squeaky toys all being stepped on at once.

Iris and I manage to secure a spot where the palm trees are casting long, welcome shadows. Jake and Kaden peel off their clothes down to their board shorts and race each other into the water. I emerge in my black one-piece swimsuit, feeling awkward, like a turtle without its shell. I'm bony in my hips and shoulders, and my legs are solid from all the hiking and bicycling I do. The swimsuit is the only one I own, and I rarely swim. Even though there's a pool in the basement of my father's house, I never go in it.

Piper and Audrey splash through the shallow water at the edge. Piper stops to execute a series of perfect leaps and spins on the sand. In her white racer-back swimsuit and high ponytail, she looks like a child model. Audrey stands back, watching.

Taking out a camera, Iris photographs Piper midspin. Piper smiles at her mother and strikes a pose. Delighted, Iris keeps snapping photos. She then requests a picture of her twins together, almost as an afterthought. Piper wraps her arms around her sister for the picture.

"Lovely," Iris says. "Okay, be careful out there, you two. Stay away from creeps. Oh, and, Piper, look out for Audrey?"

In response, Piper turns and runs deep into the water and swims away. Audrey shrugs and follows her sister—though at the pace she's keeping, it seems she has no hope of catching her.

Iris tucks her camera back into her bag. "Piper can be a little cow sometimes."

"She's certainly different to Audrey," I remark.

"Yes, they are *so* different. But you know, I would love to have had Piper's confidence back when I was eleven. She's simply amazing on stage."

"She's certainly confident. Well, I'm baking here. I'm going in." As I wade into the water, I call out to Iris. "Fair warning, I'm not leaving the pool until the temperature drops into the '70s."

Iris joins me, wearing a print bikini with a high waist. She's thicker around the middle these days but still has her long, lean dancer's legs. "I admit I have to mentally swap Fahrenheit to Celsius. I've forgotten the system I grew up with. I mean, we'd be cooked like gooses if this was seventy degrees Celsius. You poor thing—you're really suffering in this hot weather, aren't you?"

"Yes, and I'm trying not to be a baby about it. But I'm used to the cold. I mean, I was standing knee-deep in snow the day before Jake and I flew out here."

She quietens, tracing her fingers along palm tree shadows on the water's surface. "I can barely remember what it was like to have those snowy winters."

"Jake and I were helping Dad dig out the garden path. Dad was telling Jake he was doing it wrong."

"Sounds like Dad. Gosh, I can't even picture Gabe and me having to deal with snow season. We're so busy all the time. Snow would just... slow everything down."

She leans herself back in the water, almost floating, closing her eyes. "I haven't been totally honest about this trip, Lily."

I swallow. What is she about to tell me? Something about the past? Something about what she was doing the night Mom vanished?

"I think Gabe is cheating on me," my sister says flatly.

I suck in a breath, mentally adjusting. "Oh, Iris. I don't know what to say."

"We had the trip to Thailand all planned, and I thought I could do it. I thought I could go on pretending that everything is okay. For the kids' sake. And because... well, I don't want to leave Gabe. I don't want our marriage to end. But when you came along with your road-trip idea, I jumped ship. It was a way out for me. I don't have to look at his face for a whole six weeks."

The revelation shocks me from both angles—Gabe cheating and it being what made Iris want to do this trip. Strangely, the thought of Gabe behaving that way immediately makes me bristle and want to protect Iris.

"How long have you known?" I ask her.

"Oh, maybe for the past six months. I keep thinking how awful it'd be for the kids to find out. I keep wondering who else knows. Well, apart from the other woman, that is."

"Do you know who it is?"

"Nope. Don't want to know, either. Maybe it'll just burn out and Gabe and I will go back to normal. I never thought I'd be that kind of person—you know, who'd put up with something like this. But how would I cope on my own? And I don't want Gabe to just become one of those weekend dads. I don't want that for the kids. That'd be cheating them out of a father. I want them to have a normal life—the kind of life you and I didn't have, little sister."

I pluck a leaf from the water. "What about you, Iris? What do you want?"

Her eyes open, and she gazes at the sky. "I don't know. My life has been Gabe and the kids. I wouldn't have a clue about anything else."

I wish I had some kind of answer for her, but I've got nothing. She and I are both damaged by the past, and I don't know if my view on life is any better than hers. I do the only thing I can think of, which is to lie in the water and just float there alongside her.

26

In the late afternoon, we find a place to park overnight. The kids are excited by the prospect of their first sleep on the bus. We haven't gotten very far on this trip yet, but that's intentional. It's Iris's first day driving this monster of a vehicle, and the plan was to take it super easy.

The next morning, I rouse to the sound of pelting rain, unsure of where I am.

I snap fully awake, realising that I'm on a bus, with my sister and our children, at the beginning leg of some crazy odyssey. I take out my phone and check for messages. There's one from Van. It simply says, *Bon voyage*. Outside, rain is pouring down the windows of the bus.

After Iris and the kids wake, I make everyone scrambled eggs and toast. Jake sneaks small smiles at me. He seems different since we've been in Australia and especially since getting to know his cousins.

By the time breakfast is done and cleared away, hot sun peers through the clouds and turns the air thickly humid.

We roll into the next town—Surfers Paradise—when it's still morning. When I check the GPS, I see more water canals than land.

That surprises me at first. I've never seen this place from an aerial perspective before.

I fill pages of my scrapbook with old photos. Mom took a lot of pictures here. I linger on an image of Grace smiling broadly at our jewellery stand.

I'm bemused to see that Surfers Paradise is much the same as in 1998. Some things are gone, and some things are new, but mostly, it's just glitzier. I have strong memories of this place. We spent weeks selling jewellery in street markets here.

Back in 1998, when Iris and I first spotted the sign for Surfers Paradise, we expected yet another small coastal town that probably didn't even have a movie theatre. But this town proved itself to be anything but that. It was a long stretch of opulent, gleaming high-rises met by a blue ocean. There were stores to rival Beverly Hills's Rodeo Drive but also a proliferation of cheap dollar stores and the remains of failed, idealistic creations. There were wealthy locals with leathery skin who'd spent too long in tanning solariums, gold jewellery clinking on their arms and their hair dyed either too dark or too blond. And meter maids roamed the streets in gold bikinis and tiaras.

It's time to find a spot where we can park. The bus is a monster of a vehicle, and parking is going to be severely limited almost anywhere we go. I finally find one on the GPS. People stare as we walk off the bus, probably wondering who we are to be touring about like this. Iris quips about us being the Partridge Family, but none of our kids get the joke.

It's the smell of summer that hits me first as we walk onto the main streets—fried food, sunscreen, perfume, and the ocean. Maybe I'm imagining it, but those scents seem the same as I remember from 1998.

We spend the day here. As the afternoon turns to twilight and twilight turns to night, the whole place shines. Signs glow everywhere. Glittery palm trees line wide streets. Girls wear short, tight dresses in yellow, pink, and blue. The boys wear Hawaiian shirts, with warm breezes fluttering them open. All the while, the dark ocean booms, and music pounds from every nightclub and street café.

Piper looks entranced as three teenage girls pass us, wearing heavy makeup and satiny dresses. "Mum, can we go shopping? I need some new clothes. Please?"

"This isn't a shopping expedition," Iris reminds her.

Piper is undeterred. "But what about when we go to the dance comps in Sydney in February? I need to look good. And you love going clothes shopping. The boys can go to a games arcade if they get bored."

"Sorry, Piper," Iris says with a tired edge to her voice. "No shops. No clothes."

Piper stands her ground—literally—stopping and crossing her arms. "You don't appreciate me."

"Say what?" Iris shoots back.

"You don't appreciate me as a daughter," Piper says defiantly.

Iris waves her on. "Keep walking. I'm too exhausted to deal with this right now. March!"

Piper strides to the front of the group with her arms still crossed high on her chest—reminding me of her mother at the same age.

There's a message from Detective Dawson on my phone. Stepping away slightly, I call him.

He picks up quickly. "Lily, how are things?"

"We haven't gotten far yet. We're at Surfers."

"Taking it easy?"

"As far as road-tripping goes—yes. As far as kid wrangling goes—no. I'd say hiking a mountain is less tiring."

He laughs. I realise that I really like the sound of his laughter. If it's possible to miss something you last heard mere days ago, then yes, I miss it.

"I've got an update on your case," he tells me.

"Okay, what have you got?" I say in surprise.

"I admit I haven't had much time, but I've still been chasing up leads on the woman in the Polaroid photos. I came up with a few people who remember her. And one person who said her name was Merry. M-E-R-R-Y."

"Van, that's great. You have a name. Doesn't seem to fit that her name was Merry, though, because she looked damned scary in those photos."

His voice grows worryingly grim as he says, "I've actually got a bit more than a name."

"Oh?"

"I'm sorry, but I've put together a theory that Merry might have died—of a drug overdose—quite a few years back."

"Damn. It's a blow if it's true."

"Yeah, it is. There was a Merry who grew up in a suburb called Potters Village. A woman overdosed there some years back, and her name was recorded as M. Higgins. But I have no more information than that at the moment."

I look up Potters Village on my phone. "That's just a little south of here. Iris and I can stop and check the cemetery."

"No, that's okay. I'll do it when I get a minute."

"Van, we're almost there. Please, let me do this. If I find anything, I'll snap a photo and send it to you."

He sighs. "Look, okay, go for it."

After the call ends, I gaze out at the street, mentally crossing my fingers. *Whoever you are, Merry, please be alive. I have a lot of questions for you.*

27

THE NEXT MORNING DAWNS GREY, and it's raining again. This time, the rain has set in. It's still raining when we cross the border from the state of Queensland to the state of New South Wales. We drive on for a full hour after that.

The kids are blasting Nirvana's "Smells Like Teen Spirit" over the sound system, singing along at the tops of their lungs. If I close my eyes, it seems just like the old days with Mom on our road trip.

Snapping back to the present, I realise with a start we're almost at the turnoff for Potters Village. I call out to Iris to make a lefthand turn. We drive through some scrubby bushland and a modest township. I'd pictured the village as being cute and quaint, but it isn't that. It's more rough and ready than anything.

People stop and peer at us as the bus rumbles through town. Everything in town seems to be located on the one main road, even the cemetery. We find it easily. It's overgrown and poorly maintained.

The kids are happy to stay on the bus as Iris and I head away to the gravesites.

"At least it's small," Iris grumbles. "Shouldn't take long."

Rain is still pattering down, the dark clouds signalling a storm.

We gravitate to the headstones that look older. The new section won't have what we're looking for. I'm hoping that Merry won't be here at all.

Iris and I check the inscriptions of each headstone and plaque, pulling away the grass and weeds to see them better. One headstone is so low that we have to crouch and shift aside a bunch of dried flowers to see the inscription. I read the headstone out loud:

Meredith Higgins

You were loved more than you knew

1966 to 2006

"Merry could be short for Meredith," Iris whispers.

"Damn. I think you're right."

"So, what now?"

"I don't know." I pick up the dried-flower arrangement. The tag on the flowers belongs to a florist in Potters Village. "You know what? I'm going to go ask the florist if they know who bought these."

Iris pulls a face. "How would the florist know that?"

"Have you seen the size of the town?"

"I'll drive you."

"I think I'll walk. The bus was already attracting too much attention. Back soon, okay?"

I snap a photo of the grave and flowers then jog along the road. The florist is right next to the liquor store. I'm guessing men buy a case of beer and then grab a bunch of flowers next door for their wives.

I walk in, trying to smooth my hair, which has been blown about in the wind and rain. The woman behind the florist's serving counter is middle-aged and plump, her hair cut in a smart short style.

"Hi, how can I help you?" she asks.

"I've just been down to the cemetery," I start, showing her the photo. "I'm interested in finding friends or family of this woman. Meredith Higgins."

She's shaking her head before I even finish speaking. "I'm sorry—no, I don't." She has a singsong voice and ends her words as if she's asking a question.

"Well, would you know who you sold the flowers to?" I ask.

"Hmmm? No, no, I wouldn't."

"Is there someone in town who might have known Meredith?"

"Maybe not. Family lines die out sometimes, and then there's no one left to remember the dead. Pretty sad, but that's how it is."

"Yes, it is sad."

She frowns. "Did you know Merry?"

"I knew *of* her. Wait, you called her Merry?"

"Wasn't that her name?"

"The gravestone says Meredith."

"Oh, I got confused. Sorry. And I'm sorry I couldn't be of more help. I'm sorry, I have to go. I'm got a lot of orders to prepare." She heads off into the back of the store.

I have to stop myself from following her and asking if she knew more than what she was saying. But I leave and wander about town, trying the small selection of stores and asking about Meredith. Either no one remembers her, or no one wants to say they do.

I call Iris to come and pick me up on her way out of here. As I wait, I send Detective Dawson the photo I snapped of the gravesite, along with the message, *Found her*.

28

A STORM BREAKS as we head back out on the highway. The downpour is relentless, the traffic slows, and we're crammed between trucks. I'm glad when we reach our next destination—a town named Byron Bay. Our original plan had been to visit the farm and then this town, but the cemetery expedition has taken us off course.

Iris drives straight up to the Cape Byron Lighthouse. I remember Mom visiting it because it's the most easterly point on mainland Australia. I find two old photographs taken here. There is one of all of us and one of just Iris and me leaning on each other's shoulders and making peace signs. It was rainy that day too.

Piper immediately wants to recreate the photo of her mother and me. She and Audrey set about braiding our hair in the way we had it on that day all those years ago. The delay proves to be a blessing. A rainbow spans the grey sky while the rain becomes a trickle and then stops.

We make the trek up the hill. Piper and Audrey fuss about, positioning their mother and me so that we match the original poses. The kids think it's hilarious, so it's a win, I guess. It almost feels like the kids are trying to push Iris and me back together. I'm sure it makes no sense to them that two sisters hadn't spoken for so many years.

After the lighthouse trip, we have a quick look at the area's beautiful coastline. The kids start making noises about being hungry, and Iris and I decide on an early lunch. The best we can find for the six of us is a rowdy beer garden.

I glance out at the street with interest. The town is looking a lot different to what I remember. When I was a child, Byron Bay was a small counterculture town made up of hippies and city escapees seeking a simple way of life. The buildings are still low-rise and modest, but there is a distinct sense of wealth here now.

The kids fill up on burgers and fries, chatting animatedly to each other.

"Haven't been here in about three years," Iris tells me over the surrounding clatter and voices. "Gabe and I used to come away to Byron sometimes... on date weekends. His mother would mind the kids."

I sip my wine, smiling at her. "Sounds lovely."

Her eyes sadden. "It was. It was like being teenagers, you know? It was like we were still discovering new things together. We hadn't got old and boring yet."

"You're hardly old and boring," I scoff. "You're still young."

"I don't feel it." Iris sighs.

Jake points out at the street. "Is that... *Thor*?"

"Thor?" I ask. I turn my head as two sandy-haired men walk between the beer garden and the crowd, a small tribe of blond kids following them.

"That's Chris and Liam Hemsworth," Piper tells Jake. "And Chris's kids."

Iris nods, watching the family continue along the street. "They live here, a bit out of town. Enormous house. A compound, really."

Jake grins shyly. "Can't believe I just saw Thor."

"We should take Jake for a film studio tour," Piper says. "At the Village Roadshow studio, next to Movie World. That's where they made Thor. And Aquaman. That's not far from here."

"We'd have to backtrack to go there," Iris protests. "And they're probably not even running tours. You only went there because of your acting class."

Piper turns to Jake, her chin tilted upward. "I did acting classes during the winter holidays. I'm going to be in movies when I grow up."

"Shame your acting is crud," Kaden remarks.

Audrey leaps straight to her sister's defence. "Don't be rude, Kaden. She's amazing."

Iris pushes the remainder of her lunch away. "Okay, I think it's time to go."

We leave the beer garden and walk to the grocery store to load up on food. Then we catch a taxi big enough for six people and head back to the bus. With the fridge and cupboards packed with groceries, Iris settles back into the driver's seat. The kids play a game of Monopoly at the table.

I notice Iris's mood lifting as soon as she starts driving. It's as if the hum of the motor lends her some kind of peace.

Van calls me on my phone. "I didn't want to be right about Meredith," he says. "Damned shame."

"At least we know," I reply. "I had a feeling a few of the people in Potters Village might have known her, but no one wanted to say anything."

"You went around asking?"

"I did. I shouldn't have, but I was there, and—"

"Lily, you didn't need to do that. I'll head down there in a couple of days and see if I can find out anything. I'm stuck here at the moment. Let me know when you find the farm. And be safe. By that I mean, make sure there's lot of people at the farm before you enter. If it's just Bennett living there on his own now, call me."

"We'll stay safe," I assure him.

As the call ends, I glance out the window. We're heading deeper and deeper into the hinterland. It's raining again, but that doesn't diminish the beauty of the area. Everything seems to grow lush here.

Vines race along fences and up poles. The sunflowers by the roadside seem to be growing bigger and taller than they have any right to.

About an hour after leaving Byron Bay, we arrive in the Nimbin township. I gaze though the bus window with interest. The stores on the main street resemble a carnival—a mix of vintage and modern grunge—in which all signs and buildings are intricately hand painted. Rainbows and peace signs abound in psychedelic colours. Among the goods being sold are hemp, tie-dye clothing, CBD oil, and vegan fare.

When we lived at the farm with Mom, we used to come here to sell jewellery and buy clothes. I remember we once ventured into town during their Mardi Grass festival—and it actually was called *Mardi Grass*. Nimbin had a lot of hemp products on sale, and also, there was the not-so-secret trade in marijuana. I remember people dressing like something out of the 1960s Woodstock festival and little barefoot children running helter-skelter through the streets.

The sights of this town have me racing through to look at all the old photos. I'm astonished to discover that it's barely changed. The town is a time capsule. I paste in the pictures in my scrapbook.

Iris parks the bus just out of town. We pack water and supplies in our backpacks and set out. I snap pictures of the kids standing together and smiling in the main street. They're happy to check out the Nimbin Museum while my sister and I go looking for anyone who might remember the farm. We try a few stores. Two store owners remember the names of people that we mention, but they can't give us any directions.

Iris and I head into a hemp-clothing store. The store owner—a man with long grey hair in braids and a bandana—tells us that he used to ride horses with Bennett but hasn't seen him in decades. He thinks he might have left the area altogether.

"That's a big shame," I say. "Any idea where he went?"

The man's shrug is as languid as his manner of speech. "Nope. People come, people go."

"Did you ever go out to the farm Bennett owned?" Iris asks him.

"Hmmm. Don't think I did," he answers. "He'd come into town and sell me boxes of his craft beer—he used to make that."

I'm feeling a little desperate. "Any idea at all where Bennett's old farm could be?"

He rakes his fingers through his long beard. "Up near the Nightcap Ranges, I'd say. But I warn ya, this area is full o' farms. God's own country. Got yourselves a good four-wheel drive? Ordinary car's gonna get itself bogged on some o' those roads. Been wet lately."

"We've got a bus, actually. A full-size touring bus," Iris informs him.

That draws a cackle from him. "Better keep your wits about you, then."

Iris and I round up the kids and head off again on the bus. My sister clings to the paved roads—worried about getting bogged down—while I try to spot any landmark or street name that I can recall. After forty minutes, I'm feeling nothing but lost. Iris is starting to shake her head and blow out big breaths as she drives. The kids have gotten bored and are sleeping in their seats.

I gaze into the dull greyish distance. The rain hasn't given us much of a break today. Out of the clouds, a mountain with a high, distinctive peak comes into view.

"Hey, Iris," I say, "do you see that? The mountain—as far as you can see to the right?"

"Ummm, okay. Yep, I see it. Yeah. It does look familiar. So, you remember it?"

"I think so. Lemme look up what it is." On my tablet, I browse the internet. "Okay, so that mountain is Mount Warning—which means we're headed for the Nightcap Ranges. The old guy mentioned that area, right?"

"I think so."

"The photos of the scenery are awesome. Ever been there with your family?"

"Nope."

"Really?" I ask.

"Yeah, well, what can I say? I'm not into hiking and biking like you are. I'm into retail therapy."

I jerk my head around as we pass a large tree. "Hey, slow down. That tree back there—it pinged my memory."

She slows the bus and brings it to a stop. "A tree? Oh c'mon. You do not remember a tree."

"I think I do. Back up a little."

Iris huffs out a dubious sigh as she reverses. "Okay, which one?"

"That one. When I was a kid, I remember thinking it looked like a giant genie's bottle."

"It does look like a genie's bottle. But you know, I've seen trees like it before."

"That's the thing. You're in Australia, so trees like this don't stand out to you. But we don't have these in PA. Lemme look up what it is." I snap a quick pic from the bus window and do an image search on Google. "Okay, so *Australian Geographic* says it's a boab tree."

"A boab tree, eh? Never knew what they were called. So, you think we're close?"

"I think we're here."

"Oh yeah?" she asks.

"Yeah. As I remember it, the driveway was just past this tree."

"I can see a dirt road."

"Let's try it."

"Like, just rock straight into someone's property in a big ol' bus?"

I shrug. "Yeah."

"Fine. I guess we're doing this."

"I guess we are."

She pulls a face and then drives away again. Is it because we seem to be slipping back into our old ways of talking to each other? It feels natural and strange at the same time.

Ahead, there's a large, modern house with a wraparound porch that has the hallmarks of being a kit home. And beyond that are yet more kit homes, only smaller.

This isn't it. I was wrong.

A young guy emerges from the main house, wearing faded red pants and a shapeless T-shirt.

Iris pulls up and parks. She turns around to the kids, who are rousing from sleep and rubbing their eyes. "Stay here, crew, okay?"

Iris and I hop from the bus and go to meet the man.

"I'm Liam," he says in an accent that is distinctively Irish. "And you are...?"

"Iris and Lily," my sister tells him. "We're looking for a specific farm. From twenty-four years ago."

He grins. "I was born about that time."

"In that case," I say, "is there someone here who could help us?"

He rubs his blond goatee. "Oh yeah, there are some people here who've been on a trip around the sun more times than me. But not very many. We're mostly fruit pickers. Gluttons for punishment, you might call us. Anyway, go have a look around, if that takes your fancy."

Iris crosses her arms. "It's okay. I don't think this is the place."

"We'll just take a quick walk through," I say quickly. "Just in case."

Taking Iris's arm, I stroll away with her. "We're here. We might as well."

Iris tucks her red locks behind an ear. "Nothing here looks right. And it sounds like backpacker city."

"It's been a long time. Maybe it's just... changed."

Some things are beginning to look familiar. Like the fields of strawberries and, beyond those, the rows of citrus trees. A woman with deeply wrinkled leathery skin kneels in a vegetable patch, picking leafy greens.

"I don't believe it," Iris whispers to me. "That looks a lot like... Joyce?"

"I think you're right," I whisper back. I venture up to the woman. "Joyce?"

She wipes her forehead with the back of her hand. "Yeah?"

Her gaze switches from me to Iris and back again. "Oh, for the love of... no... it can't be. You're not those two young American girls all grown up... are you?"

I nod, smiling. "Iris and Lily. How are you? It's been a long, long time."

She struggles to her feet. "A hell of a long time. What are you girls doing back here?"

I snatch a breath. "If you can believe it, Joyce—Iris and I are recreating the trip our mother brought us on all those years ago."

Her expression changes from incredulous to sad. "I remember what happened with your mother... and the little one. You'd better come inside, and you can tell me why you're really here."

29

LILY JORGENSON, AGE 11

January 1998

It'd been a long slog around dirt roads, checking out farms we could stay at. I didn't know what Mom was looking for, but it sure was taking her a long time to find it. Ellie was complaining about as hard as a little girl could complain. Mom was trying to stay bright.

We were only two weeks into the trip. We'd been to Movie World and Surfers Paradise, and we'd thought that was how it was going to be. Beaches and fun. But now Mom had decided what we needed to do was to stay at a farm.

It had rained the whole way, and we'd been cooped up in the car —which was starting to reek to high heaven of food wrappers and muddy shoes. I was feeling carsick and homesick and every kind of sick.

We passed a fat tree that looked like a genie's bottle. And then Mom drove down yet another driveway and stopped. Even though it was still spitting rain, it was a relief to get out of the car.

Immediately, there were the smells of wet earth and woodfires and cooking. Flags in rainbow colours were hung everywhere. The sounds of bongo drums and singing came from rustic cabins. To the left, behind the cabins, a wide valley had been carved from the landscape, with mist hanging like ghosts.

A woman named Joyce took us under her wing. She looked about forty, in denim overalls and a bucket hat. She brought us into a large hall that contained an old-fashioned kitchen and lots of wooden tables.

It was busy and crowded. Joyce helped Mom wheel Grace in and set Ellie up on a chair with cushions so she could reach the table. There was a man sitting at one of them, carving something from a piece of wood. He wore faded clothes—a check shirt and cotton vest. His dark hair was back in a short ponytail. He had a presence you couldn't ignore. I could have been imagining it, but when Mom noticed him and he noticed her, they looked at each other just a little too long.

The other people in the room surged forward to introduce themselves. They were mostly young people, all with different accents and from different countries. There were a few older people and children with Australian accents. The people sat us down. Some brought us freshly baked sourdough bread and butter and drinks.

"Girls, this might just be it," Mom said to us, chewing on a piece of sourdough, her eyes bright. "Can you feel it? The vibe is right. This is us. We might stay here for a month and see how we feel—could be longer."

At hearing that, Iris dropped her mouth wide open. "No. No, it isn't. This isn't us."

"Iris, everyone's been so lovely," Mom insisted.

"Don't care. It's not my home. Home is in Pennsylvania. With Dad."

"This isn't the time to talk about that," Mom cautioned her. "I just couldn't be there anymore."

"Why?" Iris demanded. "Because something's wrong with your brain? Why do we all have to get dragged around because of you?"

Everyone heard Iris, though they pretended not to, turning their heads away. But one person looked in our direction—the man who'd been whittling the piece of wood. He strode across the room and up to our table. He turned a chair around and perched on it backward.

The man studied Iris for a moment before saying, "Why don't you put a bit of faith in your mother?"

Iris lifted her chin defiantly. "And who are you?"

"I'm Bennett."

"Bennett is a last name," Iris snapped.

"That's all you're gonna get," he told her. "That's what I'm known by."

"Well, Bennett," Iris said, stressing his name, "don't you try to give me advice. You don't even know my mother. She's crazy."

Mom looked horrified. "I'm sorry about this little... display. She's just tired. We're all tired. It's been a long trip today." Mom took Iris by the arm and guided her away and out through the door. Iris kept her arms folded the whole way.

Grace and Ellie and me were left at the table with Bennett. I didn't know the first thing to say to him, swallowing down my bread and staring hard down at my plate.

It was Ellie who broke the ice. "Whatcha makin' over there?"

A dimple appeared in his cheek. "A gift for a kid who lives here on the farm."

Ellie's brown eyes lit up. "Would you make me somethin'?"

Grace shook her head at her little sister. "No, Ellie. You can't just ask for things like that."

Bennett chuckled. "It's fine. What would you like, Ellie?"

"I want a tiger," Ellie said in a confident tone.

"A tiger it is," he replied.

Bennett introduced us to some of the other kids, who came to join us at the table. It was like we made friends within the first five minutes of entering the farm. By that night, we and the other kids were already a tight gang, hanging out around the fire and toasting shish kabobs on sticks. Grace kept her eye on a boy who I could tell she liked. She snapped photos that had him in every frame.

There were other campfires scattered around on the grounds. Again, I could hear drums and singing. Bennett pulled out a guitar and played—and people began singing. Ellie made everyone laugh and clap when she danced.

All the while, Bennett and Mom kept sneaking glances at each other. Iris eventually noticed that, too, which made her even angrier. She jumped up and left the campfire and flounced away to our caravan. I thought Mom would call her back, but she didn't. She let her go.

I felt bad for Iris. I was having fun, and I wanted her to have fun too. But I couldn't have everything I wanted. Life had never been like that.

That was how our first day went at the farm.

30

EVEN THOUGH JOYCE and Bennett said we could sleep in a cabin if we wanted, we stayed in our caravan overnight. Mostly because Iris refused to leave it.

Minutes before dawn, I woke before anyone else and headed outside. As I sat on the steps of the caravan, I watched the first fingers of the rising sun touch the valley below. The sun brushed the lingering mist away.

I breathed in the warm, sweet air—a scent that reminded me of eucalyptus candy. From the valley and distant mountain range came the warbling sounds of magpies and the cackling of kookaburras and the high, tinkling calls of bell birds. I'd heard all those birds since I'd been in Australia but never in concert like this. Something rose in my chest—a sense that I was surrounded by the sounds and scents and sights of freedom.

Mom stepped from the caravan. Her hair was messy and golden in the sunlight. And although her face was bare of makeup, it had a glow. I'd barely seen her wear any makeup since the date nights she used to have with Dad.

She sat beside me and drew me in close with an arm around my shoulders. "Penny for your thoughts, Lily?"

I smiled. "I think I'm gonna like it here."

"I'm happy. I thought you would. Now I just need to find a way to make Iris happy."

"Iris doesn't want to be happy."

"I think she does. I'm just... handling things wrong."

I opened my mouth to tell her that the way Iris was acting wasn't her fault, but then I spotted Joyce and Bennett crossing the grounds in our direction. The two of them stopped when they got to us. They talked with Mom about how the farm operated and said we could stay as long as we wanted but everyone at the farm had to contribute. Our family posed a challenge because Grace couldn't work the fields and Ellie was too young to do any jobs.

Bennett came up with two ideas. He said he could teach us either brewing craft beer or silversmithing jewellery. Mom didn't hesitate before choosing to have us make jewellery.

Over the next week, Bennett took Mom on as his special apprentice, teaching her the art of silversmithing. Iris, Grace, Ellie, and I watched and learned. Bennett was a patient instructor, teaching us step by step to design, hammer, and forge the pieces and then finish them with burnishing and buffing. Even Iris was interested, paying close attention to everything he said.

Joyce and Bennett held a special dinner for us at the end of that first week. It was meant to be a get-together in which we were accepted as part of the farm's community. After the dinner, there was a short ceremony in which we each placed a piece of special fragrant wood onto the fire. It was meant to signify that the time before we all knew each other was over. It was a new beginning.

Then came the usual guitars, drums and singing as we sat around the fire. I noticed that Mom and Bennett were sitting awfully close together, laughing and talking. It was part of the new texture of our lives.

When the music and singing died down, everyone looked at Joyce and Bennett. It seemed they were the anchors of this place.

Joyce glanced around the group in a deliberate way. "People, who are we?" she asked.

The others answered in unison. "Energy."

She nodded. "And what is energy?"

"Everything," people replied to her. "Light and motion."

I understood that these questions must be something Joyce often asked, and people knew just what to answer.

Joyce bent her head, taking in the answers, silent for a moment. "Energy is the ability to do work," she said finally. "Our life's work is who we are."

Grace put up her hand as if to ask a question.

Joyce beamed at her. "We don't need to ask permission to speak here. Just say what's on your mind."

"What if we can't do any meaningful work? What are we... if we can't work?" Grace drew back into herself, uncomfortable with the sudden attention on her.

"If you mean that you can't work the fields," Joyce replied, "don't you worry. That wasn't my meaning. We are the works. Works in progress. Your existence has changed the world. Every one of your movements—every thought you create, your effect upon others—is energy. You are enough."

Grace seemed happy with that answer. Mom put an arm around her, casting a quick warm smile at Joyce.

Bennett glanced around at our family. "Tell me—what are you tasked to be in this life? What do we put out there? What do we want to be remembered for?"

"Be the best person you can be?" I ventured. That was something I'd learned in a class at school.

"Be dangerous," Bennett told me. "Whatever you do, just... be dangerous."

Iris spoke up. "What the hell does that even mean?"

Mom frowned at Iris. "No need for that language."

"What it means," Bennett said, "is that each one of us is an idea —a dangerous idea. And it's up to each person to figure out exactly what that means. There are things that only you know and no one else does. That's where the danger comes in. And it's risky and incredible and glorious. And what are you going to do with that knowledge that only you possess? What kind of human will you grow into?"

Iris jabbed at the fire with a stick. "I'll never know."

"Why won't you know, Iris?" he asked.

She twisted her mouth, lowering her voice. "I'll never know who I was going to be before I was dragged away from my home."

"Then tell me," he said. "Who were you going to be?"

"A dancer," she answered. "That's who. Not *dangerous* enough for you?"

He gave her a smile. "Were you happy? Was it everything?"

"Dancing isn't about hippy-dippy love and roses, you know," Iris shot back. "It's about discipline and hard work. That's what it takes to make it."

"Duly noted." Bennett moved the conversation onto other topics.

Iris kept poking her stick at the firewood and making sparks fly.

Both Grace and Ellie were growing sleepy. Bennett offered to carry Grace to the caravan. Grace accepted and even looked pleased to be in Bennett's arms. Mom carried Ellie.

I remembered a book I'd borrowed from the farm's library. I went to grab it from the caravan before Grace and Ellie went to sleep. Mom and Bennett had already put the girls in their beds and were standing outside.

Mom was crying. Bennett moved closer and put his arms around her. For a moment, she bowed her head into his shoulder. But then things somehow swapped from that to kissing. A lot of kissing.

I stopped dead then half stepped behind a tree. After a few seconds, Bennett's hands were running up and down Mom's arms and down her back. And she had her hands on his shoulders, on his chest, in his hair. The kissing continued.

Were my mother and Bennett being dangerous together? Because it felt... *dangerous*.

Turning to square my back against the tree trunk, I sucked in a breath and tried to make sense of it. We'd only known Bennett for a week. And now Mom was smooching him in a way I'd never seen her smooch Dad.

I had to sneak away. If I stayed here any longer, I'd get found out. I returned to the campfire then sat and gazed into the flames.

Iris glanced at me. "Where'd you go?"

"Nowhere," I answered.

My sister's expression turned gloomy. "I'm gonna talk Mom out of staying here. She can't do this to us."

I shook my head. "Somehow... I don't think she's gonna leave now."

Iris shot me a death stare. Shutting her out, I squeezed my eyes closed and pretended I wanted to sleep—right there in my chair in front of the fire.

The next day, Bennett told Mom she was ready to create her own silver pieces. He asked her what she'd like to design first—something that was just for her and us four girls. Our mother chose to make birds for us. She said we were birds on the wing—forever free. That drew a huge grin of approval from Bennett.

Mom spent ages designing and creating the silver bird pendants, each one unique. It was the birds that turned the five of us into a family.

That night, at the campfire, we all felt it. We wore our bird pendants on silver chains, and Grace dissolved into tears. We thought she was homesick for her grandparents. But although she missed them, she was crying because she felt as if she and Ellie had become members of our family. We all sobbed and hugged. It felt solid and real. Grace and Ellie were my lifelong sisters now.

Even Iris and Mom finally made up. Mom brushed Iris's hair back from her face and told her that she was the child who'd made her a mother and that they'd forever have a special relationship because of that.

Bennett and Joyce and the others at our campfire watched us with big smiles on their faces. An elderly woman named Florence began singing with a high, clear voice—the Madonna song, "Like a Prayer."

When she reached the chorus, others began joining in one by one—all the adults and the kids, including us. Ellie didn't know the words, but she clapped along and sang the chorus. A few people started tapping drums with their hands.

Bennett's voice in the chorus was perhaps the strongest of anyone's—he was clapping and looking energised and totally unself-conscious. I'd never seen a man be like that before.

While we sang, sparks of the fire spiralled upward to the velvety dark sky. People started up song after song, with everyone joining in even if it was only to clap or hum along. Ellie sat on Mom's lap, swaying to the music. Iris was singing too.

I had never felt as secure and complete in my life as that night. I never wanted it to end.

31

As a month went by, I was proved right and Iris proved wrong. Because we were still at the farm. Iris didn't mind, though. It was probably the happiest I'd ever seen her. She turned fourteen, and the farm held a big party for her. She danced longer and harder than anyone.

Our family moved from the caravan into a cabin. The cabin was basic but better than the squishy caravan—and Mom and Iris decorated it with colourful cushions and housewares bought from the stores at Nimbin.

I didn't tell Iris about the smooching between Mom and Bennett. Mom and Bennett kept their smooches well hidden. But I guessed why Mom left our cabin late at night, claiming she needed a walk.

We continued to make the jewellery, and it didn't seem like hard work at all. We'd head into Nimbin or Byron Bay or any of a dozen other places to sell our wares at market stalls. Little Ellie became a proficient salesperson, upselling people on the more expensive pieces of jewellery. Iris especially loved the market stalls. She'd chat to all the boys and spend time at the beach in her bikini. Grace would tire quickly, and Mom always made sure the stalls had shade so Grace could sleep when she wanted without the hot sun on her.

Back at the farm, we had our little group of new friends to hang out and play board games with. Mom and Joyce taught us school lessons at the kitchen tables.

Mom made fast friends with Florence, an Indigenous Australian woman in her eighties who still worked the fields. Florence taught us all the things that school would not have. She showed us how to make good, healthy soil and how to grow crops without chemicals. She'd scowl when telling us how the new-growth forests could never make up for all the logging. She told us the fire seasons had become increasingly dangerous because of the new-growth trees—they burned too hot. We needed the wisdom of old-growth forests, with their connections deep under the soil, stretching back centuries before we were even born.

Florence had rolled into the farm six years before in her campervan, and she'd never left. She kept on living in her van. "Give the cabins to the families," she'd insisted.

Another month of living at the farm passed. It felt as if we were part of this place now. We needed it, and it needed us.

Bennett took us for walks deep into the valley and on the mountains, showing us the oldest trees and clear creeks we could swim in. We'd spot the occasional koala climbing a tree or a shy platypus in the water. And there were always wallabies. Life had become idyllic, serene.

The weather that year had apparently been ideal for strawberries, and there was a bumper crop. There were meant to be storms coming, and the crop needed picking fast. It was all hands on deck. Florence was in there, picking as fast as anyone else.

Mom sent me to find Iris. But Iris had somehow vanished in the chaos. I checked the hall and the cabin. No Iris. Next, I tried the library and the craft-beer distillery. I knew that sometimes Iris would sneak a glass of beer. But she wasn't there, either.

I don't even know why I checked the barns, because they weren't somewhere Iris was likely to be. But I did anyway.

In the one big barn that held large farm machinery, Bennett was fixing the motor of a tractor. I could see him through a crack in the wooden siding, but he couldn't see me. I went to walk on past. But then I saw someone else in there. Iris. She was sitting on the hood of another tractor, just watching Bennett, her long legs crossed.

I stood outside in the hot sun, fuming. I wanted to march straight in there and smack her in the ear. She'd just been sitting around all this time, watching someone else work. She'd even found the time to put makeup on—and this hadn't even been a market day.

Iris slid off the tractor hood and walked across to Bennett.

Bennett looked up at her. "I'm sure this can't be too interesting for you."

Iris shrugged. "I'm fine."

"Tell you what, then. You can grab me a spanner." He told her the size he wanted.

Iris went to fetch it. As she handed him the spanner, she gave him a quick smile. "Hey, I think I have something else for you."

Bennett let out a distracted laugh as he applied the spanner to the tractor's engine. "Something to get this old beast going again? That'd be great."

I couldn't see Bennett's face as Iris took two more steps toward him. But what she did was unmistakeable. She kissed him.

Bennett reeled away from her. "Hey, you can't—"

"But you wanted me to, didn't you?" she said in a shocked tone. "We were getting close, weren't we?"

I backed up like I'd been stung. Iris and Bennett had been getting close?

Maybe I shouldn't have, but I ran to tell Mom.

After that morning, things between Mom and Bennett cooled down fast. I'd see Mom and Bennett look at each other and then turn away quickly.

Iris became moody again. She gave everyone the silent treatment, barely did any of her chores, and even started shirking the making and selling of the jewellery.

When I heard Joyce say to Mom, "You're giving the squeaky wheel too much oil," I was certain she was talking about Iris.

And then, overnight, Iris changed again. She made friends with three sisters who lived on a farm down the road. And she began hanging with them. The girls were in their late teens. Iris would come back stinking of cigarette smoke.

Life went on like this for two more weeks, until the day Mom gathered us together and announced that we were hitting the road again. Grace, Ellie, and I protested—but it was Iris who protested the loudest. Iris told Mom she'd played her stupid game and couldn't now just rearrange us like pieces on a chessboard. It felt as if Iris was on our side and was going to bat for us. But it was hard to tell for sure.

I didn't know why we were leaving. I didn't know if it was because of Iris or because of Bennett or because of something going bad inside Mom's head. I couldn't figure it out. All I knew was that suddenly, we were packing up, and Bennett was giving our car a tune-up for the road.

And then we were gone from the farm, driving out through the gates and headed for places we'd never been before, the earth swept away from beneath our feet once again.

32

Present Day

All the old memories flash through my mind as Iris and I walk with Joyce to the main house of the farm. Joyce tells us that all the cabins and structures that used to be here got beyond repair and had to be torn down. They'd been replaced with kit homes.

She makes Iris and me chamomile tea and sits at a table with us. "Now," she says, "after what happened to your family, this can't just be some happy holiday. So, level with me."

I nod. "We... we were hoping to find answers. Some kind of resolution."

She raises her eyebrows. "The only real kind of resolution is ever going to be found in here." She taps her thin chest.

"I know," I concede.

"Anyway, tell me what you're after," she says.

"Well," I begin, "the first thing is a journal my mother was keeping. We only recently learned that she was keeping one—but the thing is, it's nowhere. I thought she might have left it here, but..."

"That's quite a thing to be looking for after twenty-something years," Joyce tells me. "But it can't be here. We even had to let go of the library. The families all moved on. It's almost all backpackers who pick the crops now."

Iris presses her teeth into her lip. "I'm guessing Bennett isn't still here?"

Joyce shakes her head. "No. Long gone. After your mother left, the wind seemed to go out of his sails. And a year later, when your mother went missing, Bennett took the news very hard. And then the cops started hounding him—especially that sergeant from Nautilus."

"Sergeant Mullard?" Iris asks.

"Yeah, that's the one." Joyce combs wisps of hair back from her face, which is still red from having been out in the sun. "He was relentless. He had the cops tear this place apart, searching behind every stinkin' blade of grass. The farm got stained by the case, as if we all had something to do with Elsa and the little one vanishing. The farm changed after that. Bennett started coming and going, until he didn't come back at all."

I touch her arm. "I'm sorry, Joyce."

"Ah, not your fault. You're not to blame. And we found a way to keep going. What else can you do? Life smacks you one way, and then before you know it, it smacks you into the middle of next week. You just have to keep picking yourself up."

"True words," Iris says. When she looks away, I wonder if she's thinking about her husband and what she told me about him.

Joyce gazes at me with serious eyes. "Bennett's got cancer."

I stare back at her in shock. "Cancer?"

She nods. "In the bones. Got him good."

It feels as if all the air has been removed from my lungs. "It's terminal?"

"Well, we're all terminal," she says. "But yeah, his time was coming sooner than it should."

"Then... he might not still be alive?" Iris asks.

Joyce sighs, glancing down at her hands. "I'd say that's the case. But I don't know for sure. Sorry to give you that news."

"Do you have any idea where he went after he left here?" I ask.

"Nope, no idea," she answers. "Bennett was a free spirit. He told no one nothing."

"Like our mother," says Iris grimly.

"Don't be too harsh," Joyce chides. "Everyone's got—"

"Don't give me that stuff about invisible battles," Iris says sharply. "I'm over it. When you keep everything to yourself, people get hurt."

I can't help but cast a hard glare in Iris's direction. Iris has kept so much to herself. She doesn't notice my glare, but Joyce does.

"I know you two would've gone through a lot," Joyce says. "Don't let it make you bitter."

I look away, unsure if her words are for me or for Iris. It feels strange to sit here and talk to a woman who knew us when we were still children.

We talk for a few minutes longer, and then Joyce invites us to stay on the farm overnight. Iris and I decide to take Joyce up on her offer. We spend the afternoon picking strawberries with the kids and taking them on a walk down to the valley to swim in the same creeks we used to swim in. I take lots of photographs for my scrapbook. In the end, this scrapbook might be all I'm left holding.

Jake, Kaden, Piper, and Audrey are like bottomless wells when it comes to hearing old stories about the farm. Joyce, Iris, and I tell them the best of it—the fun stories and the good times. It's bittersweet to be here with Iris once again, under such different circumstances.

After dinner, once the kids are asleep, I step out of the bus to go for a short walk the way that Mom used to at night. I call Van to tell him we made it to the farm. We chat for a while, and I find myself wishing he were here in person. When my conversation with Van ends, I remain outside. I like the quiet and the cool night breezes.

The wheels have already fallen off this trip. Meredith is dead, and most likely, Bennett is too. And the farm holds nothing of the past apart from Joyce.

I should have taken this trip a long time ago. Instead of wasting money on private investigators—and trying to save my relationship with Jake's father—I should have been here. Before almost every path available to me was swept away.

33

IRIS and I get the kids up early for the next leg of the trip. They grumble at being roused when the sun has barely begun to rise.

Joyce gifts us a big box of fruit, vegetables, and eggs. She makes us promise to keep in touch. I mean it when I say I will. Iris, I'm not so sure of.

My sister seems happier as we drive away from the farm. The kids have picked the song of the morning—"Under the Bridge," by the Red Hot Chili Peppers. The kids play it over and over again, singing it loudly each time. Iris and I give up and start belting it out ourselves.

The music makes the time go faster between visits to the towns on our itinerary. I might have forgotten the names of places, but I remember their landscapes. Red Rock, with intense red headlands at sunset, and Angourie, with the enormous swimming hole called Blue Pool, where we jumped from a high rock platform with the local kids. And all the others. The textures and colours are still rich in my mind.

Anywhere I can manage, I ask the locals if they know Bennett. But I come up empty-handed each time. Desperation starts to gnaw at me, like rats on a bone.

Iris doesn't help. She just watches, at one point making a comment about me being too driven. She and I will never understand each other.

After six hours of town hopping, we reach a large, sprawling place called Coffs Harbour. This town I remember well. Mom treated us to a stay in one of the large beachside resorts here. And I remember there was a big statue of a banana along the highway. From memory, I would have said the banana was one hundred feet long. But now, as Iris drives up and parks near the statue, I'd say it is half that.

I paste the single picture I have of it in my scrapbook.

The spot is now called the Big Banana Fun Park. I recall that there used to be acres of banana plantations surrounding the café. Now, it seems, they've added a theme park. We head to the café, where we feast on banana splits. Everything is bananas here—fresh bananas, dried bananas, banana muffins, banana pickles, and banana jelly.

Jake wipes cream from the tip of his nose, reading a tourist brochure. "Hey, wanna know somethin'? They built the big banana in 1964 'cause they wanted people to stop and buy their bananas. And 'cause they heard about the big pineapple in Hawaii."

I smile at my history-nut son.

"It's bun-AH-nuhs," Piper drawls at Jake, "not ban-AN-az."

Iris screws up her face at her daughter. "You do know that I used to pronounce bananas like that when I was a kid? Don't be rude."

Piper pops a strawberry in her mouth. "I'm just saying."

"Yes, you are," Iris retorts. "And you don't have to."

Jake gets an impish grin on his face. "How come you guys don't say 'pot-AH-toes'?" he asks Piper. "You say, 'pot-AY-toes.' Just like we do."

Piper fixes her ponytail. "How would I know?"

Kaden smirks at Piper. "Gotcha, sis."

We leave the café and drive back onto the highway. We're headed for a place called Limeburners Creek National Park. We were there with Mom for two weeks or more, and Iris and I are planning on staying for at least a night. We have lots of photos taken here —most of them snapped by Grace. I'm grateful for that, because it means there are so many pictures of Mom. There's Mom in a red bathing suit, sitting against a palm tree, asleep. Ellie is curled up in her lap, also asleep.

Mom, I wish we could have had more time with you. The years we had just weren't enough. Not nearly enough.

Exhaustion is making my muscles tight. The past is weighing on me heavily today. So many memories. So many unanswered questions.

The kids seem to have burned themselves out too—probably from all the running around they did at the farm yesterday. They're dozing in their seats. Iris has some soft, slow music playing over the sound system. I don't mean to fall asleep, but my eyes drift shut.

I wake with a jolt—flung like a rag doll to my hands and knees. For a moment, I'm disoriented, half in a dream and confused. The air fills with cries and screams as the bus veers sharply.

And then I'm wide, wide awake.

The bus careens off the road, almost hitting the guard rail. With a shudder and screech of brakes, the bus comes to a stop. My first thought is that Iris fell asleep while driving.

Struggling to get on my feet, I turn to check the kids. They're still in their seats. They're okay.

I rush to Iris. "My God, what happened?"

She has both hands going white on the wheel, her expression frozen. "A car tried to overtake a truck and got it very wrong, and then the stupid driver swerved in front of me. I had nowhere to go. I only just missed hitting him."

"Are you okay?"

"Yeah. But I think I heard the bus blow a tyre." She draws a deep breath. "Are the kids all right?"

"I think so. I'll go check."

The kids are standing now, peering out the window, shock on their faces.

"Anyone hurt?" I ask as I run down the aisle to them.

"I'm okay, Mom," Jake says.

"Great. Kaden, Piper—are you hurt? Wait, where's Audrey?"

Piper pulls a face. "In the bed."

"The bed?" I ask.

"Yeah." Piper nods with a fearful expression. "The bunks."

"Oh no." I race to the back of the bus.

Audrey is lying in a ball on the floor, whimpering. As soon as I look at her, I know something is seriously wrong. Her arm juts out at an odd angle.

Iris is behind me now, breathing hard. Kneeling beside her daughter, she touches her arm. "What the hell, Audrey? I told you no one's allowed in the beds while I'm driving. Oh my God, you were in the top bunk, weren't you?"

Audrey bursts into a sob. "I had a headache. I just wanted to sleep."

"I'll call an ambulance." I move to a seat and dig my phone out from my pocket.

"It's triple zero," Iris tells me.

As I call the ambulance, I realise I have no idea where we are, and I have to pause to ask Iris. Audrey turns her face away from her mother, still crying.

I crouch beside Audrey again. "You'll be okay, honey. The hospital will know exactly what to do. We can't move you—we need to wait for help."

Iris's eyes brim with tears.

An hour later, we're all at Port Macquarie Base Hospital. Iris went ahead in the ambulance with Audrey while I waited for roadside assistance with the rest of the kids. Iris is now in the operating room while the surgeons put Audrey under general anaesthetic. Jake and Kaden are off finding vending machines to buy snacks.

I'm alone with Piper. She sits next to me, her arms locking tight around her knees on the chair.

"You don't feel like anything to eat, Piper?" I ask.

"No. Snacks make you fat."

"Okay. Got it. Well, if you want anything, let me know."

"I want to go home."

"Because of what happened to Audrey?" I say gently.

"I just don't want to be here. I know that it was my mother who forced this trip. You wanted to do it with just you and Jake, didn't you, Aunty Lily? But Mum pushed in."

I take a breath before figuring out an answer. "The idea did start out with it just being Jake and me. But I've loved the chance for us to get to know all of you."

"You and my mother don't get on together. You're both faking."

That hits me straight between the eyes—the fact that she knows that and how blunt she is. It seems she's been watching every interaction between Iris and me.

"Piper... your mom and I are getting to know each other again. Look, maybe this isn't the best time to talk about this stuff. Everyone's feeling upset about Audrey."

She looks away as she mumbles, "Mum's going to blame *me*."

"What was that, Piper?"

"Audrey. Mum always makes out like I should be taking care of her."

"Oh. No, she won't blame you for what happened."

"Yes, she will. She always puts me in charge of her."

"But you two are exactly the same age," I say in confusion.

"Yeah, but she treats Audrey like a baby. She treats Dad like he's a baby too. She's always telling him what to do and how to do it."

Not knowing how to deal with that piece of information, I stay quiet, trying to think of what to say that won't sound condescending. Talking to Piper seems like a conversation with a teenager. Her speech is so measured, as if she filters everything before saying it.

Piper eyes me past her thick curtain of hair. "I knew Audrey went to the bunk bed."

"You did?"

"Yeah. I told her not to. But she said she'd only do it for ten minutes."

"Do what, exactly?"

"Exercise. She was doing stupid sit-ups. To get rid of her tubby tummy."

"Oh. Oh no..."

"Yeah. I told her Mum said stay out of the beds while she's driving. But Audrey wouldn't listen. And then I fell asleep."

"Is that something Audrey does often—exercising to flatten her tummy?"

"Yes. All the time. But then she goes and eats everything in the cupboard."

We're interrupted as a woman in hospital scrubs walks up. It's Iris. She'd had to suit up just to enter the operating room.

"How's she doing?" I ask Iris.

Iris blinks tiredly, her eyes still red from crying. "She's in surgery now. She was brave going under the anaesthetic. But scared. Poor kid. She's got a dislocated shoulder and a fractured humerus—her upper arm. She didn't hit her head, thank goodness."

I shake my head in sympathy. "I feel for both of you. Scary stuff."

Iris exhales heavily, her shoulders hunching as she crosses her arms. "I haven't had a cigarette in decades, but man, do I feel like one now. Just after I left the operating room, two social workers took me aside to question me about what happened. I think I must have explained ten times over that she fell out of a bunk bed on a bus. It was like they thought I was making stuff up. Like I freaking hurt my own daughter or something."

"That's terrible," I tell her, jumping to my feet. "Look, if you need me to go and talk to them—"

"No, I think I finally got it through their knuckle heads that we *are* actually travelling on a bus."

"Can I get you a coffee? Or a cold drink?"

"I think I just need... to go for a walk," she says. "I don't even understand this whole thing. I mean, Audrey said she had a headache and wanted to sleep. Couldn't she just have stayed in her damned seat and asked us for a painkiller?"

Piper casts a guilty glance in her mother's direction.

Iris catches the look and tilts her head in a confused gesture. "Okay, Miss Piper, seems like you've got something to tell me. Let's go for a little walk."

Piper leaves her seat like a condemned criminal and steps away with Iris. Within seconds, I hear Iris exploding at Piper. I make a guess that Piper has told her mother the real reason why Audrey was in the bunk, and it seems she was right about what her mother's reaction would be.

Piper storms off and goes to sit by herself on a bench seat at the far end of the hall. Shaking her head, Iris walks back along the hall.

"Iris," I say, "you know that what happened isn't Piper's fault, right?"

"She told you?"

"Just a few minutes ago."

"I've had it—that's all. Everything is so out of control. I've been trying to keep it together for so long—for the kids' sake. Life is damned busy between work and the kids. And then on top of all that, I'm headed for a divorce."

"Hey... one step at a time."

"You're right. I have to think about Audrey."

"Iris... I'm guessing this is where the trip ends. You'll have to go home to take care of her." My stomach lurches as I say those words. We haven't yet reached a space in which I can try to turn Iris around, to get her to spill her secrets. But Audrey's welfare has to come first.

"I don't know what to do," Iris answers. "When they were taking Audrey away for the operation, she was freaking out because she thought everyone would blame her for getting hurt and ending the trip. I had to calm her down by promising her the trip would continue."

"But... do you think you'll be able to do that?" I ask.

"I need to talk with Gabe. I called to tell him about Audrey, but I didn't tell him what I promised her. I know Piper wants to go home, but Kaden will be devastated. I don't even know if the insurance will cover the busted tyre on the bus. What a mess."

"Hey, we'll figure it out. But right now, your little girl's having surgery. It's okay to just sit here and wait for her. You don't have to do anything else."

Iris sinks into a seat near me. "You're right. You are. That's all I need to do for now."

"Is Piper okay over there by herself, or d'you want me to go talk to her?"

"She's fine. She wants her own space. She gets like that." Iris shrugs out of the scrubs, shooting me a wry look. "Remember last time we were in a hospital together?"

"Yeah. When Ellie fell out of the tree. Mom worried it'd be a fracture, but it ended up just being a sprain."

"Ellie used to climb like a little monkey."

"She sure did."

Iris stretches her long arms. "I gotta say, it's been a lot more comfortable on this trip than when we did it with Mom. I mean, we've got a whole damn bus."

"Yep. Can't tell you how many times I used to wake up with your elbow in my face. Or Ellie's feet in my stomach."

"It *was* cramped. Strange that, because it was also lonely."

"Lonely?" I ask.

"Yes. I mean, Grace was the closest one to my age, and I loved her to bits, but she couldn't do things with me. We couldn't go off together into town or go for a swim at the beach. She was in the wheelchair, and she needed to sleep a lot each day. It was hard."

"Well, Ellie wasn't anywhere near close to my age. I didn't have someone my age to hang with, either."

"Yeah, but that's different. You were happy to just go off by yourself. You were always the kid with dirt and sticks in your hair, and... well, I don't even know what you did half the time. What did you do?"

I shrug, thinking back. "Collect shells and sea glass, find sticks for the fire, look for birds' nests... make shelters for the possums. That kind of stuff."

"Right. Well, I wanted to go clothes shopping and go to my first high school dance. I wanted to compete in dance competitions. I didn't get to do any of those things that year."

"But it was fun some of the time, wasn't it?"

"Yes. Yeah, it was. But that doesn't make up for all the things it wasn't."

"I'm sorry it was like that for you."

She sighs. "I think I'm loading too much... of myself... onto my girls."

"What do you mean?" I ask.

"I wanted them to have all the opportunities I didn't. Piper has the best chance of having the life I wanted. And maybe I've built her up too much. No, not maybe. I have. Audrey's a sweetheart, and she tries hard, but she just doesn't have what it takes. And that shouldn't matter." Iris shakes her head. "What the hell have I done? She was trying to slim down. At age eleven, no less. She shouldn't even be thinking about things like that. She should be... like you were, Lily."

"It was a different time when I was a kid. No internet. None of the same pressures on young girls."

Iris isn't listening. "I feel like the worst parent in the world right now."

"Welcome to the bad-parent club," I say. "I've been a member of that for a while now."

Angling her head around, Iris shoots me a sceptical look. "What are you talking about? Jake's a great kid. C'mon—you do not have any parenting issues."

"Of course, I do. You remember Alice Eloise Dixon?"

"Uh, yeah, sure. How could I forget *her*?"

"She's the counsellor at Jake's school now."

"Oh, hell no. That's all the poor kids need—a dose of Alice Eloise."

"Yeah. And just a few weeks ago, she had Jake in her office, trying to stick him into a class for kids with bad behaviour. Kids have been harassing Jake... about what happened with Mom and Ellie. And Jake's started to push back."

"Well, so he should. Alice can suck on a lemon," Iris says.

"Don't worry. I put her in her place. She and her sister don't scare me anymore."

"Oh God—Alice and Trixie. The terrible two."

"They sure were. And still are. But I feel like I'm getting something really, really wrong with Jake. Like, maybe I've tried too hard to make sure he didn't turn out like his devil-may-care dad—or like me. When I was a kid, I was, like, *smack 'em, and ask questions later*."

"Yeah, you were like that."

I shoot her a wry look. "I think I've made Jake anxious. He's an anxious kid."

"He is a bit anxious. But have you considered that staying in that town isn't your best option?"

My sister's words hit me between the eyes harder than any physical blow. And I don't have a ready answer for her.

Iris's expression grows distant. "Do you know what the kids at Forestview used to chant at me about our dad? I'd be walking down the school hall, and they'd be saying, 'wife killer, child killer... stab her, choke her, drown her, kill her.'"

I cover my mouth in horror. "That's awful."

"Yeah. And the kids who were saying that stuff have grown up to be the adults in our hometown, including Alice and Trixie. And they're the parents of the kids at Forestview school. Think about that for a minute."

Iris's words force an image into my mind of Jake the last time I dropped him off at the school gates. He hadn't just looked sad—he looked resigned. He'd been fighting a battle that wasn't his to fight.

34

I WAIT with Iris as the clock ticks down. Jake and Kaden return with their pockets full of candy and snacks. And Piper steals down the corridor to sit next to them and share in their bounty.

A surgeon arrives to give my very anxious sister an update on her daughter. The operation went smoothly, and he expects Audrey to make a good recovery. It's the news we were hoping for.

We all stay in a hotel in Port Macquarie overnight, while the bus is being repaired and while Iris and her husband figure out what to do about Audrey and this whole trip. In the morning, I catch a taxi into town with Jake, Kaden, and Piper.

The kids have brought their skateboards with them, and they spend an hour in the outdoor skateboard rink that looks out on a wide park and the ocean. After that, we head along a boardwalk. A memory jolts me. On either side of the boardwalk as far as I can see are painted rocks, each about as high as my thigh. They're painted with amateur designs from many people. And I remember that Ellie and I painted one of these rocks back in 1998. I guess it has been painted over, as I can't find it—but still, I know our work must be there, underneath the layers.

We end up staying in Port Macquarie for three days. Iris and

Gabe have made their decision—the trip will continue. The bus hire insurance covered the damage to the tyre and wheel, and it's all fixed.

In my mind, the clock resets. I think about the wine I've stashed in a cupboard in the bus, ready for a night when the kids are asleep. I'll sit Iris down, share a few glasses of wine with her, and then I can lead her back to that night in the past when she ran through the rain with a yellow jacket over her head.

Iris gets back in the driver's seat again, and we head onto the highway. We backtrack to Limeburners Creek National Park—we had to bypass it before when Audrey fell from the bunk bed. It's a short trip, under an hour.

"Why's it called Limeburners?" Jake pipes up.

I search it on my phone. "Hmmm. Seems it was a penal settlement during the convict days. Lime was needed to make mortar for the buildings, so huge quantities of oyster shells were burned."

"That makes lime?" Jake queries.

"Seems so," I reply. "And it says here that for thousands of years before Europeans sailed in, Indigenous people ate the shellfish and kept a stone quarry to sharpen their tools."

It's for Jake that I look up as many interesting tidbits as I can about the area we're driving to. But Iris's kids end up being just as interested, and they hold me to doing that every place we go to.

"If this was school," Iris says dryly from the driver's seat, "they'd be tuning out of this history lesson."

I laugh. "Yeah, it's all different when you're actually going to the place."

We reach Limeburners, and Iris parks at a camping spot. After getting dinner sorted, Iris and I take the kids out for a walk. It's not long before dark.

To the left, there's a huddle of old, small caravans and motorhomes. At first, I think it must be a large family group all travelling together. But there is a lack of children's things—no bikes or scooters or bodyboards. And it's quiet.

As I draw closer, I catch sight of a group of women seated in a circle on fold-out chairs, aged between sixty and ninety. I'm desperate to talk to anyone who might know Bennett. I approach and say a friendly good morning. I get no more than a cold response, and then they turn away from me. I decide to try them again tomorrow.

But the next morning, I get the exact same reception from the group. When I get pushy and try asking them questions, they make it clear I'm intruding on their peace.

I return to the bus, feeling deflated. Iris and I head out with the kids to the beach today. The area is as beautiful as I remember. I go crazy taking photographs of the kids and the scenery. This time, it's not just for the scrapbook.

At midday, I stay behind to grab some landscape photos while Iris walks the kids back to grab some lunch. Wandering up a hill, I begin snapping a few landscape shots from my better vantage point. A view of a wide bay opens before me.

A deep, husky voice startles me. I turn to see a woman aged in her seventies putting out a cigarette on a tree branch. "I said, nice day."

"Oh," I answer. "It sure is."

"You're American."

"Yep, I am."

"Are you camping here?"

"Kind of. We have a bus."

"Ah, you're with the family that's got the bus. Must be hard hauling that thing around."

"It's been interesting so far," I say.

"Hmmm. Well, if you want to know the best spots, talk to me. I've been to Limeburners more times than I can count."

"Good to know. I've been here once... a very long time ago. I was a child."

"Oh yeah? What brings you back?"

"A road trip. My sister and our kids and me."

"Well, how about that? Good for you," she says.

"How about you? You said you vacation here often?"

"No, I didn't say that."

"Oh, sorry."

"You would have seen the vans down near the bottom of the hill?" she asks.

"I did, yes. But I didn't see you."

"I like to go off on my own a lot. We're a group of women living in those vans. They're our homes. We're not on holidays, but people treat us like we are."

"I see."

"Sounds strange, doesn't it? I used to have a family and live the family life. My two kids grew up and moved away. My hubby died. Couldn't afford the rent anymore. So I decided to hit the road."

"And the other women—did you meet them along the way?" I ask.

"Yup. They were all in the same situation as me. Nowhere to call home, so they bought a van and headed out into the wild blue yonder. We decided to hang together for protection. They're my family now."

"It's good you found each other."

"For sure. We're the hidden epidemic of homeless women. And there's an awful lot of us. Anyway, can't waste time feeling sorry for myself. That's not my way. We've got our vans, and we've got each other. That's how it'll be till we leave this earth."

"Well, I can't think of a better place on earth to be than the coast along these highways. The year we spent travelling here was... very special to me."

A look of approval glints in her eyes. "A whole year? You'd know the van life well, then. I been on the road fifteen-odd years, myself."

"Fifteen years? This is a long shot, but seeing as you've been travelling this road so long, you might know of someone we're trying to catch up with."

"If they travel this road, there's a mighty good chance I do."

"His name is Bennett."

She stares at me for a moment then lifts her head back and laughs. "Bennett? You're looking for *him*?"

I nod, a small bud of hope growing in my chest.

She shakes her head. "Bennett's a loner. He don't wanna talk to no one. He never has anything with him but his motorcycle and a one-man tent. It's just funny someone's trying to track him down, that's all."

"When we knew him, he ran a farm near Nimbin."

"Oh yeah. He told me about the farm."

"You've spoken to him?"

"Well, he breaks down his walls sometimes and comes and talks to us. Gives us all a laugh, he does."

"I heard he's been ill," I say.

"He is? Didn't tell me. Typical Bennett."

"If you wouldn't mind, I'd really like to see him again."

"And who are you to him?"

"He was a good friend of my mother's. I'd just like to get in contact."

"Well, I feel like I shouldn't be giving out that kind of information."

"How long ago did you last see him?" I ask.

"It would have been five, six months ago."

A thread of desperation pulls at me. "Bennett has bone cancer. I was told that by the lady who runs the farm now—Joyce."

"You know Joyce?"

"Yes."

"I've known Joyce for years. We stay at her farm sometimes." She gives a husky sigh. "That's not good news about Bennett. Look, okay. All I know is that he has a house down south."

"Down south?" I ask.

"South Coast. Port Kembla. Don't tell him I told ya. Okay? You didn't hear that from me. I wouldn't have told you at all, but it sounds like his time is short, which means your time to find him is too."

"Thank you. I can't tell you how much I appreciate this."

I head back to the bus, my step a little lighter. The kids have finished lunch and are playing a game of badminton outside—all except for Audrey, who sits with her mother and watches.

Iris squints at me, the sun in her eyes. "You know something."

"You're right—I do. I just spoke with a woman who spends her life travelling up and down the coastal highways. She knows Bennett."

Iris's mouth drops open. "Does she know how we can find him?"

"She knows where his house is. South Coast, apparently. Somewhere called Port Kembla. I don't remember if we went there with Mom."

"Port Kembla? Yep, that's south, all right. We didn't go there. It's a coal-mining town. Not Mom's thing."

"Well, there's no guarantee Bennett's going to be there. She hasn't seen him for at least five months. And well, you know, he might not still be around..."

"I guess there's only one way to find out," Iris says.

I check Google Maps on my phone. "It's a six-hour drive from here. With stops, at least eight hours. We're not going to do all that today."

"We might get as far as Sydney, though. Well, let's go. We're burning daylight."

The kids are disappointed when we tell them we're moving on—all except for Piper. She knows the sooner we get to the finish line, the sooner she can go home.

35

It's a three-hour trip from Limeburners Creek National Park to a harbour city named Newcastle. We stop for lunch and to buy food to stock the fridge and cupboards. I keep a watch on the map and the time. I know Iris won't drive the bus at night.

"Where do you think we should pull up for the night?" I ask her.

"Not sure," she replies. "Jake wanted to see Sydney, right?"

"The city would be a nightmare with a bus. I've already told him we can't do it."

"Tell you what," she says, looking at a map on her phone. "I know how we can knock down all the bowling pins. I'll drive right past the harbour bridge. Can't see much from the bridge, but if I go along here—Olympic Drive—and go right under the bridge, then you and Jake will get the best view in the city. We won't even need to get out of the bus."

"But it's right out of our way, isn't it?"

"We need to stay somewhere. I've got a friend, Tash, who owns a dance-costume-supply warehouse in the city. She has trucks come in during the day, which means there's a big space there at night. I'll give her a call."

"Sounds great," I say.

Iris was always great at planning ahead. She used to have calendars marked with the month's activities—all her school subjects, afternoon dance practice, and the pageants. Mom's haphazard, spur-of-the-moment adventures must have knocked Iris for six. Iris and Mom were polar opposites.

Iris finishes her phone call and beams at me. Her friend Tash has said we're welcome to stay. We jump back in the bus and drive out of the Newcastle region and through the Central Coast. Within the next ninety minutes, we've made it to the city of Sydney. It's somewhere I've never been, and I find myself as interested as Jake is. He sits next to me, and we share the experience.

Iris turns onto Olympic Drive at Milsons Point, and we drive under the harbour bridge. A view of a glittering harbour yawns before us, with yachts and an enormous cruise ship sailing past and the white shell-like building of the Sydney Opera House gleaming on the other side. It's almost all too pretty to be real.

"Tash's dance warehouse is not far from Luna Park," Iris tells me.

At the mention of Luna Park, Iris's kids start cheering.

I turn to grin at their cheers and then back to Iris. "Okay, by the sound of that, Luna Park is an amusement park?"

"Yeah," my sister drawls. "It's a Sydney institution. Think 1930s art deco, Coney Island, that kind of thing."

As Iris drives on, Luna Park moves into view. It's right on an edge of the harbour. There's a huge face—like the one at Coney Island—about thirty feet across, below which visitors are streaming in and out of the park. Iris pulls into a narrow laneway and then in through an open garage. It's tight, but she manages it.

After a chat with Iris's friend, Tash, we trek back to Luna Park. The first ride we try is the Ferris wheel. We get an impressive view of the harbour and city as I sit next to Jake and try to pick out landmarks.

I can't help but think about Mom. She might not have enjoyed a city, but she would have enjoyed this. I wish she were here with us. The loss of her is huge, almost unfathomable to me in this moment.

We stay in the park until way after dark, watching the lights spring on around the city. Then we head back to the bus to hunker down for the night.

Van calls me late tonight—after ten. He's not impressed when I tell him what our plans are for tomorrow.

"Lily," he says in a stern voice I haven't heard from him before, "Bennett was on the police list of suspects. You can't meet with him alone. Give me a day, and I'll come down there. I'm getting close to moving in on a suspect for Mick Brown's murder."

"Van, we don't know for sure if Bennett will even be there. This is all guesswork... and maybe even a goose chase."

"But there's a possibility."

"A slim chance."

"Look, I know you've been focused on the journal, but just remember that someone out there knows what happened to your mother and Ellie, and that person could well have harmed them. You have to keep that front of mind."

"I won't put the kids in danger—that's for sure."

"You need to worry about yourself too. Don't go anywhere isolated—not for any reason, okay?"

"Okay, got it," I say, and we talk for a while longer about everyday things.

That night, sleep evades me. I have so many questions about Bennett. Why did Mom leave the farm? Did she and Bennett ever meet up again without us kids knowing? And did she give him her journal for safekeeping?

At first light, Iris and the kids and I are back on the road, bound for Port Kembla.

I look up information about the town on my phone and read it out to the kids. "Captain James Cook sailed to Port Kembla in 1770. Red Point was his first sighting of Australia's east coast, and he's the one who named it. At the start of the 1900s, the area housed a copper smelter and steelworks."

Jake grins. "Thanks for today's history lesson, Mom."

We roll into Port Kembla when it's still early morning. I'm

surprised to discover that Red Point is beautiful, with a lido-style seawater pool that overlooks a wide span of beach. After a dip, we take a walk along the shore then head back to the bus for breakfast.

All the while, I'm making plans for the day. I have no idea where to find Bennett. I know his full name from the police files—it's Zephyr Bennett. But that doesn't help because when I look up a list of phone numbers, there are none listed for that name here.

After a chat with Iris, we decide that I'll hire a small car to run around in for the next couple of days. I'll start checking out bars and asking around town to see who might know Bennett. One of the few things I remember is that he liked beer, because he used to make his own.

I spend the day zipping about everywhere I can find. It's been a long time since I went to a bar on my own. I was a lot more adventurous in my early twenties. This feels like something they do in movies—rocking up to bars and showing an old photo to people.

At the end of the day, I return to the bus without finding out a single thing. I have dinner with everyone but then feel too restless to settle in for the night. I decide to head out again.

"You don't have to do this," Iris reminds me, "and you shouldn't."

I give a small shrug that I hope looks more casual than how I feel. "But what if Bennett only goes out at night?"

"What if he barely goes out at all? What if he isn't even here? Or what if he is here, but you're the last person he wants to see? We don't really know that much about Bennett, now, do we?"

"No. I guess we don't."

"So, don't go."

"I'll just try a few more places. And I'll keep my phone on—I promise."

With my hands in my jacket pockets, I step out of the bus. Iris still doesn't understand this trip—doesn't understand *me*. I want to take this as far as it can go. Right to the limit.

I drive around town, trying a few places I already visited earlier today. I'm about to go back to the bus when I notice a little bar I didn't see before. Now that it's dark, the broken neon sign becomes distinct. I can see through the plate-glass window. It's mostly men inside.

When I walk in, I try to look like this is something I do all the time—head down to bars by myself at night to grab a drink. Heads turn, but I ignore them.

I ask the bartender for a vodka and orange. When he returns with the drink, I seize the chance to slide the photo of Bennett across to him. "Would you happen to know this guy? It's an old photo."

He takes a quick look and then shakes his head. "Sorry, no idea. I just started here last week."

I sip my vodka. The bartender made it pretty weak, and the orange juice doesn't taste quite right.

When two men appear at the bar to buy a round of beer, I show them the photo. "Would you happen to know him? His name is Bennett."

One of them lifts his chin at me suspiciously. "You're not a daughter he didn't know he had, are you?"

I shake my head and smile. "No, nothing like that."

The second man glances across the room, toward the pool tables. It's subtle, but that's enough for me to guess something. Bennett is here.

36

I MAKE a quick study of the two men who occupy the corner of the room where the pool table is. One of them is a bulky guy in a gym shirt who looks like he works out a lot. The other has shoulder-length grey hair and a brown beard and moustache. His T-shirt hangs on gaunt shoulders.

It's Bennett. He notices me watching him. He approaches, and my mind blanks on what to say. I didn't know if I'd find him at all, and I certainly didn't expect to find him tonight.

Bennett looks from the two men on my right to me. "What have I done now?"

"Bennett," I start, "it's me—Lily."

Even with his years and having grown thinner, he's still a handsome guy. His eyes and forehead crinkle in a frown. "I don't—"

"Elsa's daughter."

"That Lily?"

"Yes. That Lily."

"Whew. Well, how about you come over and sit at a table and tell me what's going on?"

I leave my vodka behind as he shows me to a table. He chooses one that's well away from the curious eyes of his friends and the other people at the bar. It seems they all know him.

"Hold still—I'll get you a drink," he says.

"No, I'm fine. How... how are you?"

"I'm getting by." He sits opposite me. "Now, tell me straight. How'd you find me?"

"I asked around a lot—everywhere I could think of. And I put together a picture of where you might be." I exhale slowly.

"Okay. Now, tell me exactly why you're looking for me. You think I did something bad, and you want to ask me for yourself—is that it?"

"No. That's not why."

"Then why?"

"This is going to sound stupid..."

He shrugs. "Everything is stupid. We're all just animals trying to find our way through the jungle."

I attempt a smile. "My sister and I—Iris—we've been on a trip together. We... we're trying to recreate the trip our mother took us on. Sounds so strange when I say it out loud."

His eyes cloud. "You're with Iris?"

"Yes. And our children."

"I see."

"Is that a problem?" I ask.

"It's not a problem for you. Anyway, go on. What's your trip got to do with me?"

"My mother—she was keeping a journal. I only recently found that out. This trip is all about finding it."

"Do you have any reason to think I have it?"

I shake my head. "I know you and Mom were close once. I thought there was a chance she left it with you. For safekeeping or whatever."

"You ever see the journal?"

"No."

"You mean you came all this way... for a journal your mother may or may not have written twenty-four years ago?"

"Please don't make this weird."

"I'm the one making it weird? I never saw a journal. She wrote me a poem once. She wanted me to understand who she was before I met her."

My voice almost fails. "Do you still have it?"

"Nope. It was childish of me, but I threw it into the fire sometime after she left."

"Oh. So… did you… understand who she was?"

"Elsa was a complex person. There was a lot to understand. And I didn't get much time with her. Your family was barely at the farm before you were gone again."

"The farm had a big impact on me. Like it was much longer in time than it was. Iris and I visited the farm a few days ago. Joyce's the only one still there."

"She's a good egg, Joyce."

"Do you still own the farm?" I ask.

"Yep. When I die, the land will become conservation land—never to be developed. Joyce gets to keep the small portion where the crops and orchards are."

"I'm glad. It's all so beautiful."

"I knew you'd feel that way. You had a special love for the land, Lily."

Tears prick my eyes, and I have to look away. I don't want him to know the effect he's having on me—the same effect he had on me when I was eleven. I don't know if it's real or if it's all charm and smoke and mirrors.

"You okay, little bird?" he says.

"Yeah, I was just thinking about all the people who are no longer there at the farm," I lie.

"No one stays forever."

"Bennett, what happened to the contents of all the old buildings? The cabins and the library?"

"You think your mum's journal might have been in there, huh?"

"I guess I had a faint hope."

"Joyce went through everything personally. If there was

anything there of your mother's, I'm sure she would have told me—or the police. Everything was donated to charity. The old vans got sent to the wreckers. I towed Florence's campervan away myself. She gifted it to me. But I still haven't got around to fixing it up." He shrugs.

"Florence was a great lady—Mom loved her."

"Yeah, she was. Lived to ninety-eight years of age. Passed away on the farm."

"Wait... did you say you still have her campervan?"

"I do."

"Could I... is it possible I could see it?" I ask.

"I know what you're getting at. But the police searched it."

"But they wouldn't have been looking for a journal. They didn't know about it then."

"You're welcome to come and look for yourself if it'd set your mind at ease."

"I'd really appreciate that."

Before I leave the bar, Bennett invites me out to his property. It's quite a distance away from town. I can't pretend that a momentary dark thought doesn't pass through my mind. How much do I really know about Bennett? Detective Dawson's warning was clear. If you push people against a wall, you have to be prepared for them to charge straight at you.

When I tell Iris about meeting up with Bennett, a mixture of emotions crosses her face—emotions I can't decipher. She insists that I can't go alone. She finds a school holiday program that can take the kids for a day—she tells me that every council runs them. The activities include games of tennis and baseball as well as crafts and movies. Audrey will have to sit out on the physical activities, but there seems to be enough quieter activities for her.

After dropping off the kids in the morning, Iris and I drive to Bennett's house in the car that I hired. I let Van know where we're going in a text message.

Bennett's house is a ranch-style wooden building that looks as if it's had lots of additions and alterations over the years. A wide veranda runs around the entire front and side. The house sits on a large expanse of land and holds two enormous barns.

"I don't know about this," Iris says as we walk up the path. "Why couldn't he just search Florence's caravan himself and then let us know if the journal was there?"

"I'm guessing he thinks we want to see it for ourselves. I got a little intense when talking to him last night. I can be that way at times."

She stops, turning to me. "I didn't think you knew that."

"Knew what?"

"That you can be damned intense."

"I didn't think that I—?"

"Lily, you are that in spades."

She goes quiet as a man emerges from the house. Bennett. His shaggy hair hangs free today. He looks healthier in the sunlight than he did under the artificial lighting at the bar last night.

Bennett approaches us, hands in the pockets of his jeans. "Lily... Iris. Good to see you."

"Hi," Iris says quickly.

"You're all grown up," he says.

It's a somewhat awkward meeting. He seems a little colder today and less friendly. I open my mouth to say something to ease the tension, but Bennett gets in before me.

"We'll cut straight to it," he says. "The campervan is this way."

I glance at Iris, and then we follow him to one of the barns. The place is stacked full of... everything. There are vehicles from past decades—even ones that seem to be from the 1930s or '40s. Motorcycles and bicycles stand near the wall to the left. On the floor-to-ceiling shelving sit crates of vintage signs. There is even memorabilia that looks like it came straight from movie sets.

"Is this all yours?" I ask, awed.

"It belonged to everyone from my great-great grandparents to my parents. Now it's just me." He leads us around a truck. "There's Florence's campervan. Have at it."

It's dark and stuffy up at this end of the barn. The van is

crammed between the truck and a car. It's going to be a squeeze just getting between the vehicles, let alone getting through the door.

Iris stalls, raising her eyes to Bennett. "The police know we're here. Just sayin'."

Bennett frowns for a second, and then he cracks a wide grin. "Really? You're really going to stand there and say that to me?"

Iris shoves her hands in her pockets in a defensive motion. "I'm just looking out for my little sister."

"Well, little sister wanted to come here," he tells her.

I inhale the warm, suffocating air. "Let's just do this, Iris," I plead.

She turns to me. "How about I go look while you wait outside the barn, Lily?"

I glance from Iris to Bennett, not understanding what's going on. Iris is about to wreck this opportunity. Bennett might decide to throw us out at any minute.

In the moment that follows, his expression switches from confusion to anger.

37

I DON'T EVEN KNOW how things suddenly went bad. Iris and I seem to have locked ourselves into some kind of invisible boxing arena with Bennett.

He leans his head back against the truck, folding his arms. "Oh, I get it. I get it now. There is no journal, is there? You two just wanted a chance to search my property. The police weren't going to get a warrant to search this place, were they? So you thought you'd come and try to find some kind of evidence. You think I hurt your mother. How am I doing?"

I hold the palms of my hands up. "Whoa, no. You've got it wrong. It's exactly how I said it was. We just want—"

"When you asked me how I was last night, Lily," he says, "I could tell that you already knew. You know I'm ill."

I lower my eyes. "Yes, I know. And I was so, so sorry to hear it."

"Save your sorries. I've accepted what's coming for me," he says. "Are you and your sister worried I might lash out because I've got nothing left to lose?"

My sister swallows and lifts her chin. "No. But there is... something. I thought... I thought you might be holding a grudge against me. For what I did."

He stares back at her for a moment. "Seriously? You think I held that against you? All this time?"

I catch my breath as I eye them both. "What are you two talking about?"

Iris shakes her head, sighing. "I'm the reason Mom left the farm, Lily. I didn't quite tell Mom the truth about the day you saw me... kiss Bennett. I let her think that maybe he was a bit into it. Instead, what happened was that he marched me out of there. I felt kind of... humiliated."

Bennett exhales. "Wait one damned minute. That's why Elsa left? That's why she went cold towards me?"

Iris nods, recoiling.

"I didn't know," Bennett says in a low tone. "When you mentioned a grudge, I thought you meant I was holding a grudge because of what you told Sergeant Mullard. That I use women. That I reel 'em in and spit 'em out. He came after me hard when your mother vanished, accusing me of being some kind of abuser."

"I'm sorry," Iris tells him. "In my mind, when I was a teenager, that's what you were. I felt... led on."

"Because I was nice to you?" he asks in an incredulous voice.

"Yes." Iris is crying now, wiping a tear from her cheek. "I didn't know that you and Mom had a thing going. And somewhere in my stupid fourteen-year-old mind, I thought you really liked me, but then you just snubbed me for no reason. I was so hurt."

I stare from Iris to Bennett. I had no clue that Iris had told the sergeant that Bennett was basically a bad guy. It feels as if a window just opened—a window that I had no clue was even there.

Bennett looks as if he's going to start yelling, but then he shakes his head and stares up at the sky. "I'm sorry you were hurt. Wish I'd known why Elsa really left." He emits a rueful, groaning sound from the back of his throat. "You know what? It's a lifetime too late, but I'm glad to know why. I'm happy to have a damned reason."

"I wish I didn't even see you two that day in the barn," I tell them both.

"What's done is done," Bennett says. "Anyway, you're here. If you still want to search Florence's van, then do it. Else, get back in your car and leave me be."

"We'd like to take a look," I say before Iris has a chance to find her voice again.

"Van's open," Bennett tells us and then walks away, out of the barn.

Iris faces me, blinking away tears. "You hate me now, right?"

"No. I just... I just wish we all talked to each other a lot more back then. Even just a few days ago, you were telling me Bennett was some kind of Don Juan."

She rakes her teeth over her lip. "It was a story I told myself. Easier to believe that than the truth."

"Let's just check the van."

She nods.

We're pinched between the truck and caravan as we edge along the narrow aisle. After we manage to get the door open, we have to squirm to get inside.

The interior is tiny. Just big enough for one or two people. But with the space there is, Florence made good use of it. Things are stuffed in tight. Her things make me remember the kind of woman she was. Books on Indigenous history and about growing crops without pesticides. Drawers full of yarn for the blankets she used to knit for the newcomers. Only a few articles of clothing—mostly hard-wearing denim.

Iris flips through Florence's collection of old vinyl records. "These would be worth a fortune."

I simply give her a nod. My chest still feels tight after that conversation we just had with Bennett. Iris had been holding onto things she should have told me. There's a refrain playing in the back of my head: *We didn't need to leave the farm.*

And what else has she been holding onto? I want to make her tell everything—right now. But it's not the place to do that. I have to continue to keep a lock on it.

"You okay?" she asks.

"I'm fine."

"I wish things didn't happen the way they did."

"Yeah, you have no idea."

"Lily..."

"No, not now."

"Sure." Iris keeps searching. She picks up the stack of records from the deep-storage compartment and sets them aside. Next, she lifts out a shoebox and opens it. Inside is a hardcover book. Gently, she begins flipping through the pages.

As I watch her, she raises her head to me. She nods, fresh tears spilling down her cheeks.

"Hide it," I tell her in a hushed tone.

"My handbag is too small," she whispers.

With trembling fingers, I take the book from her. It has a plain, dark green cover. Not something that stands out in any way. When I open it, I see my mother's name—*Elsa Jorgenson, 1997*. As I let the journal fall shut again, I close my eyes, feeling the light weight of the book in my hands.

We've got it, Mom. You probably never intended us to see this—your personal writing. Forgive me, but I'm never letting it go.

Bennett is waiting for us when we leave the barn. I don't want to let him know we found Mom's journal, just in case there's something bad about Bennett in it after all.

But he takes one look at us and figures it out. "So, you were right, little bird," he tells me.

Instinct takes over, and I run up to him and throw a bear hug around his shoulders. "I wish we'd all stayed at the farm with you." My voice cracks with emotion.

He looks surprised as I step back. "I've wished that a thousand times. In some parallel universe, maybe things happened that way."

Iris tentatively approaches Bennett. "I'm sorry for everything. Wish I could take it back."

"Look at us, all full of wishes," he says. "Let's set them free. Take care, you two."

We head back to our little hire car, and I take the wheel again.

On our drive back to collect the kids from the holiday camp, Iris and I make a pact. We're going to read the journal together. Whatever's in it, we're going to need to lean on each other.

I've got Mom's journal safely tucked inside my backpack. I don't ever want to let it go. "Iris, this means we don't need to go on—with the trip. We found what we came looking for. It's crazy, but we did it."

"We did. But do you realise what it means that the journal was in Florence's campervan? It means that Mom stopped writing in it all the way back near the beginning of that road trip. It's possible that what's in it will only hurt us, not help us, you know?"

"I guess. I mean, yeah... I know."

"I'm not sure you do. You've been pinning your hopes on this."

I take a long breath. "Before you tell me again—I do get intense."

"Yes. But I wasn't thinking of that. I just don't want to see you get hurt. What if there's stuff in there where Mom says we were a burden and she wanted to get away from us? Could you deal with that?"

"I'll just have to."

"Okay, well, get yourself prepared." Iris pauses. "Hey, you know, the kids are having a great time, and well, it's been giving me breathing space... away from Gabe. I know what was behind this trip —it was about Mom—but it's got other good things going for it, right?"

"Yeah... for sure."

"You sound distracted."

"I admit my mind's on the journal. Sorry." I offer an apologetic smile.

"Look, I just don't want to end this yet. And Audrey was asking me if she can go see the fairy penguins. She hasn't been able to do much since she broke her arm, poor kid."

"Where are the penguins?"

"The next state. Victoria."

"How far?" I ask.

"Pretty far. At our speed, two days' travel."

"Oh. Look, okay. Audrey can have her fairy penguins."

"Thanks. Seriously. It'll mean a lot to her. I'm starting to realise she doesn't get her way all that often. In fact, she hardly ever asks for anything. That has to change. *I* have to change."

I offer Iris a warm glance as I round a bend.

"Lily?" she says.

"Yes?"

"Why don't we read a few pages?"

"But we said—"

"I can read it to you out loud. Might as well start now, before we pick up the kids, right?"

"If you're sure," I say.

Nodding slowly, Iris takes out the journal and turns to the first page. As she starts reading, Mom's soft Southern accent begins to take over in my mind until her voice is all I can hear.

38

ELSA JORGENSON, 1997

Dr Rosie Moreno tells me I've got to write in this journal each day, and I trust her to know about things like that. She says that I've spent enough time telling her all my secrets. Now I need to tell them to myself.

I didn't know what she meant at first. How could I not know my own secrets, my own past? In response to that question, she set me some homework. She asked me to start by writing free-form poetry. I was not to think about what I was writing—no trying to make anything rhyme. Just let things spill.

And so I did that. And slowly... slowly, I came to understand.

I've been so detached from myself that I've been telling my stories to Dr Moreno as if they had happened to someone else.

I wrote a dozen poems, maybe even twenty. I started in the middle of my journal, hiding myself there. I tore them all out and threw them away. I wasn't being honest.

Then one night—late—when Iris and Lily were asleep and the ocean was softly crashing on the beach, I sat on a chair next to my open window and started again.

The next day, I showed it to Dr Moreno. It made her cry.

That's how I knew I was working my way back—back to some

sort of life. Those words were the first time I'd admitted my past to myself. The start of my healing journey. I took the page out of my journal and gave it to Dr Moreno. I know the poem by heart, though, because it lives inside me.

I have always been running,
especially when I'm at my most still.
I've learned silence is a trapdoor.
You fall into the room made of mirrors
where the stranger watches you
every hour, every minute.
But my mind burns bright.
I'll have a warm body again,
I know I will.
Wind, salt, and sun on my skin,
in my hair, in my lungs.
I've made many wrong turns
—so many,
and one blinding mistake.
But I can't let a mistake
become a life.

Dr Moreno understood straight away about the warm body. It's like you've managed to draw some sunshine inside yourself and hold it there.

It's taken me a long time to learn how to do that.

She had no judgement when I told her about my big, awful mistake. I was terrified of being condemned for it. I could barely stand to even think about it. I didn't understand how I'd even done that.

But she didn't condemn me. She said to go home and start writing the story of my life. And then I'd understand who I was and why I made the choices I did.

So I'm going to tell the story of my life—to myself. So that I can begin to understand.

I grew up in North Carolina with five brothers. I was the only girl. We had a farm where we grew corn and sweet potatoes.

I remember having a lot of freedom in those years. I spent the most time with my brother Davey, who was only eleven months older than me—we'd patch up old boats we found on the swamp and take them out on the still black water under the cypress trees and Spanish moss. It was a whole world of its own, with frogs and turtles and alligators to discover.

All of that swiftly changed.

We had a bad year with the crops, and my parents decided to join a farming community further north, in Pennsylvania. We moved to PA when I was ten, straight into a bitterly cold winter and deep snow. Back when we lived on the coast of North Carolina, I don't recall ever seeing snow.

Our new community had a lot of new things to get used to.

The first thing was that it was run by a strict religious group that was led by its elders. Before, my experience of religion was church on Sundays and saying grace before dinner.

I was now to sleep in a hall with the other girls. My brothers were in another hall of all boys. And my parents were in a tiny cabin on their own.

There were instructions for me to follow. Girls were not to wear makeup of any kind. No hair dye, no fitted or brightly coloured clothing. At the time, that set of rules didn't seem overly restrictive. I was too young to care about such things.

But I wasn't fond at all of the other rules.

We weren't allowed to have what they called idle time. There was only work, sleep, and Bible time. I was to help out the other girls and women in the huge shared kitchen. On top of baking and cleaning and collecting eggs from the henhouse, I had to do two hours of religious studies a day. The church leaders had their own interpretation of the Bible, and you had to accept their word as law.

My mama questioned a few things at first, but soon, she never said a word about anything. When the snow finally melted, my brothers were put to work on the farms owned by the community.

My parents started to get a beaten-down look about them, but they backed the elders and encouraged us to obey this new structure of our lives. To this day, I don't understand why my parents stayed there. Maybe their financial situation was worse than they let on.

Just about the only time I saw my brothers was at church now. But sometimes, Davey and I would find a way to sneak off together down to the river. We'd swim in it if it was warm enough, and if it wasn't, we'd search for hellbenders—huge salamanders that were as big as two feet long. The hellbenders would hide under the river rocks.

When people came looking for Davey and me, we'd duck under the water or climb the nearest tree. And we'd have to stop ourselves from laughing when they couldn't see us.

It was late summer when Davey got sick. He was getting headaches so bad he'd be in bed for hours. The elders got mad at him, saying that he was just shirking his chores.

It was the one time Mama put her foot down. I remember travelling on the train with my parents and brothers to a big hospital—the first time I'd ever been to a city. The doctors there said two words—brain cancer. Davey had a kind of cancer in his head.

When we returned to the community, everyone gathered each day to pray the cancer out of Davey's head. The elders told us that if our family had enough faith, the prayers would work.

I guess we didn't have enough faith, because the prayers failed.

Davey died.

Davey was buried next to an apple tree. In the days before he got too sick to talk, he asked to be buried there. He made me promise that when I ate the apples, I'd think about him. I told him I didn't have to because I'd never forget him. I told him I'd never leave the community and I'd always be there with him.

It seemed like a huge mistake when they buried him. How was it possible a boy who'd been running up hills in the spring could be under the ground by the fall?

39

LILY JORGENSON

I HAVE to stop Iris from reading because my eyes are too wet and blurry to drive.

Iris turns to me, her eyes glistening with tears. "Mom told us about Davey dying from the cancer but not the rest of it. She left out so much."

"Yes, why didn't she tell us about the community and what they did about Davey? I mean, it sounds like he didn't get any treatment, right?"

"That's exactly what it sounds like."

"She said her family lived in a religious community, but she never told us that it was so strict—and so damned awful."

"Dad didn't tell us either," Iris points out. "And that's where she met him. They were both close-lipped. Unless he told you? I mean, you live with him."

"No, he never mentions it."

"I wonder what his side of it is?"

I nod. "And I wonder, too, if Davey's death is what caused the rift between our mother and her family."

"You know, I think that would explain it. She said there'd been a rift, but she never told us why."

"When I get back to PA, I'm going to try to find Davey's apple tree—if it still exists."

"Oh man, I'm gonna start bawling," she says.

"Me too. Should we stop reading this stuff for now?"

"This might be our only chance for a while. Can't read it with the kids around."

"You're right, but if it gets too bad, I might have to pull over somewhere."

"Of course."

"All right, let's do this," I say.

Iris continues reading, and again, I hear my mother's voice...

40

ELSA JORGENSON, 1997

When summer came, I ate Davey's apples.

They were warm and juicy, straight from the tree. But they didn't taste as sweet as apples should. Nothing had tasted quite the same since Davey died. Life itself had a different flavour.

I turned twelve that summer.

It was then that the community started me on the mysterious lessons that were only given to the older girls—girls who'd reached puberty or were just about to.

I knew that everyone older than twelve wore braided leather necklaces with pendants—suns for the men and half-moons for the women. In the lessons, I was taught that men are suns. Their energy gave the earth warmth and life. Women were moons. Their energy came from reflected sunlight. In the same way, women reflected the glory of men. And the man was the flame that lit the woman's candle.

We were also told girls didn't notice the way boys looked—we only noticed things like how clean they were or what they smelled like.

That idea seemed as strange to me as onion snow—a kind of snow I'd learned comes in spring in Pennsylvania. What I knew to be the truth was that the other girls and I could plainly tell which of the boys we'd like to kiss—without ever smelling them. At Sunday church, I'd steal looks at a boy who had black hair and dark skin and eyes the colour of freshly stained wood.

There were lots of purity garments and accessories that girls my age had to wear. Like, special undergarments—always white—and special braided leather belts around our waists and braided leather necklaces with moon pendants. We wore special silver rings on our fingers that looked like tiny braided pieces of rope. The things I had to put on each day made me feel trussed up like a turkey dinner.

Girls in the community married as young as fourteen. And the elders chose who married who.

When I was thirteen and a half, I was given the name of my future husband. And that name was Frederick Jorgenson.

I'd barely noticed him before. He was seventeen years old, and he looked like a man already. He was tall with the sturdy look of a farmer.

One morning, the elders summoned both Frederick and me to the Bible-study building, where they formally introduced us to each other. Frederick told me to call him Freddie. He seemed kind, but I was immediately terrified of him. I would have just run away. But at the time, I truly thought I had no option but to marry him. I'd been three years in the community at an impressionable age, and my idea of normal was badly skewed.

When I turned fifteen and Freddie was nineteen, the elders held a wedding for us in the apple orchard. Apple blossoms fell on my hair, and a lady played the flute. My brothers clapped Freddie on the back, and my father shook his hand.

It all went by in a blur.

But the wedding night—that I remember in sharp focus.

I remember Freddie's pale eyes. He picked me up in my wedding dress, took me to the bedroom, and then removed me from my clothing. As if I were a piece of fruit being peeled. The embarrassment of that moment is stuck in my head.

His face fell when he saw me standing there in my underwear.

I asked him what was wrong.

And he told me.

He told me everything about me was wrong.

My boobs were too small. My body looked like a boy's. My hips stuck out. I was too pale. I was wearing granny underwear.

Mama had given me the underwear that I wore. I didn't know anything about pretty underwear. I'd never seen any. No one had told me I was supposed to have that.

I was standing there, shivering, in a body that was suddenly ugly.

41

LILY JORGENSON

Mom's account of her wedding night sends shudders trampling down my back.

Iris stops reading, letting loose with a string of swear words. "That's insane. Why didn't Mom ever tell us what her church back then was like? Why didn't she tell us she had no say in marrying Dad?"

I set my teeth together. "Maybe she wanted to forget. Or maybe Dad didn't want us to know."

"Probably. I know this must be harder on you than me because you live with our dad. But it sure paints him in a bad light."

"I'm trying to see it that he didn't have many options, either. He grew up in that community. He would have believed in the elders and everything they believed."

"Still," Iris says, "Mom was just a kid of fifteen when they got married. She told us she was eighteen. She lied."

"Yeah, she did. But she did have you when she was sixteen. That makes terrible sense now."

"Yeah, true. She was married then." Iris makes a low sound under her breath. "And my God, he was so horrible to her on their wedding night. All the awful things he said."

"I'm going to guess he'd built up some vision in his mind of what women looked like under their clothes. Unfortunately, our mother was just a kid, and she had the body of one."

"Do you remember the date nights our parents used to have?" Iris says darkly.

"Yeah, I do."

"Remember all the makeup Mom used to wear? I wonder if that was because she didn't feel pretty without it. Maybe Dad made her feel ugly."

I draw in a breath. This is a deeper walk into the relationship between my parents than I've ever trodden before.

"Lily?" Iris says. "Are you okay?"

"Yes. It's just, well, it's pretty confronting."

"It's that way for me too."

"Oh no... oh dear God."

"What?" I ask.

"I just read a little more."

"Okay, just... read it out loud."

"Hang onto your hat, little sister."

42

ELSA JORGENSON, 1997

I HAD to get into my wedding bed, knowing that Freddie was disgusted by me.

Someone had scattered red rose petals on the linen. To this day, I can't stand red roses.

Once my granny underwear was off, all I wanted to do was to hide my body under the covers. But that's not what Freddie wanted.

Freddie had other ideas.

He had lengths of braided leather ties with him. He had them ready—here in the cabin. And he tied my wrists to the bed.

And then he did things to me.

That was sex.

I'd only had a vague idea of what it would be like, but I'd never imagined my wedding night would be anything like that.

The next day, I remember being in a strange state of mind. I barely knew who I was anymore.

I found myself running. Through the orchards. Over the hills. Away.

Away...

I was found and brought back by my big brothers. I despised

each and every one of them for that. And then I was brought before the elders.

The elders spent the next two hours giving me instruction. They said it was common for a new bride to feel flighty. They told me I needed to love and trust God more. A wife must show gratitude for the gifts her husband gives her, whatever those gifts may be.

Over the next weeks, I came to know something. The women here were forever in a state of gratitude. Men were allowed to want more than they had, but not the women. And it was mostly women telling that to other women. Be grateful, be content, count your gifts, be quiet.

My husband became increasingly interested in his collection of leather ties. Each night, he'd find new ways to restrain and shackle me. I could not figure why that excited him as much as it did.

The rest of the time, away from the bedroom, he was kind. I could not put those two things together—how he could be so nice to me and then treat me like an object.

Somehow, I gathered the courage to tell my mother what my husband had been doing to me.

She listened without speaking once. At the end she said, "Men are not like us."

It was yet another thing that stuck in my mind for a long time to come. *Men are not like us*. I remember waiting for more, but nothing more came. It was as if that simple explanation absolved everything.

The day after I spoke to my mother, the one photo that had been taken of Freddie and me on our wedding day was delivered to us. It made me cry. I'd held a vision in my head that at least I'd looked beautiful on that day, despite everything else. But when I tore away the brown paper wrapping, all I saw was a towering man in an ill-fitting suit—and a little girl playing dress-up.

I remember throwing up after seeing the photo. But it ended up not being the picture so much as the fact that I was pregnant.

Over the next months, Freddie loved my growing belly. But I felt as detached from it as I felt from everything else. I was impatient for the thing inside of me to be out. I was glad when I reached eight months of pregnancy because it'd be over soon.

No one told me that giving birth could be difficult. The women simply spoke of the joy of bringing life into the world and the pain being worth it. I thought it would hurt but I'd do it and it wouldn't be a huge deal. I didn't understand at all that labour pains could feel like a truck was trying to find an exit route out of your body.

After thirteen hours of this—against the advice of the elders—my father took one of the cars, put me in it, and rushed me to the hospital. The doctors there said my hips and pelvic bones were too narrow to give birth naturally. That was the problem with many teenage bodies, they told me. They're not ready for childbirth. I could have died.

I was wheeled into an operating theatre to have a C-section. Everything felt surreal and terrifying and out of my control. I was a body to be peeled open, just the way the wedding dress had been peeled off me on my wedding night.

I felt no connection to the baby when they put her in my arms. She was like a potato with two eyes and a mouth. I hated feeding her. I hated the awful smell of her diapers. I hated her neediness. I knew it was a sin to hate what God had given me, but I couldn't make myself love her.

When the women came to me and asked what I wanted to name her, I realised I'd given no thought to it at all. Freddie didn't care about naming her—he was only interested in naming the boys we'd have.

I walked to the window, baby in my arms, and my gaze fell upon the patch of iris flowers growing outside the cabin. It seemed as good a name as any.

I told them her name was to be Iris.

43

LILY JORGENSON

Acid burns the back of my throat. I steer the car to the side of the road and park there. For a moment, I struggle to breathe, as if all the air is gone. Mom hadn't gone into the specific details of her wedding night sex, but she didn't need to for graphic pictures to paint across my mind. I don't want these images of my father right in front of me, but I know my view of him will be forever changed. And the thought of my mother escaping only to be brought back by her own brothers is vomit-inducing. No wonder there'd been a huge rift between her and them. And my grandmother was complicit in all this. Mom had nowhere to turn.

I want to somehow go back in history and comfort that lost and terrified young girl that my mother had been. At the same time, selfishly, I want her here to comfort me.

I turn to Iris, my hands still gripping the wheel. "How can all this be real? Why didn't we know any of it?"

Iris looks as shocked as I feel. "It's horrific. All of it. I understand so much more about her now. And our father. God, I can't even..."

"My heart was in my mouth hearing the part about her being rushed to the hospital. I didn't realise that baby was going to be you.

She came so close to losing her life and losing *you*." It numbs me to think how close those events came to happening.

Iris closes her eyes. "I had a wonderful introduction to the world, didn't I? A young mother who didn't want me."

"She was just a kid then, Iris. She loved you. I know she did."

"I think I hate the sound of my own name—now that I know how she decided on it."

"I like your name," I say.

She doesn't answer.

We're both going to need time to process this. Lots and lots of time.

I start up the car again and drive away.

The kids are excited but tired when we pick them up—they don't seem to notice how unnerved Iris and I are feeling.

I return the hire car and then Iris comes with the bus to collect me.

Iris surprises Audrey with the news that she and I have agreed that we'll go see the fairy penguins. Her little face lighting up is worth the detour.

Our schedule has been completely reset. We've missed many of the towns we'd planned to stop at. We have to start the schedule again, from where we are. I still want to complete my scrapbook, as much as I can. And I need to cross off the most important person on my list of names—Iris. Maybe the fact she's opened up to Bennett is a sign that her barriers are breaking down. And now we have all of our mother's deepest secrets opening up to us, too. I make a plan to question Iris the night after we arrive on Phillip Island. It's time.

But for now, our next stop is a place on the South Coast of New South Wales—called Kiama. I find four old photos taken there—rare photos in which all of us are in the shot. I love seeing us all together.

Piper comes to sit beside me, helping to paste the pictures into my scrapbook. I'm beginning to enjoy her company just as much as I enjoy the company of her siblings. I understand her so much more since we had that chat at the hospital.

Jake asks me to look up the history of the place we're visiting, but my mind is too busy to focus. I ask Kaden to do it.

"Sure, Aunty Lily." He looks up Kiama on his phone and begins reading out loud. "So, everyone, Kiama is a place named by a local Indigenous tribe—and it means, *where the ocean makes a noise*. It's got the largest blowhole in the world and was formed from lava two hundred sixty million years ago."

"Well done, Kaden," I tell him with an appreciative smile.

The kids end up loving the visit to the blowhole—we are lucky that we've arrived on a day when it's putting on one of its best displays.

Then it's back onto the bus. We head a little away from the coast in order to stay on the highway, driving through serene cattle and dairy country.

"Kaden," I say, "you did such a good job with the last history snippet. Could you do the next?"

He looks pleased and begins looking up information on his phone. "Ladies and gentlemen, we're entering the Shoalhaven region. It's got a hundred beaches and is bordered by mountains and has almost fifty towns."

"Thanks, tour guide," Iris says from the driver's seat.

We stop to eat and rest at the exact same dairy farm Iris and I visited with Mom. I watch Iris telling her kids about when she and I were here as children. It's one of the few times I've heard her talk about that year. Feeling encouraged by that, I sit next to her and show her the scrapbook I've been making. At first, she seems tense, but then she finds some pictures that make her smile and laugh.

We continue along the highway, through the green hills of Bega, which Kaden tells us produces the best cheese in Australia. We proclaim him correct when Iris pulls up at a factory where they have cheese tasting.

With the fridge and cupboards stocked with cheese and bread, we drive away again. The pretty green landscape gives way to dry-looking bushland. The road begins to seem endless. Mile after mile of featureless road.

The kids doze off one by one. I'm feeling sleepy too.

I notice Iris is looking especially fatigued.

"Maybe we should stay somewhere overnight?" I suggest.

She shakes her head. "We're really close to the border. We should keep going."

"Iris, do you hear your voice? You've obviously had enough. Look, it's been a really long day on the road. And then there's been, you know, all those revelations in Mom's journal."

"I can do it."

"But you don't have to. I'm calling it. We're stopping."

I find a beachside town called Eden and direct Iris off the highway. Iris has a nap in the bus while I take the kids outside to explore. We find a large rock pool that's safe for Audrey to paddle in. It's gorgeous here, the late-afternoon light setting off a pinkish hue on the water. As Audrey wades in, I hold her hand, in case she should slip and get her cast wet.

The sunlight puts a glow on Audrey's face as she looks up at me. "I never want to go home, Aunty Lily. I want to keep seeing places like this—like you and my mum did with *your* mum."

I put my arm around her, giving her shoulder a squeeze. "It's been a special time with all of you—that's for sure."

Once Audrey's had a paddle, I take out my camera and start taking pictures. The sun paints an amber gold on the heads of the four children as they play, water spraying around them. Through my camera lens, the scene is magical. They're all so young, all so full of hope for their futures. I hadn't anticipated moments of sheer beauty like this on this trip, and for the first time, I feel threads of doubt pull at me. I don't want to ruin what this journey has become. I have Mom's journal—couldn't that be enough? But the old, familiar sensations of grief and bitterness rise up in my chest. I deserve a resolution from Iris.

After we return to the bus, I make the kids a cheesy pasta dish, and we eat outside on our fold-out chairs and table. Iris is still sleeping.

I excuse myself when Van calls me. "Where are you now?" he asks.

"Eden. It's stunning."

"That far, huh? Lily, I've had a chat with your old neighbour on Tiger Street—Valentina. She thinks she saw someone return to the house on the night your mother and Ellie vanished."

"Oh my God. Why didn't I know that before?"

He sighs. "It seems she did tell my uncle, but I can't find any record of it."

Anger races through me at hearing that. "Well, who could it have been? Mom and Ellie?"

"That's what I need to find out. Valentina didn't get a clear look. It was raining and, of course, very late at night."

"It's driving me crazy. Ever since you found Ellie's pendant in the house, I want to know how it got there."

"It's certainly throwing up a lot of puzzles."

"I have to tell you something."

"Oh yeah?"

"Iris and I found my mother's journal."

"Get out of town."

"I know—hard to believe."

He exhales heavily. "You're telling *me*. Where was it?"

"I... look, if you don't mind, I feel like I should hold back on that for now. You're the police, Van. There was someone who didn't have to help us, but they did, and—"

"Bennett."

"What?"

"Well, you said you were going there."

"Okay, true. Yes, we found it at Bennett's house."

"Lily, I'll come to you—tomorrow if I can—and get a copy of the whole thing."

"It's really personal stuff. From when she was growing up and all of that. It's probably not going to be helpful."

"Have you read it all?" he asks.

"Not yet. We only found it this morning. I think Iris and I need a little time before we share it with the police—with you. So far, it's been... raw."

"Okay, I understand. In that case, what I need you to do is to take a clear photo of every page and send it to secure online storage. And don't let anyone else know that you have it—no matter who. Are we clear?"

"Yeah, clear."

"Until we know who or what we're dealing with, we have to be careful. From my side of things, I'm taking care with what I let get out to the media." He takes an audible breath. "Lily, I've got to go now. I've got a pretty clear suspect for the body that was found on the riverbank. I'll be making an arrest within the next hour."

"Oh my gosh—yes, go!" I say.

"Talk soon."

After the call ends, I do exactly as he suggested—I go through and snap a photo of every page.

The mosquitoes are starting to sting, so I herd the kids onto the bus. They stretch out on the bunk beds with their phones and hand-held consoles.

Iris stirs and wakes. "Ugh, how long did I sleep?"

"As long as you needed to," I tell her.

"I need some air. Smells like cheese in here."

I laugh. "It's pasta. Saved some for you."

Iris has a bowl of the pasta, and then we head out for a walk.

"I copied the whole journal," I tell Iris, stopping to spray her and myself with insect repellent. "Got a photo of all the pages and sent it to the cloud."

"Good idea. I was too whacked to think of doing that."

"It was actually Van's idea."

"Ah. Hmmm. Van, huh?"

I cross my arms. "What's that smirk for?"

"You and Van seem to be getting kind of close. Lots of little conversations."

"It's all about the case. I mean, we need that, right? We don't want him letting it go just because we've gone away."

"Maybe, but it's all between you and him. If you know what I mean." She lifts her eyebrows.

"Let's just... keep walking."

"Did he say anything about the journal?" Iris asks.

"He said not to tell anyone we have it. Like, no one."

"Right. I'm in a slightly better mood after my sleep. Maybe we should keep reading it."

I stop and stare at her. "Really?"

She nods. "When I flicked through it back in Florence's campervan, it didn't seem very long. We should just do this in case there's something that could help with the case."

"Okay, let's do it. I've got it on my phone. I can read it from there."

We find a spot at the water's edge where we can sit—while still having the bus within our line of sight.

As I begin reading, I soon find that my mother's voice speaks inside my mind just like when Iris was reading it.

44

ELSA JORGENSON, 1997

THEY FOUND MY ELDEST BROTHER, Liam, in the apple orchard, hung by the neck on the same tree where Davey was buried.

I'd believed that Liam was a faithful member of the community, but I was wrong. Very wrong. He'd been suffering all along. He hadn't agreed with me getting married, but I hadn't guessed that. He'd been pushed into marriage himself.

With Liam and Davey gone, I only had three brothers left. All three went cold on me as if I'd caused Liam to do what he did.

Freddie found me sitting by the apple tree one day after that, sobbing. He thought it was because of Liam, and it was, but it was also everything.

I told him I hated my life with him, I hated going to bed with him, and I hated being a mother. To his credit, he listened. He threw away the leather ties and didn't even ask me for sex anymore. He got up to feed the baby at night when she cried. He went swimming with me in the river just like Davey used to.

For a while, life didn't seem as hopeless.

Then three months after Liam died, on a cold winter's morning, my father went out into the snow and shot himself.

The last thread that I had tying myself to the community snapped and broke.

I told Freddie I was leaving. He panicked and told the elders, but they didn't scare me anymore in the way they used to. They threatened to take my baby from me, and I looked them straight in their shocked faces and told them I was prepared to walk away without her.

I was at the end—the very end—of what I could take.

Freddie wouldn't have it. He said he'd move away with me if that was what it took to keep us together. I told him I wanted to move to the other side of the country, as far away from the community as I could get. California. Somewhere warm, where I could swim when I wanted. He promised me we could do that.

On the day we were leaving, Freddie's uncle offered us a house that he'd been left in a will. The trouble was, it was in Pennsylvania.

Freddie said we could stay there just a while until he got on his feet financially. It was true that we had no money between us.

I reluctantly agreed.

The house was half an hour's drive away from the community, which was something, at least. I tried to convince Mama to come with me, but she refused. I had to leave her behind.

The first time I walked inside the house, it'd been shut up for a long time. It was gloomy and smelled bad in places.

The first thing I did was to start a garden and plant maple trees out front. The house needed to look friendlier and not quite so imposing. I thought maybe I could make friends here. And do normal things.

And I did make a friend—my neighbour from a few doors down. Marcy. She had a baby daughter too. Marcy was eight years older than me, but then, as I was discovering, all the mothers around here were older than me. It wasn't common to be sixteen with a baby.

Marcy and I would sit out the front and chat while our babies played together on a rug. Iris was now six months old and starting to sit up by herself.

For the first time, I found myself enjoying my daughter's smiles, enjoying watching her roll about and play. The thought that I might have left her behind with the elders made me feel hollow. The concept of me being her mother finally seemed real.

Freddie and I began having little arguments. He wasn't used to me going out in public at all, especially not without him. The only thing he'd allow me to do was to go and get the groceries each week. I didn't drive, so I had to catch the bus in and then catch a taxi back with the food.

Two years went by like this, and I turned eighteen. It was Freddie who figured out I was pregnant again. He said I had a glow and that my stomach wasn't quite as flat. He was right. He was a lot happier about that than I was. Another baby meant a strain on the finances. I'd been looking forward to Iris going to school and me finding a job. And moving to California. I'd been dreaming about our new life there, raising Iris near the beach. But I was woefully undereducated about contraception, and now I was having another baby.

I returned home from grocery shopping one day to find Freddie and his uncle digging big holes in the basement. Freddie had a huge grin plastered on his face when he told me that I was going to get a pool, and he was getting a wine cellar.

I burst out crying.

Freddie asked me what was upsetting me. And I told him. I didn't want to stay in this house at all. We were supposed to be moving out of here soon—not wasting money on a pool and cellar. I didn't even understand why Freddie's uncle was okay with us putting these things in a basement of a house that he owned.

He said it was just for now and it wouldn't cost much because he and his uncle would be doing it themselves.

While Freddie continued to dig in the basement, I continued to renovate the house—putting up bright wallpaper and sanding down the wooden surfaces and staining them in beautiful burgundy colours.

The pool was finished in time for me to swim in it when my belly got huge.

The water was nice, but swimming didn't feel anything like it did in a river. I liked to be outside under the sky and listening to the birds and wind. But Freddie said that here, inside, none of the neighbours could spy on me while I was wearing my swimming outfits.

I went into labour while swimming alone one day in the basement. I could barely haul myself out of the pool. I expected Freddie to take me to the hospital. Instead, he arranged for my mother and a group of women from the community to come to the house.

I was terrified. I told them that last time, the doctors had said that because I'd had a C-section with my first child, I might need another one with a second. Because I might tear open.

But I was refused a hospital. Instead, my mother and the women prayed for me during the labour and helped me with my breathing. The pain became overpowering, but things thankfully progressed quicker and more easily than before. I gave birth in my bedroom, with the women standing around me.

I had another little girl.

Freddie relented and took me to the hospital for a check-up. I had to lie and say that the baby had come too quick to get any medical care. I was okay. And the baby was okay. She was two months early, though, and small.

I called her Lily. She was tiny and perfect.

Iris loved her on sight. It made my heart warm to see my two daughters together.

A month after Lily was born, Freddie said we needed to try again soon—for a boy. He said girls get married and join another household, whereas a boy would stick around and help him in his business. Freddie had already started up his own stonemasonry company.

I confided in my neighbour, Marcy. She drove me to a pregnancy-planning clinic, where they gave me some low-dose birth control pills.

I hid the pills from Freddie.

My body changed a lot after the second pregnancy and birth.

My belly was now soft, with stretchmarks on either side. My hips and thighs and breasts were rounder.

Freddie seemed to like my body more now. He said that finally, I looked like a real woman. With that came a deep and sometimes enraged jealousy.

He forbade me from talking to the neighbours—even the women because they had husbands. Marcy was the only neighbour that he allowed at our house. But then she moved away—her husband got a job in another city. And I was all alone again.

Life with my husband became like walking on eggshells. I never knew what would cause a bout of jealous rage to flare up.

One day, he returned home to find me out at the front of our long driveway, at the mailbox. I was chatting with the mailman—about nothing, really. I don't even remember the conversation. What I do remember is that Freddie marched me inside and then took me to a part of the house I'd only been in twice before. The wine cellar. I had no idea what he was about to do. All I knew was that he was simmering with rage. Why did he bring me down here? Was he about to accuse me of drinking his wine while he was at work? I never did that.

I was about to find out exactly what Freddie had in mind. He took a long length of rope from a corner, and he grabbed me and then wound the rope around me, tying me to one of the thick wooden posts.

I was stunned into silence. I was gasping for air, struggling to believe he would do such a thing.

When I found my voice, I began screaming at him—screaming that he couldn't do this to me, that it was crazy and wrong.

But he left me there like that.

It was night when he untied me. It was the strangest thing. He seemed excited and somehow different. It terrified me.

I ran straight upstairs to my girls. They were both asleep in their beds. Freddie had never taken care of the girls before by himself, but that night, he did.

After checking that the girls were safe, I quietly took my shoes from the downstairs cupboard, put them on, and walked out. I almost got all the way to the police station before Freddie came in his pickup truck and found me.

He pulled me off the street.

I began raging at him—yelling that he'd left our girls alone in the house.

Two police officers responded to my screams. One male and one female.

Freddie told them I'd recently had a baby and I was having a nervous breakdown. For some reason I'll never figure, they both believed him.

Humiliated, I had to climb into my husband's truck and return home with him. I didn't know what else to do. There was no one I could go to. And Iris and Lily were all by themselves in that big house, with an open fireplace and a pool and a high staircase.

I had to go back.

45

LILY JORGENSON

Rage heats my skin. I jump to my feet, not knowing where to put myself. For the first time in my life, I want to belt my father—punch him square in the face and demand to know how he could have done those things to my mother. "I don't know what to do with this. How can I ever go back to that house, knowing what happened there?"

Iris shakes her head, staring at the ocean. "You can't. Pack up your stuff and get out. He's a monster."

"What if...?" I jam my eyes shut.

"I know what you're going to say. I'm thinking it too. And it's not as if it hasn't crossed our minds many times before. Maybe it *was* our father who's responsible for what happened to our mother."

"I just... I didn't want to think he was capable of that."

"It was always strange—him coming out to Australia without telling anyone and then trying to track us down. Damned creepy. And then not letting us know he was here—even after Mom and Ellie went missing. I mean, we only found out because you saw him on the TV."

Angry tears wet my face. "It's hard, you know? In a situation like this, you end up with just one parent, and you desperately want to believe they weren't the culprit. You have to make a decision whether you're going to believe what they're saying... or not. And we were kids having to make that decision."

She pulls herself to her feet, gazing out to the ocean. "I never trusted him. I knew there was something strange going on. I'm older than you. I could tell that things were just weird at our house."

"Oh my God," I cry, "he kept buying her roses, remember? Red roses. In Mom's journal, she said the women spread red rose petals on her wedding bed, and she said she couldn't stand the sight of them after that."

"Ugh. You're right. Remember when Mom used to leave the roses to just... rot? I was forever throwing out bunches of slimy flowers that were rotting in their vases."

"I didn't know it was you who threw them away."

"Yeah, it was me. Sometimes, when we were walking home from school, I'd run ahead and throw out the flowers and then open up the curtains—so that you didn't have to walk into a horrible dark house where things were rotting."

"I had no idea you did that," I said.

"I kept trying to make things... normal. For you. Remember when I'd take you out of the house for walks when they started arguing? And when Mom was away for days, I'd make you and Dad dinner and then clean up and try to keep things going?"

"I guess I was in my own little world a lot."

"Yes, you were, Lily. You so were." With a sigh, she glances across the grounds to the bus. "Should we... keep reading?"

I nod, my chest tight and the breath shallow in my lungs.

46

ELSA JORGENSON, 1997

And so I swam.

Every day.

In my new pool.

Doing laps. Up and down. I'd try to change my state of mind. Because I felt murderous. I had fantasies of killing my husband and telling no one and then just continuing to live in the house with the girls. I was scaring myself.

And then, late at night, I would stay awake, thinking how I could gather up my children and flee. But I hit the same dead ends. I had no money of my own—not a cent. And I had nowhere to go.

Freddie noticed how down I was, and he thought he could make it better by us having date nights. He'd buy me dresses and makeup to wear, and he'd don a suit. But we never went out. It was always dinners at home, by candlelight. He'd cook the dinners and try to be romantic.

And then, at other times, he'd get into those strange moods in which he would call me every hour to ensure that I was at home where I was supposed to be. And he'd get it into his head that one of the male neighbours had an interest in me—and he'd get so wound up he couldn't calm himself.

If I did things like doing the gardening in a pair of shorts, he'd march me down to his wine cellar. I never knew quite what would set him off.

He installed mirrors in the cellar. So that I could see myself the whole time he had me tied up down there. He said I needed to understand who I was. That was his only explanation.

The times between all that would be fine. And it was so confusing to me. I could even manage to like my husband during those times. He'd play in the yard with the girls and make the garden look nice and watch movies with me on TV.

The time came for Iris to start school. He insisted I home-school her. I managed to convince him I'd be terrible at that. Walking Iris to school and picking her up was a joy—a place away from the house. I lied and told Freddie that the teacher said the children needed to do afternoon activities. He relented and said Iris could do one—only one—activity, but it needed to be something feminine. No sports.

I knew exactly what I'd put her into.

I'd heard about the local child pageants. I knew that the pageants required that the children travel all over the place—but Freddie didn't know that.

I thought I could find a way—a place—where I could leave Freddie and start again.

Iris loved the dance classes and the pageants. I thought she would. She was always dancing around the house. She had a natural sense of rhythm. When Lily started school, I put her in the pageants too.

I told Freddie I needed a car. I couldn't take the girls the places they needed to go without one. He agreed, and he taught me how to drive.

But along with the car and a little bit of newfound freedom came more restrictions. If I was home too late with the girls, my time in the cellar grew longer. Until it became a whole day. And then two days. Sometimes a week or more. He made Iris get Lily ready for school and walk her there and back. He'd bring me down dinner and sit with me and tell me that I needed to do better.

He'd lie to the girls and tell them I'd had to go away to a hospital for a while because I was sick.

It's hard to explain why I put up with this. It was like my brain chemistry had turned to some kind of toxic soup, flooding my brain and short-circuiting my emotions. I was flat... so, so flat. All the time.

I'd go into episodes where I could barely feel. I'd stand outside in the morning sun, waving Iris and Lily off as they went off to school, and I couldn't feel the sun on my skin, and I couldn't feel the love I knew I had for my daughters. I was just... numb.

I lost count of days. Days, hours, weeks... they meant nothing anymore.

Things got worse. Because the girls began to grow old enough to start questioning everything. I hated myself for allowing all of this to happen, for how I'd let Freddie control our lives.

The girls got so tall. Like flowers in bloom.

When Iris was small, I was her sun. But little by little, she began turning away from me. I felt her disgust. She saw me the way Freddie did. Weak, strange, and not capable of being a real mother, maybe not capable of even being a real person.

Lily was in her own world. She'd go along with anything and be happy. But that wasn't going to last.

That house, that life—it was all in darkness.

47

LILY JORGENSON

I turn to Iris, blowing out a breath that feels cold on my tongue. "She never actually went away to a clinic or a hospital. She was just... in our house. In the basement."

Iris stares at me with large eyes. "I should have realised what was going on. Why didn't I check the basement?"

"Because you didn't know to check it. Why would either of us do that? And we weren't allowed to go down to the pool when Mom was away."

Iris and I are locked in each other's gaze.

"No bloody wonder he didn't want us going down there!" Iris explodes.

"What did she even do down there for days... and weeks?"

"Lily, she was away for *three whole months* once."

My sister's words make my chest hurt, as if there are jagged pieces of glass embedded in there. An image of the wine cellar embeds in my mind—small and dark, with a tiny bathroom off to one side.

Iris draws her arms across her stomach. "She was sitting in that awful cellar for all that time. How did she even get through that?"

When Iris speaks again, she doesn't turn to look at me, and her voice sounds different. "Lily..."

"Yes?"

"He did it, didn't he? We have to admit to ourselves. Everyone was right. He killed our mother."

Words are stones in my mouth and throat. "I can't... I don't know."

"How could it be anyone else? He murdered her for leaving him. He never would have thought she'd get away from him. But she did."

"But... what about Ellie?"

"Ellie got in the way—that's all."

"I can't believe that he'd do that. Not to a little girl." I've never witnessed Dad treating a child in any cruel way. And I've always believed he loved us, in his own way. These new thoughts about him are torturing me.

"We need to get real about this," Iris says. "He was there. He arrived in Australia, and within days, Mom and Ellie went missing. What do you think the police are going to say once they read Mom's journal?"

"I just... don't want this to be real."

"We'll get through this. Together. We have to." She stares upward at the clear dark sky. "This is such a different story to the one I'd painted in my head. I always thought Mom must have wanted to be a dancer herself, so she was living that life through us—and resented us. But that wasn't it at all."

"I never knew you thought that."

"I guess I was trying to rationalise it in my mind."

We both look across the grounds to the bus as the door opens and Jake peeks his head outside. He must be wondering why our walk is taking so long. It's so like him to start worrying.

"We're going to have to leave it here for tonight," Iris says. "I don't know what kind of sleep we're going to have."

I nod. "If we do get to sleep, I think all we'll have is nightmares." We walk together to the bus.

As we predicted, Iris and I have a rough sleep. We're late to get moving in the morning. But the kids are happy to sleep in.

"Are you sure you're okay to drive?" I ask Iris as I make her a coffee.

"Believe me, I want to," she replies. "All I want to do is to drive and not think."

It's midmorning when we cross the border from the state of New South Wales to the state of Victoria. Again, the highway seems endless. Endless and featureless. I realise how much I must have slept when we did this trip with Mom, because I do not remember it being this long.

My thoughts are dark and confused and in a whirlwind. Pieces of my life fly back at me again and again, battering me. I'm hurt, bruised, and wanting refuge.

There are three messages from Van Dawson on my phone. But I can't bring myself to talk to him right now. I need my head straight.

I pretend to the kids that everything's okay. They deserve for this journey to be memorable—for all the right reasons.

Kaden announces that our next stop is the Ninety Mile Beach. I bring it up on the map on my tablet. It's a ribbon of sand barely wide enough for a road, with the ocean on one side and a narrow lake on the other. Inland from that is a set of massive lakes and bays. I remember it now.

I make a show of pasting in the old photos I have of the area into my scrapbook, even though my heart isn't in it right now. I can tell that every place we go has become so much more special to the kids because of these photographs. And they're getting to know their grandmother—who she was and what she was all about. Piper lingers on a photo of Mom walking on the sand with her arm around Iris, their hair blowing in the wind. I wonder if she's thinking about her relationship with her own mother.

After Iris has a well-earned rest at the Ninety Mile Beach, we head off to our next destination—Phillip Island. It's another four hours away.

The island ends up being tiny but packed with tourist attractions. There's a Grand Prix racing circuit, an outdoor dodgem car track, a chocolate factory, and a wildlife park.

We fit in as much as we can. I want the kids to have a good day—the best day of the trip. Because I don't know what tonight will bring. Anxiety makes my stomach tight. But I need to go through with this. Iris has got to tell me what she knows.

When night falls, we head down the shore with the other tourists, and we watch the fairy penguins waddle down to the water. It's a magical sight, and I'm glad Audrey wanted to do this. It's perfect. The island feels like a place far away from everywhere else—even though it isn't.

A storm moves in as the penguin display finishes. Lighting flashes are illuminating the sky in purple and indigo hues. We race back to the bus, which for the kids only seems to add to the adventure of the day.

After a few board games, the kids settle and head off to bed. It's not long before they're asleep. Jake even seems to have fallen asleep with a smile on his face. Which brings doubts back to me yet again. How can I go ahead and spoil this trip for Jake and Iris's kids?

But I can't imagine another time when I'll be in a closed environment like this with my sister. Here in the bus, she can't slam a phone down in my ear or walk away from me.

Through the window, I watch as lightning cracks above the ocean and rain breaks loose from the clouds.

I head to the other end of the bus, where Iris is relaxing at the table. Taking out my scrapbook, I make notes of all the things we did today. Keeping my head down, I get my breathing under control.

"The kids are certainly enjoying those old photos of yours," Iris remarks. "Makes me feel bad I've never shown them the albums."

I frown, raising my eyes to her. "I thought you said you'd thrown out the photos?"

"I know. But I actually didn't throw them out," she admits. "I still have them. In storage. I just... I just thought I'd never want to see them again." She rubs her neck wearily.

I draw air deep into my lungs, my skin prickling with tension. "Hey... you look like you could use some wine."

She raises her eyebrows. "You have wine?"

"I do. Your favourite red wine. At least, you said it was. On your Instagram."

"Whoa, that wine is expensive."

I make an awkward shrug. "Special occasion."

"Well, whip it out, little sister. Post-haste."

I bring out both bottles from the place I've been storing them since the beginning of the trip. My fingers are all thumbs as I pour us each a glass of wine. Iris doesn't seem to notice.

She leans her head back. "Despite everything—against the odds—we did this trip together, Lily. We made it happen. We even found Mom's journal."

Her warm tone is adding to my nerves. I've wanted to sit and talk with her like this forever. But now that it's finally happening, I'm about to do something that will break our newfound connection.

"We did make it all happen," I agree.

She watches the downpour dash against the windows, suddenly smiling. "Remember when it used to storm when we were in Mom's caravan? Drips would get inside, and it used to sound so loud I'd think the whole caravan was gonna collapse."

My laugh sounds brittle in my ears. "It was scary. Grace loved the storms. She said she understood them because her epilepsy sometimes felt just like electricity in her head."

Iris responds with a heavy sigh. "I remember. God, I still miss Grace so much." She drinks down the rest of her wine.

"Me too." I give her a smile. "Want a re-fill?"

On the table in front of me, my phone rings, making me jump. It's Van. His timing couldn't be worse.

"I'll text to say I'll call back later," I say.

Iris waves her hand. "No, answer it. What if he has an update on that stalker woman—Meredith?"

"Okay. I'll just be a minute. We need to polish off the rest of this bottle. And the next."

I press the answer button on my phone.

"Lily, is everything okay?" Van asks. "I tried to call earlier."

"Everything's okay with the trip." I glance at Iris. "There's some difficult stuff in our mother's journal."

"Sounds rough. I've got some good news. The photos from your mother's backpack are back. The expert was able to get them apart and restore them. She explained to me that what causes photographs to stick together is this sticky, gelatine-like emulsion layer. So, with the moisture after all those years, it was tricky. Luckily, your mother's backpack was fairly waterproof."

All thoughts about my plans for tonight fly from my mind. I've been anxious to see those pictures. I know that Mom and Grace were taking them right up until the last days.

"Oh my goodness, have you seen them?" I ask Van.

"I had a quick glance. I'm exhausted, to be honest. I've been in hours of questioning with the murder suspect."

"Oh. Did he confess?"

"No. He's not going to give it up that easy. He ended up wanting a lawyer, and I had to let him call one. I'll get him in court though. Hey, with the photos, I didn't immediately pick anything out as being important. If you and Iris pick up on anything, be sure to let me know, okay?"

"Photos are back," I whisper to Iris, then return to the phone call. "Okay, we will. We can't wait to see them."

"I'll send you a text once I get them uploaded into a secure location," he says. "The password is one I think you'll remember —rockpools."

My breath is taken for a moment by the password he'd decided on. *Rockpools.*

"Thank you," I breathe. "We'll be waiting by the phone."

48

WHILE IRIS AND I WAIT, we finish the wine and then start on the second bottle. I have to put aside my plans for now. We're about to view images of the past I thought were gone forever.

Within fifteen minutes, Van messages me again. He's got the photos all uploaded and ready to go. I push my phone back into my pocket, then switch on my computer tablet and click on the link that Van has emailed. A page of thumbnail images opens.

"Ready?" I ask my sister.

She inhales and nods. "Let's do this."

I enlarge the first set of thumbnails. Immediately, a wave of memories envelops me. There's our mother, standing in knee-deep water, her white sunhat on, the sun touching her shoulders. And Grace sitting with me on the shore, our feet in the water. And there's little Ellie in a yellow swimsuit, building a sandcastle.

Iris closes a hand around mine on the table. "Gosh, Ellie was so cute."

"Cute as a button. Do you ever wonder what she'd look like now? Who she'd be?"

"I admit I try not to think about it. Hurts too much."

"I get you. The pain never goes away."

Iris and I regard each other through wet eyes.

We continue through the images. There's Grace lying on a hammock, propped up with pillows, headphones on, and listening to her music on her iPod. And Iris and I racing along the shore, trying to beat each other.

Memories return that have dulled or even disappeared. It was Grace who took most of the photos. She was talented at it too—her depictions of small towns and landscapes are stunning. It's easy to tell she loved Mom—she took so many of her. The closeups she took of Mom are especially beautiful, with Mom smiling at the camera. There was so much light in her smile. I feel a sudden dig between my shoulder blades. Iris and I had taken our mother for granted, but Grace obviously hadn't.

The last ten or so photos are all of a campfire at some caravan park. Mom is cooking over the fire. Ellie, Iris, and I are wrapped up in beach towels beside her. It must have been Grace snapping the pictures.

"I didn't know Grace had taken all these," Iris says. "I mean, why did she? They're all the same. Well, time to wrap it up. Seeing the photos is amazing, but it's almost too much, you know? Too emotional."

"I know," I reply, but then I notice something odd. In every single photo, there is a boy somewhere in the background. He's watching us—standing in the bushland with a cigarette in his hand, like a stalker.

With a start, I realise that I saw him in a previous photo. I scroll back. Yes, there he is, in the street of some town we stopped at. He's leaning against a wall, again with a cigarette in his hand. I keep scrolling. There he is again, sitting on a motorbike. I find him again and again in the photos.

"Iris... do you see this? That guy. He's everywhere—look."

She examines the images. "Probably some kid on holidays, like us."

"No. These photos are taken over a couple of weeks. Why is he in so many damned shots? I think he was following us."

Iris pours herself another glass of wine. "You're grasping at straws, Lily. Time to pack it in and head off to bed. Been a long day. Want a glass of wine to help you sleep? There's enough for one glass left."

"Wait. No, it's a pattern. Grace must have realised that guy was following us, and she kept track of him. What the hell? He's in this photo too."

I point to a picture of teenagers standing around a campfire at a camping ground. I keep enlarging the image, trying to see the boy's face clearly. But my focus switches to that of a familiar girl.

I look up at Iris. "Oh my God, that girl there—that's *you*."

She yawns. "I remember hanging out with other kids at some places we stopped at. We were all teenagers looking for some fun."

Iris is wearing denim shorts and a type of white peasant blouse that was popular back then. I remember she liked to pretend she was a local at the places where we stayed—even sometimes pretending that Mom, Grace, Ellie, and I didn't exist. She could never have passed for a local, though. Not with her American accent. She stood out, too, with her dancer's body and her long waves of chestnut hair.

I quickly scroll to the next photo of the campfire, looking for the boy. There he is. And he's holding Iris's hand.

Iris takes a gulp of her wine. "Okay... he was my boyfriend."

My stomach flips. "Boyfriend? How? We weren't there that long."

"It happened quick. At that age, kids just... hook up."

"Why didn't you just say he was your boyfriend?"

"Because I didn't want to deal with it."

"Didn't want to deal with what?" I press.

"With you asking questions. I'm just tired, that's all."

I'm not ready to let this go. It's like I've picked up yet another piece of string, again with Iris not letting me see what's on the other end of it. "Why don't I know about him? Shouldn't I know?"

"Lily, can we let this go for tonight?"

"No. We can't. These photos were taken at the town we stayed at just before Mom and Ellie disappeared. Do you realise that?"

"What are you trying to say? He was just a teenage boy who liked me."

An image returns to me—one that's been rearing up in my mind over and over through the years. It's of me in the empty caravan, with Sergeant Mullard pounding on the door and then Iris running through the rain with her yellow rain jacket ovcr her head.

Suddenly, that image merges with the image of that boy and Iris holding hands at the campfire. My stomach lurches as I realise I'm right at the place I intended to be with Iris tonight. The only difference is that this is a backdoor route, and I already know the answer to the question I've wanted answered for so, so long.

I know where Iris was that night.

My voice sounds cold and steady in my ears as I put words to my thoughts. "That's where you went the night Mom disappeared, isn't it? You were with this boy."

She inhales a sharp breath. "Yes."

I feel as if I've just slipped into ice-cold water. "Oh my God."

"Lily... please don't make a big deal of it. It wasn't important. It doesn't matter."

She jumps to her feet, and I stand to face her. "Of course it matters. You swore until you were blue in the face you never went anywhere that night."

"Keep your voice down. You'll wake the kids."

"You never told the police about your boyfriend, did you?" I accuse.

"I was fifteen. How could I face Sergeant Mullard and tell him I'd just had sex for the first time that night? I couldn't do it."

"That's what you were doing? Having sex?"

"Yes. He... my boyfriend... he booked a caravan at the park we were at. I didn't know Mom wouldn't be back. I would never have left you alone if I'd known..."

I'm barely listening now. A thought has pushed in and is gathering ground. I scroll through the photos again, back and forth, looking for the image that shows the boy's face the best. I enlarge it, examining it closely.

Nausea rises in my stomach. I know who he is. He's much older now. Back then, his face was slimmer and smoother, with rounder eyes and longer hair.

I look up at Iris. "It's your husband. It's Gabe."

She retreats a few steps down the aisle and then returns, her hands pushed deep into her pockets. "Okay, yes. It's Gabe."

I swallow. "This is why you came back to Australia. Now it makes sense. You came back for him."

"I was in love. Stupidly, crazily in love."

"And you never said a word. Not one word about why you came back to Nautilus Bay."

"Lily, stop attacking me. After the past two days we've had with Mom's journal, this is cruel."

"Cruel? How about what you did to me? All this time, I thought you were keeping some secret about what happened to Mom that night, and I thought you were hiding it. I thought—"

"You thought I knew what happened to her?" Her face twists into a bitter expression as her eyes grow distant. Then she snaps back again, focusing on me. "Oh, wait a minute. Wait one damned minute. Is this why you agreed for me and the kids to come along on this trip? You thought you could get me to spill all my secrets?"

When I don't answer, Iris stares back at me for a moment, open-mouthed. Without another word, she marches a few steps to the door of the bus and opens it. I watch her head outside and make her way over the tufty grass between the bus and the shore, where she stands under a feeble light.

I close the door behind me and follow her. The rain is light now, but an offshore breeze blows it straight into my face and hair. The black ocean smashes the sand before us.

Drawing the hood of my jacket over my head, I approach Iris. "It's not fair for you to walk away. I didn't do any of this. It wasn't me keeping secrets."

She doesn't look in my direction. "I honestly thought you wanted to fix things between us. For us to become sisters again. But that wasn't it. Having me along on this trip of yours—it wasn't about finding the journal or finding Bennett, was it? It was about me. Finding out what I knew. Yeah, that's exactly what this was. Can't believe I didn't work that out before."

"I didn't ask you to come," I remind her. "But of course I've been hoping you'd tell me the truth." It's only a half-admission. She's already shaking her head before I finish talking.

"You're still the same old Lily. Still the same vindictive sister."

"Vindictive?" I gasp. "No. I've never been that."

She faces me with a caustic expression. "Yes, you were. You hounded me. For years. About where I was that night. And then when you were older, you kept demanding money for the private investigators that you wanted. More money, more money. Always more money. Well, I didn't have any more."

"I put in as much money as you did," I say defensively.

"Yes, you did. All given to you by your trust-fund boyfriend, Terence. But I was struggling. Gabe couldn't get a job, and I had trouble getting work myself. You know what small towns are like—it's who you know. And the private investigators didn't find anything useful. It was just a big money pit. It was like it was never going to end. You put so much guilt on me, like I wasn't doing enough. I ended up not wanting to live anymore. And I told you that."

I cross my arms around my body. "You didn't put it in quite those terms. I thought you were feeling guilty about what you knew and weren't saying."

"Well, you don't know anything. You don't know the first thing about my life."

"You shut me out of your life."

"Is it any wonder?"

I soften my tone. "Look, I'm sorry. I didn't realise you'd been going through those kinds of struggles."

"Keep your sorries. I don't need them."

I inhale the cold, wet air. My thoughts are racing away from me, spinning across the black sky. One thought stops dead in front of me, and it makes my breath stall. "Iris... this means that your boyfriend was in the same area as Mom and Ellie the night they went missing."

Her lower jaw quivers. "He was with me."

"No. Not the whole time. You were with me when Mom left. You were there for a while after she left, too."

"What are you trying to say? That Gabe was involved?"

I hear a crack in her voice and catch her fearful expression as she turns from me again. It's just enough to give me a glimpse through the window. She's lying to me again.

"Oh God," I breathe. "He had a part in it, didn't he?"

She stands rigid against the wind, her hair whipping around her shoulders. "Gabe's a good man. A great father. You need to leave this alone."

"Iris, what on earth did he do? You have to tell me."

But she starts walking away. Her body soon merges with the dark.

I stride after her. "Come back to the bus. Don't go off by yourself."

She quickens her pace, and now I can't see her at all.

"Iris," I call, going after her. "Iris!"

Wind howls along the shore, a salty spray stinging my face. I stop, unsure what to do. Panic ripples through me. I've completely lost sight of the bus now. I can't leave the kids alone—not at night.

I decide to return to the kids. As I run, I take out my phone and call Iris. She doesn't answer. When I near the bus, I hear her phone's ringtone. She's left it behind.

My phone rings before I can put it away again. It's Van. I can't think why he's calling again, but I answer it, desperate now to lean on the support of his voice.

"Are you outside?" he asks. "It's damned noisy."

"Yes. It's windy and rainy, and we're right on the ocean here."

"You're outside at night—in the wind and rain?"

"I'll explain what's happening soon."

"Is everything okay?"

"Things are messy. Super messy. But look, no one's hurt or anything. I'll work it out."

"Is it something to do with the photos?" he asks.

"Yes, it is. Van, is that why you're calling? To ask how things went with them?"

"No, something else. But it can wait. Let me know when things are more settled, okay?"

"That sounds like you have news."

"I do."

The tone in his voice scares me. "What is it?"

"It doesn't seem like the right time, Lily."

"Whatever it is, just tell me."

He exhales. "Okay. It involves the Nautilus Bay house and who's been renting it out."

"Oh God. You found out? Who is it?" I ask.

There's a short silence before he says, "I need to speak with Iris."

"Iris? She's gone for a walk. But she's left her phone in the bus, so you can't—"

I break off as I realise why the tone in his voice is so dire. This time, the silence stretches out so far it feels like a whole different world, and I'm trapped inside it.

49

I SIT INSIDE THE BUS, waiting for Iris, terrified about the revelations coming to light but even more terrified Iris won't come back. I keep telling myself it's an irrational fear. This is a tiny island. Where can she go? But still, a ball of anxiety grows in my stomach. She's had at least a bottle and a half of wine, and she could decide to do something stupid, like going off for a swim in the ocean. All the years that I imagined having a confrontation with my sister about her secret, I never anticipated anything like this.

All the while, the kids sleep, oblivious. I'm grateful for that, at least.

Forty-three minutes and fifteen seconds go by before I see my sister walk out of the night. I open the bus door for her. She's soaked to the skin.

Handing her a towel, I keep my voice as low and mild as I can manage. "Have a hot shower."

She doesn't meet my eyes. "I'll wake the kids."

"They're not babies. Doesn't matter."

"I don't want them to know... anything," she says.

"So, let's not say another word tonight."

She nods and heads along the aisle to the bathroom cubicle.

When morning comes, it's Iris who's up first, making breakfast for the kids. I had a fitful sleep and ended up sleeping late. When I catch sight of my sister's face, I know she's barely slept too.

After the kids have gone outside to play, Iris turns to face me. "There's an urgent call from Van Dawson on my phone. Do you know anything about that?"

"I didn't tell him anything about last night, if that's what you're asking."

"Okay. So, it's about something else, then?"

I nod.

Her eyes narrow. "And you know what that is, don't you?"

I exhale. "Yes, I do."

"What is it?"

"He didn't tell me much. He wanted to talk with you."

"About what, exactly?"

Sweat prickles me under my tee-shirt as I begin clearing crumbs from the table. "About who was renting out Mom's house."

"What? Van knows who's been doing that?"

I nod again, avoiding her gaze.

"Why does he want to talk to me?" she demands.

I can't manage to keep a harsh tone out of my voice when I reply. "I don't know. Why don't you call him back?"

Holding me in a direct, deliberate gaze, she calls Van and then puts her phone on speaker.

"Hello, Van," she says. "You have something to talk to me about?"

A short sigh comes down the line. "Yeah, I do. Is this a good time to talk? You might want some privacy for this call."

"Yes, it'll be private. Go ahead." She casts a wary look at me.

"Okay," Van responds. "As part of my investigations, I've discovered a company that's handling the rental of the Tiger Street house. The money heads to an overseas bank account and then into a trust. From the trust, an amount is paid each month to an account back in Australia. That account, is, well—it's in your name, Iris."

I stare at my sister, horror bleaching my mind. I'm shaking my head, my hand clamped over my mouth.

"That's not possible," Iris whispers in a strained voice. "What the hell? That's not true."

"I'm afraid it is," Van says. "I've had the details checked and rechecked about six times over. I wanted to be sure."

"This is wrong," she tells him. "I did not know Mom even owned that house. So how the hell could I be receiving money from it?"

"The transit paths of the money are correct," Van says, keeping his tone even. "But I don't know the why or how of it. So I wanted to talk with you, and we can figure out what's going on."

"There's nothing to figure out. I'm telling you I don't get any money from the house," Iris insists.

"Iris," he says, "I've got an interview to conduct in another few minutes—with a witness who saw something involving the recent murder victim here. My apologies. We'll get back to this at a later point, okay?"

The call ends.

Iris is seething, throwing her hands up in the air. "I have no freaking idea what's going on here." She turns to me. "I bet you think that your wonderful Detective Dawson has solved the case. It's all me. I did everything. I confess!"

I drop into a bench seat at the table, ignoring her sarcastic words. I'm confused and terrified by these new directions. If Iris isn't behind this, then it must be Gabe. Gabe with his perfect smile and Hollywood looks.

Inhaling a long breath, Iris sits opposite me. "You don't actually believe I'd rent Mom's house out all these years, do you?"

"No. I don't think you'd do that." In truth, I don't know what I believe. I'm footless, the ground disappearing beneath me.

"It can't be Gabe... can it?" she says in a broken voice. "I mean... he wouldn't..."

I muster strength for what I'm about to say next. "Maybe you should tell me what you didn't tell me last night. About Gabe."

A tear wets her face. "I don't think I can do that."

"Iris, I deserve to know."

"You'll judge me."

"I can't promise anything."

"Fine. You do you, Lily." She glances out the window of the bus and watches the kids for a moment then focuses on her hands as she rests them on the table. "The reason Gabe was following us around when he was a teenager wasn't because of me. He was paid to do it."

"He was paid to follow us?" I breathe.

"Yes."

"God. Who was paying him? Our dad?"

"No."

"Then who?" I ask.

"This is going to come as a shock, but—"

"Just tell me."

She takes a breath. "Sergeant Mullard."

I recoil from her answer. "That's ridiculous. How can it be him?"

"The sergeant told Gabe he'd been contacted by the child protection agency—about Mom and what she was doing with us. We weren't in school, and Mom had no proper plan for our schooling. So he wanted to keep an eye on where we were and what we were doing."

"Why would a damned police sergeant use a teenager to do his dirty work?" I snap.

"The sergeant said it was to keep the agency off his back—because the police didn't have the time or resources to keep a watch on our mother."

"Iris, what if the sergeant hurt our mother and Ellie? What if it was him?"

"No, it can't have been him. He was at the station when Mom and Ellie went missing. With two other officers."

"How do you know that?" I ask.

"Because I spoke to those officers about that night. Constables Lea Ramirez and Nik Parata. Believe me, I checked. Mullard was there in his office that night."

I shake my head. "All of this... going on behind my back. Why didn't you tell the other detectives that were involved in the case—about Sergeant Mullard?"

"I had reasons."

"What possible reasons could you have?"

"Gabe and the sergeant... they already knew each other. Gabe... well, Gabe kind of had a history."

I cast a hard stare at her. "What do you mean?"

Her features pinch. "Gabe had a rough time growing up. He'd carried out a few petty crimes as a young teenager. He'd been in and out of juvenile detention centres. He was about to go in once again. But then Sergeant Mullard offered him a deal."

"Tracking our mother?" I ask.

"Yes."

"Wow."

"You can't blame Gabe. He was a kid. In an impossible situation."

"Iris, our mother and Ellie vanished that night. And your loyalty was to your boyfriend?"

"I had to keep it secret. If I'd told, the only person it would have hurt is Gabe. The sergeant told him that he'd deny it if Gabe told anyone. No one would have believed that Sergeant Mullard had a deal with a kid who'd been in and out of juvie. And a couple of months after that night, Gabe turned eighteen. If Sergeant Mullard chose to stop protecting him, Gabe would have gone to an adult jail."

"You've got to tell the police what happened back then."

"I can't. I've told you why. Can't you at least try to understand? It could ruin Gabe's business... ruin our whole family."

"No. No, I can't understand."

"Lily... please."

"What do you want from me? To say it's okay? It's not okay. Not one part of it. Your husband had a deal with the sergeant? And you've been getting money from the rental of Mom's house? It's damned horrific—that's what it is. I don't even know who you are."

"You know what? If you believe I've been making money out of Mom's house, well, go ahead and take the whole house. It's yours."

"As if that would make up for what you've done. As if. Ever since that night, I've known you were hiding something. It's haunted me this whole time."

"Haunted you? You know, you had me fooled. Like I said before, I actually thought you'd want this trip to be a kind of reunion, as sisters. How stupid was I, huh? I even got the kids involved in this charade."

That feels like a slap across the face. It's Iris who had been enacting a charade all these years, pretending to know nothing. "Look, I'm going to call the bus hire guy. We can't continue with this."

"Are you going to tell Van what I told you?" she says in a small voice.

"I can't deal with you right now, Iris."

"Sure. Whatever. Call the guy. This trip is done."

I head outside, my arms trembling. I need to get away on my own, to straighten out the maelstrom in my head.

But as I walk away, Jake catches up to me. "What's goin' on?" he asks.

"Something to do with a mix-up with the bus hire," I lie, attempting to keep my voice light. "We've got to give the bus back."

"What? No. That's not fair."

"I know. But there's nothing we can do about it."

"We can get another bus, right?" he asks.

"'Fraid not, buddy. But we had a great trip already, right? We did a lot of fun stuff."

"Kaden and I were going to go looking for crabs. And Aunt Iris said she'd take us fishing. If we can't get a bus, can't we get somethin' else? Like, two campervans?"

I answer too sharply. "No, sorry."

Jake frowns at me. "It's stupid, but I was starting to feel like the bus was my home. It's been like the trip you and Aunt Iris had with *your* mom. But, like, without any of the bad stuff."

I realise with a start that Jake is in a situation more similar to Iris and mine than he knows. On the surface, it's all sunshine and endless beaches, but dark things are brewing underneath.

"Hey... we can do something like this again at some point." As the words leave my tongue, I know full well that nothing like this is ever going to happen again. Instantly, I feel bad about that. I know what it's like to live with hope for years, only to come to the point where I realise my hopes were fantasy.

I can't make a call to the bus hire company with Jake in tow. I'll wait to make that call a little later. I return to the bus with Jake. Iris and I go through the motions of packing the kids some lunch and then taking them down to the beach for a last-chance swim.

Jake, Kaden, and Piper head straight out on the waves on body-boards. Audrey paddles though the shallow water at the shoreline, looking lost.

I approach her. "It'll be no time before your arm's all healed and you can get out there again in the water too."

Audrey shrugs. "I'm not big on bodyboarding. The waves scare me."

"Oh. Well, I'm not big on waves, either, to be honest. I prefer calm water."

"It's a big shame we have to go home, Aunty Lily."

I sigh. "I know. I wish things were different."

"Will you come back in the next school holidays? Every school holiday? You have to. I want to see you and Jake again."

I manage a bright smile. "Jake has different school holidays to you. But we'll see you again for sure."

"Good. It's been really special. Even with this stupid broken arm."

"It's been special for Jake and me too." I hate the thought of disappointing Audrey, but there's nothing I can do to change things.

Iris approaches, the sun bright on her red hair. She takes her daughter's hand. "Come on, Audrey, don't bother your aunt Lily."

"She's not bothering me," I say pointedly.

Audrey looks from her mother to me. "I'm gonna go look for shells." She trudges away in the water and then off to the sand.

"Great," Iris says to me. "I get to look like the bad guy yet again."

"Well, you didn't have to say that to Audrey."

"You know full well what's going to happen next. We're not going to see each other again. So stop trying to be nice to my kids. It's just going to hurt them more."

"Don't turn this back on me." I gaze out at the ocean. "What do you want to do about Mom's journal?"

"What do you mean?"

"I mean, physically. Do we have copies made for both of us and then keep the original in a safe deposit box at a bank?"

"You keep it," she says tiredly. "I've got more than enough going on in my own life. I don't think I can bear hearing one more thing about what Mom went through with our dad. It's too much."

"But you might want to have the journal later on."

"Maybe. But you keep it for now. It's just a shame she didn't start a new journal for the trip she took us on. She's left us in the dark yet again." Iris gives a harsh sigh. "Good one, Mom. All you've given us are more questions and no answers."

I don't have a reply. I feel the same way. Completely in the dark. And Iris has done the same thing to me—left me in the dark all this time.

She and I share this small patch of beach for the moment, but we may as well be in different countries again. There's an invisible line drawn in the sand.

I stride away, back to where we have the towels and beach umbrellas set up. I take out my phone from my beach bag, open my set of photos of the journal's pages, and begin reading again.

50

ELSA JORGENSON, 1997

My daughters were doing well at school, and they were doing well at the pageants too—especially Iris. She lived for them.

All the time I was spending away from the house, doing things with the girls and driving my own car—it did make me feel a little braver.

But at the same time, Freddie didn't like my newfound sense of independence. I started to resist being sent down to the cellar. He didn't like that, either.

He sold my car. Just like that.

He began saying we never should have moved away from the community and that it might be time to go back. To raise the girls right, to serve God properly.

I was so scared that he would actually do it. And at any moment, his uncle could decide to take his house back or sell it from under our feet.

There was no security in my life.

I fell into yet another deep depression.

Freddie spoke to my mother, and between them, they decided I should go back to the community for a week. I told him there was no way in hell I'd do that. It was then they decided I could go away somewhere else—but only if I went with my mother.

I agreed and asked to go to Miami—or even California.

My mother chose Cape Cod. Her choice felt deliberate. At this time of year, Cape Cod was too cold for swimming.

But I went with her because it was all that was on offer.

Our accommodation had a beach view. I sat outside our house on the wooden beach chairs with Mama and stared at the ocean that I couldn't swim in. She barely spoke to me. It was like she was a stranger and not someone I'd grown up with.

I'm going to try to remember the conversations I had at that time as best I can. Because I want to remember. I want a record. I'm going to have to explain all this to my girls one day. My memories might not be accurate down to the last word, but they'll be close.

"Mama, how are you?" I asked her. "I mean, how are things really?"

"Things are just fine," she answered in her thick, curt Southern accent. "I have everything I need."

"And my brothers—how are they doing?"

"All married. I've got three grandkiddies now. Besides your daughters, of course."

"Freddie told me about my brothers' children."

"Why don't you come see them?" she asked.

"I can't. I can't go back there."

"Suit yourself."

"Mama, can I tell you something?"

"You're going to tell me anyway, so go ahead."

"I don't want to be with Freddie anymore."

She sighed, adjusting her dress. "He's your husband, Elsa."

"I don't love him."

"You don't always get love in a marriage."

"You had that with Dad."

"Well, your father's long gone. What you need to do is practice gratitude. Look at all the things you have, not the things you don't."

Resentment welled in my chest. "Can't you just listen to me?

Just this one time? Don't tell me what's wrong with me. I hear enough of that from Freddie."

"You could come back to the community and see one of the elders. That'd be the right way—"

"No. I don't want to talk to them. I told you, I'm never going back there."

She was silent, but I could see her slowly shaking her head in my peripheral vision.

A tear ran from my left eye and down my cheek. "Mama, was it all too much for you? Is that why you're like this? I know it was a lot. Davey died and then Liam. And then Dad soon after that. But... I need you. I have no one. Do you understand? I need help."

"Elsa, I rebelled against the church's teaching. That's when everything went bad."

"No. That's not why things went bad."

"I don't want to talk about this. It's all in the past."

"They've brainwashed you. You don't feel anything anymore, do you? That's how you get through. That's how you go on." A sense of loneliness and despair washed through me. "I'm going for a walk."

"Once again, suit yourself."

I got up and headed along the shore. The cold air slapped my cheeks and made my eyes water.

I walked past couples and families who were chattering and laughing—all of them having better lives than me. I continued all the way to the docks. A line of yachts was moored here, but there was no one around.

Throwing caution to the Atlantic wind, I pulled off my dress and waded into the ocean. The ice-cold water took my breath, but I kept pushing forward.

A voice carried on the wind. "I wouldn't."

I jerked my head around, looking for the owner of the voice. I found him standing on the deck of a yacht. I couldn't pick the accent. South African or English, maybe? But still, his casual drawl had me confused.

"Wouldn't what?" I called back.

"Go into that water," he said.

"Well, I would. The cold doesn't scare me."

He shrugged. "Suit yourself. But try not to make too much of a mess."

"What do you mean by making a mess?" I tossed back at him.

"If the sharks getcha," he explained. "I saw a couple of fins earlier." His lazy, generous grin matched the tone of his voice.

I returned the smile. "Where are you from?"

"About six weeks across the Pacific."

"You're a long way from home."

He angled his head around, pointing out to sea. "That's my home."

"Must be nice to have a yacht."

"Why don't you come on board? You can dry off with a towel. You look frozen."

I looked back at my dress, which was in a pile on the sand.

"Don't worry. I won't look," he said.

I really was cold. I decided to take him up on his offer.

Like a gentleman, he came down to the shore to hand me the towel and didn't make me walk in my underwear all the way to him.

"Come up on deck," he said.

Wrapping myself in the large blue-and-white-striped towel, I followed him.

"Better?" he asked.

I nodded. "Very much."

His hair was a sandy kind of blond, bleached by the sun. Freckles and blue eyes and short, fair eyelashes. His eyebrows and beard stubble were dark. His teeth were square and flat as he smiled.

"Like what you see?" he said.

I was stumped for words because I really had been staring. I wouldn't have blamed him for thinking I was a bored housewife on vacation.

"If you want to get dressed, you can go into the cabin," he told me, indicating a set of steps.

"Thanks." I made a quick exit to below deck and got my dress back on.

When I returned, he was standing in the doorway, winding up a length of rope. My focus all went to the rope. I'd made a huge mistake. All men were like Freddie. I stumbled backward on the steps, crying out.

He ran down and caught me, which only made things worse. A struggle followed.

"Whoa, lady," he said, taking his hands from my shoulders, "you don't think I'm gonna hurt ya, do you? I was just coiling some marine rope—for storage. I do that all the time."

"I—I have to go."

"Of course." He walked back up the stairs, giving me room.

I walked back onto the deck, my breaths tight and shallow. The rope was lying on the floor where the man had dropped it, coiled neatly.

"I'm sorry," I told him. "I didn't mean to be so... damned stupid."

"I should have stopped to think."

"No, not your fault at all."

I don't know exactly how it happened, but I started telling him about Freddie, about what he'd been doing to me. It came out in a desperate rush—things I'd kept locked inside for so long.

The man wanted to take me to the police right there and then.

But I couldn't do it.

He tried hard to understand, but I'm not sure if he did—not completely.

We talked for the next hour. And he listened. That was a gift I never thought I'd find on this trip away with my mother. Because she certainly wasn't going to listen to me.

He helped me make a plan. In a few days, he'd drive to my house and take my daughters and me to a women's refuge.

I was desperate enough to agree.

But that night, I changed my mind. Freddie would only come after me. And he'd bring his uncle and others from the community. And then he'd force me to go back there.

In terror, I stole out of the house that Mama and I were renting and ran along the shore, all the way back to the yacht.

At first, I didn't think the man was there. But then I found him sleeping downstairs in his bed.

I told him I couldn't carry out his plan. I couldn't do it.

I know he was trying his best to understand me, with his hair askew and his voice husky with sleep.

I hadn't intended to, but I kissed him.

The kiss felt nothing like it did when I was with Freddie.

The kissing turned into more, until our clothes were on the floor, and we were in the bed together.

Afterward, his arms were around me, and I was warm beside him, and the seagulls were cawing in the sky, and the ocean was slapping against pylons outside.

That's what I remember most.

51

LILY JORGENSON

Oh, *Mom. Oh, my goodness.*

I can't believe you did that. I mean, I'm glad that you did, and I'm glad it was good. But I can't help but be a little shocked. And it was practically right under your mother's nose. I wasn't expecting to read that at all. I'm astonished and awed and full of wonder.

Was this the turning point for my mother deciding to leave Dad?

I wish Mom had put the date on her journal entries. I try to think back to how old I was when Mom went to Cape Cod. I remember it being an unusual thing, because Mom never went away with Grandma.

I was very young then. So this happened years before she packed up and left Dad. It can't have been the turning point. Still, I'd like to believe that the event on the yacht gave her strength.

My heart broke in two when I read the conversation between her and her mother. Grandma seemed like a shell—anything that had once been alive inside her had shrivelled up and died.

Was her encounter with the yacht guy the thing that Mom wrote about in her poem as being her biggest mistake? Did she feel like sleeping with him was a sin?

I want to share this with Iris. But now there's a wall between us again, and this time, the wall is staying.

A thought about Mom races into my mind—a thought so dark my chest starts squeezing. What if Dad found out about what Mom did with that guy on the yacht?

Oh God. He did. He must have. That would explain the three months Mom spent in the mental health clinic—the months that I now knew were spent in the wine cellar of our family home. Grandma came to stay with Iris and me then. Did she have any clue about what her daughter's husband was doing to her?

The brief cheer I felt about Mom finding a little happiness is dashed.

I don't want to read what comes next. Iris had the right idea—to put this journal away. Reading it is far too painful. I don't think I can bear to read about the time Mom spent in the cellar and how desperate she must have felt. I've seen that cellar a thousand times since I've been living in that house with my father. He doesn't keep anything in it anymore—not even wine. It's just a bare, featureless room. But I'm chilled now, thinking about what happened there.

But I find myself compelled to read it. For so long, my mother felt like she had no one to turn to, no one to talk to. The least I can do, as her daughter, is to read her words and know her pain.

Steeling myself, I open the journal at the place I stopped reading and turn the page.

52

ELSA JORGENSON, 1997

THE NEXT TIME I saw him, I realised I didn't know his name. And he told me. *Elias*.

It immediately seemed the most beautiful name in the entire world.

I saw him every single day that I was in Cape Cod. I'd tell my mother I was heading out for a walk, and off I'd go. It was wonderful. It was also very, very wrong.

I was as sinful as those women Freddie was scornful of—the kind of woman who threw her family away to commit adultery with some random man. Freddie constantly reminded me that he was a good family man—he'd stuck with us through thick and thin, and all he expected of me was to be a good wife and mother.

Of course, I never could be good enough in Freddie's eyes.

Every day on the yacht, Elias made me feel as if I was good, as if I had worth.

And then the vacation was over, and I had to say goodbye. He gave me his number and made me promise to keep in touch. But I knew I couldn't do that.

I went home to Freddie and the girls.

Freddie knew I was different now, but he couldn't figure out why. I know he questioned my mother about it. And he questioned me at length.

I never told him a single thing.

And then something happened that turned my world on its head.

I became ill.

It began with a bout of food poisoning. When I stayed sick for weeks, I began to suspect that Freddie was poisoning my food and trying to kill me slowly.

But then I realised what was happening. I was pregnant.

I'd been careful to use my contraceptive pill for years. Except that on the trip away to Cape Cod, I hadn't taken them with me.

I visited the clinic and asked for a pregnancy test. I needed to be sure. The doctor felt my belly above the pubic bone and estimated that I was three months gone. An ultrasound confirmed it. I'd still been menstruating, but she said that happened sometimes.

On my return home, I did something that I thought I was never going to do. I took out Elias's number from the place I had it hidden in the cellar.

"Didn't think you'd ever call," was the first thing he said.

"That's how it was meant to go, right?" I replied lightly. "When you gave me your number, you were being nice. You didn't try to make plans or anything. I—"

"Elsa. You're married. That's why."

"Of course. Forgive me."

"I'd love to see you again. But I'm afraid I'm not in the USA anymore. More's the pity." His voice somehow sounded like a cloudless summer day.

"I just... need to talk to you," I explained. "Are you busy?"

"My parents are having a birthday dinner for me, so I have to go in a few minutes. But I'm listening."

"Happy birthday."

"Thank you."

"I don't know how to say this, so I'll come straight out with it. I've been to the doctor. I'm expecting a baby."

"Say what?"

"It's yours."

"You know that for a fact?" he asked.

"I do."

"Okay. Give me a minute."

The line went quiet, and my stomach flipped, and I desperately wanted to run to the bathroom to vomit.

"Sorry," he said finally, "your news threw me. What do you want to do?"

"I honestly don't know."

"Don't take this the wrong way... but I have something to tell you too. I didn't own that yacht. I'm just a skipper. After you left Cape Cod, I sailed straight down to Panama and then across the South Pacific to Australia, where I delivered the yacht to its owner."

"Do you think I'd mind that you're a skipper?"

"I just didn't want to lead you astray."

"Oh... I get it. You think I'm pursuing you because I thought you had money?"

"Just wanted you to know."

I was about to hang up. How could he think that about me?

But he spoke again. "Elsa, we'll figure it out. Let's start with this—what do you want from me?"

"I don't want money."

"I'm not saying you do."

"I just wanted to tell you—that's all. I guess that's stupid, because—"

"Hang on. You thought you'd just tell me, and that'd be it?" he asked.

"I guess so, yes."

"Have you told your husband you're pregnant?"

"Not yet."

"Listen, I'll call you back after I do this dinner thing with my parents."

I thought he'd never call me back again. But he did.

Over the next month, it became a regular thing. During the day, we'd chat on the phone. I fell in love with him. Deeply in love.

The situation was hopeless, though. He knew it, and I knew it.

Freddie would never let me go.

53

LILY JORGENSON

My mind races in all directions. Mom was pregnant by this guy? Actually pregnant?

I don't understand this at all. Why didn't Iris and I know this? I'd never seen her pregnant in my life. Something must have happened to the baby.

From across the beach, Iris is looking at me strangely.

Breathing in deep, I walk across the sand to her. "Iris, I need to tell you what I just read."

She shakes her head. "I don't need those mental pictures in my head. No thanks."

"Then I'll ask you a question. Did you ever see Mom pregnant—sometime after she went to Cape Cod with Grandma?"

"Pregnant? What? Lily, that never happened."

"I never saw her with a big belly either. But she was pregnant after she went to Cape Cod."

"She was? God. She must have lost the baby. Why didn't she tell us that?"

"Maybe because the baby wasn't Dad's."

She stares at me with a shocked expression. "It wasn't Dad's? Then... whose was it?"

I hold out my phone. "Read it for yourself."

"It's obvious that you know. Just tell me."

"Some guy with a yacht she met in Cape Cod. A skipper."

"I don't believe it," she says.

"It's what she wrote." I tell Iris everything Mom said.

Iris exhales, expanding her shoulders and looking out to the horizon. "Okay, forget what I said earlier. I can't let you read all this stuff on your own. I mean, there was a baby involved. It sounds like something really terrible happened from this point on. I'm going to guess Dad found out."

"That thought crossed my mind too. I feel like throwing up."

From out on the water, Jake waves. I wave back and force a smile.

Iris takes the phone from me and starts reading it out loud.

54

ELSA JORGENSON, 1997

My belly was growing bigger every day. I knew I had to tell Freddie. And I'd have to pretend it was his. I hated every inch of myself already.

The only thing I had was my secret phone calls. And they were going to end soon. I couldn't keep talking to Elias like this.

But Elias wasn't prepared to end it. He surprised me with a wild proposal. He said I should leave Freddie and take Iris and Lily with me—take them right out of America. And we'd make a new, happy family.

But Freddie would never let me take Iris and Lily out of the country. They didn't even have passports—and neither did I. I could get a passport for myself without Freddie knowing, but I couldn't get them for the girls without his signature.

Again, Elias tried to convince me to go to the police. But I knew exactly what would happen if I did.

Elias came up with another plan. I needed to get proof of what Freddie was doing to me.

Once I had that proof, I'd tell him I needed to go away to a retreat—for the sake of my physical and mental health. But I'd actually go away to have the baby. With the baby born in the new country, I'd start the process for the baby and me to gain Australian citizenships. Once the baby was born, we'd fly to Pennsylvania and collect Iris and Lily.

Freddie couldn't stop us then, because we could show the police what he'd been doing to me.

It seemed like such a plan couldn't possibly work. Too much could go wrong.

But I put my trust in Elias.

I left Pennsylvania when I was just past six months pregnant. My belly wasn't showing much yet.

When I arrived at the airport, Elias was waiting for me. I hadn't seen his face in all that time, since Cape Cod. In my eyes, he was a miracle.

I wanted to meet his parents, but he was hesitant. He said his mother would have trouble accepting a woman who was currently married with two daughters. He wanted to wait until I was divorced from my husband.

He had a little apartment about an hour away from where his parents lived. It was perfect—our own place, with a distant glimpse of the sea. That was all I needed. That tiny patch of blue. Elias would hold me while we gazed out at that view together. We swam together in the mornings before he went to work. And we walked together at sunset when he came home. He told me he'd take me sailing in the future. We'd go across the South Pacific, stopping at Fiji and Bora Bora and the Galapagos Islands.

I soaked it all in. It was blissful. I never knew life could be like this.

Every day had a beauty to it. I couldn't wait to raise my baby in this new world. And I couldn't wait to bring Iris and Lily into it. The rest of my life seemed like it could be this shiny, perfect thing.

God hadn't condemned me to a life without love, after all.

55

LILY JORGENSON

Iris twists around to me. "Oh God. The baby is Ellie."

I gasp. "What? How?"

"Wake up. That has to be why Mom dragged us all the way to Australia. Because her baby was there."

"We don't know that. I was assuming Mom lost the baby—in a miscarriage or..." Snatching the phone from Iris, I try to scroll to the next pages. But there's nothing more.

"Did you photocopy all the pages?" Iris asks.

"Yes, all of them. Why would she do that—just end it there?"

"Maybe she only wanted to write it to the part where everything was good with her and Elias," Iris suggests. "And maybe she left it with Florence for safekeeping because she was scared we'd find it."

I nod, then gasp as a thought rushes at me. "God, if the baby was Ellie... that means the father is the Lowood's son. Was his name Elias? I can't remember."

"You're right," Iris breathes. "I remember Mrs Lowood calling him Eli once or twice. And think about it—Ellie might have been named after him. Maybe Mom too. Elsa and Elias. Matches with Ellie."

"This is crazy. Ellie was our mother's own biological daughter?"

Iris nods. "It fits. Everything fits."

"You're right. It does fit. I'm just... shocked out of my skin."

"Me too."

"But... wouldn't it have been on her birth certificate that our mother was Ellie's mother?"

"I don't know." Iris lets out a slow breath. "Let's figure out as much as we can. So, if Ellie is the baby, then Mom made a decision to leave her behind with the grandparents—the Lowoods. But... why would she do that?"

"Maybe because Elias died?" I suggest, uncertain. "The Lowoods said he died—a fishing-trawler accident. Without Elias, Mom might have thought she couldn't survive financially."

Iris nods. "Sounds right. My question is—did the Lowoods even know about Mom back then? It doesn't sound like they did. So... after Elias died, did Mom have the baby all on her own? And then she dropped her off at the Lowoods' house in secret?"

"Oh God, just imagine." My stomach clenches. "I think I know what Mom's big, blinding mistake was. It was leaving Ellie behind."

"That has to be it," Iris says. "And then she tried to fix her mistake by returning to Australia—to Ellie."

"You know what I just thought of? Mom mentioned mirrors in her poem. And there were mirrors down there in the wine cellar."

My sister makes a low sound from between her teeth. "I thought the mirrors were there for Dad to show off his damned wine collection. Mom must have been sitting there hour after hour, staring at herself. She was the stranger she wrote about."

I wonder to myself if it became like an out-of-body experience for her. In my mind's eye, I can see her down there in that small room, waiting, watching the woman who was tied up there. Herself. What would that do to you, to spend days and weeks feeling as if you were outside your own body?

"She must have somehow gotten some film of what he did," I muse. "With a camcorder or something. I mean, she had no money, but with Elias helping her, she might have been able to buy one."

"Yeah," Iris replies. "And you know what? It'd explain why Dad stood aside and let us go. He might have had no choice. It could have been that or go to jail. But... maybe he couldn't let her go in the end. He came to Australia and went looking for her."

The two of us stand in silence as water washes over our feet. The horror of those thoughts and mental images are too much.

Iris's eyes are red when she turns to me. "Lily, do you think Mom might have just... gone completely around the bend because of all that happened? And the night she went missing, she just took Ellie and left?"

"If her mind snapped... maybe. But people get better. She wouldn't just stay away from us like that. And what's the connection with Sergeant Mullard? I mean, what does he know? Why was he paying Gabe to track our mother? I don't believe that child protection was involved—do you?"

"I don't know. It kind of made sense to me. Mom was just so... scattered. She kept dragging us around from place to place, on a whim."

"But none of it was a whim. We know that now, right? We know why she brought us to Australia. We know why she left Nautilus Bay. And we know why she left the farm. She had good reasons. Damned good reasons."

Iris raises her tear-stained face to the sky. "Okay, yes. It's hard for me. I've seen her one way for so long—it's hard to see her in another light."

"So... what now?"

"I don't know. I wish I did."

"I guess we tell Van what we've found out, for a start?"

Her mouth firms into a straight line. "I'm not sure about that. We'd have to include telling him about Sergeant Mullard—and that's his uncle."

"Mullard isn't in the police force anymore. He doesn't outrank Van or anything."

"You don't understand. Everyone in Nautilus still sees him as the one in charge. And he still throws his weight around as if he is. People still call him Sarge, and I'm not kidding about that. They do. I think he still has a bit of control over Van too."

Iris and I eye each other through the tense air between us. I'm not sure what to think or believe or trust.

I practically jump as phone messages sound on both our phones at once.

The messages are from Van: *Just looking through the set of photographs again. I noted something possibly suspicious. There's a teen boy I need to ask you about.*

"He's noticed Gabe in the photos," Iris whispers. "It's only a matter of time before he realises who he is. Lily, I'm scared to tell him about the sergeant. It feels like a long row of dominoes is set up and ready to fall. If the sergeant did something wrong, he's going to try to cover it up. Whatever it is, I'm pretty certain he'll try to kick it to Gabe, who could get blamed for something he didn't do. Something serious. This has been hanging over Gabe's head and mine ever since Mom vanished."

"Iris..."

She holds up the palms of her hands to me. "Can I ask for one thing—just one thing? Give me some time. I need to talk to my husband. I have to tell him what's going on. We've got to get prepared." She glances across the water at the kids. "Please, Lily."

Swallowing, I nod. She's got her family to think about. But she can't delay this for long.

I pick up my phone as she walks away to call Gabe. I've got my own call to make.

56

"Potters Village Florist," the woman answers.

"Hi. My name is Lily. I came in to talk to you about a week ago. About your friend Merry Higgins."

"Merry wasn't my—"

"I think she was. When I came into your shop, I told you her name was Meredith. And you called her Merry."

"I don't have time right now for this."

"Do you know who I am?" I ask.

"Yes... you're the girl whose mother has been missing for years. I looked you up when you left your card."

"Then you know how important this is. The police have reopened the investigation. They'll be talking to you soon. But if you talk with me, they might not have to."

"Someone already called—a Detective Dawson from Nautilus Bay. Said he'd be coming to town next week."

I soften my tone. "I didn't know he'd already contacted you. Please... just talk to me."

I sit and wait, holding my breath. I'm desperate to know how Meredith Higgins fits into the picture. Why was she hanging around our mother's house when we lived in Nautilus Bay? I recall the

Polaroid Mom took of Meredith outside our kitchen window at night. She'd looked so damned creepy—like a ghost. Why was she there? What did she want from us?

"I saw an article about Merry in the news," the woman finally says, her voice cracking. "She doesn't deserve to have those bad things said about her."

"Then tell me about her."

"It's Merry's private business. Not for the whole world to know."

"The police are going to find out all about her soon. Would you rather the world hears the story from you or from people who didn't care about her?"

She sighs. "Look, okay. I'll tell you..."

"Thank you." I remind myself to stay calm, be kind. This woman doesn't have to talk to me, and I need her to tell me all she knows.

"So... we grew up on the same street," she begins. "We were good friends. Right here in Potters Village. But Merry had a troubled home life. She got into drugs when she was a young teenager, and then she ran away when she was sixteen. Next thing I knew, she was in Surfers Paradise, supporting her drugs habit any way she could. You know, sex work and that. It was so sad. I'd catch up with her sometimes and try to help her. But she didn't want help. And then she told me she was pregnant."

"Poor girl," I say.

"Exactly. I didn't see her for months. Then she came to me, crying her eyes out. She said she'd had the baby, but it was taken away from her. She was deemed unfit. But then she cleaned herself up and got the baby back and looked after her. But when her daughter was older, Merry slipped back into the drugs. And her daughter was taken away again. This time for good."

"Could I have her daughter's name? I'd like to talk with her."

"I'm afraid you can't. Her daughter died," she says.

"Oh no..."

"Merry was heartbroken when that happened. That's when she came back to live in Potters Village."

"What a tragic life."

"Very. But she wasn't a bad person. She just made... very bad decisions. I take flowers to her grave every month. She deserves that much. I paid for the plaque on her grave too."

"You were a good friend," I say encouragingly.

"I tried to be."

"Can I ask you something? You said you saw the articles about Meredith in the media recently. So, you know that she was stalking my family when we lived in Nautilus Bay. We don't know why. She hung around our house at night, and—" I stop dead as I realise something. "Oh gosh, she was Grace's mother, wasn't she?"

"Yes. She was. She loved Grace with all her heart."

"Grace used to stay over at our house in Nautilus all the time. Do I guess right that Meredith wanted my mother to let her take Grace? And my mother would have told her no."

"In your mother's defence, anyone seeing Merry at that time would have told her no. She was barely capable of looking after herself, let alone her daughter."

Thoughts spin through my head. "So, Merry would have been angry with my mother—hated her, even?"

"Yes. She was furious with her. But please don't read too much into this. Merry didn't hurt your mother. She wouldn't have done that. She wasn't violent."

"But she might have wanted some kind of retribution," I say.

"Look, you don't know Merry. Despite her failings, she was a pacifist. She let people run over the top of her. Please don't—"

"Tell me, did she say anything about my mother and Ellie Lowood—anything at all?"

"Not long after Grace died, Merry started rambling about Ellie. She said that Ellie called Grace on the phone."

I drop to my knees, straight onto the sand. "Ellie spoke to Grace? In what year?"

"It would have been the year Grace died—2004."

"In 2004?" My voice sounds raspy in my ears.

"Yes. Merry said your mother took Ellie to the faraway."

"The faraway? What in the world?"

"Faraway fields. That's what she called it. Like I said, a complete ramble. Paranoid raving. Merry wasn't well. She'd lost everything. And then, of course, she died of a drug overdose. I was the one who found her."

My throat has gone completely dry. "I'm sorry about Merry. So sorry. Thank you. Thank you so much."

I have to end the call because I can no longer breathe.

57

When Iris walks up to me, she's crying again. "Gabe said that it's time. He said to tell Van everything. Do you want to do it, or should I?"

I don't answer her—I can't. My head is busy constructing a crazy three-dimensional puzzle box with a dozen moving pieces, and I'm trying to force all those pieces to lock together.

Iris sits on the sand beside me, hugging her knees. "Gabe admitted everything else too. He said it wasn't an affair he was having—not totally. Just that a friendship with the wife of one of his friends got a bit too close. He knows it was wrong, but he said he didn't realise what was happening because there was no sex involved. Thank God for that. He said—"

"Iris, we can't talk with Van Dawson right now."

"What? Why? I thought you'd want that."

"I just talked with the florist from Potters Village—you know the one I told you I spoke with before?"

"Yes..."

"She did know Meredith Higgins. She was her best friend once. Meredith was Grace's mother."

"Our Grace?" Iris asks.

"Yes."

"That doesn't make sense. You sure she wasn't just making that up?"

"If she's lying, she's damned good at it. I need you to prepare yourself for what she said next."

Iris silently nods.

I exhale a shallow breath. "Grace told Meredith that Ellie contacted her—years after she went missing. In 2004."

Her mouth drops open. "Meredith told her that?"

"Yes. The only other thing Meredith said was that Mom took Ellie to a place called faraway fields. The florist said Meredith was rambling."

Iris shakes her head. "Yeah, that sounds like a complete and utter ramble. I guess it does add up that Meredith was Grace's mother. It'd also mean that Merry and Elias were together at one point. And maybe she hated our mother because she knew that Elias was in love with her."

"I wonder. Sounds like it could fit. Elias had Grace with Meredith but there was never any kind of relationship. And then our mother came along and got pregnant to Elias with Ellie. Meredith might have been furious about that."

"Yes," Iris says. "Mrs Lowood was always vague about the mothers of Grace and Ellie. I assumed the mothers had both dumped their daughters on her after Elias died. But I'm obviously wrong about that. Grace told us she hadn't seen or spoken to her mother for years, but maybe they were in contact sometime after Ellie went missing. But as much as I'd love to believe that Ellie really spoke to her sister, it can't be true. Grace would have told the police."

"I want to believe it... so much."

"I know. But faraway fields is not a place that exists. It's fantasy." Iris pulls a grim face and then takes out her phone and conducts a search online. "Okay, so there are a few places around the world with that name—mostly holiday houses."

I sound stupidly hopeful as I say, "Maybe not now, but what about years ago, back in 2004?"

Iris searches again. "There was a place called Faraway Fields in Tasmania. Some kind of hippie commune. It's now a winery."

"If I have my geography right, Tasmania is the island state off the bottom of Australia, right?"

She nods. "But it's nowhere near Nautilus Bay. It's—let me look it up. It's fifteen hundred miles away from there. And it's cold—freezing in winter. Mom would not have taken Ellie there."

"What's the winery called?"

"Valeria Vineyard."

I twist around so that I can see Iris's phone screen too. She finds the website of Valeria Vineyard and then swipes through the pages. There are lots of images of picturesque sunlit rows of grapevines. And happy workers. One image is of an older woman and a girl standing together in the vineyard. The photo was taken in late afternoon, and the features of the pair are hazy.

But there's something about the girl's expression—the way she's screwing up her face when she smiles and the way one of her eyes has narrowed. Touching the screen, I enlarge the faces. The woman is definitely not Mom. But the girl—the girl looks so much like Ellie that I can't take my eyes off her.

"I think we just found our Ellie," Iris says softly.

58

IRIS and I make a crazy plan. We're not going home. We're going to Tasmania—with all the kids in tow. We don't know what we're going to find there. It's probably just wishful thinking that this girl is Ellie.

For now—just for now—I'm choosing to put everything Iris told me on the backburner. I always knew she was keeping a secret, but I never believed that she herself had hurt our mother or Ellie. Not directly. And now that I know what she did, dark thoughts about Quincy Mullard and Gabe DeCarlo are on my mind—as well as everything I now know about Meredith Higgins. But I'm putting it all in a box and screwing the lid down tight until this trip is done.

I make a frantic call to the *Spirit of Tasmania*—a ship capable of taking our bus across the sea. The operator tells me they can take buses but not at short notice.

Iris and I then jump onto a travel website to book plane tickets. It's going to cost a bomb to get us all on a flight. But there's no other choice. Within minutes, we've got the tickets sorted. Iris then makes a call to Mr Ackerley to inform him we need to arrange for the bus to be picked up.

The kids are jubilant but mystified at the change of plans.

We can't tell Van Dawson—not yet. Because I know he'll tell us to hold back and wait for him to investigate. I'm terrified that if the police get involved, Ellie might run—and Mom, too, if she's there. Whatever was making them hide all these years might have them running and hiding again.

It's a two-hour drive from Phillip Island to Melbourne's Tullamarine Airport. The bus is picked up six at night. Iris and I have already packed up the sporting gear in boxes, ready to be sent back to Iris's house by truck.

We only just make our flight, racing into the airport like mad people. It takes just over an hour from there to cross the Bass Strait. And then we're there in the capital—Hobart.

I feel breathless, waves of anxiety and anticipation running down my back.

"Wait with the kids," I tell Iris, inhaling a gulp of air. "I'll go grab a hire car. And this time, I'm driving."

She gives me a direct look. "Take a moment to breathe, Lily. We don't know what we're going to find or if this is even real. We've got to accept whatever comes our way."

I nod, but I'm not really listening. I dash to the service desk and choose the only six-seater vehicle they have available.

As we drive away, Iris taps the address into the GPS. The vineyard is on the coast, in a place called the Freycinet Peninsula. I'm dismayed to discover that's a whole two-and-a-half-hour drive from here.

"Tasmania looked kind of small on the map," I tell Iris. "The vineyard is ages away."

Kaden pipes up. "It just looks small because of the size of the mainland, Aunty Lily."

"Why are we going to a vineyard?" Audrey asks. "Kids can't drink wine."

"In some countries they can," Piper says in a self-assured tone. "They're allowed to have a glass with dinner. It's normal."

"Well, that may be so," Iris says wryly. "But don't go thinking this trip is a kiddie wine festival. We're here for the scenery. And...

yes, maybe Aunt Lily and I will have a well-deserved glass of wine or two."

"You and Aunty Lily made up, didn't you?" Piper says pointedly.

"What do you mean?" Iris asks her daughter.

"You two were fighting," Piper says.

I brush a hand in the air. "No, we weren't fighting."

"I know what fighting looks like, Aunty Lily," Piper replies.

"We had a disagreement—that's all," Iris insists. "We're okay now."

I nod in agreement as I steer the car around a corner.

"Good," Piper says. "I know I had a hard time of it at first. But it's been fun. I don't want you and Aunty Lily to not see each other again for years."

"That's not going to happen," Iris says in a tight tone.

Everyone goes quiet after that. When I glance in the rearview mirror, I can see my son's eyes. I didn't think he noticed the recent tension between Iris and me, but now I can tell that he did. His look of fear is unmistakable.

The kids eventually drift off to sleep. So does Iris. It feels as if the scenery is all mine to enjoy—and it's beautiful. So very green and natural.

It's super late when we arrive at our rental house. The house is cabin style and right next to the vineyard. We stopped for pizza on the way, and everyone seems happy just to crawl into bed.

All through the night, I keep waking. My mind just won't rest. Just before dawn, I steal out to the kitchen to make myself a coffee. I need a few minutes of solitude before this day begins, so I head outside, perch on a chair, and watch the first light blink over the horizon.

Iris steps from the house and comes to join me. "Did you sleep?"

"No. You?"

She shakes her head.

I drink the last drop of coffee. "What time do you think Valeria opens up for business?"

"No idea. Maybe we could go have a look around."

"What—just barge straight onto private property?" I ask.

"We can just pretend to be blundering tourists. If we're questioned, you should answer, Lily. You can be a clueless American on your annual vacation."

"Yeah, great."

"Look, the worst they can do is tell us to leave."

I rise from my chair. "Fine. I'll just sit here and stress otherwise. Let's go find out what we came here to find out."

The morning brightens as we walk together along the road. A vineyard spreads out to our right. I'm surprised to see a couple of people already at work, both women.

Iris and I try to slip inside the gate unnoticed, but one of the women turns and sees us. She heads to the gate, dropping a pair of pruning shears into the pocket of her apron.

"Hi," I begin, "we're renting the Airbnb cottage just a little down the road—"

"Yes," she interrupts in a friendly voice. "I know the one. It belongs to a friend of mine—Donna. Hi, I'm Carla, the owner of this vineyard." She looks like the older woman from the photograph I saw on the website—just aged a few years. She's perhaps in her sixties.

"Hi. Could I... uh, could I ask that my sister and I have a little wander through your vineyard?" I ask her. "We've never visited one before."

A frown replaces her smile. "I'm afraid we're not running any tours at the moment."

"Oh, I just meant a quick walk. We'll be back later today—to buy some of your wine. I'm sure it's wonderful."

"Uh, well, of course—go ahead. Just exit by the same gates. We'll be open to the public at ten."

"Thank you," I tell her as Iris and I walk in.

"Nicely done," Iris whispers.

We head together down an aisle between the grapevines. The air holds an earthy, vaguely fruity scent. The vineyard is larger than it looked from the outside. We make a few wrong turns, realising we've lost sight of where the other woman was.

Iris and I round another aisle.

And there she is. A full-figured young woman in denim overalls, wearing the same thick work apron the other woman had. She's crouching as she tends the grapes, fixing wire. Her hat covers most of her face.

Iris and I exchange tense glances, and then we walk up the aisle side by side. The woman looks up with a smile, shielding her eyes from the morning sun with her arm. "Taking a look through Valeria?"

"Yes," I answer. "I think we might have even seen a picture of you on the website."

"The one of Mum and me? Oh, that's old," she says flippantly.

"She's your mother?" Iris seems to struggle to keep a disappointed tone from her voice.

The woman nods. "Carla Valeria."

A sinking sensation floods my body. She can't be Ellie.

It's then that she pulls herself to her feet and we can see her face clearly. I know, without a doubt, who she is. I know those round cheeks, the pointed chin, the shape of her eyes. With the sun's glare now out of her face, she looks from Iris to me. Her jaw goes slack.

"You know us, don't you?" I say in the gentlest voice I can manage.

She shakes her head, backing up a step. "I'm sorry, I don't know who you are. I think you should go."

At a loss, I turn to Iris.

Iris reaches for my hand, squeezes it, and then turns to the young woman. "In 1998, a family travelled the east and southern coasts of Australia in a car towing a caravan. That family was Elsa Jorgenson and her daughters, Iris and Lily—as well as two sisters named Grace and Ellie Lowood. You're Ellie Lowood... aren't you?"

She shakes her head again, firmly this time, but a tear runs from her eye.

59

Iris and I sit inside a cottage at the edge of Valeria Vineyard. It belongs to Tina Valeria—the woman who used to be called Ellie Lowood. The blonde curls she had as a child are now short and dark. Her baby teeth have been replaced by the teeth of an adult. Dark eyebrows and eyelashes have grown in over colouring that was once fair. Her adult body is large and curvy.

Everything about her seems like a miracle, and I keep pinching myself. She's actually here—right in front of me. I want to hug her and hold her, but so far, she's kept her distance.

She sits opposite Iris and me at the table, eyes down, picking a loose thread from her shirt sleeve. "How did you find me?"

"When you were about nine years old," I say softly, "you tried calling your sister, Grace, didn't you?"

She hesitates then nods. "I was confused about who I was. I had so many questions. But I didn't get to talk to Grace."

"Who did you speak to?" Iris asks in a confused tone.

Ellie twists the thread around her finger. "I spoke to the woman I thought was my grandmother. But she didn't believe me. She told me it was cruel and evil to prank people who are grieving."

Iris glances at me. "Grace must have overheard the call." She then turns her attention back to Ellie. "We need to know... about our mother. Where is she? What happened?"

Ellie's breathing quickens, and she hunches her shoulders as if in pain. "I don't know."

"How long since you last saw her?" Iris presses.

"I haven't seen her since... since I was little. I'm sorry... I don't know any more than that," Ellie answers.

Her response crushes me. I don't know what I was hoping for—for my mother to materialise here at the vineyard?

"It's okay, Tina," I tell her. "Please don't be sorry. You were just a little girl. I can't tell you how much we've missed you. Every day for twenty-four years. Can you tell us about your life? How did you come to live here at the vineyard?"

With a deep frown, Ellie slowly nods. "I've always lived here. I mean, after I was adopted. I have no clear memories of my life before then. It's completely hazy."

"But you remember us?" I ask.

She nods again. "When I saw your faces, I remembered. It was a shock... like something from a dream was suddenly real."

I take my computer tablet from my bag and open the photographs that Van sent. I show her a picture of a four-year-old Ellie making a sandcastle at the beach. "This is how we remember you. You were such a bright, creative child. You made the most intricate sandcastles—you'd even make moats with crocodiles. And you drew us the most wonderful pictures."

Ellie stares at the picture. "That's me?"

I nod. "That's you." Next, I begin scrolling through the pictures, showing her images of all of us. When it comes to a picture of Mom, Ellie flinches and turns away.

Switching off the computer, I catch Iris's eye.

Iris licks her lips nervously, threading her fingers together on the table. "When you called your grandmother, you said you were in the process of questioning who you were. Did you try to call anyone else —the police, even?"

"A few times over the years, I started to call the police," Ellie replies, "but I stopped myself every time. It's hard to explain. I'd have such terrible panic attacks. And the more I'd think about my past, the more the nightmares would come back..."

"Nightmares?" I gently prompt.

She exhales. "I had nightmares for many years. I needed help to get past them. My mother took me to see someone. A hypnotherapist, I think. She took the terror out of the nightmares."

Iris bluntly asks what I'm thinking. "Could the nightmares have been real?"

Ellie's reaction is immediate. She looks for all the world like someone who's about to flee. And I'm terrified she'll do just that. Irrationally, I imagine she'll disappear into thin air, and we won't ever find her again.

"Tina," I say, "did you ever wonder who your parents were before you were adopted?"

She nods, her eyes still large and fearful. "I've thought about them, of course."

"Did you ever try to find out more?" I add.

"I know who my father must have been," she tells me. "His name was Elias Lowood. He died when he was quite young. He had two daughters. Grace and me. I read an article that said Elias had an ongoing casual relationship with a woman who'd gotten pregnant by him twice. And the woman kept dumping the children on Elias's parents. I guess I didn't care about finding out who my mother was after reading that. Elias didn't sound like a great guy, either."

"You can't believe everything you read," Iris says quietly.

Ellie shoots Iris a questioning look.

"You know who I see when I look at you?" I ask Ellie carefully.

She frowns. "Who?"

"I see a little of Elias Lowood," I reply, "and a lot of my mother."

Her jaw wobbles, and she shakes her head. "Why would you say that? Why would I look like your mother?"

"You have her face," Iris says.

"You're not making any sense." Ellie thrusts her hands into the pockets of her overalls. "I have to go."

"Just a minute," Iris says. "If we were to show you the photo of our mother again, I think you'd see the likeness."

Ellie's expression goes distant. "She said... she said I was hers. But that can't be right."

"Who?" Iris asks quickly. "Our mother?"

Ellie nods, swallowing.

I watch Ellie' face carefully. "When did she say that?"

"In the nightmares," Ellie answers.

I hold my breath. "Does that mean you remember them?"

"Yes," Ellie answers. "Parts. I thought I imagined your mother telling me I was hers. I thought I imagined all of it. I don't understand what's going on."

"Would you tell it to us?" I plead.

Ellie levels her gaze at me. "It could not have happened in the way I used to dream it, okay? It's all wrong. Trust me when I tell you this—you do not want to hear it."

"Yes, we do," I say. "It doesn't have to be right or true. Just tell us what your dreams were."

Ellie lays curled hands on the table. "Okay. All right. You're here. I'll tell you." She draws a long breath before she begins. "I remember rain. A rainy night. I'm in a car with Grace, who is in the front seat. I don't know where or why, but we're parked somewhere in the dark. Your mother is outside the car. I climb into the front seat, onto Grace's lap. I get restless, and Grace sings me a song. I don't remember what the song was. And then I'm looking to see where your mother is. I can see another woman walking up..."

"Who?" Iris whispers.

"My grandmother," Ellie answers.

Iris and I stare at each other. Ellie was right about her dream being an imagining. Mrs Lowood was in hospital when Ellie and Mom went missing. It could not have been her.

"I jump out of the car and run to Grandma," Ellie continues, squeezing her eyes shut. "Grace calls me back. But I don't listen. Grandma is yelling at your mother, saying, 'She belongs to us, not you. Not you, Elsa.' Your mother sees me, and she takes my hand.

She tells me she's my mother and she loves me. I don't remember what happens next. But in my dream... your mother is suddenly on the ground in the grass... and Grandma... Grandma has a rock in her hand. And when I look at your mother, there's blood on her forehead, but the rain washes it away. And she... she doesn't close her eyes... even though the rain is coming down on her face. And I know... I know she's dead."

It feels as if all the oxygen is sucked from the room. I'm trembling, and I can't draw a breath. The images in my head are so dark that I rush outside to be in the sun and under the sky.

60

Iris and Ellie step outside and come to stand beside me. I'm sobbing, and I can't make myself stop.

"I warned you," Ellie says in a lost voice. "It's the worst kind of nightmare."

"We need to find out if Mrs Lowood could have left the hospital that night," Iris says grimly.

"She was very sick, wasn't she?" Ellie says. "She'd had a stroke?"

"Yes, a stroke." I wipe my wet face with my hands. "But if this is the way it happened, I don't understand how Mom went running down the road with Ellie, leaving Grace behind in the car..."

Iris seems to understand. "Lily, what if it wasn't Mom chasing Ellie along the road—what if it was Mrs Lowood? Maybe she wasn't as sick as she made out?"

I'm shocked as Ellie nods, bowing her head. "In my nightmare, Mrs Lowood is like a monster. Trying to grab me. Just all hands, grabbing and grabbing. But she can't get me. And I think she'll do to me what she did to your mother. And then I'm running—just, like, through a black sky. Everything is black. And she's coming after me, calling my name. I'm wet and soaked to the skin, but I can't stop running. Because she'll catch me. That's all I can remember. I'm sorry... I'm so, so sorry..."

I lock eyes with Iris. I can tell that Iris thinks what Ellie is telling us is real and true. I don't want it to be. With every fibre of my body, I don't want it to be.

In my peripheral vision, I notice that someone is walking down the vineyard aisle. It's Carla Valeria.

She throws a suspicious look in the direction of Iris and me. "I thought you two had left. Tina, is everything okay?"

"Everything's okay, Mum," Ellie answers.

"You've been crying," Carla states as she nears us. "You've all been crying. What on earth is going on?"

"Mum..." Ellie ventures. "I think these two women might be my sisters."

Carla gasps, shrinking back. "I think you'd all better come into the house."

"Just a minute," Iris says. "I want to call my eldest and check on the kids—he's thirteen, but still..."

Nodding, Carla catches her breath and gazes at Ellie with trepidation in her eyes.

Ten minutes later, we're sitting in Carla's farmhouse-style kitchen. I'm at a loss to speak, and it's Iris who comes to the rescue, leading the questions. I think I know why Iris is steadier than me. She has long thought our mother was dead. But I'd kept a candle burning in the dark. That flame has just been cruelly extinguished, and my chest feels hollowed out and burned.

Carla puts a glass of wine in front of each of us and then sits at the large round table. "It's our finest aged red. I think we need this right now."

Iris sips her wine. "Mrs Valeria—"

"Carla," the woman tells her.

"Carla," Iris corrects, "you haven't told us how it happened that Ellie—Tina—turned up here at your vineyard."

With a finger, Carla traces the gold rim of her wine glass. "As you found out, this place used to be called Faraway Fields. Some people thought of it as a commune. I guess that's fair. We had a lot of idealistic people here who thought we could form our own little society. I was one of them. Anyway, some foreign backpackers came to us one night. They'd come to help build a project—a mudbrick house. It wasn't unusual for us to get backpackers dropping in. People do that, you know—travel around the world to help with sustainable projects. Of course, we had to house and feed them and teach them all we knew about how to live off-grid."

Ellie stares at Carla. I'm guessing it's the first time she's heard this story.

Carla bites the side of her bottom lip, frowning. "The backpackers were a couple who looked about eighteen. They had a little girl with them, a tiny blonde girl with dirt in her hair and scratches all over her body—and dark red lines all the way around her neck. I was horrified. This little tot had been tortured. I couldn't get any information out of the tourists—they didn't speak English, and they were high as kites. I later found them injecting meth, and I threw them out. We didn't accept any hard drug users at Faraway. I wouldn't let them take the girl—but they seemed happy to leave her, anyway."

"Mum," Ellie says in a hushed tone. "Who were they? What did they do to me?"

Carla's eyes fill with pain. "I don't know. You didn't speak for the first months you were here with me—barely for the first year."

Iris crosses her arms. "That's shocking. Those people tortured her? Why didn't you go to the police?"

"Because I was terrified they'd give her back to her parents," Carla explains in a thin voice. "You hear stories all the time where the child is forced to go back to abusive parents, and the next thing you know, the poor child is dead."

"But... didn't you hear about us?" Iris presses. "I mean, in the news? It was big news back then. Didn't you hear that a woman and a little girl were missing? All you had to do was look at a photo of Ellie on the TV or in a newspaper, and you'd have known it was her."

"We didn't have televisions or newspapers at Faraway Fields. That was the whole idea of it," Carla responds. "I did hear a snippet of news—second-hand—at a bakery in town. About an American family going missing. I didn't know the details, but I didn't think it could have anything to do with two backpackers who didn't know English, and their little girl. And that happened all the way up in Queensland. I mean to say, that's so far from here. Two thousand miles or whatever. Honestly, I didn't connect the two."

"So, you just... kept her?" Iris asks incredulously. "How did you manage to adopt her?"

Carla's chin dimples as she draws her mouth down. "We home-schooled the children at Faraway. I used to be a teacher—it wasn't a problem. And Tina wasn't the first child here in Faraway not to have a birth certificate. But I did register her in the name of Valeria when she was eight. I'd already given her a first name. She didn't tell me hers when she arrived here—I told you, she wasn't speaking at all."

My throat feels dry as paper, and I take a gulp of wine. "I think I might know how Tina got the lines around her neck."

Iris, Ellie, and Carla look across to me.

"If I'm right," I say, trying to picture the scene in my head, "then the tourists didn't hurt her. Tina, you said your grandmother was trying to grab you? But it was raining hard, and she couldn't keep hold of you. I'm thinking that she did get hold of your necklace, but in your struggle to get away, the chain cut into your neck. And then it broke in your grandmother's hand. After you ran away, you went to hide in the woods. We know that because there was a witness—a man named Jared Keller. Because you were running through the woods at night, you probably got pretty scratched up. And the rain would have made the ground muddy, which would explain the dirt all over you. And maybe, once your grandmother gave up on chasing you... you ran to get help, and that's when the backpackers picked you up. They might have taken one look at you and thought you needed to get away. And if they were very young and high on drugs, as Carla said, they might not have made the best decisions."

Iris huffs, her eyes flashing in anger. "I think Lily's right.

Because I'm guessing that sometime that same night, Mrs Lowood drove to our house to look for the journal, and she still had Ellie's necklace... and the pendant slipped off the chain and fell between the floorboards..." Iris closes her eyes tightly. "And I don't even want to think about what she did between chasing Ellie and driving to our house..."

Carla looks at Iris and me in horror. "You girls have got to go to the police." She reaches out and closes her fingers over Ellie's hand. "Whatever happens, please know I did what I did out of love for you."

61

I STAND OUTSIDE THE LOWOODS' house in Nautilus Bay. The morning is bright and fresh—which seems all wrong for what's about to happen. Iris and Ellie step up to stand beside me. With Ellie in the middle, we reach to hold each other's hands.

Van emerges from the police car with another officer—Detective Lea Ramirez. A little further down the street, three other police vehicles are parked, with police officers ready and waiting.

"Just follow my lead," Van tells my sisters and me. "As we discussed, only Tina is going to get a chance to speak. We can't discuss the other side of it, okay?"

We nod in unison. Then we walk together to the front door.

It's Mr Lowood who answers the door. Startled at the sight of us with the detectives right behind, his mouth drops open. "What is all this?"

"Mr Lowood," Van says, "may we enter? We have a matter to discuss with your wife."

"What could you possibly want with Joan?" Mr Lowood responds. "No. No, you can't come in."

"We actually can." Van holds out a search warrant for him to inspect.

His jaws quivers as he moves back from the doorway, his rheumy eyes growing large and wild.

Mrs Lowood is in the living room, ironing shirts on an ironing board. It's such an ordinary sight that my mind rebels at the horrific scenes that Ellie painted. But my heart knows that they are true.

Mrs Lowood almost drops the iron as she sets it down. "What are you all doing here?"

"Mr and Mrs Lowood," Van says, putting a hand on Ellie's shoulder, "do you know who this is?"

A faint look of recognition passes through Mrs Lowood's eyes before they dull again. "Should I know?"

Ellie speaks up. "I used to be known as Ellie. Ellie Lowood."

Mrs Lowood gives only a brief glance to Ellie before her gaze slides back to Detective Dawson. "Is that what this is about? The identity of this young lady? Well, I'm sorry to say that she isn't our granddaughter, Detective. She looks nothing like her. You've all been fooled."

"We've not been fooled, Mrs Lowood," says Detective Ramirez in her terse, quick tone. "And the reason we're here is not because of your granddaughter. But she requested a chance to speak to her grandparents."

Ellie stares at her grandmother. "I called here when I was nine years old. You wouldn't let me talk to Grace. And you denied being my grandmother."

Mrs Lowood stumbles back a step, splaying a hand over her chest. "No such thing happened. And I don't know who you are or what you want. But you all need to get out of my house."

Mr Lowood hobbles across on his walking stick to help his wife onto the couch. He looks back at Ellie. "Just give her a minute. She's in shock. Are you really our Ellie?"

She nods, tears streaming down her face. "I remember you, Granddad. You used to call me your sunshine girl."

His eyes grow wet. "I think it is you. Joan, it's our granddaughter. She's come back."

Mrs Lowood looks down at her hands, twisting the wedding

rings on her finger. "You're a half-blind old fool. That's not her. I'd know."

Ellie gazes directly at Mrs Lowood. "I never got the chance to speak to Grace again. And when I called, you insisted that Ellie was dead—you told me that's why I couldn't be her."

"Joan?" her husband queries. "Tell me this isn't true."

She doesn't answer him.

Ellie's hand tightens on mine. "I know what you did, Grandma—everything you did. I'm sure you hoped that when I wasn't found, it meant that I had died. That made it easier for you, didn't it?"

Mr Lowood eyes his wife in horror. "Oh no, no. Good God. Joan, what is she talking about?"

"Stop making up these terrible, terrible lies! I want all of you out of here." Mrs Lowood turns to her husband. "Why are you letting them do this to me? Get them out!"

He looks stricken, frozen. He doesn't respond. Mrs Lowood drops her head, twisting her rings again.

"Grandma chased me down the road," Ellie says. "I thought she was going to kill me too. I thought if she ever found me, she would. It took every ounce of strength I had to call your house back when I was nine. I was hoping to talk to you or Grace. But she answered the phone every time I tried. She hung up on me after the first time."

Mr Lowood studies his wife, his expression slack with horror. "Joan, tell me you didn't do the things they're accusing you of?"

When Joan Lowood raises her head, her face has transformed into a cold, bitter mask. "Don't you speak to me like you've got the high moral ground."

Mr Lowood recoils from her.

"Why don't you tell them all what you did?" Mrs Lowood spits. "Grace was yours, not Elias's. Tell them. Tell them that you... you were going to see that young drug-addled prostitute. Meredith."

I catch my breath, turning to Iris.

"You and your great friend Quincy Mullard," Mrs Lowood mutters darkly. "I know full well that Meredith was only sixteen when the two of you began... using her services. I've had to live with that all this time. And then I was lumbered with the product of your debauchery—your daughter, Grace."

"That's enough, Joan. No one here believes you," Mr Lowood warns, but his skin has gone a chalky-grey shade.

"Is it enough? No, no I don't think it is," Mrs Lowood replies in a chilled tone. "No one should be asked to put up with what I've had to live with. No one. I wanted to send Grace away—far away from us and away from Meredith—and have her adopted out. But no. Meredith got what she wanted. She knew she was too much of a hopeless drugged-up street urchin to look after Grace, but she wanted us to get stuck with her so that she could just flit in and out of her life whenever she chose. And I didn't get a say in the matter. I know full well that Meredith was bribing you and Quincy because you'd both gotten into bed with her when she was just a minor, and she was holding that over your stupid heads."

Mr Lowood sinks into an armchair, his eyes unfocused and his arthritic knuckles tight on his walking stick. My heart races against my chest wall. Iris tightens her grasp on my hand, instinctively comforting me.

"It's time to head down to the station, Mrs Lowood," Van says. "I'll give you ten minutes to get yourself ready. I warn you that you might not find yourself back here at your home ever again. Do you understand?"

I catch a moment—a fleeting moment—in which Mrs Lowood looks defiant, as if Detective Dawson has no right to do this to her. She has, after all, spent twenty-four years pretending to everyone that she's a tragic innocent. It's been her whole identity. I don't know if she ever expected Ellie to resurface. But then her expression shifts to sheer terror.

Detective Ramirez stands watch inside Mrs Lowood's bedroom door as she changes her clothes. Then Van and Ramirez escort Mrs Lowood to the front door. Mrs Lowood casts one last look in Ellie's direction before she's taken out to a waiting police vehicle.

62

One week after Mrs Lowood was taken into police custody, she confessed everything. All the awful, horrifying details came to light. That same week, Detective Ramirez arrested the former sergeant Quincy Mullard. So far, Quincy had chosen to remain silent, insisting that he didn't even know Meredith Higgins and hadn't known the teenage Gabe DeCarlo.

I'm not going to get my time to sit down with the sergeant—as an adult—and question him. But it doesn't matter, because Iris and Gabe have told me everything I need to know. I'm discovering there are sometimes alternate paths to the truth.

Van ended up finding a briefest of entries in Quincy Mullard's case files about the psychologist, Rosie Moreno. All it said was, *R.M —weekly visits*. That was it. The sergeant had just wanted the whole case to go away quickly, so that his involvement with Meredith Higgins and Gabe DeCarlo was never discovered.

Detectives Dawson and Ramirez called Iris, Ellie, and me into the station. They explained how the story of the night that Mom and Ellie vanished had unfolded.

During our road trip, our mother had frequently called Mr Lowood to let him know where she was and how Grace and Ellie were doing. Mr Lowood had spoken about those calls to his friend, Quincy Mullard. That year, Meredith Higgins had been insisting that Sergeant Mullard bring Grace back to her, saying that if he didn't, she'd report him for having sex with her when she was just sixteen years old. Mullard had met her halfway, paying the teenage Gabe DeCarlo to keep tabs on our family in the first months after we left Nautilus Bay and when we had almost returned. Gabe DeCarlo couldn't refuse—he was a kid who was terrified of the sergeant.

Iris met Gabe during the last two weeks when we were at the farm. She had no idea he was stalking us. The two of them fell hard for each other. Mom and I had thought Iris was spending time with the girls who lived on the farm next door, but she was actually spending time with Gabe.

Toward the end of our road trip, when we were nearing Nautilus Bay, Mom called the hospital and spoke with Mrs Lowood to tell her she was going to bring Grace and Ellie to see her. At this time, Mrs Lowood checked out of the hospital and booked herself into an expensive facility that had a nurse on staff. Mrs Lowood's stroke had been minor, but she didn't want anyone to know she was out of the hospital yet. Mrs Lowood told our mother she could keep Grace but she wanted Ellie back.

When our mother refused to hand Ellie over, Mrs Lowood came looking for her. And she found her in the parking lot of a small shopping centre. In a blind rage, Mrs Lowood advanced upon our mother while she was outside her car, hugging Ellie. She hit her twice on the back of her head with a rock. After our mother fell to the ground, Mrs Lowood made repeated blows to her head with the rock, killing her.

When Ellie backed away in terror, Mrs Lowood grabbed her necklace and broke it. Ellie raced away into the night. Mrs Lowood chased her along the road as far as she was able, until Ellie vanished into the forest.

Giving up, Mrs Lowood made her way back to the closed shopping centre, where there was a pay phone. She called the police, pretending to be a concerned driver named Mrs Deauville. She told the police she'd seen a young woman and a child running down the road, making sure her description of the woman matched with Elsa Jorgenson. The witness, Jared Keller, had mentioned in his statement he thought the woman looked older, but Sergeant Mullard had chosen to believe Mrs Deauville over him—even though he never got to speak with her in person.

Mrs Lowood then hauled our mother's body into her car and drove away, leaving Grace behind in Mom's car. Grace never saw a thing, and the fierce rain had concealed the shouts between Mom and Mrs Lowood earlier.

Mrs Lowood knew of a place where she could take the body—a deep crevice between rock platforms on a cliff edge. She drove along a dirt road to the cliff and then rolled our mother's body over and over until it fell into the crevice. Mrs Lowood then pushed layers of dirt, twigs, and branches on top. The heavy rain that night covered her tracks and washed away all evidence.

On the way back, Mrs Lowood realised she had Mom's backpack still in her car. She stopped and threw it out into the shrubs by the roadside. Mrs Lowood then drove to Mom's house on Tiger Street. The rain had eased by this time. Before entering the house, she removed her raincoat and shoes. She had seen Mom writing in her journal one time and knew she was keeping one. So, she searched the house for it, worried that Mom might have spoken about Ellie being her own child, and worried Mom might have revealed the deal that Mrs Lowood had struck with her.

Oh yes, *the deal.* Mrs Lowood confessed that to Detective Dawson too. After Elias died of an accident on a fishing trawler, Mom went into an early labour, and she had Ellie at home alone.

Mom wanted to stick to her plan to keep the baby and bring Iris and me back to Australia. But Mrs Lowood was desperate to keep Ellie, who was her beloved dead son's only child. She told Mom she'd ruin the lives of all three of her daughters if she tried to take the baby away. Mrs Lowood swore she'd tell the police that Mom had seduced Elias and had deliberately gotten pregnant then abandoned her daughters in America and followed Elias back to Australia.

Iris and I guessed that the fact Mom had no money was also a deciding factor. She'd have gotten nothing in a divorce from Dad—our house still belonged to Dad's uncle at that time. Mrs Lowood offered Mom money to go home to America—without the baby. She convinced Mom it'd be better for everyone.

Mom left the baby behind and returned home. She put the money in a secret bank account and left it there. But Mom couldn't bear being apart from Ellie for long. When Ellie was three years old, Mom returned with Iris and me, using the money to buy a house.

The night that Mrs Lowood murdered our mother and searched our house, she didn't find the journal. She lost the pendant from the necklace that she'd torn from Ellie's neck while she was cleaning up her footprints with a towel. She knew it didn't matter if she'd touched any of the surfaces in the house—she'd been in there a few times before.

Mrs Lowood then returned to the care facility—where, the next day, she pretended to have developed vertigo. She used a wheelchair for the following two months, even though she had no need of it.

And that was it. All the ugly details that Mrs Lowood had kept locked up tight from the world for so long.

Two days after Mrs Lowood told Detective Dawson everything, my mother's bones were retrieved from the burial site. Iris, Ellie, and I wanted to be there. We didn't want Mom to be alone when she was brought back into the light. We were the ones who were rich in the memories of who she'd been. She was not just a collection of bones long buried on a cliff edge.

Detective Dawson allowed us to gather on the cliff but not close to the retrieval site. We had to wait while the forensic recovery crew completed their task. The only bright points in that day were the sunshine and the fact that Mom had been buried on a clifftop overlooking a beach, where she could hear and smell the ocean. Of course, she could do neither of those things. But it felt as if it could be true, and it was things like that you clung to in the face of so much dark despair.

Van approached us afterward and let us know that they had her and would take good care as they carried her away. And then he left with the teams of police.

63

WE HOLD Mom's funeral in early February. The day is scorching hot, as February in Australia is. We requested that no one wear sombre colours. Instead, we asked that people come in their bright, colourful, comfortable clothes.

Mom never told us whether she wanted to be buried or cremated. She'd been far too young to think about dying. But we chose cremation, because then we could take her to the ocean. She was buried a long time, and we knew that the water was what she loved best.

We've chosen a beautiful but isolated spot for the funeral, where there are lots of palm trees for shade. We didn't expect so many people from Nautilus to turn up. They didn't know Mom personally, but it seems that everyone knows our story now. I'm certain that some people have come to gawk, but the rest are here to tell us how sorry they are that one of their own caused our family such grief.

Our Tiger Street neighbour, Valentina, and her family turn up with smiles and tears. Joyce is here, too, and she gifts us some jewellery that Mom made when she was on the farm. I'm surprised to see Bennett turn up on his motorcycle—but I shouldn't be. His one concession to wearing bright colours is a red bandana. Bright colours were never his thing.

The Dawson family arrive together. Van whispers that he wishes he could hug me, but he stays back, understanding my need to not start rumours about us through the town. I'm not ready for that.

My father is absent from the funeral. He knows it is being held, but he's also aware that Iris and I have Mom's journal—a journal that details the terrible things he did to her. I'm glad he decided not to come.

With everyone now gathered, Iris and Ellie and I take turns to talk about our mother's life and what she meant to us. We tell them how much Mom loved the sun, salt, and sand of the coast. She was a seeker of life and light.

Valentina speaks, too, saying she adored our mother and our family. At the end, we add a memorial for Grace, who Mom loved like a daughter and who we never got to say any proper goodbye to.

With the speeches complete, everyone steps into the water together and scatters tiny wildflowers. Then my sisters and I walk into the ocean together and take Mom's ashes to the gentle waves.

I feel a small hand slip into mine. It's Jake's. I know he's finding all this especially hard. The funeral is a reminder that mothers can die—and that is a strong fear Jake holds. I wish he didn't have that worry. I will have to figure out what to do about it.

After the service, we hold a gathering at Mom's house on Tiger Street. The music is from the nineties—all our mother's favourites. We didn't want a sad occasion. We wanted to celebrate our mother's life.

Valentina and her family spent ages putting up fairy lights all around the trees and fences, and they brought over lots of their chairs and fold-up tables. Mrs Dawson and Anna made and brought all the refreshments. I'm awed by how much people have gone out of their way to make this day easier for Iris, Ellie, and me.

The celebration goes on into the night. People are spilling out of the house and across to the ocean. Jake and his cousins are in the pool, just like Iris, Grace, Ellie, and I used to do during the hot summer nights.

Iris approaches, silently putting her arms tight around me. "You okay, Lily?"

"I'm one big puddle of emotions. The ceremony was beautiful. I just wish it didn't have to be. I wish—"

"I know."

"I'm glad she's finally at rest, though. At least we have that."

"Yes, we have that. And that's a lot." Iris strokes the back of my head and then steps back. "Hey... I need to tell you something. About the rental payments for this house."

"Look, I don't care. Honestly. We'll just put it in the past, and—"

"Lily. It wasn't me."

"It was Gabe?"

"No. Haven't you worked it out yet?" she asks.

"I'm lost."

"You know those payments Dad gives us each month? Guess where they've been coming from?"

"What? No..."

"I'm afraid so. Dad was still legally married to Mom—so he got sent all her legal documents after she went missing. Some time back, he finally bothered to look over the papers. And he discovered that Mom owns this house. He decided to have it cleaned up and restored, and then he just went ahead and rented it out."

"Oh my goodness. That's why the house looks just the same. Dad is so stuck in the past. That's his signature move—to keep things just as they are. I should have guessed."

"Apparently, he hasn't made a dime out of it. He's sent all the money to us. Van pulled me aside and told me earlier."

I inhale a deep breath of salty ocean air. "Mind blown."

Glancing across the yard, I notice Gabe looking back and smiling.

"How are things with Gabe?" I ask Iris in a half whisper. "I know you tried telling me before, but that was right at the time when everything went crazy. And there hasn't been a spare moment since."

"It's certainly been a crazy time. Gabe and I are good. We've had a deep conversation, and we've figured out what we need to do going forward."

"I'm happy for you, Iris."

"Thank you."

Iris returns to her husband, and I'm alone again. Suddenly, I'm feeling overwhelmed by everything this day has been. I retreat upstairs to my old bedroom. I drag a wooden chair across the floorboards to the window and then sit looking out at the smooth dark sky. A tear travels down the length of my face and falls—probably all the way down to the floorboards, where it's absorbed by the old dry wood.

Mom said to me once that to find peace, you have to look for the quiet places. Lots of things in life will shout at you and demand your attention. But you can't let them keep turning your head.

A line from Mom's poem edges into my mind and I whisper it to myself: *I've learned silence is a trapdoor. You fall into the room of mirrors, where the stranger watches you.*

I understand that better now. Silence is a double-edged sword. It's an escape from the noise that surrounds you, but it's also a window into your own soul. It's a room of mirrors. And if you don't like what you find there, it will cut you to pieces.

The things I've done and haven't done weigh on me. What have I done with my life? What am I doing with Jake's life? Have I been doing with Jake what Mom did? Have I been running? My job requires constant travel. I'm never still. I take Jake with me when I can, but most of the time, I can't. Does he worry every time I leave that I won't return? And how long can I keep doing this for?

A figure stands in the doorway. Somehow, I know before I turn my head that it'll be Van Dawson.

He has an apologetic expression on his face. "Just wanted to find you—make sure you're okay. Uh, I can leave you alone again..."

"No, I'm okay. I just..."

"I can guess. It's been a big day for you and your sisters."

"Yeah. It has been."

"You want me to go?" he asks.

"No. Actually, it'd be nice if you'd come sit with me."

"I can do that." Van crosses the room and picks up the stool from the dressing table. He plants himself next to me. A smile creases his face as he looks out the window. "I remember walking past here with my friends a few times. I saw you."

I frown. "I don't think I ever noticed you."

I realise that if he used to see me when I lived here, then he witnessed some of the happiest days of my life, and then when I came to live with his family, he witnessed me at my worst, with my childhood innocence disintegrating. I don't know what to make of this or who he sees when he looks at me now.

"I'm not surprised you didn't notice me," he says. "There was always lots going on here. Lots of people and music. Kids everywhere. I remember seeing your mum here too—usually doing some gardening out the front. Pretty lady."

"She was. I'd give anything to go back to that time and have just one day with my mother."

"I wish you could, too. I felt so sorry for you and your sister when you arrived at my house. You were a little kid who was scared out of her mind. And Iris was trying to get away from us every second she could."

"All those times she left your house—it ends up she was going to see Gabe DeCarlo," I tell him wryly.

"Figures," he says, "knowing what we know now."

"I held onto an anger about those days for so long," I admit. "I'm ashamed to say it, but when I found out you'd gone into the police force, I didn't trust you. I thought... I thought you'd be just like your uncle, just a younger version of him."

"You had a right to think that," he says. "All you knew of me was how I was back in those days when you lived at my house. I didn't deal well with what was going on with you and your sister. In my defence, I was fifteen."

I smile. "I hated you."

"I know."

"Van... I'm sorry... about your uncle Quincy. That must be difficult for your family."

He exhales hard, glancing down. "Mum, Anna and I never liked him. And he deserves whatever's coming his way next. He had personal information about a case he was investigating, and he didn't disclose it. Not to mention Mrs Lowood's claim that he sought sex from a minor—Meredith. That's criminal too. All very serious stuff."

"You know, it feels like Meredith was the key. If Sergeant Mullard had come clean that she'd been blackmailing him, the case might have been solved quickly. But at least, even after all this time, there were threads connected to her."

"Yeah. I've found that to happen sometimes on the job—important things are still connected to the past. Well, on the job, and once or twice outside of that." His dark eyes flick up and hold me in their gaze. He looks away again quickly. "So, what's next for you? I know you said you were staying on for the funeral. But that's over now."

I nod. "I have to go back home soon."

"How soon? You didn't get a chance to tell me about your mother's journal."

"I guess that'll have to come out in court, won't it? When Mrs Lowood's trial comes up."

"I'd say, yeah, it would."

"It was harsh, reading it. There's a lot I didn't know." I stall, taking a breath. "Hey... Van?"

"Yep?"

"I don't know if I'd have stayed sane on that bus if we didn't have our little talks each night."

He smiles. "Glad to hear it. Anytime you need someone to talk to, even if it's in the early hours, I'm your man."

That draws a surprised laugh from me. "Thanks. I'll remember that."

"I have to say, though—you kept a lot to yourself while you were on that bus trip."

"Well, you're the police. There was no getting around that."

"When you don't know who you're dealing with or what you could be walking into—"

"I know, I know—you have to be careful." I don't say what I'm thinking. There were no dangerous people out there on the road trip laying any kind of traps. In the end, it came down to just us—Iris and me. I haven't yet come to terms with my part in making Iris feel like she couldn't tell her secrets. I was a child when we lost our mother—but so was she.

I cover up my thoughts with a quick smile. "Yes, leave it to your friendly neighbourhood detective."

He laughs. "Is that what I am?"

"You were my lifeline." The words leave my tongue with an earnest intensity that immediately makes me want to snatch them back. Because I don't know if I'm ready for him to see inside. But I suddenly can't look away from him.

In the still, sultry dark, I study his face—his brown eyes and the deep lines between them—that look if he's always thinking hard on something. And I follow the curve of his mouth—the mouth that flicks upward so easily when something amuses him.

I feel myself shift, maybe shifting into something like the warm slipstream of air I sensed myself living in when I was a child at this house, back when good things just happened and when I didn't live inside my own mind so much.

Without thinking on it, I find myself touching his arm and then leaning in to kiss him.

He hesitates, shifting back. "I wanted to do that—so much I can't even tell you—but it felt like—"

"You're not the kind of guy to kiss someone at their mother's funeral?"

"Yeah. Exactly that."

This time, it's Van who moves in close and kisses me.

64

Ellie has made an important decision. She's going to keep her last name of Valeria—because it's who she's been since she was four years old, and she also sees it as her future. But she changed her first name to a mix between Ellie and Tina. She's now Elina Valeria.

Iris and I love it because we can still call her Ellie for short. Iris lobbies hard for Ellie to move to Nautilus Bay, but Ellie says she could never see herself moving from her home in Tasmania.

It comes time for Ellie to catch her flight. But we can't let her go —not yet. It feels too soon to lose sight of our little sister. So Iris and I fly back to Tasmania with Ellie so that she can share her part of the world with us.

During the daytime, Ellie shows us around the Freycinet Peninsula, where she grew up. And at night, we sit and drink wine from her vineyard and look through her photograph albums—pictures of Ellie at every age she's been since she went missing. We discover that Ellie has a girlfriend named Astrid and they're planning on getting married one day soon. Ellie and Astrid give us a tour of the vineyard and teach us how to make a good bottle of red wine.

This morning, Iris, Ellie, and I sit together on a rocky outcrop that overlooks a place called Wineglass Bay, in the Freycinet

National Park. Below us is a scoop of crystal-blue water edged with a rind of white sand. Beyond that is a low set of mountains coloured in soft shades of pink and brown in the sunrise, and in the distance sits a glimpse of the Tasman Sea. The scene is unimaginably pure.

Ellie threads wildflowers together, making flower crowns for us just the way she used to when she was little. I feel myself sinking into the moment, swimming in its sheer beauty.

I'm reminded so strongly of the year we spent wandering the coast with our mother. We were free-roaming spirits, untethered from everything. Before the very last night, that year had been strange and intense, but not even Iris could deny that it'd also been filled with beauty and discovery.

I take Ellie's hand and squeeze it. "This is everything."

"All this time," Iris says to Ellie, "this is where you were, and we never knew."

A smile flits across Ellie's face. "It feels kind of amazing to know that people were thinking of me. It was lonely a lot of the time, growing up. It was Mum, me, and the workers."

I adjust her flower crown. "We've got each other now."

Ellie locks her arms around her knees. "I can't help but imagine how different life would have been if your mother—*my* mother—had just kept driving that night. If she hadn't stopped. If she hadn't called my grandmother. We would have continued our trip. All of us."

Iris picks a leaf from Ellie's hair. "Don't spend too long thinking about what might have been. Mom used to say that people get stuck going around and around a hill... and then die on it. She'd said she'd done that for far too long, wearing a trail around the same hill. She said you have to climb the hill one step at a time until you have a better view, and then you can see the road out."

Ellie laughs ruefully. "You sound just like a big sister."

"You'd better believe it," Iris says.

With a sigh, Ellie rests her chin on her knees. "I don't want to let either of you go. I've only just got you back. But I don't know what to do about that. You both have your lives, and I have mine here. And Lily, you'll be on the other side of the world."

"I've got decisions of my own to make," I say quietly.

Iris eyes me with interest. "What does that mean? And what about Van? He'll be devastated when you leave."

I give an offhand shrug and a smile. "Oh, c'mon. What?"

"You don't have to hide it," Iris says, grinning. "We know."

Ellie nods. "Clear as a bell."

"So, what are you two gonna do—a long distance relationship?" Iris asks. "They never work out. It'll just end up in heartache. You're just gonna have to come and live in Nautilus."

I gaze out to the mountains. "That would be a huge move."

I'm not ready to tell my sisters yet, but I'm seriously considering doing just that. I'm not even ready to tell Van that yet. He's laid his cards on the table, telling me how he feels and what he wants. But do I really know how I feel about him? The adult Van Dawson came into my life as the lead detective of the case involving my missing mother. I'm not sure if I'm able to separate him from that role yet. And then there's Jake to consider. He's my priority. I already know what he'd choose, but he's a child, and he can't make those kinds of decisions.

I need to go home first, back to Pennsylvania, and make sure I'm not too caught up in a time and a moment to see clearly. And I need to confront my father about the things Mom wrote in her journal.

Dad never treated Iris and me badly... except he did. Because how he treated our mother was always going to affect us. Mom's constant struggles, her absences, her apathy, her endless laps in our basement pool—those all formed the fabric of our childhood. And that all stemmed from Dad.

Perhaps, in time, I might come to a place where I can square up the environment Dad grew up in—that strict, strange community and its focus on restraining women in all possible ways—and the fact that Dad was forced to commit to marriage before he was even an adult.

Ellie takes out a bottle of red wine and glasses from her picnic basket. She pours each of us a drink. "Are we ready?"

The three of us stand on the rock platform, in our flower crowns, each holding a glass of wine.

"To the daughters of Elsa Jorgenson. May we have her strength," Ellie says.

"May we have her strength," the three of us repeat. We touch glasses.

"You say the next words," Ellie whispers to me. "You know them off by heart."

A tear tracks down my face as I nod. "I've added a last line to Mom's poem. Does anyone mind?"

Iris's voice is soft when she says, "Go for it, sis."

I wipe my tear and recite her poem:

I have always been running,
especially when I'm at my most still.
I've learned silence is a trapdoor.
You fall into the room made of mirrors
where the stranger watches you
every hour, every minute.
But my mind burns bright.
I'll have a warm body again,
I know I will.
Wind, salt, and sun on my skin,
in my hair, in my lungs.
I've made many wrong turns
—so many,
and one blinding mistake.
But I can't let a mistake
become a life.

I am a bird in flight.

AUTHOR'S NOTE

I hope you enjoyed BIRDS IN FLIGHT!

Writing this book was a long, emotional journey for me—over a year. I wasn't sure where it would end up, but I was certain that Lily would find the answers she was so desperately seeking—for better or worse.

Find your next thriller reads & upcoming books on my website: *annitaylor.me*

BOOKS

What to read next!

STRANGER IN THE WOODS

Emotional suspense. A photographer travels to the Scottish Highlands for a dream job—only to find herself trapped in a snowstorm with dangerous residents of a small town.

THE GAME YOU PLAYED

Emotional suspense. Cruel notes in rhyme taunt Phoebe about her missing two-year-old son, Tommy. The game has just begun.

ONE LAST CHILD - Book 1 Tallman's Valley Detectives

Suspense. Five nursery-school children vanish from a picnic. The kidnapper returns them years later. All except for one last child—the granddaughter of homicide detective Kate Wakeland. Speculation grows that the kidnappings were a revenge plot.

THE LULLABY MAN - Book 2 Tallman's Valley Detectives

Suspense. A decade ago, The Lullaby Man preyed upon young girls in Tallman's Valley. He stole into their lives, whispered in their ears, spoke of love. They think he died... but did he?

THE SILENT TOWN - Book 3 Tallman's Valley Detectives

Suspense. Detective Kate Wakeland senses dark undercurrents swimming in the depths of her beloved town of Tallman's Valley. A sizzling end to the Kate Wakeland series.

THE SIX

Dark horror/suspense. Young mother, Evie, is desperate to find a way to repay her secret gambling debt. But travelling to an island that runs a mysterious program for addicts is the worst mistake of her life.

POISON ORCHIDS

Dark horror/suspense. Two backpackers arrive at a remote fruit farm, desperate for work. They find a strange cult and a charismatic owner who seems to be hiding his true intentions.

ACKNOWLEDGMENTS

Much appreciation as always to my family & friends for listening.

Many thanks to my readers for your beautiful comments & messages & reviews. It all helps more than I can put into words!

Thanks also to my line editor, Sarah.C, and my proofreader, Caroline. And lots of thanks to the first readers of my draft version—Tim, Kirsten, Chris & Louise.

Made in United States
Troutdale, OR
01/10/2024

16865882R00224